TERMS OF ENDEARMENT

Larry McMurtry

A STAR BOOK
Published by
the Paperback Division of
W. H. ALLEN & Co. Ltd

A Star Book
Published in 1984
by the Paperback Division of
W. H. Allen & Co. Ltd
A Howard and Wyndham Company
44 Hill Street, London W1X 8LB

First published in Great Britain
by W. H. Allen & Co. Ltd, 1977
Reprinted 1984 (twice)

Copyright © Larry McMurtry, 1975
Distributed by Gordon and Gotch Ltd., exclusively.
Made and printed in Australia by
The Dominion Press—Hedges & Bell, Victoria

ISBN 0 352 31476 1

A portion of this book has appeared in *Playboy* magazine

TERMS OF ENDEARMENT

'I'm pregnant! That's what I've been trying to tell you for an hour.'

'What!' Aurora said, looking at Emma. Her daughter was smiling, and had said the word "pregnant".

'Oh, God,' she said, clutching her stomach with both hands. 'Oh, God!' she said, wrenching herself into a sitting position.

'Momma, stop it, I'm just pregnant,' Emma implored.

'Just pregnant!' Aurora cried, confusion turning suddenly to rage. 'You . . . negligent . . .' But words failed her.

'What did I do?' Emma yelled, beginning to cry. 'Why can't I be pregnant? I'm married.'

Aurora's lips began to tremble. 'Emma, it's not the point . . . Who will I ever . . . get now? What man would want a grandmother? Now I'll lose all my suitors!'

Larry McMurtry is the author of many books including:

THE LAST PICTURE SHOW
MOVING ON
HORSEMAN, PASS BY

TERMS OF ENDEARMENT

BOOK I

Emma's Mother

1962

CHAPTER I

"THE SUCCESS of a marriage invariably depends on the woman," Mrs. Greenway said.

"It does not," Emma said, not looking up. She was sitting in the middle of her living-room floor sorting a large pile of laundry.

"It most certainly does," Mrs. Greenway said, assuming a stern expression. She tightened her lips and narrowed her brows. Emma was letting herself go again—a breach of standards—and she had always endeavored to meet any breach of standards with a stern expression, if only briefly.

Sternness, she knew, did not become her—at least it didn't *entirely* become her—and Aurora Greenway, as she herself knew quite well, was not one to do the unbecoming—not unless it was a matter of strictest duty. Yet strange as it sometimes seemed—to both of them—Emma *was* her daughter, and her behavior *was* a matter of strictest duty.

Aurora's face was more plump than not, and despite forty-nine years that seemed to her to have consisted largely of irritations and disappointments, she still almost always managed to look pleased with herself. The facial muscles necessary to a display of true sternness were called into play so seldom that they were somewhat reluctant to stir, but nonetheless, when the need arose, she could be for short periods extremely stern. Her forehead was high, her cheekbones strong, and her blue eyes—usually so dreamy and, Emma would have thought, vacantly complacent—were capable of sudden angry fires.

In this case, she felt that only a little narrowing of the brows would be necessary.

"I don't believe there's a decent garment in that whole pile of laundry," she said, with her own light and slightly arrogant contempt.

"You're right, there isn't," Emma said. "It's a crappy bunch of clothes. However, they do cover our nakedness."

"I'd rather you didn't mention nakedness to me, I'm not concerned with it right now," Aurora said. Her brows were getting tired of being wrinkled, and her mouth of being tight, so she relaxed, conscious of having done a mother's duty. It was unfortunate that her daughter had been too stubborn to look up and notice, but then that was Emma. She had never been duly attentive.

"Why can't I mention nakedness?" Emma asked, looking up. Her mother dipped two fingers into what was left of a glass of iced tea, extracted what was left of an ice cube, and sucked on it while she watched her daughter work. Making Emma feel guilty had never been easy, but it was the one maternal task left to her, and Aurora attacked it with relish.

"You have a fine vocabulary, dear," she said, once the ice cube was gone. "I personally have seen to that. There are certainly better ways to use it than the discussion of naked bodies. Also, as you know, I've been a widow for three years and I don't wish certain things called to my attention."

"That's ridiculous," Emma said. Her mother calmly extracted another ice cube. She was, as she would have put it, recumbent, lying at ease on Emma's ancient blue couch. She was dressed in a loose elegant pink lounging robe that she had picked up on a recent trip to Italy, and she looked, as usual, faintly bemused and smugly happy—happier, Emma thought, than either she or anyone else had a right to be.

"Emma, you really should diet," Aurora said. "You're such an unyielding person, dear. I want you to know that I'm *raather* vexed."

"Why?" Emma said, poking in the clothes pile. As usual, several socks had failed to mate.

"*Raather* vexed," Aurora repeated, on the chance that there was something wrong with her daughter's ears. She had put the full weight of Boston behind her "raather," and was not disposed to have it ignored. Emma, who possessed—among other unladylike qualities—an annoying interest in precision, would have insisted that it was only the full weight of New Haven, but quibbles of that sort cut no ice with Aurora. Boston was hers to employ, and the full weight of it was meant to strike thunder. Had they been in Boston, or perhaps even New Haven—any place where life could be kept in hand—no doubt it would have; but the two of them, mother and daughter, were in Emma's hot, muggy oversmall living room in Houston, Texas, where the full weight of Boston seemed to strike nothing at all. Emma went on distractedly counting socks.

"You're letting yourself go again," Aurora said. "You're not taking pains with your appearance. Why won't you diet?"

"Eating makes me less frustrated," Emma said. "Why won't you stop buying clothes? You're the only person I know who has seventy-five of everything."

"The women of our family have always prided themselves on their dress," Aurora said. "All except you, at least. I am not a seamstress. I do not propose to sew."

"I know you don't," Emma said. She herself was wearing jeans and one of her husband's T-shirts.

"That garment you have on top of you is so disgusting I scarcely know how to refer to it," Aurora said. "It belongs on a pickaninny, not on a daughter of mine. Of course I buy clothes. The selection of a tasteful wardrobe is a duty, not a pastime."

With that, Aurora lifted her chin. When justifying herself to her daughter she often liked to assume a touch of majesty. Emma was seldom impressed, and the look on her face at that moment smacked of defiance.

"Seventy-five tasteful wardrobes is a pastime," Emma said. "I reserve judgment about the tasteful part too. Anyway, what happened about your female problem?"

"Stop it! Don't talk about it!" Aurora said. In her indignation she not only sat up but attempted an outraged flounce, causing the old couch to creak loudly. It was not merely the moral weight of Boston that she embodied.

"All right!" Emma said. "Good God! You told me you were going to the doctor. I just asked. You don't have to break the couch."

"You needn't have mentioned it," Aurora said, genuinely upset. Her lower lip was trembling. She was not ordinarily a prudish woman, but lately all mention of sex upset her; it made her feel that her whole life was wrong, and she didn't like to feel that way.

"You're absolutely ridiculous," Emma said. "Why do you have to be so touchy? Shall we correspond about it?"

"I am not ill, if you must know," Aurora said. "Not ill in the least." She held out her glass. "However, I should like some more iced tea."

Emma sighed, took the glass, got up, and left the room. Aurora lay back down, almost depressed. She had her strong days and her weak days, and she had begun to feel a weak day coming on. Emma had not anticipated her wants in any way—why were children so incapable of keeping their minds on parents? She was in the mood for a fit of despond, but her daughter, determined to thwart her at every turn, came back immediately with a glass of iced tea. She had stuck a sprig of mint in the glass and, perhaps as a gesture of contrition, had brought a little dish of sassafras candy—one of the several candies that her mother particularly enjoyed.

"That's sweet," Aurora said, taking a piece.

Emma smiled. Her mother, she knew, had been about to go into a fit—a lonely-widow, unappreciated-mother fit. The candy had been a brilliant stroke. The week before she had squandered a whole dollar and sixty-eight cents on a variety of it, all of which

14

she had hidden and about half of which she had already eaten herself. Flap, her husband, would not have looked kindly on such an expenditure. He professed strict ideas about tooth decay but would undoubtedly just have spent the money on his own vices, which were beer and paperbacks. Emma was devil-may-care when it came to teeth, and liked to have candy around to stave off fits—her mother's or her own.

Aurora, her little sinking spell conquered, had already drifted back into happy indolence and was gazing around the living room, hoping to find something new to criticize.

"The reason I brought up the doctor was because I went yesterday myself," Emma said, settling herself on the floor again. "Maybe I've got some good news."

"I hope he's persuaded you to diet," Aurora said. "No one should be so intractable as to reject the advice of their physician. Dr. Ratchford has had long years of experience and except where I am concerned it's been my observation that his advice is invariably good. The sooner you start to diet the happier person you'll be."

"Why do you always make an exception of yourself?" Emma asked.

"Because I know myself best," Aurora said serenely. "I certainly wouldn't allow a physician to know me this well."

"Maybe you've got yourself fooled," Emma suggested. The laundry really was depressing. All Flap's shirts were worn out.

"I have not," Aurora said. "I do not permit myself delusions. I never try to whitewash the fact that you married badly."

"Oh, shut up," Emma said. "I married okay. Anyway you just said two minutes ago that the success of a marriage invariably depends on the woman. To use your very words. Maybe I'll make this one a success."

Aurora looked blank. "Now you've made me lose my train of thought," she said.

Emma snickered. "That was thought?" she said.

Aurora took another candy. She looked aloof. Sternness might present problems, but aloofness was her element. Life often required it of her. In gathering after gathering, when her sensibilities were affronted, she had found it necessary to raise her eyebrows and cast a chill. There was little justice. It sometimes seemed to her that if she were remembered at all it would probably only be for the chills she had cast.

"I have often been complimented on the clarity of my expression," she said.

"You didn't let me tell you my good news," Emma said.

"Oh, yes, you've decided to diet, just as I'd hoped," Aurora said. "That *is* good news."

"Damn it, I didn't go to Dr. Ratchford to talk about dieting," Emma said. "I don't want to diet. I went to find out if I'm pregnant, and it looks like I am. That's what I've been trying to tell you for an hour."

"What!" Aurora said, looking at ,Emma. Her daughter was smiling, and had said the word "pregnant." Aurora had just taken a sip of iced tea—she almost choked. "Emma" she yelled. Life had struck again, and just when she was almost comfortable. She sprang up as if jabbed by a pin, but fell back heavily, breaking the saucer and causing her almost empty tea glass to spin around erratically on the rugless floor, like a child's top.

"You're not!" she cried.

"I think so," Emma said. "What's the matter with you?"

"Oh, God," Aurora said, clutching her stomach with both hands.

"What's wrong, Momma?" Emma asked, for her mother looked genuinely stricken.

"Oh, my iced tea jiggled when I fell," Aurora said. "I don't know." Blood was rushing to her head, and she began to hyperventilate. She could only breathe in gasps.

"Of course that's wonderful for you, dear," she said, feeling terrible. It was a shock, it wasn't right—something was out of order, and she felt confusion closing in on her. Always she fought confusion, yet it seemed to lie in wait for her, no matter where she went.

"Oh, God!" she said, wrenching herself into a sitting position. Her hair, which she had more or less caught in a bun, came completely loose, and she opened the neck of her robe to assure herself more air.

"Momma, stop it, I'm just pregnant," Emma yelled, angered that her mother would indulge herself in a fit after she had been so generous with the sassafras candy.

"Just pregnant!" Aurora cried, confusion turning suddenly to rage. "You . . . negligent . . ." But words failed her, and to Emma's intense annoyance she began to smite her forehead with the back of her hand. Aurora had been raised in an era of amateur theatricals and was not without her stock of tragic gestures. She continued to smite her forehead vigorously, as she always did when she was very upset, wincing each time at the pain it gave her hand.

"Stop that," Emma cried, standing up. "Stop smiting your goddamn forehead, Momma! You know I hate that!"

"And I hate you," Aurora cried, abandoning all reason. "You're not a thoughtful daughter! You never have been a thoughtful daughter! You never will be a thoughtful daughter!"

"What did I do?" Emma yelled, beginning to cry. "Why can't I be pregnant? I'm married."

Aurora struggled to her feet and faced her daughter, meaning to show her such scorn as she had never seen before. "You may call this marriage but I don't," she yelled. "I call it squalor!"

"We can't help it!" Emma said. "It's all we can afford."

Aurora's lip began to tremble. Scorn got lost—everything was lost. "Emma, it's not the point . . . you shouldn't have . . . it's not the point at all," she said, suddenly on the verge of tears.

"What's the point then?" Emma said. "Just tell me. I don't know."

"Mee!" Aurora cried, with the last of her fury. "Don't you see? My life is not settled. Me!"

Emma winced, as she always did when her mother cried "Mee!" at the world. The sound was as primitive as a blow. But as her mother's chin began to shake and pure fury began its mutation into pure tearfulness, she understood a little and put out her arm.

"Who will I ever . . . get now?" Aurora cried. "What man would want a grandmother? If you could . . . have waited . . . then I might have . . . got somebody."

"Oh, dear," Emma said. "Aw, Momma, stop that." She went on crying herself, but only because she had a sudden fear of laughing. Only her mother did that to her, and always at the most unlikely times. She knew she was the one who ought to feel outraged or hurt—probably she would when she thought about it. But her mother never had to think; she was just outraged or hurt, immediately, and with a total purity of feeling that Emma had never been able to command. It always happened.

Emma gave up. She let herself be beaten once again. She dried her eyes just as her mother burst into tears. The whole fit was ridiculous, but it didn't matter. The look on her mother's face—an utter conviction of utter ruin—was too real. The look might not last five minutes—seldom did—but there it was, on a face that Emma felt sure must be the most helplessly human face that she or anyone she knew had ever had to confront. The sight of her mother looking blank with distress had always caused whoever was handy to come rushing up at once with whatever love they had available in them. No one had ever been able to stand to see her mother looking that way, Emma least of all, and only love would change it. She began immediately to make loving sounds, and her mother, as usually, tried to fight her off.

"No, get away," Aurora said. "Fetuses. Ugh. Yick." She recovered her capacity for motion and floundered across the room, waving her hands and making swatting motions, as if she were knocking tiny batlike embryos out of the air. She didn't know what was wrong, but it was a blow at her life. She knew that much.

"See! Now I'll lose all my suitors!" she yelled, turning for a last moment of defiance.

"Now, Momma . . . now, Momma, it's not that bad," Emma kept saying as she advanced.

When Emma finally cornered her, in the bedroom, Aurora took the only course open to her: she flung herself on the bed, and her light pink garment billowed down after her like a sail falling. She sobbed for five minutes uncontrollably, and for five more with varying degrees of control, while her daughter sat on the bed beside her rubbing her back and telling her over and over again what a dear, wonderful person she was.

"Now, aren't you ashamed of yourself?" Emma asked when her mother finally stopped crying and uncovered her face.

"Not in the least." Mrs. Greenway said, pushing back her hair. "Hand me a mirror."

2.

EMMA DID, and Aurora sat up and with a cool, unsentimental eye inspected the damage to her face. She rose without a word and disappeared into the bathroom; water ran for some while. When she emerged, a towel around her shoulders, Emma had just finished folding the clothes.

Aurora settled herself on the couch again, mirror in hand. There had been doubtful moments, but her image had somehow struggled back to where she thought it ought to be, and she merely glanced at herself thoughtfully a time or two before turning her gaze upon her daughter. In fact, Aurora felt quite ashamed of her outburst. All her life she had been prone to outbursts, a habit which ran contrary to her preferred view of herself as a rational person. This outburst, considering its cause, or at least its starting point, seemed particularly unworthy of her. Still, she did not propose to apologize until she had considered the matter carefully—not that her daughter expected an apology. Emma sat quietly by her neatly folded clothes.

"Well, my dear, I must say you've behaved rather independently," Aurora said. "Still, the times being what they are, I suppose I should have expected it."

"Momma, it has nothing to do with the times," Emma said. "You got pregnant, didn't you?"

"Not consciously," Aurora said. "Not with unseemly haste either. You're only twenty-two."

"Now stop it, just stop it," Emma said. "You're not going to lose your suitors."

Aurora's expression was once again a little bemused, once again a little aloof. "I can't imagine why I should care," she said. "All of them are miles beneath me. I'm not at all sure that's why I

19

cried. The shock may have made me jealous, for all I know. I always meant to have more children myself. Is Thomas coming home soon?"

"I want you to call him Flap, please." Emma said. "He doesn't like to be called Thomas."

"Sorry," Aurora said. "I don't like using nicknames, even charming ones, and my son-in-law's is hardly charming. It sounds like part of a loincloth."

Emma gave up again. "He should be here any minute," she said.

"Thomas is not likely to be prompt," Aurora said. "He was late on several occasions while you were engaged." She stood up and picked up her purse.

"I'm leaving at once," she said. "I doubt if you'll mind. Where are my shoes?"

"You didn't wear any," Emma said. "You were barefooted when you came in."

"Remarkable," Aurora said. "They must have been stolen right off my feet. I am hardly the sort to leave my house without shoes."

Emma smiled. "You do it all the time," she said. "It's because all seventy-five pairs of them hurt your feet."

Aurora didn't deign to reply. Her departures, like her moods, were unpremeditated and always quite abrupt. Emma got up and followed her mother out the door, down the steps, and along the driveway. It had come a little summer shower and the grass and flowers were still wet. The lawns up and down the street were a brilliant green.

"Very well, Emma," Aurora said. "If you're going to contradict me I suppose it's a good thing I'm leaving. We should inevitably quarrel. I'm sure you'll find my shoes the minute I'm gone."

"Why didn't you look for them yourself if you're so sure they're there?" Emma said.

Aurora looked aloof. Her seven-year-old black Cadillac was parked, as always, several yards from the curb. She had had a lifelong horror of scraping her tires. The Cadillac was old enough, in her view, to pass for a classic antique, and she always paused a moment before she got in, to admire its lines. Emma walked around the car and stood looking at her mother, whose lines, in their way, were also classic. West Main Street, in Houston, was never very busy, and no cars disturbed their silent contemplation.

Aurora got in, adjusted her seat, which never seemed to stay the same distance from the pedals, and managed to insert her key in the ignition, a trick only she could manage. Years before she had been forced to use the key to pry open a screen door, and since then it had been slightly bent. Perhaps by now the ignition was bent too—in any case Aurora was firmly convinced that the bentness of the key was all that had kept the car from being stolen many times.

She looked out her window and there was Emma standing quietly in the street, as if waiting for something. Aurora felt inclined to be merciless. Her son-in-law was a young man of no promise, and in the two years that she had known him his manners had not improved, nor had his treatment of her daughter. Emma was too poor and too fat and looked awful in his T-shirts, which, had he any respect, he would not have allowed her to wear. Her hair had never been one of her glories, but at the moment it was a distinct stringy mess. Aurora felt inclined to be quite merciless. She paused a moment before putting on her sunglasses.

"Very well, Emma," she said once again. "You needn't stand there expecting congratulations from me. I was not once consulted. You have made your bed. You no longer have an open destiny. Besides, you're far too stubborn to be a parent. Had you cared to take me into your confidence a little sooner, I could have told you that. But no, not once did you consult me. You haven't even a proper residence—that place you live in is just the top of a garage. Infants have enough respiratory problems without having to live with cars beneath them. It isn't likely to do much for your figure either. Children never think of these things. I am still your mother, you know."

"I know, Momma," Emma said, stepping close to the car. To Aurora's surprise she didn't argue, did not defend herself. She merely stood by the car, in the awful T-shirt, looking, for the first time in years, mild and obedient. Emma looked down at her quietly, in the manner of a proper daughter, and Aurora noticed again something she was always forgetting: that her child had the loveliest eyes, green, with lights in them. They were the eyes of her own mother, Amelia Starrett, who had been born in Boston. And she was so young, really, Emma.

Suddenly, to Aurora's terror, life seemed to bolt straight from her grip. Something flung her heart violently, and she felt alone. She no longer felt merciless, she just— She didn't know, something was gone, nothing was certain, she was older, she had not been granted control, and what would happen? She had no way to see how things would end. In her terror she flung out her arms and caught her daughter. For a moment the only thing she knew was the cheek she was kissing, the girl she was hugging to her; and then, abruptly, her heart settled back and she noticed, quite to her surprise, that she had pulled Emma half through the window of the car.

"Oh, oh," Emma said repeatedly.

"What's wrong?" Aurora asked, releasing her.

"Nothing," Emma said. "I just bumped my head on the car."

"Oh. I wish you weren't so careless, Emma," Aurora said. She had never that she could remember lost so much dignity so quickly, and she scarcely knew what to do to recover it. Ideally she would have driven straight away, but the shock, or whatever it was, had left her shaken. She didn't feel quite up to working the pedals. Even when at her best she sometimes forgot to work them, and did inconvenient things to cars that stopped in her way. Often people shouted at her at such times.

Besides, it was not the moment to drive away. In her panic she felt sure she had given her daughter the upper hand, and she was not disposed to leave until she had it back. She twisted her rearview mirror around until she could see herself in it, and she waited patiently for her features to compose themselves again. It certainly was not turning out to be one of her better days.

Emma watched, rubbing her bumped head. She had gotten her due, more or less, but she could see that her mother had no intention of letting her keep it.

"You don't have to tell your boy friends for a while, you know," she said. "You rarely let me meet them anyway. I could probably have the kid off to prep school before they suspect a thing."

"Humph," Aurora said, combing her hair. "In the first place the child, if there is to be one, will almost certainly be a girl. That's customary in our family. In the second place they are not my boy friends, they are my suitors, and you will please refer to them as such, if you must refer to them at all."

"Whatever you say," Emma said.

Aurora had wonderful hair—it was auburn and abundant, and had always been her daughter's envy. Arranging it invariably left her looking pleased, and soon she looked pleased again. Despite all, she had kept her looks, and looks were a great consolation. She rapped the steering wheel with the back of her comb.

"You see, I told you Thomas would be late," she reminded Emma. "I can't wait any longer. If I don't rush I'll miss my shows."

She elevated her chin several degrees and bestowed upon her daughter a slightly impish grin. "As for you," she said.

"As for me, what?"

"Oh, nothing," Aurora said. "Nothing. You've brought this upon me now. There is nothing more to say. No doubt I'll manage somehow."

"Stop trying to make me feel guilty," Emma said. "I have my rights, and you're no martyr. It's not like the stake and the pyre await you around the corner."

Aurora ignored the remark—it was her custom to ignore all cleverness of that sort.

"No doubt I'll manage somehow," she said again, in a tone which was meant to indicate that she considered herself absolved of all responsibility for her own future. She was, for the moment, rather cheerful, but she wanted it clearly understood that if anything bad happened to her in what remained of her life the fault must be laid at doorsteps other than her own.

To forestall argument, she started the car. "Well, dear," she said, "at least it may force you to diet. Please oblige me and have something done to your hair. Perhaps you ought to dye it. Honestly, Emma. I think you'd look better bald."

"Leave me alone," Emma said, "I'm resigned to my hair."

"Yes, that's the trouble with you," Aurora said. "You're resigned to far too much. That garment you're wearing verges on the pathetic. I wish you'd go take it off. I've never allowed myself to be resigned to anything that wasn't delightful, and nothing about your life is delightful that I can see. You must make some changes."

"I think they're being made for me," Emma said.

"Tell Thomas he might be more prompt," Aurora said. "I must sail. My shows won't wait. I hope I don't meet any policemen."

"Why?"

"They look at me wrong," Aurora said. "I really don't know why. I've never hurt one." She took another gratifying look at her coiffure and twisted the mirror more or less back into place.

"I imagine it's that negligent look you cultivate," Emma said.

"Pooh, I'm going. You've delayed me long enough," Aurora said. She dismissed her daughter with an airy wave and peered down the street to see whether any obstructions had been put in her path. A small green foreign car had just chugged past, but that was minor. Probably if she honked loudly enough it would turn into a driveway and let her by. Such cars ought to be driven on sidewalks anyway—there was little enough room in the streets for American cars.

"Bye, Momma, come again," Emma said, for form's sake.

Aurora didn't hear. She seized the steering wheel commandingly and poked her foot at the appropriate pedal. "Little Aurora," she said fondly as she drove away.

3.

EMMA HEARD her and smiled. "Little Aurora" was an expression her mother used only when she considered herself alone against the world—alone and supremely adequate.

Then she jumped. Her mother had begun immediately to honk at the Volkswagen, and the Cadillac had a very loud horn. Hearing it unexpectedly gave everyone, Emma included, apprehensions of emergency. Against such honking the little green car had no chance—the Cadillac swept it aside as easily as an ocean liner might sweep aside a canoe. The driver, assuming that catastrophe had overtaken someone, turned into a driveway and didn't even honk back.

Emma stretched the T-shirt as far down her legs as it would go. The trees overhead were still dripping from the summer shower, and drops of water fell on her bosom, such as her bosom was. The T-shirt did emphasize certain of her inadequacies. Her mother had not been entirely wrong.

As usual, after one of her mother's visits, Emma found herself feeling antagonistic, not merely toward her mother but also toward her husband and herself. Flap should have been there to defend himself, or her, or them. Her mother hadn't really been on the attack; she had just been exercising her peculiar subtle genius for making everyone but herself seem vaguely in the wrong. There was never any peace with her mother around, but somehow, once she left, there was even less. Her most absurd remarks had a habit of hanging in the air. They were always uncalled for and outrageous, but never, for Emma, simply dismissible. Hair, diet, the T-shirt, Flap, and herself—no matter what she said in retaliation she was always left with the feeling that she had let her mother get away with murder. Actually, Flap was no great help, even when he was there. He was so scared of losing what little standing he had with Mrs. Greenway that he wouldn't fight.

Two minutes later, while Emma was still standing in the driveway feeling dim-witted and slightly annoyed with herself, running through in her mind the brilliant rejoinders she might have made to her mother, Flap and his father drove up. His father was named Cecil Horton, and when he saw Emma he turned his neat blue Plymouth right up beside her, close enough that he could reach out and squeeze her arm without getting out of the car.

"Hi, Toots," he said, smiling broadly. Cecil was a man of the 1940s—"Toots" was his customary gallantry. Emma hated it and looked forward to the day when Cecil forgot himself and used it with her mother. His smile also annoyed her, because it was automatic and completely impersonal. Cecil would have smiled broadly at a fire hydrant if he had had occasion to greet one.

"Toots yourself," she said. "Did you buy the boat?"

Cecil didn't hear the question. He was still smiling at her. His graying hair was neatly combed. He was only sixty, but he had grown a little deaf; in fact, he had stopped expecting to hear most of what was said to him. When he found himself being addressed by someone he was supposed to like, Cecil held his smile a little longer and if possible patted a shoulder or squeezed an arm to assure whoever it was of his affection.

Emma was not sure she believed in his affection, since it carried no real attention with it. She was convinced that she could have stood in the driveway dripping blood, both arms amputated at the elbow, and Cecil would still have driven up, said "Hi, Toots," smiled broadly, and squeezed her stump. Her mother couldn't stand him and left wherever she was at the mention of his name. "Don't argue with me. When you talk about people they soon appear," she would say, going out the door.

A few minutes later, when Cecil and the Plymouth had gone their way and she and Flap were walking up the driveway, Emma felt piqued enough to raise the issue.

"It's two years now, and he's never really noticed me," she said.

"It's not just you," Flap said. "Daddy doesn't pay much attention to anybody."

"He pays attention to you," Emma said. "Strict attention. I only enter his consciousness when he notices that I've failed to provide you with something he thinks you should have, like a clean shirt. You've told me that yourself."

"Stop picking on me," Flap said. "I'm tired."

He did look it. He had a long nose, a long jaw, and a mouth that turned down easily when he was depressed, which was often. Perversely, when she had first known him, it was the fact that he was so frequently and frankly depressed that had attracted her to him—that and his long jaw. His depression had seemed touching and somehow poetic, and within two days Emma had become convinced that she was what he needed. Two years had passed and she was still reasonably convinced of it, but there was no denying that Flap hadn't really responded as she had expected him to. She was obviously what he needed, but nine days out of ten he was still depressed. Time had almost forced her to admit that his depression wasn't something that was going to go away, and she had just begun to ask herself why. She had also begun to ask Flap the same question. Not for nothing was she Aurora Greenway's daughter.

"You shouldn't be tired," she said. "All you've done is help your father look at a boat. I've done a laundry and had a fight with mother, and I'm not tired."

Flap held the screen for her. "Why was she here?" he asked.

"That's an odd question," Emma said. "Why do you ask?"

"I don't know," Flap said. "You weren't very friendly to Daddy. I'd like a beer."

He went into the bedroom and Emma held her peace and got the beer. His touchiness about his father didn't really upset her—the two of them had always been very close and she was an intrusion into their relationship that Flap hadn't learned to handle gracefully, that was all. There were times when he was comfortable with her, and she assumed there were times when he was comfortable with his father, but there had never yet been a time when all three of them had been genuinely comfortable together.

Still, Cecil at his worst couldn't make her a tenth as uncomfortable as her mother could make Flap without even trying.

He was stretched out on the bed reading Wordsworth when she brought the beer.

"What do I have to do to get you to stop reading and talk to me?" she asked.

"I'm just reading Wordsworth," he said. "I hate Wordsworth. Almost anything will get me to stop reading him. You ought to know that. The smell of cooking would probably do it."

"You're a difficult man," she said.

"No, just selfish," Flap said. He closed Wordsworth and gave her a nice friendly look. He had brown eyes and could look hopeless and friendly at the same time. It was his best look, and Emma had never been able to resist it—almost any sign of friendliness was enough to win her over. She sat down on the bed and took his hand.

"Did you tell her you were pregnant?" Flap asked.

"I told her. She had a fit." She described the fit in full detail.

"What an absurd woman," Flap said. He sat up suddenly, smelling of beer and salt water, and began to make a pass. His passes were always sudden. Within five seconds Emma was flustered and breathless, which seemed to be exactly the effect he wanted to make.

"What is it with you?" she asked, struggling to get at least partially undressed. "You never seem to want to give me time to think about it. I wouldn't have married you if I wasn't willing to think about it."

"One of us might lose interest," Flap said.

It was the one thing he did quick—everything else took him hours. Sometimes, in cool moments, Emma wondered if it might not be possible to reverse his priorities, get him to do sex slow and other things quick, but when put to the test she always failed. At least, though, when he sat up afterward to take off his shoes he looked really happy. Ardor seemed to stay in his face longer than it did elsewhere, which was actually all right with her.

"You see, doing it my way neither of us loses interest," he said over his shoulder while on the way to the bathroom.

"Getting laid by you is more like getting sideswiped," Emma said. "Interest has little to do with it."

As usual, she finished undressing after the fact and lay with her head propped on two pillows, looking at her feet and wondering how long it would be before her stomach rose and blocked them from view. Hot as it was, the late afternoon was still her favorite time. She was cooled for a few minutes by her own sweat, and a long slanting shaft of sunlight fell across her, right where her panties should have been. Flap came back and flopped on his stomach to resume his reading, which made her feel slightly left out. She put one of her legs across his body.

"I wish your attention span were longer," she said. "Why are you reading Wordsworth if you don't like him?"

"He reads better when I'm not so horny," Flap said.

"Momma isn't really absurd," Emma said. Her body had somehow been rushed off far from her mind, but that was over and her mind wanted to go back and have the conversation it had been beginning when the rush occurred.

"I'd like to know what she is then." Flap said.

"She's just absolutely selfish," Emma said. "I wish I knew whether that was bad or not. She's a great deal more selfish than you are, and you're no slouch. She may even be more selfish than Patsy."

"Nobody's more selfish than Patsy," Flap said.

"I wonder what would have happened if you two had married one another," Emma said.

"Me and Patsy?"

"No. You and Momma."

Flap was so startled that he stopped reading and looked at her. One of the things he had always liked about Emma was that she would say anything that popped into her head, but he had never expected that particular thought to pop into anyone's head.

"If she heard you say that she'd have you committed," he said. "*I* should have you committed. Your mother and I may not have much integrity but we at least have enough to keep us from marrying one another. What an abhorrent thought."

"Yes, but you're a classicist, or something," Emma said. "You think people only do reasonably normal things, or reasonably abnormal things. I'm smarter than you and I know that people are apt to do anything. Absolutely anything."

"Especially your mother," Flap said. "I'm not a classicist, I'm a romantic, and you're not smarter than me."

Emma sat up and scooted over near him so she could rub his back while he read. The sun had moved down her legs and onto the floor, and she had stopped being sweaty and cool and could feel the mugginess of the evening coming through the open window. It was only April, but already so hot at times that the patches of hot air were almost visible. Emma sometimes thought of them as having shapes, like Casper the Ghost, only these were unfriendly little hot ghosts that settled on her shoulders or curled around her neck, making her splotchy with heat.

After a while she began to try to decide what might make the coolest possible supper. She decided cucumber sandwiches, but it was only an abstract choice. Flap would never eat them and she didn't have any cucumbers anyway. Unless she cooked something great he would probably read for hours without saying a word; after having sex he almost always read for hours without saying a word.

"It would have been strange if one of us had married someone who didn't like to read, wouldn't it?" she said. "There must be millions of interesting people in the world who just don't like to read."

Flap didn't answer, and Emma sat looking out the window at the deepening evening, turning supper possibilities over in her mind. "The only thing I don't like about sex is that it always means the end of a conversation," she said.

"Still, I guess it's what keeps us together," she added, not really thinking.

"What?" Flap asked.

"Sex," Emma said. "We don't talk enough for it to be conversation."

But Flap hadn't really heard her. He had just spoken in response to her voice, to be polite. Emma got off the bed and began to gather up her clothes and his, feeling suddenly that she didn't know quite what to make of things. Her own chance remark disconcerted her. She had no idea why she had said it, and no way of knowing whether she meant it or not. In the whole two years of their marriage she had never said anything similar, anything to indicate that she felt their being together was something less than a part of natural law. She had forgotten how to imagine life apart from Flap, and besides she was pregnant. If there was anything neither of them needed to think about it was the basis of their being together.

Emma looked at him, and the fact that he still lay sprawled on the bed reading, perfectly content, perfectly solid, and completely oblivious to her, tipped her back from her strange momentary list toward the unreal. She padded off and showered, and when she came back Flap was poking in the chest of drawers looking vainly for a T-shirt.

"They're on the couch," she said. "They're even folded."

She felt inspired to make a Spanish omelette and hurried off to try, but it was one of the fairly frequent occasions when her inspiration didn't quite carry her through a dish. Flap contributed to what proved a minor debacle by sitting at the table and tapping his foot while he read, something he often did when he was really hungry. When she set the dish before him he looked at it critically. He fancied himself a gourmet. Only the fact that they had no money kept him from being a wine snob as well.

"That doesn't look like a Spanish omelette," he said. "That's just Tex-Mex scrambled eggs."

"Well, my mother was too patrician to teach me to cook," Emma said. "Eat it anyway."

"What a great day this has been," he said, looking at her with his nice friendly eyes. "Daddy bought a new boat, I got home too late to see your mother, and now I get scrambled eggs. A perfect run of luck."

"Yeah, and you also got laid," Emma said, helping herself to some of the omelette. "It happened so fast you may not remember it, but you did."

"Oh, stop pretending you're neglected," Flap said. "You aren't neglected and you couldn't look bitter if you tried."

"I don't know," Emma said. "I might learn."

It had begun to shower again, heavily. While they were finishing the omelette it stopped, and she could hear the trees dripping. The darkness outside was wet and deep.

"You're always saying, 'I don't know,'" Flap said.

"Yes," Emma said. "It's true too. I don't know. I don't think I ever will. I bet that's what I'll do when I'm old. I'll sit in a chair somewhere saying 'I don't know, I don't know.' Only then I'll probably drool when I say it."

Flap looked at his wife, once again a little startled. Emma had unexpected visions. He didn't know what to say. Though unorthodox in appearance, it had actually been a very good omelette and he felt unusually content. Emma was staring into the wet night. Her quick face, which was almost always turned toward him—to see what he might be thinking, or might be wanting—was for the moment turned somewhere else. He had been about to compliment her but didn't. Emma could sometimes make him feel reticent, at odd times and for no reason he knew, and it had just happened. A little baffled and very reticent, he fiddled with his fork for a while, and they sat and listened to the dripping trees.

CHAPTER II

1.

"You WILL be pleased to know that I've softened," Aurora said, quite early the next morning. "Perhaps, after all, it isn't entirely to be lamented."

"What isn't?" Emma asked. It was only seven-thirty, and she was barely awake. Also, she had stubbed her toe getting to the telephone, which was in the kitchen.

"Emma, you do not sound alert?" Aurora said. "Have you been taking drugs?"

"Momma, for God's sake!" Emma said. "It's dawn. I was asleep. What do you want?"

Even in a confused state and with her toe hurting she realized it was a stupid question. Her mother called every morning, and never wanted anything. The fact that the phone was in the kitchen was the only thing that had saved her marriage. If it had been by the bed and had rung every morning at seven-thirty Flap would have divorced her long ago.

"Well, I hope I don't have to remind you again about drugs," Aurora said firmly. "I read about them everywhere I turn."

"I don't take drugs, I don't take drugs," Emma said. "I don't take anything. I haven't even had coffee yet. What did you say to begin with?"

"That perhaps it isn't entirely to be lamented."

"I don't know what you're talking about," Emma said. "What isn't?"

"Your state," Aurora said. Sometimes she was plain-spoken and sometimes she wasn't.

"I'm all right," Emma said yawning. "I'm just sleepy."

Aurora felt mildly exasperated. She was not being given credit for what seemed to her highly admirable intentions. Fortunately she had a cruller to hand, on her breakfast tray, so she ate it before saying anything more. Her daughter, a mile and a half away, dozed a moment with the phone held to her ear.

"What I was referring to is the fact that you are with child," Aurora said, making a fresh start.

"Oh, that's right, I'm pregnant," Emma said.

"Yes, if you must use plain words," Aurora said. "Speaking of words, I have been reading the news. Your friend the young writer seems to be publishing a book."

"Danny Deck is," Emma said. "I told you that months ago."

"Humph. I thought he was living in California," Aurora said.

"He is, Momma," Emma said. "The two things aren't mutually exclusive."

"Please don't be philosophical, Emma," Aurora said. "It makes no impression on me at all. It says in the paper he is to be here tonight, autographing his book. You might have married him, you know."

Both bolts were from the blue, and Emma flushed, half with embarrassment and half with anger. She looked out the window at their little snatch of back yard, half expecting to see Danny sleeping in it. He had a habit of passing out in back yards, particularly theirs. He also had a habit of catching her in her nightgown, and the news that he was around made her feel immediately shy. At the same time she was furious with her mother for having found out about the autograph party first.

Danny was hers, and her mother had no right to know things about him that she didn't know.

"You shut up," she said fiercely. "I married who I wanted to marry. Why would you say that? You always detested him and you know it. You even liked Flap better than you liked Danny."

"I certainly never cared for Daniel's attire," Aurora said placidly, ignoring her daughter's anger. "That much is undeniable. He dressed even worse than Thomas, which is hardly conceivable. Still, facts are facts. He's proven himself a man of accomplishment, and Thomas has not. It may be that you chose unwisely."

"Don't say that to me!" Emma yelled. "You don't know anything about it. At least I chose! I didn't let five or six men trail me around for years, like you're doing. Why are you criticizing me? You can't make up your mind about anything!"

Aurora promptly hung up. There was clearly no point in continuing the conversation until Emma had had time to cool off. Besides, André Previn had just stepped onto the *Today* show and André Previn was one of the few men alive to whom she immediately yielded her undivided attention. Vulgarly put, she was mad for him. For the *Today* show he was wearing a polka dot shirt and a broad tie, and he twinkled and kept his dignity at the same time. Aurora sipped her coffee and had another cruller while hanging on to his every word. The crullers came to her airmail every week in a white box from Crutchley's of Southampton, the gift of her second-dullest suitor, Mr. Edward Johnson, the vice-president of her bank. Edward Johnson's only redeeming feature was that he had grown up in Southampton and knew about Crutchley's; arranging for her weekly package of crullers was, as far as Aurora knew, the most imaginative thing he had ever done in his life.

André Previn was a fish of another water. He was so adorable that at moments Aurora found herself envying his wife. A man who possessed both dignity and a twinkle was a rare find—it was a combination for which she herself seemed fated to look in vain. Her husband Rudyard, through no fault of his own, had had neither. The very fact that his name was Rudyard was no fault of his own; his ridiculous mother had never gotten over a schoolgirl

35

crush on Rudyard Kipling. Indeed, looking back on her twenty-four years of marriage to Rudyard—something, admittedly, that she seldom did—Aurora could not remember a single thing that had been his fault, unless it was Emma, and even that was questionable. Rudyard had been without the slightest capacity for insistence; he had not even insisted that they marry. A plant could not have been easier to relate to, or less exciting. All he really needed was a tub of water to soak in at night—Aurora had often told him as much, and he had always agreed. Fortunately, he had also been tall, handsome, beautifully mannered, and possessed of a patent on a minor chemical for which the oil industry paid him comfortable sums of money. Had it not been for the minor chemical, Aurora felt quite sure they would have starved; Rudyard had been much too well mannered to hold a job. His approach to existence had been to decline comment whenever possible; if he had a genius for anything it was for minimums. Even while he was alive Aurora had sometimes found herself forgetting that he was alive, and then one day, without a word to anyone, he had sat down in a lawn chair and died. Once he was dead, even his picture didn't serve to call him to mind. Twenty-four years of minimums had left her only a scattering of usable memories, and, in any case, in her heart of hearts she had long since given herself up to thoughts of others—singers, usually. If she were ever forced to put up with a man again she intended to see to it that he could at least make noise.

André Previn's great appeal was that he was both musical and dimply. Aurora herself was devoted to the Bach Society. She watched him closely, determined to get some fresh movie magazines and find out how things stood with his marriage. She had never been able to keep away from movie magazines; they seemed to accumulate in her grocery bag. Emma heaped much contempt on her for reading them, so much that she was forced to keep them in her laundry basket and read them behind locked doors, or in the dead of night. The minute the show was over she called her daughter again.

"Guess who was on the *Today* show?" she said.

"I don't care if Jesus was on the *Today* show," Emma said. "What do you mean, hanging up on me? First you wake me up, then you insult me, then you hang up. Why should I even talk to you?"

"Emma, do be civil," Aurora said. "You're much too young to be so difficult. Besides, you're going to be a mother."

"I don't even want to be one now," Emma said. "I might turn out like you. Who was on the *Today* show?"

"André," Aurora said.

"Groovy," Emma said sulkily, not very interested. She had gotten dressed but had not been able to calm down. Flap was sound asleep, so there was no real point in cooking breakfast. If Danny would only turn up she could make him some pancakes and hear all about the trouble he had managed to get himself into; she was dying to see him, dying to hear what had happened to him, but at the same time the thought that he might suddenly be standing outside the door filled her with apprehension.

"Why are you so nervous?" her mother asked, keying in on the apprehension instantly.

"I'm not nervous," Emma said. "Don't you start prying into my life. You shouldn't be talking to me now anyway. It's time for your suitors to be calling."

Aurora observed that that was true. None of her suitors would have dared call before eight-fifteen, nor would they dare neglect her past eight-thirty. In various parts of Houston, at that very moment, men were fidgeting because her line was busy, each wishing that he had been bold enough to call at eight-fourteen, or even eight-twelve. Aurora smiled; all that was satisfying knowledge. Still, she was not about to let the fact that her fellows were calling stay her from her maternal investigations. Her daughter was being much too secretive.

"Emma, I smell a rat in your tone," she said firmly. "Are you contemplating adultery?"

Emma hung up. Two seconds later the phone rang again.

"Even Stephen," Aurora said.

"I'm contemplating murder," Emma said.

"Well, we've never had a divorce in our family," Aurora said, "but if we have to have one, Thomas is a good place to start."

"Goodbye, Momma," Emma said. "Speak to you tomorrow, I'm sure."

"Wait!" Aurora said.

Emma waited silently, chewing a nail.

"Dear, you're so abrupt," Aurora said. "I'm eating, you know. It can't be very good for my digestion."

"What can't?"

"Being spoken to abruptly," Aurora said. She would have liked to sound despondent but was so perked up from seeing André that she couldn't manage it.

"It's a very disappointing way to start the day," she went on, doing her best. "You seldom let me finish and you never say kind things to me anymore. Life is so much pleasanter when people say kind things to one another."

"You're wonderful, you're sweet, you have gorgeous hair," Emma said tonelessly and hung up again. Once she had tried to write a short story about herself and her mother; she had described the world as one vast udder from which her mother spent her life milking compliments. The figure hadn't really worked, but the basic premise was accurate enough. It had taken her years to get to the point where she could hang up when she didn't feel like being milked.

She went outside and sat on the steps of her little porch in the bright sunlight, waiting for Danny. It was his hour—he loved to come for breakfast and would sit in the kitchen quietly ogling her while she cooked. He always pretended to be deeply exhausted from his various adventures, but he was never too exhausted to ogle—as she knew and as Flap knew too. They were all one another's best friends and had been for three years, and they inspired one another to heights of talk they were otherwise seldom inspired to; still and all, there were romantic nuances in the friendship, and the fact that Danny had gotten married didn't seem to affect the nuances at all. No one with a grain of sense expected his marriage to last, or even to count particularly. He had married on a typically feckless impulse, and it might have already stopped lasting, for all she knew.

The fact that Danny had actually managed to get his novel published seemed more astonishing to Emma than the fact of his marriage. It was an equivocal, ambiguous thing, and her mind

nibbled at it while her legs grew hot from the sun. Almost everyone she knew had hoped at one time or another to become a
writer. It had been Flap's only ambition when she first met him.
She herself had written fifteen or twenty vague, girlish short
stories, but she had never let anyone see them. Most of their
college friends had poems or short stories or fragments of novels
secreted away. Danny even knew a janitor who wrote screen-
plays. But Danny actually *was* a writer, and it made him different. Everyone treated him as if he weren't quite a normal person,
or the same as they were. It was probably true, and Danny
probably knew it was true, but it bothered Emma a little. She
was the only person, so far as she knew, to treat him as if he were
the same as everyone else, which was why they were such special
friends. But being married to Flap and treating Danny as if he
were the same as everyone else weren't simple things to combine,
she had discovered. Areas of the friendship and areas of her
marriage had become almost all nuance.

The sun got too hot to sit in pleasantly, and she scooted back
into the shade of the eaves to brood about it. While she was
waiting for Danny, Flap appeared. It didn't surprise her. She
knew perfectly well that he could feel her thinking about things.
He opened the screen door about a foot and looked at her with
no great friendliness.

"What about breakfast?" he asked. "Are we married or aren't
we?"

Emma kept sitting in the shade. Only her toes were in the
sunlight. Her toenails were getting hot. "I don't think you should
bully me," she said, not moving. "No one was awake to cook
breakfast for, so I didn't cook it yet."

"Okay, but Dad and I are leaving after a while," he said. "You
don't want to send me off on an empty stomach, do you?"

"I didn't know you were leaving," she said quickly. "I don't
really want to send you off at all. Why are you leaving?"

Flap was silent. He was in his underwear and couldn't come
out on the porch.

"You didn't tell me you were leaving," Emma repeated. "Why
didn't you say something about it last night?"

Flap sighed. He had hoped she would be cheerful about it. so he wouldn't have to feel guilty for two days, but it had obviously been a forlorn hope.

"Well, we wouldn't buy a new boat and not go try it out, would we?" he asked. "You know us better than that."

Emma pulled her toes in out of the sun. She had been extremely happy for a few minutes, with just herself and the warm boards and a few vague thoughts of Danny. It was such happiness to be alone on her porch that she had been quietly expecting the whole day to be complete delight. Perhaps warm boards and cool shade were the best parts of life, after all. Flap had only to open the screen door to tip everything out of kilter again. All the life that went on in the house itself came out on the porch, and Emma felt cornered. She also felt angry.

"I didn't know I married Siamese twins," she said. "Can't you two go anywhere without one another?"

"Now don't start that," Flap said.

"No, you're right, why should I?" Emma said, getting up. "I haven't got the paper yet. What would you like for breakfast?"

"Oh, anything," Flap said, greatly relieved. "I'll get the paper."

He was very guilt-ridden during breakfast and talked constantly, hoping he could somehow manage to atone for what he was doing before he did it. Emma was trying to read the classifieds, and his attempts to mollify her with conversation began to irritate her more than the fact that he was deserting her to go fishing with his father.

"Look, just shut up and eat," she said. "I can't read and listen, and you can't taste your food when you're talking like that. I'm not going to divorce you because you prefer your father's company to mine, but I might divorce you if you don't quiet down and let me read."

"I don't understand why you read the classifieds anyway," Flap said.

"Well, they're always different," Emma said.

"I know, but you never do anything about them," he said. The sight of her patiently going down the columns of ads always annoyed him. It was hard not to feel intellectually superior to someone who spent half her morning reading classified ads.

"You see things you want but you never go buy them," he added. "You see jobs you want but you never go get them."

"I know, but I might sometime, if I feel like it," Emma said. She did not intend to be bullied out of her pleasure, and in any case she had once bought a beautiful pale blue lamp at an estate sale she had noticed in the classifieds. It had only cost seven dollars and was one of her greatest treasures.

Cecil came while Flap was shaving, and Emma put aside her paper and got him some coffee. She managed to press some toast and jam upon him, every crumb and speck of which he ate. Watching Cecil eat always fascinated her, because his plates ended up as clean as if they had never had food on them. Her mother had once observed that he was the only man she knew who could wash a dish with a piece of bread, and it was true. Cecil was a kind of Japanese farmer of eating: he concentrated on his plate as if it were a tiny plot of land, every millimeter of which it was up to him to utilize. Left with one bite of toast, one bite of egg, and one bite of jam, he would first put the egg on the toast, then put the jam on the egg, and then carefully wipe the plate with the bottom side of the piece of toast before putting the bite in his mouth. "How's that for making things come out even?" he would say with a touch of pride. Usually he would even manage to wipe his knife and fork on the edge of the toast at some point, so that everything would look exactly as it had looked when the meal began. When she and Flap had first married, Cecil's ability to make things come out even had often disconcerted Emma badly. In those days she had been too shy to watch anyone eat her cooking, and she would look up at the end of a meal and see Cecil's shining white plate and be unable to remember whether she had fed him or not.

Flap came in while his father was finishing his coffee. He looked so miserable that for a moment Emma was touched. Being torn between a wife and a father obviously wasn't much fun. Why he had to be torn was a mystery to her—she had certainly never been torn between him and her mother—but clearly he was, and there was no point in her making things worse for him. She lured him into the bedroom so she could give him a nice kiss, but it didn't work. He was too miserable to be interested, and he didn't really like being kissed anymore, anyway. Thwarted, Emma tried rubbing his stomach to show him she had no hard feelings.

"Would you please try not to look so woebegone?" she said. "I don't want to have to sit around here feeling guilty because I've made you feel guilty. If you're going to desert me you might at least learn to be arrogant about it. Then I could hate you instead of having to hate myself."

Flap just looked out the window. He couldn't stand Emma when she tried to analyze things. The only thing that he was really miserable about was that the fact that he was married to her made him feel obliged to ask her to come with them.

"You could come if you really wanted to," he said unemphatically. "You don't really want to float around all weekend arguing about Eisenhower and Kennedy, do you?"

"No thank you," Emma said. "I certainly don't."

By dint of much hard work she and Cecil had hacked out Eisenhower and Kennedy as *their* subject of conversation. In Cecil's view, Ike had been the only good president since Abraham Lincoln. He loved everything about him, particularly the fact that he had risen from humble beginnings. It took a thrifty man to rise from humble beginnings. Those Kennedys, as he called them, offended him at every turn. It was clear that they wasted money, and the fact that some of it was their own mitigated nothing, in Cecil's eyes. He doubted that those Kennedys could even be trusted to clean their plates.

Emma didn't care. She was frankly glamour-struck, and she adored the Kennedys. Her mother, who paid no attention to presidents at all, had grown so tired of hearing the two of them argue about Eisenhower and Kennedy that she had forbidden them to so much as mention a president at her table again.

"Well, maybe we'll bring home some good fish," Flap said lightly.

Emma took her hand off his stomach. His face had lightened as quickly as his tone. All it had taken to cheer him up was her polite refusal of his little *pro forma* invitation. He turned and bent over and began to drag his fishing gear out of the bedroom closet, and he began to whistle "The Wabash Cannonball." One or another of her dresses was always getting snagged on his fishing gear, but it was their only closet and he had no other place to keep it. When he bent over to get his tackle box the T-shirt he was wearing rode partway up his back. Emma stood looking at the bumpy lower part of his spine. It was a place her hand loved, at certain times. But she felt chilled and sullen. She would have liked to have a heavy chain in her hand, and if she had had one she would have hit him with it, right across the lower part of his spine. If it broke his back, so much the better. He had somehow made her betray herself by refusing her own right to go with him; then he had offered her the possibility of a fish to cook as a reward for refusing her own right. She had done nothing really honest all day, and she stood looking at him, feeling that she didn't know how to begin to do anything honest. Only a chain would have made it possible for her to do something honest, and she didn't have one.

All she had was a sullen coldness, and the secret of Danny. Flap could have found out the secret if he had read the morning paper as attentively as her mother had, but he had only glanced at the headlines and read the sports page. He knew he was going away fishing and hadn't even looked to see what was on at the movies. At two or three points during breakfast Emma had almost confessed what she knew, not exactly out of loyalty but because a strange wavery apprehension came over her and went away and then came over her again. If Flap had ever once looked at her right, she would have come right out with Danny, but she could tell from the happy way he was whistling "The Wabash Cannonball" that he was not going to be thinking about her much for a couple of days. She made no effort to look any way but hostile as they were leaving, but it made only a dim impression on him.

"You look sort of resentful," he said, pausing a moment on the steps. The tone he used was the tone he would have used if all he had said was "Nice weather."

"I am," Emma said.

"Why?" he asked politely.

"It's not my place to say," Emma said. "If you really care, then it's your place to find things out."

"Well, you're just impossible," he said.

"I don't agree," Emma said. "I'm possible when I'm handled with a little care."

Flap was in perfect spirits. He didn't want to fight, and didn't answer; nor did he notice that when he waved to her from the car she didn't wave back.

Cecil didn't notice her omission either. He too was feeling very good. "That girl's the cat's meow," he said. "Marrying her was the smartest thing you've done with yourself yet. Hope we can bring her some good fish to cook."

2.

THE GIRL who was the cat's meow went in and attempted to arm herself against the alternating senses of anger and futility, emptiness and apprehension that had invaded her heart and spoiled her pleasure in what she had thought might be a wonderful morning. All she had wanted was for Flap to face up to her for a minute—maybe just look really friendly, and not friendly-guilty, as he had looked. He knew what a pushover she was, how easy she was to please. Two nice minutes would have done it, and it seemed disgraceful to her that he had married her and yet didn't care enough to produce two nice minutes when she needed them.

She pushed the dirty dishes out of the way and sat down by the window where she had sat the night before to listen to the rain. For weapons she had coffee and cigarettes, the want ads and the crossword puzzle, and even her old shabby copy of *Wuthering Heights*. The book was one of her unfailing comforts in life, but for once it failed her. She couldn't lose herself in it, and all it did was remind her of what she already knew too well: that in her life nothing that total would ever be at stake. No one would ever think she was that crucial—not truly or absolutely, not life or death, commit or die.

While she was staring at the want ads the phone rang.

"You again," she said, knowing perfectly well who it was.

"Of course. You didn't let me have the last word," her mother said. "That was rather selfish of you, dear. You know how much I enjoy the last word."

"I was busy," Emma said. "Also, I was thinking of your fellows."

"Oh, them," Aurora said. "Emma, you still sound resigned. Honestly. Here you are about to have a nice baby and you don't even sound happy. You have your whole life before you, dear."

"You've been telling me that for ten years," Emma said. "Some of it must be behind me by now. That's what you told me when I got braces, as I recall. It's also what you told me when I got engaged."

"Only to bring you to your senses," Aurora said. "Unfortunately, I failed."

"Maybe I'm just a resigned person," Emma said. "Ever think of that?"

"I'm hanging up," Aurora said. "You're very unrewarding today. I don't think you like me when I sound gay. I may have erred on occasion in my life, but at least I've kept a healthy attitude. You have responsibilities now. No child wants a mother who's resigned. If you ask me you'd do well to diet."

"You'd better stop picking on me," Emma said flatly. "I've had enough. You weigh more than I do anyway."

"Humph," Aurora said, and hung up again.

Emma stared at the want ads, quivering slightly. She had stopped feeling angry at Flap, what she could not stop feeling was disappointed. Life had far too little of *Wuthering Heights*. Now carelessly, now meticulously, she peeled an orange, but it lay on the table uneaten until late that afternoon.

CHAPTER III

1.

By TEN A.M., after a short nap to calm her nerves, Aurora had made her way downstairs and onto her patio. Rosie, her maid for twenty-two years, found her there, recumbent on a chaise.

"How come all the phones in this house is off the hook?" Rosie asked.

"Well, it's not your house, is it?" Aurora said defiantly.

"No, but the world could be comin' to an end," Rosie said serenely. "Nobody could call an' tell us. Maybe I'd like to get a runnin' start."

"I can see the world from where I'm lying," Aurora said, glancing at it. "It does not appear to be coming to an end. You've been listening to your preachers again, haven't you?"

"I still don't see no point in having four phones if you're gonna go around leavin' them off the hook," Rosie said, ignoring the question. Rosie was five one, freckled all over, and weighed ninety pounds, sometimes. "I might not be no bigger than a chicken, but I got fight," she often said. "I ain't afraid to work, I can tell you that."

Aurora knew that. She knew it only too well. Once Rosie let herself loose on a house, nothing was ever quite as it had been. Old and familiar objects disappeared forever, and those that were allowed to remain were consigned to places so unlikely that it was sometimes months before she came across them. Having Rosie for a maid was an appalling price to pay for cleanliness, and it was perpetually unclear to Aurora why she paid it. The two of them had never got on; they had fought tooth and nail for twenty-two years. Neither of them had ever intended for the arrangement to last more than a few more days, and yet years passed and no good stopping place appeared.

"So?" Rosie inquired. It was her way of inquiring if it was all right to hang up the phones.

Aurora nodded. "I was punishing Emma, if you must know," she said. "She hung up on me twice and was not apologetic. I don't regard that as forgivable."

"Aw, I do," Rosie said. "My kids hang up on me left and right. That's just kids for you. Kids don't know what manners is."

"Well, mine knows," Aurora said. "Emma didn't grow up in the street, like some people's children." She lifted her eyebrows and looked at Rosie, who squinted back at her undaunted.

"All right, just keep off my younguns," Rosie said. "I'll light into you like a rat terrier, first thing you know. Just because you was too lazy to have but one doesn't mean other people ain't got a right to a normal-sized family."

"I'm certainly glad all Americans don't share your view of what's normal," Aurora said. "If they did we'd be standing on top of one another right now."

"Seven ain't a one too many," Rosie said. She snatched several pillows off the chaise and began to pound them. Aurora seldom moved without eight or ten of her favorite pillows. Trails of pillows often led from her bedroom to whatever part of the house she came to rest in.

"Can't you leave me my pillows?" she yelled. "You're no respecter of a person's comfort, I must say. I didn't like your tone just now, either. You're a fifty-year-old woman and I don't intend to see you through another pregnancy."

Rosie's fecundity was a source of constant apprehension to both of them, but particularly to Aurora. The youngest child was only four, and there seemed reason to doubt that the tide had really been stemmed. Rosie herself was ambivalent. She scarcely gave her children a thought for months on end, but when she did give them a thought she found it difficult to give up the notion of having another one. It had pepped her up too many times. She moved around Aurora in a crouch, snatching every pillow she could reach. Those that had pillowcases she instantly stripped.

"Emma was probably just washing her hair and never wanted to talk," she said to divert Aurora's attention. "Anyhow, she's got a heavy cross to bear. That sickly dog of a husband of hers ain't fit to kick off the porch."

"I'm glad we agree on something," Aurora said, kicking out at her idly. "Straighten up. You're far too short as it is. No one wants a maid who's two feet tall."

"Got a date for lunch yet?" Rosie asked.

"As a matter of fact, yes," Aurora said. "If you don't stop hovering around me I'm going to swat you."

"Well, if you're goin' out I'm having Royce in then," Rosie said. "I just thought I'd clear it with you."

"Of course," Aurora said. "Have him in. Make free with my food. I don't know why I don't just deed the house to you. I'd probably be happier in an apartment anyway, now that I'm an aging widow. At least no one would snatch my pillows."

"That's just talk," Rosie said, still grabbing and shucking. Naked pillows lay everywhere—the only ones that weren't naked were the three Aurora was lying on.

"In point of fact it's not just talk," she said. "In point of fact" was one of her favorite phrases. "I ought to move. I don't know what's to stop me, unless I marry, and this is far from likely."

Rosie snickered. "You may marry but you ain't gonna move," she said. "Not unless you marry some old coot with a mansion. You got too many doodads. There ain't an apartment in Houston that'd hold this many doodads."

"I'm not listening to any more of your twaddle," Aurora said, rising and clutching her three remaining pillows to her. "You're as difficult as my daughter and your grammar is worse. Now that you've spoiled my rest I have no choice but to go outside."

"I don't care what you do as long as you don't get in the way of my work," Rosie said. "You can go poo-poo in the frog pond for all I care."

"No choice," Aurora muttered, abandoning the field. It was another of her favorite expressions, and also one of her favorite states. As long as she could feel robbed of all choice, then nothing that went wrong could be her fault, and in any case she had never really enjoyed choosing, unless jewels and gowns were involved.

She kicked several naked pillows out of the way and left the patio with as bad a grace as possible to go out in the sunny back yard and inspect her bulbs.

2.

WHEN SHE came down from her bedroom two hours later, dressed for her luncheon date—or nearly so—Rosie was in the kitchen having lunch with her husband, Royce Dunlup. In Aurora's view Royce was even less inspired than Rudyard had been, and it was a wonder to her that Rosie had somehow prompted him to seven kids. He drove a delivery truck for a company that sold packaged sandwiches, pigs' feet, barbecue chips, and other horrible foods. Somehow or other he always managed his deliveries so as to be in the Greenway neighborhood at lunchtime, so Rosie could feed him a home-cooked meal.

"There you are, Royce, as usual," Aurora said. She was carrying her shoes in one hand and her stockings in the other. Stockings were one of the banes of her existence, and she only put them on at the last minute, if at all.

"Yes, ma'am," Royce said. He stood in great awe of Aurora Greenway, and had remained in awe of her despite having eaten lunch in her kitchen almost every day for twenty years. If she was home, she was usually still in her dressing gown at lunch-time—indeed, it was her custom to change dressing gowns frequently during the course of the morning, more or less as a prelude to serious dressing. Often, proceeding quite frankly on the premise that any man is more interesting than none, she would descend to the kitchen and attempt to get a conversation out of Royce. It never worked, but at least she got to consume her rightful share of whatever Rosie had cooked—usually an excellent gumbo of some sort or another. Rosie was from Shreveport and had a fine touch with shellfish.

"You're looking thinner, Royce. I hope you're not working too hard," she said, smiling at him. It was her traditional opener.

Royce shook his head. "No, ma'am," he said without taking his nose out of his gumbo.

"My that looks good," Aurora said. "I believe I'll just have a cup to bolster me before I start. Then if I get lost on the way to the restaurant I won't have to drive around feeling hungry."

"I thought you never got lost," Rosie said. "That's what you always claim."

"Lost is not the right word," Aurora said. "It's just that I sometimes don't arrive very directly. I don't see that it's nice of you to bring it up anyway. I'm sure Royce doesn't want to hear us argue while he's eating."

"Let me worry about my own husband," Rosie said. "Royce could eat in an earthquake and never miss a bite."

Aurora fell silent in order to consume the gumbo. "I really do think I'm allergic to stockings," she said when she finished. "I never feel quite well when I have them on. Probably they inhibit my circulation, or something of that nature. How is your circulation these days, Royce?"

"Pretty well," Royce said. When pressed about almost any aspect of his personal well-being, Royce might commit himself to a "pretty well," but that was his absolute limit.

He probably wouldn't have said much more if he had dared, but the truth was he didn't dare. Twenty years of watching Aurora bumble around the kitchen in hundreds of dressing gowns, always barefooted and usually only haphazardly coiffed, had filled Royce with a vast doomed lust. She kept a large pile of blue pillows in a particularly sunny corner of the kitchen, and she usually ended up flopped on them, eating gumbo and singing little snatches of opera while she looked out the window and admired the yellow roses in her garden, or watched the midget TV from which she was seldom long separated. She had bought the little TV the minute she had seen it, and considered that she used it to "keep up," something she had always felt obliged to do. Usually she plopped it on a pillow of its own so she could keep up and admire her roses at the same time.

The minute she finished the gumbo she put her cup in the sink and went over and piled the blue pillows as high as they would go. "I think I'll sit for two minutes," she said, sitting. "I don't like to go out when I'm not feeling quite settled, and I'm certainly not feeling very settled."

Rosie was properly disgusted. "You're the biggest sissy I ever seen," she said. "Besides, you're already late."

"You hush," Aurora said. "I have a right to look at my own yard for a moment, don't I? I'm gearing myself up for my stockings."

She looked at her stockings and sighed. Then she started to put one on but got only as far as her calf before she lost her impetus. Once she lost her impetus with a stocking there was very little hope, and she knew it. She began to feel very melancholy, as so often happened just before her luncheon dates. Life was far from romantic, luncheon dates or no. She stuffed her stockings in her purse, feeling very fitful. Then she sang a snatch of Puccini, hoping it would improve her mood. "I should have done more with my singing," she said, sure that no one cared.

"Well, you better not do no more with it in my kitchen," Rosie said. "If there's one thing I ain't in the mood for today it's I-talian music."

"Very well then, you've driven me out," Aurora said, rising. She snatched up her shoes. In fact, the singing *had* improved her mood. "Goodbye, Royce," she said, pausing at the table to give him a big smile. "I hope your meal hasn't been spoiled by all this dissension. You know my car, of course. If you should see that

I've had a flat I do hope you'll stop and help me. I don't think I could do very much with a flat, do you?"

"Uh, no, ma'am, uh, yes, ma'am," Royce said, not quite sure which question he was supposed to reply to, or in what order. He was so bedazzled by Aurora's presence that he could scarcely remember anything. He was smitten, and he had been smitten for years—hopelessly, of course, but deeply. She passed out the back door, full of impetus again, but her fragrance lingered near the table for a bit. She was just the size woman Royce had always meant to marry. Rosie was not much more buxom than a doorjamb—a freckled doorjamb—and not much more yielding either. Royce had kept himself going for longer than he could remember with the entirely ignoble fantasy that someday Rosie might be killed, tragically but as painlessly as possible, and that Aurora Greenway, bound to him by twenty years of gumbo and unanswered questions, might accept him, countrified though he was.

More practically, he also, unbeknownst to everyone, kept himself going with the favors of a part-time barhop named Shirley, who was more nearly Aurora's girth. Unfortunately she neither talked as nice nor smelled as good, and their exertions didn't affect Aurora's place in his fantasy life. There her place was secure.

Rosie, for her part, was not five one and an East Texan for nothing. She had no inkling of Shirley, but she knew perfectly well that her husband had been peeking at her boss underneath his soup spoon for years. She resented every ounce over ninety pounds that Aurora weighed, and there were a lot of them. She had no intention of dying, certainly not before Royce, but if she did anyway she meant to leave him so encumbered with debts and children that he would have little chance to enjoy life without her—not, in any case, with a woman who did little more than traipse around from one pile of pillows to another all day long.

Rosie's theology was hardbitten and oriented toward punishment rather than reward. In her world view, contented indolence was the worst abomination of all, and Rosie, whether the Lord did or not, knew that Aurora Greenway was about as contentedly indolent as anyone alive. Nothing brought out the vengeance-seeking streak in Rosie like watching her husband spill gumbo on his pants because he happened to be watching Aurora loaf around the kitchen watching TV and singing Italian songs.

She had told Royce many times precisely what she meant to do to him spiritually, financially, and anatomically if she ever caught him emerging from one of Aurora's dressing gowns. As soon as the back door closed she marched over to the table and told him again.

"Whut?" Royce said. He was a large, indecisive man and looked aggrieved at his wife's accusation. He offered to swear on the Bible that he had never in his life entertained the one thought that he had entertained almost constantly for two decades.

"I don't know why a grown man would sit there an' offer to swear to a lie," Rosie said. "Then you got me and the Lord both against you, and havin' me against you is bad enough. Aurora ain't worth it, even if she was to cotton to you, which she don't."

"I ain't said she did, Rosie," Royce said with a pained look in his eye. He wished his wife wouldn't so bluntly destroy his one remaining dream.

"Hell, we got seven kids," he added. He always added it—it was his major defense. "Why don't you look at it that way?"

"Because it don't impress me no more than snappin' peas," Rosie said. She had gone back and perched herself on a stool by the sink and was at that moment snapping peas.

"Nice kids," Royce added hopefully.

"I don't know what makes you think so," Rosie said. "You know how lowlife they are. We're lucky they ain't all in the pen, or reform school, or runnin' whorehouses or something. Don't stand there looking at me with your thumbs in your belt. If you got some time to spare you can help me snap these peas."

"Seven kids ought to mean somethin'," Royce insisted. He did take his thumbs out of his belt.

"Yeah, seven accidents," Rosie said. "Means you can't hold your liquor, or nothin' else either. We've had seven car wrecks too—maybe more. An' for the same reason."

"Whut reason?" Royce inquired. He looked out at Aurora's large sunny back yard and thought somberly of how nice it would be to be living in her house with her rather than in his house with Rosie. He and Rosie and the two kids that were still underfoot lived in a four-room frame crackerbox in the Denver Harbor area in North Houston, not far from the Ship Channel. Every morning, almost, the Ship Channel sent its terrible smells their way. It was a citybilly section, full of bars and liquor stores and dangerous alleys that were likely to come out in black neighborhoods or Mexican neighborhoods—places where tipsy rednecks were often deprived of their wallets and their consciousnesses, and sometimes deprived of their lives. It was a wonder to him that Rosie had escaped a tragic death as long as she had in such a neighborhood.

"For the reason that you ain't got a precaution in you after eight or nine beers," she went on, snapping vigorously.

"I guess you never wanted a one of 'em, did you?" Royce said. "I guess it's ever' bit been my fault."

"Why no," Rosie said. "I ain't above enjoyin' an accident now an' then, specially if it happens after dark. Of course I wanted kids. You know how afraid I was of endin' up an old maid. What I was pointin' out to you, Royce, is that seven kids don't mean we're still sweethearts, like we was at first, and it sure don't mean you wouldn't take a little shine to Aurora if she was to get sweet on you."

Royce Dunlup would have been the first to admit that he didn't know much, but he did know that he couldn't outtalk his wife.

"Ain't nobody been sweet on me in a hunnert years," he said gloomily, looking into Aurora's refrigerator. He even liked her refrigerator better than any other refrigerator.

"Quit moonin' an' pay attention to me," Rosie said. "I got my hair set this mornin' and you never said a word."

Royce looked, but it had been so long since he had noticed Rosie's hair that he could not remember how it might have looked before she had it set. In any case he couldn't think of a word to say about it.

"Well, I guess all this will keep till suppertime," he said. "I got to get to Spring Branch."

"That's fine, Royce," Rosie said. "I just got one thing to say to you, and that's if you see any Cadillacs with flats with fat women sittin' in them, just play like you got a gnat in your eye and keep on truckin', okay? You owe me that."

"Why?" Royce asked. Rosie was always suddenly calling in debts he didn't know he had accumulated.

Rosie didn't answer. The only sound in the kitchen was the sound of peas snapping.

"Rosie, I swear," Royce said. "You just make me feel at a total loss." He made the mistake of looking for about one second into two steely gray East Texas eyes—they were squinting slightly, and they held no mercy.

"Gotta go," he said faintly, quelled, as usual, before he had done anything to be quelled for.

Rosie stopped squinting, confident, for the afternoon at least, that she had him. She left off snapping for a minute and made a nice kissing sound for her bewildered spouse. "Bye-bye, honey," she said. "That's sweet, you droppin' in for lunch."

3.

MR. EDWARD JOHNSON, first vice-president of the most tasteful little bank in River Oaks, was trying to think of some way to keep from looking at his watch so often. It was not really seemly for a bank officer to look at his watch every thirty seconds, particularly not when he was standing in the foyer of the most exclusive French restaurant in Houston, but that was what he had been doing for almost forty minutes. It was only a matter of time, and not much of it, before he would start looking at his watch every fifteen seconds, or even every ten seconds; the people coming in would see his wrist keep jerking up and would probably think he had some kind of muscular disorder. That was not good at all. No one wanted a banker to seem spastic. He kept telling himself he ought to contain himself, but he couldn't contain himself.

He had spoken to Aurora that morning and she had seemed almost affectionate. Her tone at times had been a tone to stir hopes, but of course that had been three hours ago, and Aurora had always felt free to change her plans as abruptly as a cricket, though of course in all other respects she was nothing like a cricket at all. Still, Edward Johnson knew there was absolutely no reason to assume that she hadn't suddenly had a change of heart. She might, that very morning, have decided to marry any one of his rivals. She might have eloped with the old general, or the rich yachtsman, or one of the oil men, or even the completely disreputable old singer who continued to tag her around. It was conceivable that some of her suitors had dropped out without his knowledge, but then it was just as likely that new ones had already been added to replace them.

Such thoughts were not easy to live with in the foyer of an exclusive restaurant, under the annoyed eye of a maitre d' who had been grimly holding a table for forty minutes. The only way Edward Johnson could have kept his wrist from jerking up would have been to clench it between his legs, which struck him as being even less seemly than having it jerk. It was not a happy position to be in, and the moment came when he could bear it no longer. He waited until the maitre d' was busy with the wine steward and quickly stepped outside, hoping against hope to spot Aurora.

To his immense relief he did just that. The first thing he saw was her familiar black Cadillac, parked well away from the curb in the nearest bus zone. His heart swelled—for once his timing had been superb. Aurora loved little attentions, like having her car door held for her.

All cares forgotten, Edward Johnson rushed to hold it for her. He ran into the street, yanked the door open, and looked down on the object of his fondest hopes and strongest desires—only to note, too late, that she was in the process of putting on her stockings. One was on and the other one was halfway up her leg. "Aurora, you look lovely," he said, a second before he realized he was looking down upon her partially naked lap—more naked lap, at least, than he had so far been allowed to see. The blood that had been rushing to his head at the prospect of pleasing her made a sudden U-turn and vanished completely.

To make matters worse, a very large bus bore down upon him, honking furiously. The Cadillac, of course, was parked in its zone. When the bus driver saw that he couldn't dislodge the Cadillac he pulled up adjacent to it and stopped barely eighteen inches away. Edward Johnson, thinking for a moment that he was about to be crushed, tried desperately to crowd closer to the car without actually falling into the lap of his date. The front door of the bus whooshed open, and two hefty Negro women managed to squeeze their way between the two vehicles and onto the bus. The driver, a lanky white boy, looked down at Edward Johnson with dull, passionless annoyance. "You-all got your fuckin' nerve," he said. "Whyn't you get a motel room or some-thin'?" Then the door whooshed shut and the bus roared away, filling the air with brown exhaust.

Aurora, aside from pulling her skirt down and tightening her lips slightly, made no movement at all. She did not look at Edward Johnson, she did not look at the bus driver, and she did not so much as frown. She gazed ahead with a pleasant but slightly aloof expression and allowed a small silence to grow. She was adept at small silences, and knew it. Silences were the equivalent, in her repertoire, of the Chinese water torture—they fell, second by second, upon the most sensitive nerves of whoever had been so foolish as to occasion them.

The man who had occasioned this one was not, as Aurora knew, any sort of stoic. Five seconds were quite enough to break him.

"What did he say?" he asked witlessly.

Aurora smiled. Life, she knew, was something one had to make the most of, but there were certainly times when it was difficult to know how to go about it.

"The young man's remarks were quite distinctly put," she said. "I don't think I care to repeat them. I have a date with a gentle-man *inside* a nearby restaurant, I believe. I have never yet made a date that required anyone to wait on a curb, that I can recall. Late as I usually am, one of my escorts might grow dizzy from hunger and fall in front of a bus if I did that. Given a choice, I'd far rather my escorts applied their time to seeing that we get a good table."

"Oh, sure, sure," Edward Johnson said. "You take your time. I'll just run back in and see about ours right now."

Ten minutes later Aurora stepped into the restaurant and smiled at him as if she had not seen him in weeks. "Why there you are, Edward, as usual," she said. Thanks to nervousness his kiss landed somewhere between her cheek and her ear, but she seemed not to notice. Her stockings were on, but the backdraft from another passing bus had blown her abundant hair into a wild upward shape, and she paused a moment to comb it down.

Aurora never allowed herself to take the slightest notice of the reputation of restaurants—not in America, at any rate—and in her view it was quite obvious that no self-respecting French restaurant would have allowed itself to be in Houston anyway. She soon swept on toward the dining room, trailing Edward Johnson behind her. The maitre d' saw them coming and rushed to confront them—Aurora had always unnerved him, and she did it again. He saw her patting a few vagrant locks into place and failed to realize that in her view her appearance was quite as it should be. He himself was fond of mirrors and at once suggested one.

"Bonjour, madame," he said. "Madame would like the ladies' room?"

"Thank you, no, and it's not quite your place to raise such topics, monsieur," Aurora said, walking right past him. "I hope we're going to be seated well, Edward. You know how I adore watching people come in. I've been rushing, as you can see. Probably you're very annoyed with me for being so tardy."

"No, of course not, Aurora," Mr. Johnson said. "Are you feeling well?"

Aurora nodded, glancing around the restaurant with happy disdain. "Why yes," she said. "I hope we're having pompano, and as soon as it's practicable. You know I love it above all fish. If you had a bit more initiative you might have ordered it in advance, Edward. You are rather passive, you know. If you had ordered it in advance we could be eating it now. There was little enough likelihood that I would have wanted anything else."

"Certainly, Aurora," he said.

"Uh, pompano," he said to the first passing busboy, who looked at him blankly.

"That's a busboy, Edward," Aurora said. "Busboys do not take orders. The waiters are the ones in the dinner jackets. I do think a man in your position ought to keep these distinctions a little more clearly in mind."

Edward Johnson could have bitten his tongue off. Almost always Aurora's mere presence was enough to cause him to say things that made him want to bite his tongue off. It was absolutely inexplicable. He had known the difference between waiters and busboys for at least thirty years. He had even been a busboy himself once, as a teenager in Southampton. Yet the minute he sat down beside Aurora Greenway foolish remarks of a sort he would never otherwise have made seemed to pop out of his mouth with no warning. It was some sort of vicious circle. Aurora was not one to let foolish remarks pass, and the more she didn't let them pass the more he seemed compelled to make them. He had been courting her for three years and could not remember a single foolish remark that she had ever let pass.

"I'm sorry," he said humbly.

"Well, I don't think I want to hear about it," Aurora said, looking him in the eye. "I've always thought that people who are too quick with their apologies can't have a very healthy attitude."

She took off a few of her rings and began to shine them up with her napkin. Napkins seemed to work better on rings than anything else, and as far as she could see, the fact that the restaurant had nice napkins was about the only justification for having lunch with Edward Johnson. A man who would order pompano from a busboy was hardly inspiring. On the whole, men who stood in awe of her were even worse than men who didn't, and Edward Johnson seemed mired at least hip deep in awe. He had lapsed into nervous silence and was munching a piece of celery that seemed to her much too wet.

"You had better put a napkin in your lap if you intend to keep eating that celery, Edward," she said. "I'm afraid it's dripping on you. On the whole you don't seem quite attentive to things today. I hope you haven't had setbacks at the bank."

"Oh, no," Edward Johnson said. "Everything's going just fine, Aurora." He wished some real food would come. If there was some real food on the table to talk about he might stand a chance of saying something sensible; there would be less risk that ridiculous remarks would pop out of his mouth to embarrass him.

Aurora quickly found herself driven to the wall with boredom, as was usually the case when she lunched with Edward Johnson. He was so afraid of making a fool of himself that he said nothing at all; the best he could offer in the way of conversation was to munch his celery as loudly as possible. She took refuge, as was her custom, in a minute examination of everyone in the restaurant—an examination that was hardly reassuring. A number of well-dressed and obviously influential men were lunching with women much too young for them. Most of the women were young enough to be their escorts' daughters, but Aurora doubted very much that that was the case.

"Humph," she said, offended by the sight. "All is not well in the land."

"Where?" Edward Johnson said, jumping a little. He assumed that he had spilled something on himself, but he couldn't imagine what, since he had stopped eating celery and was sitting with both hands in his lap. Perhaps the busboy had spilled something on him in revenge.

"Well, I must say the evidence is all around us, Edward, if you'd only open your eyes and look," Aurora said. "I distinctly dislike seeing young women debauched. A great many of them are probably secretaries, and I doubt they can have had much experience of the world. I suppose when I am not able to lunch with you you resort to younger women, don't you, Edward?"

The accusation left Edward Johnson momentarily speechless. It was, in fact, true, and he hadn't the slightest notion how Aurora had found it out, or any hint of how much she knew, not that there was much to know. In the four years since his wife's death he had wined and dined at least thirty of the youngest and most inexperienced secretaries he could find, hoping that some one of them would be impressed enough with his rank or his table manners to sleep with him, but it had been a forlorn effort. Even the greenest little eighteen-year-olds, out of Conroe or Nacogdoches, had no trouble finding ways around him. Scores of fancy meals and hours of his suavest conversation had not so far swayed any of them even to the point of holding hands with him. In truth, he was not far from despair with it all, and his most cherished dream was that maybe someday Aurora Greenway, through some whimsy of the heart, would suddenly decide to marry him and save him from such punishing pursuits.

"You don't seem to be speaking up, Edward," Aurora said, looking at him closely. She had not really meant anything by her accusation—it was her habit, on occasion, to toss out nets of accusation just to see what she could drag in. Those with any sense denied everything at once. The denials might fall on deaf ears; but more often the ears they fell on were just disinterested, Aurora's thoughts having wandered away in the time it took the accused to frame his denial.

The only thoroughly stupid tactic possible when faced with one of Aurora's accusations was to confess; it was the tactic Edward Johnson immediately took. He had meant to lie—he almost always lied to Aurora about everything—but when he looked up and attempted to face her she seemed so convinced that he faltered. She was the only woman he knew who could look absent-minded—distracted, even—and yet seem utterly convinced of the truth of whatever lay uppermost in her mind. She was continuing to inspect the restaurant's clientele, continuing to polish her rings, all with a happy hauteur, but she shot him a look out of the corner of her eye that said plainly enough, he was sure, that she knew all about his secretaries. Confession seemed his only hope, so he blurted one out.

"Oh, not often, Aurora," he said. "Once a month maybe. No more."

Aurora stopped polishing her rings. She looked at him, quite silent. In an instant her look had become grave. "What did you say, Edward?" she asked.

"Very infrequently," he said. "Very infrequently, Aurora."

He was aware from the way her face had changed that he had made a real blunder, something far more serious than ordering from the busboy. She was looking him in the eye and she wasn't smiling. He felt a coward suddenly. He often had, with Aurora, but never so much. Something was wrong—it had never been right. He was a bank vice-president, an important man, he controlled millions, he was known and looked up to; an Aurora Greenway was none of those things. She was well known to be flighty; he didn't even know why he was courting her, why he wanted to marry someone whose mere look made him quail inside. But it was happening. Why was he wasting time, spending money, making a fool of himself, all for a woman he was scared to death of. It made no sense, but he was sure he was in love with her. She was an awful lot livelier than his wife had ever been—his wife had never been able to tell a pompano from a carp—yet there was terror at the heart of it, simple terror. He didn't know what to do or say when Aurora leveled her blue eyes at him. Why wasn't he the man he seemed to be when he was around men? Why didn't he defend himself better, or attack her in return? Why did he have such a feeling of not knowing what to do?

"You mean to say, Edward," Aurora said quietly, "that you bring young women here, where you've brought me?"

"Oh, trivial, Aurora," he said. "Of no consequence. Not relevant at all, really. Just secretaries. I mean for company."

He paused. The pompano arrived. Aurora received it in total silence. The maitre d' had started to suggest a wine, but she chilled him with one look. She considered the fish for a moment but did not pick up her fork.

"What's a man to do?" Edward Johnson said nervously, thinking out loud.

Aurora sat quietly looking at nothing for what seemed to Edward Johnson like a very long time. She did not touch her fork, and he didn't dare touch his.

"I believe you have proposed marriage to me, haven't you, Edward?" she said, looking at him quite expressionlessly.

"Of course, of course," he blurted. His stomach had stopped being a sac—it felt more like a kernel.

"Did you mean it?" Aurora asked.

"Of course, Aurora," he said, his heart suddenly leaping up irrationally. "You know I'm nearly. . . crazy . . . to marry you. I'd marry you this afternoon, right here in this restaurant."

Aurora frowned, but only slightly. "The best marriages are not performed in cheap restaurants, Edward," she said. "Though it isn't really a restaurant, is it? It's more a sort of seraglio, if I'm not confusing my terms. And I've let you bring me to it, haven't I?"

"Marry you this afternoon," Edward Johnson repeated passionately, thinking from her strange manner that there must be some chance.

"Uum," Aurora said with no expression at all. "I do hope my memory isn't failing me, Edward. I'm a little too young to have my memory fail me just now. If it hasn't already begun to slip, then I seem to recall that you have often said I was the only woman in your life."

"Oh, you are," he said urgently. "No doubt of that, Aurora. Why even before Marian died I was crazy about you."

Aurora frowned again, still very slightly.

"I should think insulting me would be quite enough for you, Edward," she said. "I don't believe it's necessary for you to go on and insult the memory of your dead wife. I'm sure she had more than enough of that to put up with while she was alive."

"Oh, no, I'm sorry, you misunderstood. No insult," Edward Johnson said, lacking any clue as to what he ought to say. "Last thing I would ever do."

Aurora began matter-of-factly to fold her napkin. "In point of fact it is not the last thing you'll ever do, Edward," she said, looking at him coolly, "not, at least, unless you propose to perform hari-kari with that butter knife. You're holding it in the wrong hand, by the way. At least it's the wrong hand for buttering—I'm not versed in the etiquette of hari-kari." She stopped and looked at him silently. Edward Johnson changed hands with his butter knife.

"Speak to me, Aurora," he said, completely panicked. "Don't look like that. Those women were just kids. Just teenagers. Inconsequential. I just take them out because they're young."

Aurora chuckled dryly. "Edward, I can assure you you don't have to convince me they were young," she said. "No doubt some of them are seated here under my very eyes. I imagine you and your fellow executives have worked out some satisfactory method of exchange between yourselves. In any case it's your business, not mine. I'm only curious about one thing. If you have been telling me, as you admit you have, that I'm the only woman in your life, what am I to think you've been telling your teenagers?"

"Uh, nothing," Edward Johnson said. "I never promise them anything." He could not at that moment remember anything he had ever said to a secretary. A nightmare was happening—he had been a lunatic to ask such a frightening woman to lunch when he could have gone to his club and had a nice game of golf. And yet he couldn't stand the thought of losing her completely. He wanted desperately to wrest control of the situation, to show Aurora that he was a man she could respect. She was looking at him with a strange, remote expressionlessness, as if in her view he was of less account than the parsley that lay uneaten on their two plates.

At that point, to his great relief, the wine steward appeared with a bottle of white wine. He showed it briefly to Edward Johnson, who nodded cheerfully; then the steward whipped out his corkscrew.

"I don't believe we chose a wine," Aurora said at once.

"I chose, madame," the maitre d' said, popping up at her elbow with a thin smile. The very sight of Aurora filled him with spleen.

Aurora took her eyes off Edward Johnson for a moment and faced the maitre d'. "That's twice you've acted out of turn, monsieur," she said. "I would rather you didn't stand so close to my elbow."

The maitre d's smile grew even thinner. "Madame should eat her fish," he said. "Very excellent pompano, and it's getting cold."

Without the slightest hesitation Aurora took her plate and turned it upside down. "So much for your fish, monsieur," she said. "The gentleman seated across from me has just confessed to statutory rape, which makes you little more than a brothel keeper. I am prepared to be quite vehement in insisting that you don't presume to choose my wines."

"Please, Aurora, please," Edward Johnson said. "None of us want a scene."

"Why, I don't expect you do," Aurora said, "but the fact is I have already made one. I was brought up never to flinch from a scene when a scene is called for. All that remains to be determined is the extent of the scene I shall make."

The maitre d', judging correctly that there was nothing to be done but back away from her, accordingly backed away. Aurora gathered up her keys and pointedly ignored the many heads that were turned. Edward Johnson sat stupefied, aware that the principal hope of what remained of his life was in the process of being crushed.

"Aurora, I never did anything," he said. "I never did anything."

"Why not, Edward?" Aurora asked. She looked in her mirror for a moment and then looked back at him.

"None of them would let me," he said simply. "I just don't know how to talk when I'm around you," he added. "I guess you do something to me and it makes my brain stop working."

Aurora stood up, met the maitre d's outraged eye once more, and then looked down at what remained of her bank vice-president.

"Well, it's extremely fortunate for me that I have that effect on you, Edward," she said, standing up to leave. "Otherwise I don't know how long it would have taken me to find out the truth about you. Those girls you've been misleading are the age of my daughter, or younger. I'll have to ask you to cancel my crullers at once."

For a moment Edward Johnson couldn't remember what crullers were. Whatever had happened had all been too brutal. He had planned what he thought would be an exceptionally nice lunch, and now suddenly his relationship with Aurora Greenway seemed to be ending, right at one of the best tables in the best French restaurant in Houston. He was wearing his nicest suit, and somehow he had been sure Aurora would finally be impressed. He tried desperately to think of something to say that might put things right.

"I'm a widower," he said. "You don't know how it is."

"You're speaking to a widow, Edward," Aurora said, and left.

4.

WHEN SHE arrived at her home, unfed, the indefatigable Rosie had finished with the house and was washing down the driveway and watering the grass. It was a hot day—the smell of wet concrete and wet grass was pleasant on such a hot day. Aurora stopped the Cadillac and sat in it for several minutes, neither moving nor thinking.

When Rosie had watered to her satisfaction she turned off the hose and came over. "What are you sittin' there for?" she asked.

"Don't nag me right now," Aurora said.

"I guess somethin' went wrong," Rosie said. She walked around and got in the front seat of the car, in the mood to sit for a minute with her boss.

"Yes, you're extremely perceptive," Aurora said.

"He run off with a twelve-year-old, or somethin' like that?"

"I'm sure I should be grateful," Aurora said. "He was so scared of me he couldn't look me in the eye anyway."

"What'd you do to get back at him?" Rosie asked. She couldn't read well enough to enjoy *True Confessions*, so she had to make do for excitement with whatever was happening to Aurora.

"Very little," Aurora said. "I turned a perfectly nice fish upside down, but that was to annoy the maitre d'. Edward got off lightly."

"I doubt it," Rosie said.

Aurora sighed. "He was so apologetic it brought out my mean streak," she said. "I guess I'm down to three."

"That's plenty," Rosie said. "One fella with his tongue hanging out's always been as much as I could put up with."

"Yes, but yours hasn't died," Aurora said. "If God were ever to take Royce you'd be in the same pickle I'm in."

"God's got a million like Royce," Rosie said unromantically.

The two of them sat in comfortable silence for a few minutes. When she thought about it, Aurora decided that being free of

Edward Johnson left her feeling more relieved than not. The crullers had been too rich, besides.

"You better get out of this car if you expect me to wash it today," Rosie said. "I ain't washing no cars after three o'clock."

"All right, all right," Aurora said. "I never told you you had to wash the car. But have it your own way. You always do. I'm going in to see which of my possessions you've lost or hidden."

"Nothing wears a piece of furniture out quicker than leavin' it in the same place," Rosie said a little defensively. "That's a home truth, and you can believe it."

"It's a home truth that's stripped me of most of what I started out with," Aurora said. "I hope you've left me some gumbo at least. He was not even forceful enough to see that I stayed and ate my lunch."

She took off her sunglasses and looked at Rosie. Edward Johnson was no great loss, but despite the nice smells of spring she felt slightly downcast. While she was sitting she had allowed herself to wonder what the point of it all was—a mistake she seldom made.

"Pore thing," Rosie said. Nothing touched her sympathies like Aurora having lost a beau. It made her think of all the beaus she herself would probably have lost if Royce hadn't been around. She became sad herself at the mere thought of the injustices that might have been done her. Also, Aurora was easier to like when she was down. The minute her spirits rose she became contrary again.

The words of sympathy were scarcely out of her mouth before Aurora became contrary again.

"Don't you poor thing me," she said, looking Rosie over critically. "You're the one who only weighs sixteen pounds. I'll have you know that I'm in perfect mental and physical health, and I'm not at all to be pitied. You'll be lucky to last another five years, at the rate you smoke, and I don't think your husband is very happy either. Every time I see Royce he's looking gloomy, and I see him every day. Doesn't he ever look happy?"

"What's happy got to do with it?" Rosie said hotly. "I don't know what Royce Dunlup has got to be happy about."

"That's an awful thing to say," Aurora said. "What kind of wife are you?"

"One with some sense," Rosie said. "Royce has got bills to pay and me and the kids to look after. That man's got to keep his shoulder to the wheel—he ain't got time for sport. Besides, all he wants to do is shack up with you, and you know where I stand on *that*."

Aurora smiled. "Still jealous, are you?" she said.

"You know me," Rosie said. "I ain't one to take nothin' lightly."

"Well, it must be an awful way to be," Aurora said, tapping the steering wheel thoughtfully with a fingernail. "The more things one can take lightly, the better chance one has. In any case, you're probably wrong about me. I doubt that Royce entertains masculine thoughts about me, at my age."

"You're full of prunes if you think he don't," Rosie said. She opened the glove compartment and began to weed its contents. Aurora watched with some interest. She seldom remembered having a glove compartment herself, and its contents were something of a revelation to her. A pair of sandals emerged, as well as an amber necklace that she had been hunting for months.

"Why there it is," she said. "What a place for it to be."

"You're full of prunes if you think he don't," Rosie repeated. She dragged out a fistful of costume jewelry and a number of income tax statements.

"Oh, well, I'm sure we've talked of this before," Aurora said. She gave Rosie a lazy look in which there was much unconcern for the topic at hand.

"It's not always easy to tell when men are having masculine thoughts," she added. "I suppose I've stopped noticing. You're welcome to keep him out of my kitchen if you're so worried."

"No, then he'd just take up with some slut," Rosie said. "Them bars he delivers to is full of sluts. No telling what would happen then."

Aurora opened her door. "There is very little telling what will happen ever," she said. "I believe I'll muddle on in."

"Gumbo's on the stove," Rosie said. "I'm taking the green stamps if I find any. I'm saving up for one of them home beauty parlors. Maybe what I need to be is a beautician."

"Anything you want, just keep it away from me," Aurora said. She slipped off her shoes and stockings before she got out. The bright green grass of her lawn was nice and wet and she took her time walking across it. Somehow being barefoot always made her feel more the way she liked to feel. It was so much easier to be enthusiastic when her feet were touching something besides shoes. Time and again she had had to fight down an urge to throw all her shoes in the garbage and begin a retreat from life—it was one of her strongest if most unladylike urges. She had never gone and done it, but she was not above throwing away five or six pair when she thought Rosie wouldn't notice. All her life she had looked for shoes she liked, but the truth was there just weren't any; it seemed to her that the only events that made shoes worth it at all were concerts. At concerts, if the music was truly good, shoes ceased to matter; social engagements were a different matter. No matter what the scale or tone of the engagement, she seldom felt quite right until she was back home and the wood of her floors or the tile of her patio or perhaps the velour of her bedroom rug was under her bare feet again.

She lingered on her lawn, feeling better and better about things, and by the time she actually got to her doorstep she looked back and saw that Rosie, that demon of energy, had already got a chamois and a bucket and some water and had covered half the Cadillac with soapsuds. She went in and got a large bowl of gumbo and a piece of nice bread that had come from an Argentine bakery nearby and went back to sit on her steps and eat while Rosie went at the chrome. "You'll have a fit, working so hard in that sun," she called out, but Rosie flapped the chamois at her contemptuously and went on happily about her work. She had just finished polishing the chrome when Royce Dunlup drove up in his baby blue delivery truck to take her home.

CHAPTER IV

1.

EMMA HAD learned something about heat from life in Houston. Heat was an aid to suspension, and there were times when suspension was an aid to life. When she really didn't know what to do with herself, she had learned to do nothing at all. It was not an approach her mother would have approved of, or Flap either, but then neither of them was ever around when feelings of purposelessness seized her, so it didn't matter. If it was very hot and she felt really purposeless, she did nothing at all. She took off most of her clothes and sat on her bed staring at the bureau. The reason she stared at it was because it happened to stand against the wall, exactly opposite her bed. She didn't read at such times, though often she took a book along for a prop. What she did was suspend herself and stare at the bureau. She ceased to have definite thoughts or feelings, definite wishes, definite needs. It was enough to sit on the bed staring at the bureau. It was not really like living, but it didn't hurt. It was not boredom, not despair, not anything. It was just sitting. It was certainly not a state she tried to guard. Anyone could interrupt it if they chose, but she herself didn't particularly try to avoid it.

When Flap had gone away, and her mother had called, and she had peeled half the orange and not eaten it, she thought of a number of things she might do. She was a senior biology major, and there was all sorts of lab work she could be doing. She had a part-time job in the zoology lab and could always go over and prepare specimens when she wanted company. There was always company to be had in the lab. What kept her home was simply a liking for home. Perhaps it was an inheritance from her mother, for her mother had a hundred possible outlets too and seldom used any of them. Both of them liked staying home, but then her mother had every reason to like it, since her house was one of the nicest places in Houston. Immediately upon moving from New Haven, her mother had decided that good Spanish Colonial was about the best one could do architecturally in the Southwest and had made her father buy a lovely Spanish Colonial house on a fairly old, fairly unfashionable one-block-long street in River Oaks. It was open and airy, with thick walls and rounded doorways. There was a small patio upstairs and a long one downstairs, and the green yard behind the house backed up against a heavily wooded gully, rather than another street. The trees along the gully were immensely tall. Her mother had the house painted every few years to keep it white. She had never air-conditioned, except, after long argument, her husband's den and the little guesthouse in the back yard, where her father, Edward Starrett, had lived his last years and died. Aurora loved her house so much that she seldom left it, and Emma could sympathize. Her own cluttered garage apartment was hardly that lovable, but it was an easy enough place to be suspended, and when Flap went off with his father that was what she did.

She washed her hair first, and then sat on the bed with her back to an open window, letting the hot midday Houston air blow it dry.

It was late that night, while still somewhat in her suspended state, that Emma seduced her old friend Danny Deck, the writer. Her first impulse the next morning—once Danny was gone and she had time to think—was to blame Flap for it, although she told herself at the time that the only real reason he was to blame was that he hadn't been there to stop her.

It was a night, though, that she was to brood on intermittently throughout her life; and years later, while she was living in Des Moines, Iowa, she managed to articulate Flap's culpability more to her own satisfaction. He had not said anything honest to her before going away with his father. If he had she would have had his honesty to be loyal to, and that, she felt, would have stopped her somewhere short of seduction. Still, by the time she came to that articulation she had other, rather more serious things to worry about than one night of confusion ten years back. The awareness that his dishonesty might have been part of what was working in her that night was no more than a small click that caused her to think of Danny for a moment, and of Flap as he had been then, before going on with her day.

Emma was working her way backward through the newspaper when Danny finally came. He had called in the afternoon, sounding hard up—his wife had left him months before and he was looking for her, since their child was about to be born—also he had an autograph party to go to and he had just driven non-stop from California, or practically so, and he was tired and at the end of his rope. Since Danny made a practice of living at the end of his rope, Emma paid it no mind. Periodically, almost day to day, Danny Deck managed to convince himself that he was finally and totally defeated, but that had never worried Emma. She knew quite well that it only took a beautiful or a friendly woman to cause him to change his mind; she didn't let his end-of-my-rope tones affect her day.

Since she had been suspended most of the day, she had still not finished the morning paper, but she had managed to work her way from the want ads almost to the front page. Flap hated to see newspapers read that way, so she had a better time with the news when he was gone. She had worked her way back to page three and was absorbed in a story about a rich gun collector whose wife had shot him with one of his own guns when she heard Danny's old car pull up outside. The sound only made her read faster. The reason the gun collector's wife had shot him was because in a fit of rage he stuffed her favorite earrings in the garbage disposal and ground them up. For some reason the story gave her a strong sense of déjà vu. Things seemed to happen over and over again. It seemed to her she was always reading stories about some crazy Houston killing just as Danny chose to arrive. While she was waiting for him to walk up the driveway she said hello to the mirror a couple of times, to be sure her voice would work.

It had come a terrific thunderstorm that evening, and the driveway and the wooden steps up to her apartment were still wet. In the years ahead she remembered the wet smell of the steps, and only a few other things. The second time they made love was around seven-thirty the next morning and she couldn't concentrate because she was feeling the phone was about to ring. It was just at the time her mother always called. It was drizzling; Emma hurried and the phone didn't ring. They went to sleep with the rain around them like a kind of curtain, very restful, though they only slept about half an hour.

When she awoke, Danny was sitting up in bed looking out the window at her dripping back yard. "I see you still have hummingbirds," he said. "I see your feeder."

"Yep. I feed them Kool-Aid," she said. "You're too skinny."

"It's because I'm at the end of my rope," he said mischievously, well aware that she took a light view of his little desperations.

Emma sighed. He had come in looking like a bedraggled and hopeless washout. His father-in-law had just beaten him up, his suit looked like he had crossed a swamp in it, and he had been forbidden to see his newborn daughter, ever. Also one of his ears was bleeding. She had been bathing it when she decided she had to kiss him. Mostly what followed was that she squirmed fearfully all night and got out of bed a dozen times to see if Cecil's car was pulling into the driveway. It was partly Flap's handiwork anyway, since he was the one who had conditioned her to feel that sexual intercourse had to follow kissing within two minutes or less.

"Now we're both at the end of your rope," she said. "I must be losing my mind. All I really wanted was to kiss you."

"I think your motherly nature just undid you," Danny said,

grinning. "What you really wanted was to get me out of that wet suit. Mortal sin probably seemed a small price to pay."

When she sat up he learned over and rubbed his cheek against hers, pleasantly. He had done that the night before too. It was part of the start of the trouble. Then he looked out the window into the veil of rain and started to explain his latest theory, which had something to do with love being radical and sex being conservative. Emma snuggled against him, too cozy to listen, but glad at least that he was sounding like a promising young author again instead of a beaten young man. "Radical acts are done with the heart," he said. "I might be able to write better now. I have more to forget."

Emma moved her fingers over the smooth skin that covered his arm muscle. "Why is it that that's always the smoothest part of a man?" she asked. "That area right there?"

At breakfast they sat on the same side of the table and played hands while they talked. As regards his wife and daughter, Danny seemed to face an impenetrable wall; his wife's parents would only have him arrested if he tried to see them. Emma became slightly melancholy at the thought of how everyone's life was being lived—also she had begun to feel a strong wifely nervousness again, expecting Cecil's car to pull in the driveway any second.

"I'm leaving before you explode with nervousness," Danny said at once. "Are you feeling very guilty?"

"Not very," Emma said. "I have too bad a character for that."

His car was filled with junk, but he managed to find a copy of his novel for her. "Don't those bottles rattle when you drive?" she asked, referring to the twenty or thirty Dr. Pepper bottles in the back seat. Danny was trying to think of something to scribble in his novel for her and didn't answer. Emma knew that it was not very likely she would ever know a man with whom she had more accord—during breakfast they had had a lot of accord. He seemed to be the one person whose estimate of her had never wavered.

"Best I can do," he said tightly, handing her his book. It was called *The Restless Grass*.

"Please don't marry for a while," she said. From the look on his face it seemed to her he was likely to marry in the next day or two, bigamously, if he met anyone he could win.

"You mean until I get smarter?" Danny asked, grinning. His hair had gotten quite long.

Emma couldn't stand it. Her mother was right. He ought to have been hers. She turned, feeling she had to go.

"Oh, Danny," she said. "Nobody cares about that."

2.

WHEN HE drove away she went in and removed all traces—she even emptied the wastebaskets. Then she felt such a deep relief at having been allowed to get away with it that she relaxed and dozed on her steps too long. The morning clouds had blown away and she got sunburned. She decided to say that his book had come in the mail. Flap was someone to whom—if he had caught her—she would have owed an explanation; since he hadn't, she was not sure that she owed him anything. She and Danny had been caught, all right, but caught by one another: the absence of those feelings she could only feel with him was going to be the punishment that fit her crime.

The moment Danny left she stopped expecting Flap. If he hadn't had instinct enough to come home and catch her sinning he was not likely to come home just to keep her company. The fish were probably biting. She put some cream on her sunburned cheeks and worked her way rapidly backward through the paper to the follow-up story on the man who had ground up his wife's earrings. While she was reading it the phone rang.

"Well, I hope you're in a better mood than you were in yesterday, dear," her mother said.

"I don't know if I am or not," Emma said. "We'll have to see how things develop. How are you?"

"Beset," Aurora said. "Harassed as well. I'm summoning you and Thomas to dinner, pre-emptorily. I didn't call this morning, because I allowed the General to take me to breakfast, which was a good deal more trouble than it was worth. I hope you aren't feeling sluggish as a result."

Emma remembered how strongly she had felt the phone about to ring while she had been trying to feel Danny.

"Sleeping late doesn't make me feel sluggish," she said.

"Well, having to watch that man eat eggs made *me* feel sluggish," Aurora said. "I suppose he eats them in the correct military manner, I don't know. The two of you will be here at seven, won't you?"

"No," Emma said.

"Oh, God," Aurora said. "Don't tell me you're going to be difficult two days in a row. Why do you need to be difficult when I am harassed?"

"You're jumping to conclusions, as usual," Emma said. "I'll be glad to be there at seven, but Flap happens to be gone."

"He's left you?" Aurora asked.

"Don't get your hopes up," Emma said. "I don't think he'd leave me without waiting to see how this child turns out. He's off with his father, fishing. They have a new boat."

"Oh, foolishness," Aurora said. "It would have been less trouble for all of us if that boy had been born a fish. I'm growing more irritable by the minute."

"Who's your date?" Emma asked.

"Oh, Alberto," Aurora said distractedly. "I consider that I owe him a dinner. He's been plying me with concerts lately."

"Good. I adore Alberto," Emma said.

"Well, I won't have you singing his praises. He sings them loudly enough, as you know. Incidentally, he has been forbidden to sing this evening, so don't ask him. Also he has been forbidden to mention Genoa, so don't you mention it either."

"Keep him on a tight leash, don't you?" Emma said. "Why can't he mention Genoa?"

"Because he's excessively boring on the subject," Aurora said. "The mere fact that he was born there makes him think he has the right to describe every cobblestone in it. I have already heard him describe every cobblestone in it, and it's quite unnecessary. I've been to Genoa and you couldn't tell it from Baltimore.

"I know," she added. "I've had a stroke of brilliance. Your young friend Daniel is in town—you must bring him. A young writer would make a very nice fourth. Besides, I'm anxious to see if he's dressing any better."

"No, Flap wouldn't like me bringing him, even if I could find him," Emma said. "I think he's jealous of Danny."

"My dear, that's entirely his problem," Aurora said. "Don't give it a thought. I am your mother and it's perfectly proper for a friend to escort you to my table in your husband's absence. Civilized procedure takes allowance of the fact that husbands are sometimes absent."

"I don't think mine is very impressed with civilized procedure," Emma said. The unexpected ironies of the situation made her feel bold.

"Do you really think all that's a good idea?" she said. "I mean generally. Married ladies being escorted by men they aren't married to. Doesn't it sometimes lead to problems?"

Aurora snorted. "Naturally," she said. "It often leads to disgrace. I hardly know why I wasn't led to disgrace myself, considering how active I am and how reluctant your father was to take me to parties. You're taking up too much of my time, asking these questions. Disgrace abounds, if I may coin a phrase, but good dinner parties are rare. I will expect you and young Daniel at seven and I hope you'll both be witty and scintillating."

"Hold it," Emma said. "I don't know where he is and I don't think I can find him."

"Oh, Emma," Aurora said. "Stop that. I happened to be passing your street this morning and I saw an extremely disreputable car sitting in front of your house. It could only have been Daniel's. Just fish him out of whatever closet you've hidden him in and clean him up as much as possible and get him over here. Don't slow me down with nonsense when I have cooking to do."

Emma stopped feeling relaxed. She hadn't gotten away with it, after all. The picture was changed—worse yet, it was ambiguous. She felt hostile suddenly, but she tried to choke it down. She had to find out what game her mother wanted to play.

"You're a snoop," she said hotly, despite her resolve. "I wish I lived in another town from you. I demand privacy. And I can't bring Danny. So far as I know, he's left town."

"Humph," Aurora said. "It seems to me he ought to keep you informed of his movements if he's going to jeopardize your reputation. I have little respect for men who aren't around when they're needed. Your father was always around when I needed him, though of course he was also around when I didn't. I'm hanging up now. I suppose I'll have to allow Alberto to bring his wretched son."

"I don't like you driving down my street," Emma said as the phone clicked.

CHAPTER V

1.

By THE time Emma arrived Aurora had done everything and, having nothing more to do than finish dressing, had suffered a small loss of impetus, of a sort that was particularly apt to afflict her in the evening when guests were expected. She was standing in her bedroom looking at her Renoir. It was a small Renoir, true, and early, but still it was superb: a small oil of two gay women in hats standing near some tulips. Aurora's farsighted mother, Amelia Starrett, whose eyes had been a Renoir green somewhat unsuited to Boston, had bought the picture in Paris when she herself had been a young woman and Pierre Auguste Renoir quite unknown. It had been the dominant painting of her mother's life, she felt quite sure, as it had been of hers, and as it would be, she hoped, of Emma's. She had resisted all pressures to hang it where others could see it. Others, if they were worthy, might come to her bedroom and see it, but her bedroom was the only place she would allow it to be. The dresses of the women were blue; the painting's colors were light blue, yellow, green, and pink. Still, after thirty years, tears sometimes came to her eyes when she looked at it for too long, as they might have that evening had not Emma appeared at her bedroom door just when she did.

"There you are, you spy," Emma said. She had decided attack was the best plan—it was certainly the easiest, since she still felt full of hostility. Her mother was wearing one of her many trailing gowns, this one deep rose, belted with a turquoise belt she had found somewhere in Mexico. She was holding an extraordinary necklace in one hand, amber with silver, that had come from Africa and that Emma understood had been lost.

"Hey, you found your amber necklace," she said. "That's so lovely. Why don't you give it to me before you lose it again?"

Aurora looked at her daughter, who was dressed creditably for once in a nice yellow dress. "Ha," she said. "Perhaps I will, when you acquire presence enough to wear it.

"I've just been looking at my Renoir," she added.

"That's nice," Emma said, looking at it herself.

"It certainly is," Aurora said. "I'm afraid I had a good deal rather be looking at my Renoir than talking to Alberto. I was forced to ask his son, thanks to you. Probably we're in for a good deal of Genoa, no matter what."

"Why do you see him if you don't like him?" Emma asked, following her mother, who had drifted out on her second-floor patio. "That's what I can never understand about you. Why do you see all these people if you really don't like them?"

"Luckily for you, you aren't old enough to understand that," Aurora said. "I have to do something with myself. If I don't, old age will set in next week."

She rested her hands on the balcony of her patio and stood with her daughter watching the moon rise over her elm, over the cypress that she loved above all trees in the world, over the tall wall of pines that bordered her back yard.

"Besides, I do like them," she said thoughtfully. "They are mostly quite charming men. I seem to have been bred for either more or less than charm. I've had less and I can't find more. You yourself have certainly settled for considerably less than charm."

"I hate charm," Emma said at once.

"Yes, you're much too immature for my necklace," Aurora said, putting it around her neck. "Would you help me fasten it?"

She considered the moon a moment longer with a restful expression. Emma had noticed the expression often, usually before social occasions. It was as if her mother was suspending herself for a little while in order to be the more energetic later.

"Besides," Aurora said, "it is not really a great disparagement to say that I prefer my Renoir to a given man. It is a very fine Renoir. Few enough can measure up."

"I like it but I'd still rather have the Klee," Emma said. It was her grandmother's other good picture, bought when she was a very old lady. Her mother had never loved it, though she allowed it to hang in the living room. Apparently it had been the last of many subjects of controversy between Amelia Starrett and her daughter Aurora, for at the time it was purchased Klee was no longer cheap. Her mother had not wanted her grandmother to spend such a sum on a picture she had not found congenial, and the fact that the picture had multiplied in value many times over had not diminished her resentment at all. It was a striking, stark composition, just a few lines that angled sharply and never quite met, some black, some gray, some red. Her mother had allowed it a panel on the white wall near the piano, and too near the large windows, Emma thought. At times the picture was overwhelmed with light and became almost invisible.

"Well, you may have it as soon as you acquire a proper residence," Aurora said. "I don't dislike it enough to consign it to a garage, but if you ever have a whole house you must take it at once. It was one of your grandmother's two serious mistakes, the other, of course, being your grandfather."

"Now there was charm for you," Emma said.

"Yes, Father was charming," Aurora said. "No one reared in Charleston has ever lacked charm, that I can see. He never raised his voice to me until he was eighty, but then I must say he certainly attempted to make up for lost time. He screamed at me for the last ten years of his life."

"Why?" Emma asked.

"I wouldn't know," Aurora said. "Perhaps Charlestonians are only granted eighty years of charm."

"I hear the doorbell," Emma said.

Aurora stepped into her bedroom and looked at her clock—a beautiful old brass ship's clock that she had inherited from an uncle who had been to sea.

"Drat that man," she said. "He's early again."

"Just ten minutes," Emma said.

"You go let him in, since you adore him," Aurora said. "I intend to stand on my patio for another ten minutes, just as I'd planned. You might tell him I'm on the phone."

"I think you're awful," Emma said. "You're already ready."

"Yes, but I intend to see a bit more of the moon," Aurora said. "After that I will do my best by Alberto. Besides, he's Genoan through and through. If you'd read any history you'd know how calculating they are. They almost stole America, you know. Alberto's always ten minutes early. He's hoping I'll mistake that for wild impetuosity—something he once actually possessed. Go let him in and make him open the wine."

2.

WHEN EMMA opened the front door most of a flower shop walked in, in the arms of two short Italians, one young and one old. Alberto the wildly impetuous staggered in carrying red roses, blue irises, a small potted orange tree, and some anemones. His son Alfredo bore an armful of white lilies, some miniature yellow roses, and what appeared to be a bundle of heather.

"Big load," Alberto said, gritting his teeth to keep from losing his grip on the orange tree.

"I'm bringing her flowers tonight, oh boy," he said. He and Alfredo, both of whom, heightwise, had only an inch on Rôsie, lurched into the living room and began to distribute the flowers in piles on the rug. As soon as he was relieved of the orange tree Alberto turned and came quickly to Emma, holding out his arms. His eyes shone and his smile seemed full of spirit.

"Ah, Emma, Emma, Emma," he said. "Emma. Come and kiss

her, Alfredo. Look at her—gorgeous yellow dress, gorgeous hair, what eyes! When you havin' your baby, honey? I love you."

He embraced her, squeezed her tightly, kissed her loudly on both cheeks, patted her behind for good measure, and then, as abruptly as he had assumed it, dropped his ham-Italian manner completely, as if five seconds of it had been all he had energy for.

Alfredo, round-cheeked, popeyed, and nineteen, bustled up to do his part of the kissing, but his father abruptly stiff-armed him aside.

"What do you flatter yourself for?" he said. "She doesn't want to kiss you. I was teasing. Go and make us some Bloody Marys; we gonna need them if we're not lucky."

"You haven't been to the store lately," Alfredo said, ogling Emma with his goggle eyes. He was starting at the bottom of the family business, which happened to be musical instruments. The bottom happened to be the harmonica department, and Alfredo would talk harmonicas at the drop of a hat.

"Why do you bring that up?" Alberto said to his son. "She doesn't need a harmonica."

"Anyone can learn to play one," Alfredo said. It was a statement he made eighty times a day.

Emma put her arm around Alberto and led him off to the kitchen to find vases and open the wine. He looked up the stairs longingly when they passed them. It had been many years since he had been allowed up them, except once for a hasty look at the Renoir, and then, much to Aurora's annoyance, he had spent most of his time looking at her bed. Once things had been different between them, and Alberto could never forget it, though since then he had had two wives. The direct approach had worked with them, but with Aurora he could no longer find a direct approach to the direct approach. Even in his fantasies he could no longer quite attain to the upper reaches of her house; such conquests as he could still imagine always took place in the living room.

"Emma, will she ever have me?" he asked. "Am I dressed enough? Is she happy today? I think she will like my flowers, at least I can hope, but I don't think I should have brought Alfredo. I try to keep him from talking about harmonicas, but what can I do? He is young, what else does he know to talk about?"

"Aw, don't worry, I'll take care of you," Emma said. Alberto had given her voice lessons when she was fourteen. He had been a respected tenor once and had sung in every important opera house in the world, but an early stroke had ended his career and forced him into the instrument business. Where her mother was concerned, his suit was doomed, and yet he kept on, which was partly why Emma loved him. No gallantry touched her quite like that one. He had already managed to rumple himself badly. His old gray suit was floppy and too heavy for the hot night, his tie was knotted awkwardly, and he had spilled dirt from the potted orange tree into one cuff. Worst of all, he was wearing Kiwanis cufflinks.

"Why are you such a fool, Alberto?" she said. "You know how Momma massacres people. Why don't you find somebody nice? I can't be here to protect you all the time."

"Ah, but fantastic woman," Alberto said, frowning at the wine. "Best woman of my life. I have you on my side now, maybe we get her for me."

Suddenly from the living room came the wail of a harmonica—and a harmonica being played as loudly as possible. Alberto sprang to life and flung the corkscrew into the sink.

"Idiot!" he yelled. "Traitor! This is the last stroke. He has ruined me. My hair stands up at this!"

"Oh, God," Emma said. "Why'd you let him bring it?"

"Listen! Listen!" Alberto insisted. "What is he playing?"

They listened a moment. "Mozart!" Alberto cried. "This is the last stroke!

"I'll box him one," he added, heading for the door. "Maybe she has gone deaf." He rushed out of the kitchen, Emma just behind him.

The scene they came upon was even more amazing than the scene they had expected. Aurora, instead of being at the head of the stairs looking horrified, was sitting on her living-room sofa, resplendent in her rose gown and amber necklace, her wonderful hair shining, holding the miniature yellow roses in her hands and

84

listening with every appearance of happiness and interest as Alfredo—who had planted himself squarely in the middle of the floor, next to the bundle of heather—blasted away at something that only a professional musician could have recognized as Mozart. Alberto already had his fist doubled up, and he was forced to undouble it and wait out the little concert with as much grace as possible.

As soon as Alfredo was finished Aurora rose with a smile. "Alfredo, thank you," she said. "That quite charmed me. I think perhaps you've not got quite the delicacy of phrasing you might aspire to if you're going to play Mozart, but then you know as well as I do that perfection never comes easy. You must keep working, you know."

She gave him a pat on the hand in passing and came over to his startled father. "Al-berto, as usual," she said. "That's the most wonderful heather, dear, and I haven't had any for such a while." She kissed him on both cheeks, and to Emma's surprise, seemed to be beaming at him.

"All this is little short of overwhelming, Alberto," Aurora said. "You have the most wonderful florist. I don't know what I do to deserve such abundance."

Alberto was just recovering himself from the shock of the harmonica performance. He was not quite yet able to believe the evening still had a chance, and he could not keep himself from glowering at Alfredo, something Aurora noted at once.

"Now, Alberto, just stop scowling at that boy," she said. "I wouldn't scowl at a wonderful boy like Alfredo, if I had one. I was very devilish with him, in any case. He showed me his new symphonic harmonica and within two minutes I had tricked him into playing it for me. I do hope you're going to see that he gets proper musical training, and I do hope too that you got around to opening the wine.

"And if you didn't, it was Emma's fault," she added. "Her instructions in that regard were quite precise." She gave her daughter an airy smile.

"It was my fault," Emma agreed. The evening was young and Alberto still had plenty of time in which to accumulate black marks.

"I can play rock too," Alfredo said, causing a vein to bulge out on the side of his father's nose.

"No, you've done enough," Aurora said. "Your father's not likely to tolerate any more of my little indulgences just now. Besides, I've fixed us some trifles to nibble on while we watch the evening, and I'm sure we'd all like a drink. You look like you've been having your nervousness again, Alberto. I don't know what's to be done with you."

She took Alberto's arm, and with a glance at her daughter that left her with the responsibility for anything that might need to be done she meandered off toward her lower patio. Alfredo treaded behind her as closely as he dared.

3.

ALBERTO HAD come in like a lamb and Emma fully expected to see him slaughtered and cooked. Instead she saw him turned, for an hour or two at least, back into the lion he must once really have been. She had known that her mother was not without charm, and had suspected that she was not without sympathy either, but she had never expected to see those qualities exercised so generously on Alberto's behalf.

Her meal was wonderful, starting with mushrooms stuffed with pâté and proceeding to cold watercress soup, endive, and a veal dish Emma didn't know the name of, in a tart sauce and with ratatouille, followed by cheese, a pear, and coffee, at which point Alfredo put his head on the table and went to sleep, leaving them to have brandy without the threat of his harmonica.

They had eaten on the patio, and by some miracle Aurora had even arranged for a minimum of bugs. Alberto was so buoyed by his nice reception that for a time he recovered his energy and rose to great heights of Italian charm. He popped up every two minutes to keep the wine glasses filled, patted Aurora every time he passed her chair, and stopped eating after every third bite to praise the food. Aurora accepted both the compliments and the patting without complaint, ate a healthy amount of her own food, and pressed no attacks at all, though she did devote a certain amount of attention to Alfredo's table manners. It was all so pleasant that Emma might have scintillated a bit herself, if she could have got a word in edgewise.

Then, for no visible reason, while they were all sitting quietly holding their brandy, Alberto's spirits suddenly plunged. One minute he seemed fine and the next he was crying. Tears ran down his cheeks, his chest was heaving, and he shook his head mournfully from side to side.

"So good," he said, gesturing at the remains of the meal. "So beautiful . . ." and he turned his eyes to Aurora. "I don't deserve. No, I don't deserve."

Aurora was not surprised. "Alberto, surely you're not going to cry," she said. "A wonderful man like yourself—I'm not going to have it."

"But no," Alberto said. "You feed me this meal, you are so nice, Emma is so nice. I don't know . . . I am old and crazy. I don't sing no more. . . . What do I do? I sell bassoons, electric guitar, harmonica. Is no life. What am I gonna offer?"

"Alberto, I'm taking you right out in my garden and you're going to get a lecture," Aurora said, rising. "You know I'm not going to allow you to disparage yourself this way." She took his arm, made him get up, and walked him off into the darkness. Emma sat for a moment. Alberto must have gotten worse, for she could hear him sobbing, and her mother's voice over the sobs.

When the sobs were silenced and the two of them still didn't reappear, Emma got up and began to clear the table. One of her mother's firmest principles was that Rosie was not to be burdened with the remains of her parties. While Emma was scraping the plates her mother stuck her head in the kitchen door.

"That's nice of you, dear, but it can wait," she said. "Could you come and make your goodnights? My friend is better, but he is still somewhat crestfallen. We had better walk them to their car."

Emma left the dishes and followed her mother. Alberto was standing in the living room looking small and sodden, and Alfredo, barely awake, was yawning on the front porch. Aurora had stuck the heather in a great green vase and put it by the fireplace, and the irises and anemones were on the window ledges of the deep curved windows.

"Emma, I am sorry, honey, I have ruined the party," Alberto began, but her mother went up to him and imperturbably tucked his arm in hers and began to lead him toward the door.

"Hush, Alberto," she said. "We've heard quite enough out of you this evening. I don't know how I'll be able to sleep now, your banter has stirred me up so. Why a man with your taste in flowers wants to stand there belittling himself is more than I can fathom. But then I don't know that I'll ever understand the male of the species, clever as I am."

They all walked out and stood for a moment on the front lawn, Alfredo dozing, Alberto standing sadly with his arm around Aurora's waist. There was a soft breeze, and thin clouds were moving overhead.

"I do love the nights this time of year," Aurora said. "The air here is at its best just now, don't you think, Alberto? I've always supposed it was because of the trees that our air is so soft. It has a kind of weight, you know. I believe trees have something to do with the making of air."

She looked down at Alberto fondly. "How are the nights in Genoa, dear?" she asked. "You've hardly mentioned your own birthplace all evening, you know. I'm afraid you sometimes take my little strictures a bit too seriously. You really can't allow me to suppress you, Alberto. It can't be good for you, that I can see."

"Yes, in Genoa I was another man," Alberto said. "We were there . . . you remember?"

Aurora nodded and put him into his car. Alfredo was guided down the driveway without incident. The car was a Lincoln, and even older than Aurora's Cadillac. It was a relic of Alberto's heyday as a tenor.

"All right now, you call me at the crack of dawn," Aurora said once Alberto was under the wheel. "Otherwise I shall worry about you. I'm sure we can devise something pleasant to do next week. I do think you ought to promote Alfredo, though, dear. He's your own son, and he's been in harmonicas too long. If he grows discontent, then the next thing you know he'll follow in my daughter's footsteps and start having babies by someone you may not approve of. I'm not sure I'd care to see Alfredo have a baby just yet."

"Maybe he could sell guitars," Alberto said doubtfully, looking out at the two women. He tried to gather himself for a last gesture.

"Was wonderful," he said. "The mother is wonderful, the daughter is wonderful, just alike, my darlings. I am starting." And as the car shot forward he took both hands off the wheel and began to blow them both kisses.

"Oh, dear, there goes Alfredo, it seems," Aurora said, watching him slump onto the floorboards as the Lincoln pulled away. It only pulled away from them, however; as soon as Alberto removed his hands from the wheel it veered straight for the curb. Alberto wrested it into the street, but not before there had been a hideous scraping of tires.

"There, you see what happens?" Aurora said to Emma, gritting her teeth at the sound. "I trust you won't be so quick to criticize my parking after this. In all likelihood he will have a flat in the next few days."

She had put on her sandals to dine but kicked them off at once.

"You were awfully nice to Alberto," Emma said.

"I don't see why that should be worthy of comment. After all, he was my guest."

"Yes, but you're so mean about him when he's not around," Emma said.

"Oh, well, that's just my way," Aurora said. "I've been allowed to become sarcastic, I suppose. Your father made little effort to correct me in that regard. It's a general failing in our family—the men are never adequate to correcting the women when they need it. It's certainly not likely that Thomas will ever correct you."

"I'm not sarcastic," Emma said.

"No, but you're young," Aurora said, going in the front door. She stopped in the living room for a moment to admire her flowers.

"He does have wonderful taste in flowers," she said. "Italians often do. What you don't seem to comprehend is that people of any substance are often much better in person than they seem in the abstract, when one is merely left to think about them. Everyone likes to gripe about people who aren't there. It doesn't mean one has no feeling, you know."

Together they attacked the kitchen and dispatched their chores rapidly. Emma took a big sponge and went out to the patio to wipe off the table, and Aurora soon trailed after her carrying a hairbrush and a final bowl of watercress soup. She also had some scraps of bread to put in her bird feeder. Emma sat at the table and watched her mother crumble the bread, humming as she crumbled.

"I do believe I hum Mozart better than Alfredo can play him," she said when she came back from the yard. She sat down across from her daughter and ate every last drop of her soup. The night had a hum of its own and mother and daughter listened to it awhile and were quiet.

"Are you as nice to all your suitors as you are to Alberto?" Emma asked.

"By no means," Aurora said.

"Why not?"

"Because they don't deserve it," Aurora said. She began to brush her hair.

"Would you ever marry him?"

Aurora shook her head. "No, that's quite out of the question," she said. "Alberto is just a fragment of himself now. I'm not sure but what that stroke might just as well have killed him, because it robbed him of his art. I heard him at his best and he was very fine—first rate. He behaves well, for a man who has lost the best thing he ever had—and that is saying much."

"So why do you rule him out?" Emma said.

Aurora looked at her daughter and continued to brush her hair. "No, I'm far too difficult for Alberto," she said. "I knew both his wives and they were empty as birds' nests. He never had the skill to handle me, and now he hasn't the energy either. In any case his tradition has only prepared him for compliant women. I'm deeply fond of him but I doubt that I could remain compliant very long."

"Then don't you think it's wrong of you to lead him on?" Emma asked.

Aurora smiled at her daughter, who was sitting demurely in her nice yellow dress and challenging her motives.

"You're lucky to have caught me when I'm mellow, if you're going to say such things to me," she said. "I'm afraid our points of view are twenty-five years apart. Alberto is not an adolescent with his life ahead of him. He's an aging man who's been seriously ill, and he might drop dead tomorrow. I have told him many times that I couldn't marry him. I am not leading him on, I'm merely doing the best I can by him. It may be that he cherishes impossible hopes—I suppose he does—but at his age impossible hopes are better than no hopes at all."

"I still feel sorry for him," Emma said. "I wouldn't want to love somebody I couldn't get."

"It's not the worst fate, whatever the young may think," Aurora said. "There is at least a certain stimulation in it. It is certainly a good deal better than getting somebody you find you can't love, when all is said and done."

Emma thought about it for a moment. "I wonder where I'll be when all is said and done," she said.

Aurora didn't reply—she was listening to the sounds of the night. Apart from a drop more soup, there was for the moment nothing she really wanted, nothing she really missed. Few things gave her quite the same sense of serenity as knowing that her food had been well prepared and well received, and that her dishes were done and her kitchen clean. In such a mood nothing could vex her deeply. She looked over at Emma and saw that Emma was looking at her.

"Well, what?" she asked.

"Oh, nothing," Emma said. Her mother was so often outrageous that it was almost troubling to have to think of her as someone who was possibly just as normal as she was—or conceivably even more normal. Seeing her with Alberto had made her realize that her mother had had a life about which, in essence, she knew nothing. What had she done with Alberto when he was younger and could still sing? What had she done in her marriage for twenty-four years? Her mother and father had been simply *there*, like trees in the back yard—objects of nature, not objects of curiosity.

"Emma, you're being somewhat evasive," Aurora said. "That can't be proper."

"I wasn't," Emma said. "I just don't know what I want to ask."

"Well, I'm at your service, I'm sure—if you can decide before my bedtime."

"I guess I'm just curious to know what you liked best about Daddy. It just occurred to me that I don't really know that much about you two."

Aurora smiled. "He was tall," she said. "It wasn't always helpful, in view of the fact that he spent such an inordinate amount of his life sitting down, but on those occasions when I could manage to get him on his feet it was an asset."

"I don't think that explains twenty-four years, surely," Emma said. "If it does I'm appalled."

Aurora shrugged and licked her soup spoon. "I was appalled to find such a disreputable car parked in your street this morning," she said. "It would be more decorous of Daniel to stick it in a parking lot the next time he decides to sneak in on you at dawn."

"That wasn't what we were talking about," Emma said quickly. "That's completely beside the point."

"No, as I perceive it the point is taste," Aurora said. "You are far too romantic, Emma, and if you're not careful it will bring you to rack, at the very least, and quite possibly to ruin as well."

"I don't follow you," Emma said.

"You aren't trying," Aurora said. "You're hoping to be allowed to keep your most cherished notions—in my day they were called illusions—but you won't get to. In the first place I am afraid you vastly underrate appearance. Your father's appearance was somewhat to my taste, and since he never worked hard enough or felt violently enough to cause it to deteriorate, it continued to be to my taste for twenty-four years—at least whenever he would stand up. Aside from that he was mild and had manners and was never disposed to beat me. He was much too lazy to transgress, so in general we got on."

"You make it sound awfully general," Emma said. "You don't make it sound deep at all."

Aurora smiled again. "As I recall, we were speaking of longevity," she said. "I hadn't realized that we were speaking of depth."

"Well," Emma said. She had the beginnings of the odd and not entirely pleasant feeling she often felt when her mother, in her own strange way, set out to lecture her. It was a sensation almost of shrinking, of fading quietly backward into girlhood. She didn't like it, and yet to her distress she didn't entirely dislike it either. Her mother was still there, someone to face things with.

"Emma, you are so remiss about finishing your sentences." Aurora said. "You speak vaguely enough, at best, but I really think you ought to try harder to finish your sentences. You are always saying things like 'Well,' and then you go no further. People will think you suffer from a mental vacuum."

"Sometimes I do," Emma said. "Why should I have to speak in complete sentences?"

"Because complete sentences command attention," Aurora said. "Vague grunts do not. Also, because you're about to be a mother. People who lack the decisiveness to finish their sentences can hardly pretend to the decisiveness necessary to the raising of children. Fortunately you have several months in which to practice."

"What am I supposed to do?" Emma asked. "Stand in front of a mirror and speak to myself in complete sentences?"

"It wouldn't hurt you," Aurora said.

"I didn't want to talk about me," Emma said. "I was trying to get you to talk about you and Daddy."

Aurora tilted her head a few times to exercise her neck. "I was quite willing," she said. "I'm unusually mellow tonight, perhaps because I drank my own wine instead of allowing Alberto to fill me up with something inferior. Perhaps I'm so mellow that I missed the point of your question, if you had one. Or then again perhaps you phrased it too vaguely for me to get."

"Oh, Mother," Emma said. "I just wanted to know what you really felt."

Aurora waved her hand lightly, swinging the empty soup spoon. "My dear, doubtless there are hundreds of edifices in this world that rise from shallow foundations, if I may speak elliptically," she said. "When I'm mellow and the air has a nice weight I do so love to speak elliptically, as you know. Many edifices, some of them even taller than your father, might well crumble if someone came along and gave them a few healthy kicks. I myself am still capable of healthy kicks, I assure you. As for your question, which happily you phrased grammatically, if rather dully, I can tell you quite distinctly that I don't care if I never hear the phrase 'really felt' again."

She looked her daughter right in the eye.

"Okay, okay, forget it," Emma said.

"No, I've not finished," Aurora said. "I may have new heights to rise to. For all I know, my dear, good grammar provides a more lasting basis for sound character than quote real feeling unquote. I would not presume to claim that definitively, but I must say that I suspect it. I also suspect, if you must know, that it was lucky for your father and me that none of my admirers had much capacity for kicking. The difference between the saved and the fallen, I have always maintained, boils down to adequate temptation."

"What's adequate?" Emma asked.

"Adequate is a kind that's hard to come by in these parts, unhappily for me," Aurora said. "Or happily for me, as the case may be. I've not given up the search though, I assure you.

"I suppose it's something of an enigma," she added reflectively.

"What?"

"Adequacy." Aurora smiled at her daughter, and a touch of mischief was in her smile.

"I only hope your brilliant young friend is adequate to maintain you, if it should prove that he's adequate to tempt you," she said.

Emma flushed and jumped to her feet. "Shut up," she said. "He's gone. I don't know if he'll ever come back. I just wanted to see him once. He's an old friend—what's the harm in that?"

"I don't believe I suggested there was any harm in it," Aurora said.

"Well, there wasn't," Emma said. "Don't sit there and make

complete sentences at me. I hate good grammar and I think you're awful. I'm going home. Thank you for the dinner."

Aurora waved her soup spoon, smiling at her furious daughter. "Yes, thank you for attending, dear," she said. "Your dress was quite well chosen."

They looked at one another for a moment. "All right, if you're not going to help me," Emma said. At once she wished she hadn't said it.

Aurora looked at her daughter calmly. "I doubt seriously that I shall fail to help you if I'm called upon," she said. "What is far more likely is that you'll be too stubborn to call upon me at the proper time. I wish you would sit back down. In fact, I wish you would spend the night here. If you go back home you're surely going to fret."

"Of course I am," Emma said. "I can fret if I want to."

"Listen!" Aurora said commandingly.

Emma listened. All she could hear was the flutter of wings from one of the several birdhouses.

"Those are my martins," Aurora said. "I imagine you've disturbed them. They are quite responsive to agitation, you know."

"I'm going on," Emma said. "Good night."

When she had gone Aurora took her spoon and her bowl to the kitchen and washed them. Then she returned to the patio and walked out in her back yard. The martins were still fluttering in the martin house, and she stood beneath them and sang softly for a little while, as she often did at night. It occurred to her, thinking of Emma, that she had no real wish to be younger. Few enough of the rewards of life seemed to belong to youth, when one considered. She leaned against the pole of the martin house, happily barefoot, and tried to remember something that would induce her to want to start again where her daughter was. She could think of nothing, but she did remember that she had a couple of new movie magazines to read, tucked away by her bed—a little reward for having done her duty by her old lover and good friend Alberto. He had been such a fine singer once. No doubt he had more reason than she did for wishing to be young again.

The grass, as she walked in, was just beginning to be wet from the moist night, and the moon that earlier had shone so nicely on her elm and her cypress and her pines was curtained and faint in the mist—that mist that the Gulf breathed over Houston almost every night, as if to help the city sleep.

CHAPTER VI

1.

"PHONE'S RINGING," Rosie said.

The news came as no surprise to Aurora, whose hand was less than a foot from the instrument in question. Midmorning had come again and she was ensconced in a sunny little window nook in her bedroom, almost her favorite place in the world. She had the sunlight and an open window and a great many pillows around her, for moral support, and she needed them all, since she was in the midst of one of her least favorite of all tasks: paying bills. Nothing filled her with quite such a sense of indecision as the sight of her bills, more than fifty of which lay scattered about the window nook. None of them so far had even been opened, much less paid, and Aurora was staring fixedly at her checkbook, trying to get her balance solidly in mind before tearing into the many ominous envelopes.

"Phone's ringing, I said," Rosie repeated, since it still was.

Aurora continued to stare at her checkbook. "How like you to state the obvious," she said. "I know the phone is ringing. It's my sanity that's being destroyed, not my hearing."

"It could be good news," Rosie said brightly.

"That is a remote possibility, in the mood I'm in," Aurora said. "It is far more likely to be someone I don't want to talk to."

"Who would that be?" Rosie asked.

"That would be anyone insensitive enough to call me when I don't wish to be called," she said. She made a dark face at the phone.

"You answer it," she said. "It's making it difficult for me to keep my mind on figures."

"It's got to be the General, anyway," Rosie said. "He's the only one with the gall to let it ring twenty-five times."

"Well, let's test him," Aurora said, laying down her checkbook. "Let's see if he has the gall to let it ring fifty times. That much gall amounts to arrogance, and if there's anything I don't need right now it's arrogance. Do you suppose he's watching?"

"Yep," Rosie said, borrowing a little of her employer's hand lotion. "What else has he got to do?"

The General's home, as luck would have it, was at the end of Aurora's street, and his bedroom window commanded a clear view of her garage. He had only to pick up his binoculars to determine if her car was there, and his binoculars were seldom far from his hand. His wife's death and Rudyard Greenway's had come only six months apart, and the General and his binoculars had been a constant factor in Aurora's life ever since. Even working in the flowerbeds in her front yard became a problem; she could seldom do so without the thought that two greedy, cold blue military eyes were fixed upon her.

Her phone continued to ring.

"I certainly think military training must destroy the finer instincts," Aurora said. "Are you keeping count of the rings?"

"He ain't my boy friend," Rosie said. She was exploring Aurora's dressing table, looking for things she might need.

"Answer it," Aurora said. "I'm growing faint from listening to it ring. Be acerbic."

"Be what?" Rosie asked. "Talk English."

"Don't let him push you around, in other words," Aurora said.

Rosie picked up the phone and the scratchy masculine voice of General Hector Scott immediately began to grate on the ears of both. Even amid her pillows Aurora could hear it distinctly.

"Hi there, General," Rosie said blithely. "What are you doing up so early?"

Everyone who knew him knew that Hector Scott rose at five A.M., summer and winter, and ran three miles before breakfast. He was accompanied on his runs by his two Dalmatians, Pershing and Marshal Ney, both of whom, unlike the General, were in the prime of life. The dogs enjoyed the runs—again unlike the General, who ran because his standards would not permit him not to. The one member of his establishment who absolutely loathed them was his man. F.V., who was forced to follow the morning runs in the General's old Packard sedan car in case the General or perhaps one of the Dalmatians dropped dead along the way.

F.V.'s last name was d'Arch, though few knew it. Rosie happened to be one of the few, the reason being that F.V. hailed from Bossier City, Louisiana, which was right next to her own home town of Shreveport. Occasionally, when she was caught up with her work, Rosie would trip down the street and spend a happy morning in General Scott's garage helping F.V. tinker with the old Packard, a car so over-the-hill and generally unreliable that it was usually broken down by the time it got home from following the three-mile run. Rosie was a great comfort to F.V., partly because they both loved to reminisce about the good old days in Shreveport and Bossier City, and partly because she understood Packard engines almost as well as he did. F.V. was a thin little fellow with a pencil mustache and a good deal of native Cajun melancholy; his old home ties with Rosie might have grown into something stronger if they hadn't both been convinced that Royce Dunlup would walk in with a shotgun and mow them both down if, as F.V. put it, "anything ever happened."

"Yeah, they mowed down Bonnie and Clyde," Rosie observed happily whenever the conversation drifted into such channels.

General Scott, however, knew quite well that Rosie knew quite well that he had been up since five A.M., and her remark fell somewhere between impertinence and insult. Under ordinary circumstances he would not have tolerated either from anyone, but unfortunately nothing involving Aurora Greenway and her household, if it could be called a household, seemed to align in any way with ordinary circumstances. Faced with the usual irritating and extraordinary circumstances, he made his usual effort to be restrained but firm.

"Rosie, we won't go into the question of why I'm up," he said. "Could you put Mrs. Greenway on at once?"

"It don't look like it," Rosie said, glancing at her boss. Her boss had a cheerful but rather distant look on her face as she sat among the litter of bills.

"Why not?" the General asked.

"I don't know," Rosie said. "I don't think she's made up her mind who she's talkin' to today. Wait a minute while I find out."

"I do not want to wait, and I won't," the General said. "This is childish nonsense. You tell her I want to speak with her at once. I have waited thirty-five rings already. I'm a punctual man myself and I was married for forty-three years to a punctual woman. I don't appreciate delays of this kind."

Rosie held the receiver away from her ear and grinned at Aurora.

"He says he won't wait," she said loudly. "He says it's childish nonsense, and his wife never made him wait in his life. She was right on time for forty-three years."

"What a ghastly thought," Aurora said with a dreamy wave of her hand. "I'm afraid I've never marched to any man's drum and I'm far too old to start now. Also I have observed that it's generally weak-minded people who allow themselves to be slaves to the clock. Tell the General that."

"She ain't marching to no drum and she ain't no slave to no clock," Rosie said to the General. "And she thinks you got a weak mind. I guess you can hang up if you want to."

"I do not want to hang up," the General said, gritting his teeth. "I want to speak to Aurora, and I want to speak to her now."

Invariably, attempts to get through to Aurora caused him to

grit his teeth at some point. The only saving aspect was that they were still, at least, *his* teeth: he had not yet been reduced to gritting dentures.

"Where is she?" he asked, still gritting.

"Uh, she ain't far," Rosie said cheerfully. "Uh, some ways she's far and some ways she's close," she added after another glance at her boss.

"That being the case," the General said, "I would like to ask why it was necessary to allow the phone to ring thirty-five times. If I still had my tanks this wouldn't have happened, Rosie. A certain house I know would have been leveled long before the thirty-fifth ring, if I still had my tanks. Then we'd find out who's to be trifled with and who isn't."

Rosie held the receiver away from her ear. "He's off on his tanks agin," she said. "You better talk to him."

"Who's there, who's there?" the General said loudly into his silent receiver. In his prime he had commanded a tank division, and attempts to get through to Aurora almost always brought his tanks to mind. He had even begun to dream of tanks, for the first time since the war. Only a few nights before he had had a very happy dream in which he had driven up River Oaks Boulevard standing in the turret of his largest tank. The people in the country club at the end of the boulevard had all come out and lined up and looked at him respectfully. He was the only four-star general in the club, and the people there looked at him respectfully even without his tank; but it had been a satisfying dream nonetheless. General Scott had many dreams involving tanks, many of which ended with him crunching through the lower walls of Aurora's house, into her living room, or sometimes her kitchen. In some of the dreams he merely tanked around indecisively in front of her house, trying to come up with some method for getting a tank up the stairs to her bedroom, where she always seemed to stay. To get into her bedroom he would need a flying tank, and everyone who knew anything about generals knew that Hector Scott was a realist where ordnance was concerned. There were no flying tanks, and even under duress his subconscious refused to supply him one. As a result he continued to find himself in conversations with Aurora Greenway or her maid that put him in the mood to try and break the telephone receiver over his knee.

He was just arriving at that state when Aurora stretched out her hand and took the phone. "I might as well talk to him," she said. "I'm really not in any great hurry to pay my bills."

Rosie yielded the receiver with some reluctance. "It's a good thing they took his tanks away when they let him out of the army," she said. "What if he got ahold of one someday an' come after us?"

Aurora ignored her. "Well, as usual, Hector," she said, uncovering the mouthpiece, "you've frightened Rosie rather badly with all your talk of tanks. It seems to me that at your age you would have learned what frightens people and what doesn't. I wouldn't be surprised if she gives notice. No one wants to work in a household that a tank's apt to burst into at any moment. It does seem to me you'd realize that. I'm sure F.V. wouldn't like it if he thought I was likely to smash in on him any any moment."

"That's exactly what F.V. does think," Rosie said loudly. "He knows how you drive. A Cadillac can kill you just as dead as a tank. I've heard F.V. say that many a time."

"Oh, shut up," Aurora said hotly. "You know how touchy I am about my driving."

"I haven't said anything, Aurora," the General said firmly.

"Well, I wish your voice weren't so scratchy, Hector," Aurora said.

"It's just F.V.'s bad luck to live right there at the corner," Rosie went on, taking up her dustcloth. "The kitchen's right where you'd end up if you was ever to forget to turn."

"*I shall not forget to turn!*" Aurora said with great emphasis.

"I didn't say you would!" General Scott said, his temper rising.

"Hector, I'm hanging straight up if you're planning to shout at me," Aurora said. "My nerves are not all they might be today, and you have not helped any by letting my phone ring thirty-five times. If you wear out my bell I won't appreciate it, I can tell you that."

"Aurora, my dear, all you need do is answer it," the General said, striving to bring moderation and mellifluousness to his voice. He was aware that his voice was scratchy, but it was only a natural consequence of the fact that he had been stationed in the tropics when he was young and had impaired his vocal apparatus in the line of duty, or by yelling at idiots too loudly and too often in a humid climate. Ignorance and incompetence on the part of his subordinates had always caused him to yell sooner or later, and he had encountered so much of it in his career that his voice had been little more than a croak by the time World War II ended. It seemed to him to have recovered itself well enough, but it had never pleased Aurora Greenway, and it seemed to please her less as the years went by. At the moment it didn't seem to be pleasing her at all.

"Hector, I do think you ought to know better than to admonish me," she said. "I am not a member of an army and am hardly interested in being treated like a private, or a sophomore, or whatever rank you've assigned me in your thoughts. It is my phone, you know, and if I am not disposed to answer it that is *my* business. Besides, I am frequently gone when you ring, I'm sure. If my bell is going to have to ring sixty or seventy times every time you take it into your head to call, then it's certainly going to wear out. I'll be lucky if it lasts the year."

"Aha, but I knew you were there," the General said quickly. "I've got my binoculars here and I've been watching your garage. Nothing's left it since six o'clock this morning. I fancy that I know you well enough to know that you're not likely to go anywhere before six in the morning. So in effect I have you. You were there and you were just being stubborn."

"That's a rather demeaning deduction," Aurora said instantly. "I certainly hope you didn't conduct your battles like you're conducting what might loosely be called our courtship. If you had I'm certain we would have lost whatever wars we happened to be in."

"Oou, my God," Rosie said, wincing a little for General Scott.

Aurora didn't so much as pause for breath. The thought of Hector Scott, who was sixty-five if he was a day, sitting in his bedroom with his binoculars glued to her garage since six in the morning was more than enough to make her see red.

"While I've got you, Hector, let me point out to you certain possibilities you seem to have overlooked in your reasoning, or whatever you do," she said. "First, I might have had a headache and not have wished to speak, in which case hearing a phone ring sixty times would hardly have contributed to my ease. Second, I might well have been in my back yard, beyond the sound of my phone or the reach of your binoculars. I'm very fond of the act of digging, as you ought to know. Often I dig. I must have *some* relaxation, you know."

"Aurora, that's fine," the General said, feeling a short retreat was called for. "I'm glad to have you out there digging—it's fine exercise. I've dug a great deal myself in my day."

"Hector, you've interrupted," Aurora said. "I was not speaking of your day, I was enumerating possibilities you had overlooked in your impetuosity to talk to me. A third distinct possibility is that an invitation had taken me beyond the sound of my phone."

"What invitation?" the General said, sensing trouble. "I don't like the sound of that much."

"Hector, at this moment I'm so annoyed with you that I don't really give a twit what you like and don't like," Aurora said. "The plain fact is that I frequently, indeed habitually, receive invitations from a number of gentlemen other than yourself."

"At six in the morning?" The General asked.

"Never you mind when," Aurora said. "I'm not as old as you, you know, and I'm far less fixed in my habits than your good wife seems to have been. In point of fact there is very little telling where I'm apt to be at six in the morning, nor is there any particular reason why I should be required to tell, if I don't choose to. I'm no one's wife at the moment, as I'm sure you realize."

"I realize it and I find it a patent absurdity," the General said. "I'm ready to do something about it too, as I've told you many times."

Aurora covered the receiver with one hand and made an amused face at Rosie. "He's proposing again," she said. Rosie was poking in a closet, trying to find a pair of shoes that might be worn out enough that she could appropriate them for her oldest daughter. The General's latest proposal surprised her not at all.

"Yeah, he probably wants you to get married inside a tank," she said.

Aurora went back to the General. "Hector, I don't doubt your readiness," she said. "A number of gentlemen seem to be ready, if that means anything. The point I must insist upon is that you aren't able, however ready you may think yourself to be, and I don't quite like the term 'patent absurdity' used as you chose to use it just now. I see nothing patently absurd in being a widow."

"My dear, you've been a widow for three years," the General said. "For a robust woman like yourself that's long enough. Too long, in fact. There are certain biological needs, you know—it doesn't do to ignore biological needs too long."

"Hector, are you aware of how rude you're being?" Aurora said with a flash in her eyes. "Do you realize you let my phone ring a great many times, and now that I've been considerate enough to answer it all you can think of to do is lecture me about biological needs. You could hardly have put matters less romantically, I must say."

"I'm a military man, Aurora," the General said, trying to be stern. "Blunt speech is the only thing I know. We're both adults. We needn't beat around the bush about these things. I was merely pointing out that it's dangerous to ignore biological needs."

"Who says I ignore them, Hector?" Aurora said with a devilish tone in her voice. "Happily there are still some nooks and crannies of my life your binoculars can't reach. I must say I'm not especially happy with the thought of you sitting there day after day speculating about my biological needs, as you call them. If that's what you've been doing it's no wonder you're usually so disagreeable to talk to."

"I'm not disagreeable to talk to," the General said. "I'm not unable, either."

Aurora opened one bill, the one from her least favorite dressmaker. It was for seventy-eight dollars. She looked at it thoughtfully before she replied.

"Unable?" she said.

"Yes. You said I was ready but unable. I resent that, Aurora.

I've never allowed anyone to cast slurs on my ability. In fact, I've always been able."

"Well, you've lost me somewhere, Hector," Aurora said vaguely. "It's quite careless of you. I think what you must be referring to is my remark about marriage. It would be very hard for you to deny that you aren't able to marry me, since I simply won't have it. I don't see how you can consider yourself able in that regard, when it's obvious to both of us that there's not a thing you can do about me."

"Aurora, will you shut up?" the General yelled. His temper rose abruptly, and at about the same time, though not so abruptly, his penis also rose. Aurora Greenway was infuriating, absolutely infuriating; except for one or two lieutenants, no one in his life had been able to make him so angry. No one in his life had been able to cause him to have erections just by talking to him on the phone, either, but Aurora could. She was almost infallible, too—some timbre in her voice seemed to do it, whether she was being argumentative, or whether she was just being happily vague and talking about music and flowers.

"Why yes, Hector, I will shut up, though I think it's rather rude of you to suggest it," Aurora said. "You are being exceptionally rude to me today, you know. I've been paying my bills and trying to concentrate on my accounts and you sound very scratchy and military and aren't helping me at all. If you don't stop being so rude I'm going to have Rosie talk to you in my stead, and she is apt to be far less polite than I've been."

"You haven't been polite, you've been very goddamn irritating!" the General said, only to hear a click on the line. He put the receiver back on its hook and sat tensely for several minutes, quietly gritting his teeth. He stared out the window toward Aurora's house, but he felt too dispirited to bother lifting his binoculars. His erection lingered a bit and then subsided, and shortly after things were back to normal he picked up the phone and called again.

Aurora answered on the first ring. "I certainly do hope you're in a nice mood now, Hector," she said at once, before he even spoke.

"How did you know it was me, Aurora?" he asked. "Aren't you

taking a big chance? It very well could have been one of your other habitual callers. It might even have been your mystery man."

"What mystery man, Hector?" she asked.

"The one you strongly hinted at," he said, not with much asperity. A feeling of hopelessness had come over him. "The one whose bed you are presumably sharing on those occasions when you don't happen to be home at six A.M."

Aurora opened two more bills while the General was cooling off; she was trying to remember what she had done with the forty dollars' worth of lawn supplies she had apparently bought three months before. The General's accusation glanced off her lightly, but the tone he made it in was slightly more serious.

"Now, Hector," she said, "you're sounding resigned again. You know how I hate to hear you sounding resigned. I hope you haven't allowed me to beat you down again. You're just going to have to learn to defend yourself a little more vigorously if you want to get along with me. I should think a military man like yourself would have more skill at self-defense. I can't quite think how you survived all your wars if this is the best you can do."

"I was inside a tank most of the time," the General said, remembering how cozy it had felt. Aurora sounded suddenly very friendly and warm, and his erection began to come back. It had often amazed him how quickly she could begin to sound friendly and warm once she knew she had someone on the ropes.

"Well, I'm afraid all that's past, dear," she said. "You're just going to have to get by without your tanks from now on. Say something to me and put some snap in your tone, if you don't mind. You can't imagine how depressing it is to have a resigned voice coming over one's telephone."

"Right, I'll get to the point," the General said, miraculously his own man again. "Who's the new fellow?"

"What are you talking about?" Aurora asked. She was gathering up all her unopened bills. She had decided to put the unopened ones in a neat stack before opening them. The sight of neat stacks of things sometimes went a long way toward convincing her that her life was really in order, despite how she felt. She had decided the seventy-eight-dollar bill was probably legitimate and was waving at Rosie to bring her her fountain pen, which was on her dressing table instead of where it ought to be. Her dressing table was not amenable to neat stacking—hundreds of objects had found their way to it and gotten no further, and Rosie was holding up perfume bottles and old invitations and eyebrow pencils, hoping to come up with whatever it was Aurora wanted fetched.

"The fountain pen, the fountain pen," Aurora said, before the General could reply. "Can't you see I'm writing a check?"

Rosie found the pen and pitched it to her carelessly. She loved to investigate Aurora's dressing table—it always yielded products she had never heard of. "Tell him you'll marry him if he'll trade off that Packard," she said, sniffing at some cucumber oil. "I swear, that car costs a mint of money and he don't go nowhere in it even. F.V.'s tried to tell him but it don't do no good."

"Rosie, I'm sure General Scott is capable of deciding what automobile he wants to drive," Aurora said, writing the check forcefully. She had a strong sense just then of being in command of her fortunes. "What was it you were saying, Hector?"

"I asked you who you were spending the night with," the General said tightly. "I've asked you several times. Of course if you don't choose to answer, that's your business."

"Oh, pooh, you're much too touchy, Hector," Aurora said. "I was merely trying to make you realize that my whereabouts at six A.M. is somewhat subject to whimsy. I might have decided to dance until dawn, or then again I might be off taking a cruise in the Caribbean with one of your rivals. You really don't seem to have much sense of sport, you know. It's something you really might try to cultivate before you get any older."

The General felt deeply relieved. "Aurora, can I ask you one favor?" he said. "If you're going out today would you give me a ride to the grocery store? I'm afraid my car has broken down."

Aurora smiled to herself. "Well, that's rather a prosaic favor, Hector, when one considers all you might have asked for," she said, "but it's certainly one I can manage. If you're sitting over there starving, my bills can certainly wait. I'll just pull myself together and you and I can go out for a nice drive. Who knows but what you'll weaken and buy me lunch."

"Aurora, that would be wonderful," the General said.

"Tricked him into it, didn't you?" Rosie said when her boss hung up. "Didn't take much trickin', did it?"

Aurora stood up, scattering her neat stack of bills back into disarray. She went to her window and looked out on the sunlit back yard. It was a brilliant day, with deep patches of blue between huge snowy April clouds.

"Men who are free all day have such an advantage over men who aren't," she said by way of reply.

"You like 'em randy too, don't you?" Rosie said.

"You hush," Aurora said. "I like a great many more things than you do, apparently. You don't seem to want to do anything except torment me and poor Royce. If you ask me, you're lucky to have kept that man so long, the way you treat him."

"Royce'd sink like a rock if he didn't have me to rag him," Rosie said confidently. "What you gonna wear? You know how quick the General is. He's probably already standing at the door. His wife never made him wait in forty-three years. He'll probably whop you with his umbrella if you don't hustle right over."

Aurora stretched and opened her windows a little wider. It was really exhilarating to be going out into such a day, even with someone as importunate as Hector Scott was apt to be. Rosie came over and looked out the window with her. She too was perked, and what perked her was the knowledge that Aurora was going out. It meant she had the whole house to herself to poke around in. Besides, Aurora would do almost anything to avoid paying her bills, and if she stayed home she would just avoid it by flirting with Royce. With Aurora gone she herself could spend a pleasant lunch hour lecturing Royce on his many shortcomings.

"Now look at this day," Aurora said. "Isn't it splendid? If I could only get myself into the right state of mind I'm quite sure I could be happy just with the trees and the sky. I only wish Emma responded to such things the way I do. Probably she's sitting over there in that miserable garage right now, gloomy as she can be. I don't know what she's going to do with a baby if she doesn't learn to take advantage of a day like this."

"She better bring it over here and let us raise it," Rosie said. "I hate for any kid of Emma's to have to grow up around Flap. If you an' me had a couple of Emma's kids to play with I might not have to have no more."

"Well, anything to slow you down," Aurora said, though actually on such a lovely day even the thought of Rosie pregnant couldn't drag her spirits down. "I believe I'll wear that dress I just paid for," she said, and went to the closet and found it. It was a flowered silk dress, light blue, and it did practically everything a dress should, both for her flesh and for her spirit. Without further delay she flung herself into dressing, happily convinced that seventy-eight dollars, at least, had been well spent.

2.

Something over an hour later she eased the Cadillac into the General's driveway. F.V. was standing in his chauffeur's pants and an undershirt idly watering the lawn. He was incorrigibly addicted to going around in his undershirt, a Cajun habit even the General's iron discipline had not been able to affect. He was a short little fellow and he looked perpetually mournful.

Aurora didn't care. "There you are again, F.V.," she said. "I do wish you wouldn't go around in your undershirt. No one I know likes the sight of a man in his undershirt. Also I don't quite see why you've chosen to waste water that way. In a city where it rains twice a day it is hardly necessary to water lawns."

"Ain't rained in two weeks, Miz Greenway," F.V. said mournfully. "The General put me to doin' it."

"Oh, the General's too impatient," Aurora said. "If you want to stay on my good side I think you should turn that hose off and go iron yourself a nice fresh shirt."

F.V. only looked more mournful and swished the hose around indecisively. One of the things he prayed for, on the rare occasions when he prayed, was that Mrs. Greenway would remain unyielding in her refusal to marry the General. The General was a stern taskmaster, but at least with him a man knew where he was. F.V. never had any idea where he was with Mrs. Greenway. It seldom took her more than two minutes to put him between the horns of a dilemma, as she just had, and the thought of having to live his life between the horns of thousands of dilemmas was more than F.V. could face.

Fortunately just at that moment General Scott stepped out of his house. He had been watching Aurora's approach through his binoculars and he was ready. He wore, as he always had since laying aside his uniform, an expensive charcoal gray suit and a blue-striped shirt. Even Aurora had been forced to admit that he dressed impeccably. His ties were always red, and his eyes always blue. The only thing about him that wasn't precisely as it had been was the hair that ought to have been on his head; to his annoyance most of it had vanished between his sixty-third and his sixty-fifth year.

"Aurora, you look wonderful," he said, coming around to her side of the car and bending in to kiss her cheek. "That dress was made for you."

"Yes, literally, I'm afraid," Aurora said, looking him over. "I just paid the bill this morning. Do get in right away, Hector. Doing so much addition has given me a ravening appetite and I thought we might just drive into the country and eat at our favorite little seafood house, if that suits you."

"Perfectly," the General said. "Quit swishing that hose, F.V. You almost swished me. Just keep it pointed at the yard until we're gone."

"Miz Greenway told me to turn it off anyway," F.V. said. "She wants me to go iron a shirt."

He dropped the hose, as if so many and such conflicting responsibilities had suddenly crushed out the last of his spirit, and to the General's amazement went slogging through the wet yard toward the house. He disappeared without so much as bothering to turn off the hose.

"He acts like he's going in there to commit suicide," the General said. "What did you say to him?"

"I admonished him about wearing those undershirts," Aurora said. "My traditional admonition. Perhaps if I honk at him he'll come back out."

Aurora had always considered the horn to be practically the

most useful part of the car, and her use of it was frequent and uninhibited. It took her only ten seconds to honk F.V. back out of the house.

"See here, turn off that hose if you're not going to water," the General said, a little confused. Aurora's honking unnerved him, so that he could think of no other instructions. He associated loud noises with battles and didn't know quite what to make of one when it was occurring right in his own driveway.

F.V. picked up the hose again and approached the car so distractedly that both Aurora and the General were afraid he was going to poke it in the window and douse them both. Fortunately he stopped just short of the driveway.

"Miz Greenway, can I borrow Rosie?" he asked plaintively. "I ain't never gonna get that Packard fixed unless she helps me. It sure does prey on my mind."

"Yes, of course, anything—help yourself," Aurora said, backing suddenly. The hose was considerably too close for comfort, and F.V. seemed to be losing his grip on things. In five seconds she and the General were safely on their way.

"You know, F.V. was never in the service," the General said wistfully, once they were gone. "I wonder if that's the reason he's the way he is."

3.

HALFWAY THROUGH lunch Aurora realized she was being too nice, but the food was so delicious that she couldn't stop. Excellent food had been her undoing more than once in life. The thing that had attracted her to Rud, aside from his height, was that he had known the whereabouts of every good restaurant on the East Coast; though, unhappily, as soon as they married he forgot them all and developed a fondness for pimento cheese sandwiches that was to prove lifelong. Excellent food swept away her defenses—she could not eat well and bristle too—and by the time she had lapped up every drop of her lobster bisque and started on her pompano she was feeling extremely gay.

With the seafood so excellent, it was necessary for both of them to consume quite a lot of white wine, and by the time Aurora had worked her way into a salad and had begun to think in vague terms of the problem of getting home, the General was feeling even gayer and had begun to reach across the table every two minutes to squeeze her arm and compliment her on her dress and her complexion. Nothing was more apt to bring out her best lights than a fine meal, and long before this one was over her best lights were flashing so brilliantly that the General was just short of being in a state.

"Evelyn always pecked at her food," he said. "Somehow she always just pecked. Even in France she didn't seem to want to eat. I never knew why."

"Maybe the poor thing had something stuck in her windpipe," Aurora said, happily scooping up the last of some cherries she was having. If the food hadn't been so good she would have endeavored to damp her glow a little, but there was really no knowing where her next cherries jubilee would come from and she was not inclined to waste any. When she finished she poked her tongue into the several corners of her mouth, hoping to locate whatever particles of the meal that might have strayed; while she was searching she sat back and surveyed the restaurant merrily. She had been too busy eating even to observe who was there. It was an unrewarding survey, however; while they had been eating, the lunch hour had ended, and only she and the General and two or three stragglers were left.

With the food gone there was no way she could avoid noticing that her friend General Scott was approaching a state. His face was almost as red as his necktie, and he had begun to talk of foreign climes—always one of the worst signs with him.

"Aurora, if you'd just come with me to Tahiti," he said as they were walking to the car. "If we could just be together in Tahiti for a little while I'm sure you'd see matters in a different light."

"Why, Hector, look around you," Aurora said, gesturing toward the blue sky. "The light is wonderful here. I don't know that I'd trade it for the light in Polynesia, if that's where you want me to go."

"No, you misinterpret me," the General said. "I meant that

with a little more time you might come to think differently about me. Foreign climes sometimes do wonders. Old habits fall by the wayside."

"But, Hector, I'm quite fond of my habits," Aurora said. "It's nice of you to think of me, dear, but I really don't see why I should have to go all the way to Tahiti to get rid of habits I'm perfectly comfortable with right here."

"Well, I'm not perfectly comfortable with them," the General said. "I'm goddamn frustrated, if you want to know the truth." Seeing that the parking lot was empty except for their car, he immediately demonstrated the nature of his frustration by launching a quick assault. He disguised it for two seconds by pretending that all he meant to do was hold the door open for her, but Aurora wasn't fooled. The General was seldom able to restrain himself completely, particularly not when he had grown so red in the face, but she had had a good deal of experience with his little physical blitzkriegs and knew they posed no serious threat either to her person or her mood.

She squirmed right through the one in progress, searching in her purse for her keys all the while, and aside from having to straighten her dress a bit and comb her hair—things she would have had to do in any case—she got through it with her gaiety intact.

"Hector, you do beat all," she said happily, putting her twisted key in the ignition. "I can't think why you'd think I'd go to Tahiti with you if you're going to leap on me in every parking lot in town. If that's the way you behave I don't see why you think anyone would want to marry you."

The General's passionate state had curdled somewhat from lack of success, and he was sitting on his side of the car with his arms crossed and his lips compressed. He was not so much annoyed with Aurora as he was at his dead wife, Evelyn. The crux of his annoyance with Evelyn was that she had been such poor preparation for Aurora. To begin with, Evelyn had been petite, whereas Aurora was large. He could never quite figure out where to grasp her, and before he could get anything like a secure hold she managed to squirm her way into some corner or other, where she could not possibly be embraced. Evelyn had failed to provide him with any practice at all, since she was the soul of patience and docility and had never squirmed in her life that he could remember. She had always stopped whatever she was doing the minute he touched her, and in some cases even before he touched her. In fact, she was never doing much anyway and considered his embraces to be a nice change of pace.

Aurora's kind of pace was something else again, and in retrospect he couldn't imagine why Evelyn had been so docile.

Aurora, for her part, was keeping one eye on him and the other on the road. The sight of him sitting with his arms crossed was so comical that she couldn't repress a chuckle.

"Hector, you can't know how amusing you are at these times," she said. "I'm not sure your sense of humor is quite all it ought to be. There you are sulking, if I'm not mistaken, just because I won't let you work your will upon me in a parking lot. I've heard that teenagers go in for that sort of thing, but you and I are some ways out of our teens, you must admit."

"Oh, hush, Aurora, you almost hit that mailbox," the General said. "Can't you drive a little closer to the center of the road?" Her penchant for driving with one wheel off the pavement annoyed him almost as much as her penchant for parking three feet from the curb.

"Well, just to oblige you I'll try," Aurora said, verging left a tiny fraction. "You know I don't like to be too close to the center line. Suppose I wobbled just as I was meeting someone. Frankly if you're going to sulk all the way back home I don't care if I do hit a mailbox. I was not brought up around sulky men, I can tell you that."

"God damn it, I'm not sulking," the General said. "You're making me desperate, Aurora. It's easy for you to talk about parking lots and working my will, but in fact you know damn well I never get a chance to work it anywhere else. You won't let me in your house and you won't come in mine. I haven't worked my will in years anyway. I'm not drinking from the fountain of youth, you know. I'm sixty-seven. If I don't work it pretty soon it's not apt to be workable."

Aurora glanced over at him and was forced to sigh. He had a point. "Dear, you put that rather sweetly," she said, reaching over and making him uncross his arms so she could give his hand a squeeze. "I do wish I was feeling more compliant these days, but the fact is I'm just not."

"You don't try!" the General burst out. "I should think you'd at least try! How many four-star generals do you think are going to come your way?"

"Now, you see, you always go one sentence too far, Hector," she said. "If you'd just try shortening your speeches by one sentence each I might find myself feeling a little more compliant one of these days."

Despite her earlier promise, the Cadillac's right wheels were off the pavement and edging farther and farther toward the ditch all the time, but the General compressed his lips and said nothing about it. He considered that the responsibility was mostly his anyway—he was well aware that she wasn't to be trusted on the open road and should not have let her bring him to a restaurant thirty miles out of town.

"Be that as it may, I still think you might try," he said irascibly.

Aurora ignored his tone and drove a mile or two in silence. Then she reached over and squeezed his hand again.

"Trying is not precisely what's required, Hector," she said. "I am not by any means the most experienced woman in the world, but I do know that much. You have such wonderful taste in food, dear, that I really hate to let you go, but I'm afraid I may have to. I seem to be very set in my attitudes these days, and I don't think even a trip to Tahiti would change me very much."

"What are you talking about, Aurora?" the General asked, disturbed by what he was hearing. "Why would you let me go, and where do you think I'd go if you did?"

"Well, as you pointed out, I'm behaving in a rather frustrating manner," Aurora said. "I've no doubt you'd be better off if I let you go. I'm sure there are any number of nice ladies around Houston who'd simply be delighted to have a four-star general come their way."

"Not as nice as you," the General said, almost before her mouth was closed.

Aurora shrugged and glanced at herself briefly in her rearview

116

mirror—as usual it was turned so she could see herself better than she could see the road.

"Hector, that's very romantic of you," she said, "but I think we're both aware that whatever charms I may have are more than offset by my difficulties. Everybody knows I'm impossible, and you might just as well admit it and quit wasting what time you've got left. I'm afraid I've come to share the general view. I'm haughty and willful and very sharp-tongued. You and I irritate one another in a number of ways and I don't think we could keep the same roof over our heads for six days, even if we tried our best. Anyone as particular as myself deserves to have to live alone, as I shall probably have to. It's purely self-defeating for you to sit there training your binoculars on my garage and dreaming your dreams. Find some nice woman with a taste for good food and whisk her right off to Tahiti. You're a military man and I think it's high time you regained the habit of command."

The General was so amazed by what he was hearing that he forgot to remind Aurora that they were approaching the turn that would bring them back to Houston.

"But, Aurora, I still have the habit of command," he said angrily. "It just so happens that you're the only woman I want to command."

Then he noticed that she hadn't noticed the turn and was about to sail right past it. "Turn, Aurora!" he yelled, loud enough to have turned a column of tanks.

Aurora drove straight on. "Hector, this is no time to show off," she said. "Your voice just isn't what it used to be and that is not precisely what I meant when I spoke of the habit of command, anyway."

"No, no, Aurora," the General said. "You missed the road. As many times as we've driven out here, God damn it, it does seem to me that you'd know the way. I've had to show you the way every single time."

"You see, that's just what I meant by us being unfitted for one another," Aurora said. "You always know your way to places and I never do. I'm sure we'd drive one another mad in a matter of days. Can't I just turn at the next road I come to?"

"No!" the General said. "The next road you come to leads to El Paso. Turn around."

"Oh, well, all right," Aurora said. "You spend half your life talking to me about foreign climes and now you won't even let me try a new road. I don't think that's very consistent Hector. You know how I hate to retrace my steps."

"Aurora, you have no goddamn discipline," the General said, losing his temper. "If you'd only marry me I'd fix that in no time."

While he was losing his temper Aurora executed one of her most masterful U-turns, sweeping from bar ditch to bar ditch.

"You didn't signal," the General said.

"That may be true, but it's your car that's always broken down," Aurora said, lifting her chin. Hector had suddenly become unrewarding to talk to, so she stopped talking. The effects of her excellent meal had not worn off, and she was still in a fine mood. They were on the great coastal plain southeast of Houston. Flights of gulls were going over and the smell of the nearby ocean mingled with the smell of the tall coastal grass in a pleasant way. It was a very nice road to drive on, it seemed to her, and it was easy enough to look at the strings of white gulls and the extraordinary masses of clouds that were beginning to pile up on one another, certainly far pleasanter than looking at Hector Scott, who had his arms crossed again and was obviously quite annoyed with her.

"Hector, I don't believe you were nearly as sulky before you went bald," she said. "Don't you think a hairpiece might improve your spirits, dear?"

Without a moment's warning, the General sprang at her. "Turn, Aurora!" he yelled. "You're missing the road again!"

To her annoyance he actually leaned over and started to grab the wheel himself, but she quickly slapped his hand away. "I'll turn if that's all you can think about, Hector," she said hotly. "Just let me do it."

"No, it's too late," the General said. "Don't turn now, for God's sake."

But Aurora had had enough of such talk. Without further ado

she turned, too late to quite hit the road she was aiming at but just in time to avoid hitting the barbed-wire fence that ran beside it. What she did not fail to hit was a large white car that, for no reason in the world that she could see, was parked right in the ditch by the fence. "Oh, my," she said, braking.

"I told you!" the General shouted just at the moment that they hit the rear end of the parked car.

Aurora never really drove very fast, and she had had time to do quite a bit of braking, but still when she hit the white car she hit it with quite a loud wham. She herself experienced no discomfort from the wham. Almost immediately there was another wham—she had no idea where that one came from—and then to her surprise the car seemed to be enveloped in a cloud of dust. She hadn't noticed any dust before the accident.

"My goodness, Hector, do you suppose we're in a sandstorm?" she asked, and noticed that the General was holding his nose.

"What's wrong with your nose?" she asked as the Cadillac lurched back in the direction of the barbed-wire fence. It stopped before it got to the fence, but the cloud of dust remained. After a while it settled and Aurora took out her brush and began to brush her hair.

"Don't talk to me, Hector, just don't talk to me," she said. "I'm sure you're going to say I told you so, and I refuse to hear it."

The General was still holding his nose, which had bumped on the windshield.

"Aren't those nice sea gulls, though?" Aurora said, noticing with some satisfaction that they were still flapping along overhead, probably giving no thought at all to a world in which pedals were constantly having to be worked.

"Well, now you've done it," the General said. "I always knew you'd do it and now you have."

"Well, Hector, I'm glad to have given you *that* satisfaction at least," Aurora said. "I should hate to have been a disappointment to you in every way."

"You're a ridiculous woman!" the General burst out. "I hope you realize that. Just ridiculous!"

"Well, I sometimes suspect it," Aurora said quietly. "All the same I wish you weren't quite so eager to turn me against myself."

She continued to brush her hair, though with fading spirit. The dust had settled, and she had had at least one accident, if not two. Hector Scott, far from being a help, was settling back to gloat, and her instincts were confused and subdued. Ordinarily when things went wrong her instinct was to attack, but in this case she had too strong a feeling that whatever had happened had been entirely her fault. Perhaps, as Hector said, she was ridiculous—that and nothing more. She felt rather lost, in her heart, and would have liked for Rosie or Emma to be there, but neither of them was.

"Hector, I do wish you'd let me try the next road I came to," she said sadly. "I don't think I'd have hit anybody if I hadn't had to retrace my steps."

At that moment, to her surprise, a small man of no pretensions appeared at her window. It was obvious at once that he had no pretensions. "Hello, ma'am," he said. He was short and had sandy hair and a very freckled complexion.

"Yes, hello, sir," Aurora said. "I'm Aurora Greenway. Are you one of my victims?"

The small man reached a freckled hand in and shook hers. "Vernon Dalhart," he said. 'You folks ain't hurt, are you?"

"I bumped my nose," the General said.

"No, we're fine," Aurora said, ignoring him. "Were you injured?"

"Aw, no," Vernon said. "I was just lying in the back seat talking on the phone when you popped into me. I ain't hurt an' the phone never even went dead. We got to work out our story quick, though, because that boy that hit you was a highway patrolman."

"Oh, dear," Aurora said. "I knew they didn't really like me. I never thought one would run into me, though."

"You glanced off my tail end and skidded up on the highway, you know," Vernon said. "I seen it. He just happened to be coming along right then. He's all right, but it kinda knocked the wind out of him. It'll take him a minute or two to get cracking on this thing."

"Oh, dear," Aurora said. "I suppose it means jail. I wish I could remember my lawyer's last name."

"Aw, nobody'd take a nice lady like you to jail," Vernon said, smiling at her rather nicely. "All you have to do is tell him it was all my fault."

"Be careful, Aurora," the General said. "Don't commit yourself."

Aurora paid him no mind at all. "But Mr. Dalhart," she said, "it was quite evidently all *my* fault. I'm known the world over for my erratic driving. I certainly wouldn't think of putting the blame on you."

"Won't hurt a thing, ma'am," Vernon said. "I play poker with the boss of the highway patrol just about every week of the world, an' he ain't won in years. You just tell this boy that you was idlin' along and I backed into you. All I got to do's drop the ticket in the next pot. It's simple as that."

"Uum," Aurora said, considering. The small man, Mr. Dalhart, seemed unable to stand still. He shifted from one foot to the other, fiddling with his belt buckle. Yet he smiled at her as if she had done nothing wrong, and that was so refreshing that she felt inclined to trust him.

"Well, Mr. Dalhart, you make it sound very practical, I must say," she said.

"I don't trust this man, Aurora," the General said suddenly. He didn't like the way Aurora was perking up so quickly. If only the catastrophe had deepened a little bit more she would have been forced to come to him for comfort, he felt sure.

"Mr. Dalhart, this is General Scott," Aurora said. "He's a good deal more suspicious than I am. Do you think I can carry off this little deception, really and truly?"

Vernon nodded. "No problem at all," he said. "Them old boys who drive patrol cars got simple minds. It's just like bluffin' a dog, you know. Just don't act scared."

"Well, I'll try," Aurora said, "although I can't claim to have bluffed very many dogs."

"Now stop it," the General said, straightening himself up and making the knot in his tie a little neater. "After all, I was a witness to this accident. I also happen to be a man of principle.

Suppose I don't happen to want to sit here and listen to you give false evidence. Lie, in other words. That is what you were about to do, isn't it?"

Aurora looked down at her lap for a moment—she sensed real trouble. She stole a look at Vernon Dalhart, who was still bobbing around outside the car, and still smiling at her. Then she turned and looked the General in the eye.

"Yes, Hector, go on. I'm listening," she said. "I'm not so noble but that I lie on occasion. Is that the point you wish to make against me?"

"No, but I'm glad you admit it," he said.

"You're not getting to the point, Hector, and I wish you'd hurry," Aurora said, not taking her eyes off him.

"Well, I saw the accident too, you know, and I'm a four-star general," he said, a little unnerved by her look but not quite unnerved enough to back away.

"I don't think you saw a bit more than I did, Hector, and all I saw was dust," Aurora said. "What does this come down to?"

"What it comes down to is that I'll support your little lie if you'll take a perfectly proper, perfectly respectable trip to Tahiti with me," the General said with an air of triumph. "Or if Tahiti doesn't suit you it can be anyplace else in the world that you might want to go."

Aurora looked out the window. Vernon was still fidgeting, but he was also looking at the ground, as if embarrassed to be privy to such conversation. She could hardly blame him.

"Mr. Dalhart, could I ask you a great favor, point blank?" she said.

"Why sure," Vernon said.

"If your car is still working, after that lick I gave it, I wonder if you'd mind giving me a ride to town?" Aurora asked. "After we're finished with the police, I mean. I don't think I'm quite up to driving in the state I'm in."

"Your car won't run anyway, ma'am," Vernon said. "The back fender's mashed against the tire. "I'll run you right in as soon as we've settled with the law.

"Be glad to run the General in too," he added a little hesitantly.

"No, not the General too," Aurora said. "I've no interest at all in how the General gets home. As he's fond of pointing out, he's a four-star general and I doubt in a country like ours a four-star general is going to be left to starve by the roadway. I've found my ride and he can find his."

"That's goddamned high-handed of you, Aurora," the General said. "All right, I won't challenge your story. My little effort was in vain, I see, but I don't see why I have to be derided for it. You can just stop acting like that."

Aurora opened her door and got out. "You shouldn't have tried to blackmail me, Hector," she said. "I'm afraid it's had a very destructive effect on my feeling for you. You can sit in my car if you like, and as soon as I'm home I'll tell F.V. where you are. I'm sure he'll come and get you. Thank you very much for the lunch."

"Now stop it, God damn it!" the General said, growing seriously angry. "We've been neighbors for years, and I won't have you walking off from me this way. I didn't do anything so bad."

"No, nothing, Hector, not a thing," she said. She bent and looked in at him a moment. They had, after all, been neighbors for years. But there was nothing of neighborliness in the General's eyes. They were cold blue and angry. Aurora straightened herself and looked across the miles of grass that stretched toward the Gulf.

"Then get back in here and stop acting like a goddamn queen," the General said.

Aurora shook her head. "I have no intention of getting back in," she said. "The reason you didn't do anything just now, Hector, was because you couldn't, you know. You have no power at the moment. It's the thought of what you might do if you were granted some that worries me. I certainly don't intend to grant you any. I have to be going now. You look after yourself."

"I won't forget this, Aurora," the General said, very red in the face. "I'll get even, I assure you."

Aurora walked away. The ground was somewhat uneven and she reached out and took Vernon's arm, which seemed to shock him. Nonetheless, he let her.

"I'm sorry about that little argument," she said. "I've added awkwardness to injury, I'm afraid."

"Well, I always heard that generals was nothing but trouble," Vernon said.

"*Were* nothing but trouble," Aurora said. "Generals is plural and were is plural. It really sounds better, you know."

Vernon didn't know. He looked at her uncertainly.

"Oh, well," Aurora said quickly. "I really shouldn't be criticizing your grammar just after I've wrecked your car. It's just a habit of mine."

She was abashed that the remark had slipped out, and also somewhat disconcerted to discover that when she turned to speak to Vernon she looked right over his head.

"The law's managed to catch its breath," Vernon said. "I guess we gotta face the music now."

A very thin, very young patrolman was walking around and around behind Vernon's car. The car was a huge white Lincoln that seemed to have a television antenna on top of it.

"Why he's so slim," Aurora said, looking at the young patrolman. "He's just a boy." She had expected someone large and angry, and the sight of such a slight young man was very reassuring.

"Why is he walking around and around?" she asked. "Do you suppose he's dizzy?"

"He might be a little dizzy," Vernon said. "Most likely he's just looking at the car tracks, tryin' to figure out what happened. He's the one that's got to explain smashing up that patrol car."

"Oh, dear," Aurora said. "Perhaps I should plead guilty. Otherwise I may have ruined his career."

Before Vernon could do more than shake his head the young patrolman walked up to them, also shaking his head. He carried a clipboard.

"Hello, folks," he said. "Hope one of y'all know what happened to us. Me, I ain't got a clue."

"My fault, first to last," Vernon said. "You an' the lady here never stood a chance."

"I'm Officer Quick," the young man said, very slowly. Then he shook hands with both of them.

"I knew I ort never to have got up today," he said with a

pained grimace. "You know how some days you get a kinda feeling of doom? That's just how I been feelin' all day, an' I was right as rain. I hope I didn't hurt your car too much, ma'am."

Aurora had to smile, he was so harmless. "Not seriously, Officer," she said.

"Well, I ain't making no excuses," Vernon said. "Just write me out a ticket and that's that."

Officer Quick surveyed the whole area slowly, the pained expression still on his thin face. "Mister, I ain't sweatin' the ticket," he said. "I'm sweatin' drawing the map."

"What map?" Aurora asked.

"Regulations," the young man said. "We gotta draw maps of these accidents we find, and if there's one thing I can't do it's draw. I couldn't draw a straight line with a ruler, and I ain't no good at crooked lines either. Even when I figure out what happened I can't draw it, and this time I can't even figure out what happened."

"Oh, well, let me draw it for you, Officer," Aurora said. "I studied drawing quite seriously when I was a girl and if it will be any help to you I'll be glad to draw our little accident."

"All yours," Officer Quick said, handing her his clipboard at once. "Most ever' night I dream about some accident happenin' and me havin' to draw the map. That's mostly what I dream about now, drawin' maps."

Aurora felt quite strongly that the moment had come to improvise. She took the pen that Vernon immediately offered.

"Goodness," she said, for it was the only pen she had ever seen that had both a clock and a calendar on it. Once she got over the novelty of that she propped herself against the back of Vernon's car and began to draw the accident. Apparently there was going to be no one to say her nay—Hector Scott was still sitting in her car—so she proceeded to draw the accident precisely as she would have preferred it to occur.

"You see, Officer, we were watching the sea gulls," she said, sketching them in first, along with a cloud or two.

"Oh, I see, bird watchers," Officer Quick said. "Say no more. That explains everything."

"Yep, that's the whole story in a nutshell," Vernon agreed.

"You bird watchers is always running into one another," Officer Quick said. "I think this here whole emphasis on not drivin' while you're drinkin' is all wrong. Why I can go down to the dancehall on my night off an' tank up till my ol' bladder won't hardly hold it and still be steady as she goes there at the wheel. I ain't never hit nothin' while I was drinkin', but they ain't no tellin' what I'd hit if I was to drive along an' try to watch a bird. I think they oughta put up a few signs sayin' 'Bird Watching Don't Drive.'"

Aurora saw that the young man had bought the story before she had even had time to make it up. She did a hasty little drawing in which Vernon was backing up beneath some sea gulls while she was advancing on them obliquely. She depicted Officer Quick and his patrol car as perfectly innocent passers-by, and was not too successful at drawing her car in the process of whirling around and around. She also drew in a sizable cloud of dust, since that was her chief memory of the accident.

"It was awful dusty, wasn't it?" Officer Quick said, studying the picture intently.

"I ort to have been a fireman," he added wistfully while he was struggling to write Vernon out a ticket.

"Perhaps it's not too late," Aurora said. "I must say I don't think it's very healthy for you to lie in bed dreaming about maps all night."

"Naw, no hope," the young man said. "There ain't even a regular firehouse in our town. It's all just volunteer work, an' you know what that pays."

As Vernon was helping Aurora into the white Lincoln she bethought herself once more of General Scott. It hardly seemed fair to go off and leave such a nice boy at the mercy of Hector Scott.

"Officer, I'm afraid the man sitting in my car is very angry," she said. "Actually he's angry at me, but he's a retired general and it wouldn't surprise me if he was in the mood to say ugly things to anyone who comes around."

"Oh," Officer Quick said. "Y'all just gonna go off and leave him sittin' there, huh?"

"Yes, that's what we'd planned," Aurora said.

"Well, I ain't goin' near him," Officer Quick said. "If he gets out an' flies into me I'll call a couple of my local col-leagues an' we'll arrest him. Y'all folks try to keep your minds off birds now."

"Yes, we will, thank you very much," Aurora said.

Officer Quick had extracted a toothpick from his shirt pocket and was chewing on it with an air of quiet melancholy. She and Vernon both waved at him, and he returned the wave in a listless fashion.

"One last thought, folks," he said. "Come over me like a flash. Maybe what y'all need to do is move to Port Aransas. You know they got that big bird sanctuary there. Millions of our little . . . feathered friends. If y'all was to move down there an' get you one of them little houses that sits there on the bay with little balconies on them you wouldn't even have to drive at all, in order to keep up with sea gulls an' all that. You could just sit there with your feet propped up on the rail and watch birds night an' day. Be easier on the public too. Adios, amigos." And he waved again and plodded off toward his patrol car, rubbing his head as he went.

"What an amazing young man," Aurora said. "Are all police-men like him?"

"Yep, ever' one of them's crazy," Vernon said.

CHAPTER VII

1.

BEFORE AURORA could more than catch her breath Vernon was going ninety. She thought it felt very fast and looked over to make sure. Ninety it was. They had zipped past her Cadillac so fast she had barely had time to glance at Hector Scott, who was sitting there rigid as ever. The car itself was unlike any she had ever ridden in. It had two telephones and an elaborate radio of some kind, and one of the doors in the back had a television set built into it. Vernon handled the wheel rather casually, she thought, considering how fast they were going. Still, she felt more amazed than frightened. Vernon seemed perfectly confident of his driving and the car was so impressive and well-padded that it was probably more or less impervious to the vicissitudes that might befall normal cars. The doors locked themselves, the windows rolled themselves up, and it was all so comfortable that she found it hard to worry about the world outside, or even to remember that there was a world outside. The seats were covered in very soft leather, and the general color scheme was maroon, which suited her fine. The only thing tacky that she could see was the paneling of the dashboard, which was in cowhide—the sort with the hair still on.

"Well, I'll have to call you Vernon, I believe," Aurora said, settling back. "This is a very nice car. In fact, I don't know why I don't have one like this myself. The only thing wrong with it is that dreadful cowhide. How did that happen?"

Vernon looked abashed, which was rather affecting in a small freckled person, Aurora thought. He was pulling nervously at one ear.

"My idea," he said, still pulling.

"I must say I think that was a small lapse of judgment," Aurora said. "Don't do that please, you'll just stretch your earlobes."

Vernon looked even more abashed and stopped pulling at his ear. Instead he began to pop his knuckles.

Aurora held her peace for thirty seconds, but the sound of popping knuckles was more than she could tolerate.

"Don't do that either," she said. "It's just as bad as stretching your ears, and it makes a noise. I know it's dreadful of me to be so outspoken, but I will try to be fair. You can criticize me as soon as I do something that you find intolerable. I just don't think you ought to go around pulling on various parts of your body all the time. I noticed you doing it just after we had our wrecks."

"Yeah, I get the fidgets," Vernon said. "Nervousness is what it is. I can't slow down. The doctor says it's my metabolism." He stared hard at the road, trying to keep himself from pulling anything.

"That's a vague diagnosis at best," Aurora said. "I really think you might consider changing your doctor, Vernon. Everybody has a metabolism, you know. I have one too, but I don't pull on myself. You're obviously not married. No woman would allow you to fidget like that."

"Naw, never settled down," Vernon said. "Always been restless as a jack rabbit."

Ahead, to the northwest, the skyline of Houston had appeared, with the afternoon sun shining on its tall buildings, some silver, some white. Soon they were in a river of traffic, flowing with it toward the city. Vernon managed to control his fidgets by keeping both hands on the wheel, and Aurora leaned back in the wonderfully comfortable maroon leather seats and watched the city flash by with a good deal of contentment.

"I've always liked being driven better than I like driving," she said. "This is obviously a trustworthy car. Perhaps I ought to have been driving Lincolns all these years."

"Well, this here's my home," Vernon said. "Kind of a mobile headquarters. It's got a writing desk that pops out in the back seat. Got an icebox back there an' a safe under the floorboards to keep my winnings in."

"Goodness, Vernon, you seem to have my fondness for gadgets," Aurora said. "Could I make a call from one of your telephones? I'd just like to call my daughter and tell her I've been in a wreck. It might make her a little more considerate."

"Help yourself."

"How delightful," Aurora said, a sparkle in her eyes as she dialed. Something new was happening.

"I really don't know why I haven't had a phone put in my car," she said. "I guess I supposed it was something only millionaires could have." She paused, reflecting on her remark.

"I must be in shock from my wreck or I wouldn't have put that quite so stupidly," she said. "Of course I don't mean to imply that you aren't a millionaire. I do hope you won't consider anything I say an insult while I'm in this state."

"Oh, well, I got a few mil, but I ain't no H. L. Hunt," Vernon said. "Don't like to work that hard."

Just at that moment Emma answered the phone.

"Hello, dear, guess what?" Aurora said.

"You're getting married," Emma said. "General Scott's won you at last."

"No, quite the contrary," Aurora said. "He has just been removed from my life. I'm calling you very briefly, dear. You'd never guess it, but I'm in a moving car."

"Are you serious?"

"Yes, a moving car," Aurora said. "We're on the Allen Parkway.

I just wanted to inform you that I had a small car wreck. Happily it wasn't anybody's fault and no one was hurt, though the young patrolman did have the wind knocked out of him for a few minutes."

"I see," Emma said. "Whose moving car do you happen to be in?"

"The gentleman I had the wreck with has very considerately offered to drive me home," Aurora said. "His car is equipped with phones."

. "Lots of food for thought here," Emma said. "Rosie said you went off with General Scott. What became of him?"

"I'm afraid he's been left to cool his heels," Aurora said. "I'm hanging up now. We're coming to a light. I'm not used to talking in traffic. If you care to call me later I can give you more details."

"I thought you were going to stay home and pay your bills today," Emma said.

"Bye. I'm hanging up before you spoil the conversation," Aurora said, hanging up.

"I wonder why my daughter insists on reminding me of the very things I don't want to be reminded of." she said to Vernon. "If you've never been married, Vernon, I don't suppose you've ever experienced that vexation."

"I never been married, but I got nine nieces and four nephews," Vernon said. "I get to play uncle a lot."

"Ah, that's nice," Aurora said. He absentmindedly popped his knuckles once or twice, but she let it pass.

"On the whole I think I was fonder of some of my uncles than I've ever been of anyone," she added. "A good uncle is a godsend in this day and time. May I ask where is your home?"

"This here's mostly it," Vernon said. "These seats lay back, you know. All I got to do is find a parking place an' I'm home. These seats make right nice beds, and I got my TV and my phones and my icebox. I keep a couple of rooms down at the Rice Hotel, but that's mostly just to pile my dirty clothes in. The only things this car ain't got is closet space and a laundry."

"My goodness," Aurora said. "What an extraordinary way to live. I wouldn't be surprised if it didn't contribute to your fidgets,

131

Vernon. Comfortable as your car is, as a car, it can hardly take the place of a home. Don't you think it might be wise to put some of your money into a proper residence?"

"Wouldn't be nobody to take care of it," Vernon said. "I'm gone half the time. I got to go up to Alberta, tomorrow. If I had a house I'd just be worryin' about it. Might make me fidget worse."

"Alberta, Canada?" Aurora asked. "What's up there?"

"Oil," Vernon said. "I can't fly much. Gives me an earache. Usually I just drive wherever I go."

To Aurora's amazement he found her street, and without taking a single wrong turn. It was only a one-block street and a great many of her guests were unable to find it even when given precise instructions. "Well, here we are, aren't we?" she said when he pulled up in her driveway. "I can't believe you found it on the first try."

"No trick to that ma'am," Vernon said. "I play a lot of poker in this part of town."

"You don't have to call me ma'am," Aurora said. "In fact, I'd rather you wouldn't. It's not a locution I've ever been fond of. I'd far rather you called me Aurora."

It occurred to her, though, that there would be no further need for him to call her anything. She was home and that was that. He was going to Alberta in the morning and there was no telling where he might go from there. Certainly she had no business asking him what he meant to do.

With very little warning, her spirits began to fall. The mood of contentment she had felt while they were driving in had proved very insubstantial—probably it had only happened because the Lincoln's seats were comfortable, or because Vernon, fidgety as he was, was friendly and uncritical, and on the whole a nice change from Hector Scott. Vernon didn't seem to be quick to take offense, which was unusual in her experience. The men she met seemed frequently to take offense almost at once.

The sight of her nice house made her feel quite gloomy somehow. The nice part of the day was over, and the dregs, in a sense, were what remained. Rosie would be gone and there would be no one to fuss at at all. Her soap operas were over, and even if she called Emma and told her the story of the wreck in great detail it wouldn't really take up much more than an hour. Before very long she would have nothing to do but contemplate her bills, and it was not really very pleasant to have to pay one's bills in an empty house. Paying bills always gave her a feeling of panic anyway, and it was much worse when there was no one around to distract her. Also, she knew that once she got off to herself she was going to start worrying about her car wreck, and how to get her car home, and the law, and Hector Scott, and all sorts of things that she was not likely to worry about as long as someone was around.

For a moment, looking at Vernon, she had a strong impulse to ask him if he would like to stay to supper and talk to her while she paid her bills. Fixing him a meal was only a fair return for his courtesy in bringing her home, not to mention getting her off with the law; but asking a man to talk to her while she paid her bills was a curious thing to do, at best, and rather forward. It was obvious that Vernon was no ladies' man—how could he be, living in a car?—and if he was about to set off for Canada he probably had last-minute things to do, as she always did before she set off somewhere.

There was something about him that she liked—perhaps it was only that he had been able to find her street—but she didn't feel that whatever it was ought to be pushed quite so unconventionally. The circumstances of their meeting had been unconventional enough. Aurora sighed. She had begun to feel quite downcast.

Vernon waited for her to get out, but she didn't. Then it occurred to him that he was supposed to get out and open her door for her. He looked to see if that was what she was waiting for and saw that she was looking sad. She had looked happy only a moment before, and the sight of her looking sad frightened him badly. He knew a great deal about oil, but nothing at all about sadness in ladies. It startled him badly.

"What's the matter, ma'am?" he asked at once.

Aurora looked at her rings a moment. She was wearing a topaz and an opal. "I don't know why you won't call me Aurora." she said. "It's not a very difficult name to pronounce."

She looked up, and Vernon grimaced and looked abashed. He

was so abashed, in fact, that it was painful to see. His look made it quite evident that he was no sort of ladies' man at all. Aurora felt somewhat relieved, but also, suddenly, a little perverse and quite determined.

"I gotta work up to it, Miz Greenway," he said. "It ain't easy."

Aurora shrugged. "Oh, well," she said, "it's perfectly easy, but 'Mrs. Greenway' is somewhat of an improvement. 'Ma'am' makes me feel like a country schoolteacher, which I am far from being. I don't know why it should matter anyway, since you're about to run off and leave me. I don't blame you at all; I've been nuisance enough today. I'm sure you'll be happy to be on your way to Alberta, so you won't have to sit around with me."

"Well . . . no," Vernon said. He paused, confused.

"No," he said again.

Aurora turned her gaze upon him. It was not fair, she knew—he was such a nice little man—but she did it anyway. Vernon didn't know what was happening. He saw that his passenger was looking at him in a strange way, as if she expected something. He had no idea what it might be that she expected, but her look told him that it depended on him, and that it was very important. His car, which was usually so peaceful and empty, suddenly seemed like a pressure chamber. The pressure came from the strange look on Mrs. Greenway's face. She looked like she might be going to cry, or else get mad, or else just be very sad—he didn't know which. It all depended on what he came up with to do, and she hadn't stopped looking him in the eye for what seemed like many minutes.

Vernon felt a cold sweat coming on, only instead his palms got very dry. He didn't know the lady from Adam or Eve, and he didn't owe her a thing in the world, and yet suddenly he felt that he did owe her something. At least he wanted to owe her something. He didn't want her to be as sad, or as mad, as she seemed about to be. There were lines in her face that he hadn't noticed earlier, but nice lines. The pressure got worse; he couldn't tell if the seams of the car were about to burst, or if he was, and the need to fidget became so intense that he could have popped every knuckle on both hands in ten seconds if he hadn't known that that was the worst thing he could do.

Aurora, unrelenting even for a second, kept looking at him; she was turning the rings on her fingers, waiting for something, looking straight at him. It seemed to Vernon suddenly that everything was different. All his life people had insisted that someday a woman would come along and change him before he knew what was happening to him—and now it had come true. He would not have believed a human being would have had the power to change him so much so quickly, but it was so. Everything changed, not slowly, but at once. His old life had stopped just after he parked, and the ordinary world that he had known up to then had just stopped counting. Everything that stopped had stopped so abruptly that it took his breath. He felt that he would never see or need to see or even want to see another face but the face of the woman who was looking at him. He was so stunned that he even said what he felt.

"Oh, lord, Mrs. Greenway," he said. "I'm in love with you—plumb in love. What am I gonna do?"

The feeling in what he said wasn't lost on Aurora—his words seemed to be formed of emotion rather than breath, and she had seen them struggle out of real depths of fear and surprise.

Immediately she relaxed, though she too was surprised and for a moment rather flustered—flustered partly because such words and feeling had become unfamiliar to her and also, partly, because she knew that she had demanded them of him. In her loneliness and out of momentary inadequacy in regard to her life she had exerted herself and demanded love from the only person who was at hand to give it; and there it was, all over Vernon's windburned, freckled, and panic-stricken face.

She smiled at him, as if to say wait a minute, and looked away for a moment, at the sunlight on the pines behind her house. It was late and the sun was falling; the light filtered through the pines and fell across the lengthening shadows in her yard. She turned back to Vernon and smiled again. Her other suitors proposed and they cajoled, but they were afraid to say such words—even Alberto, who had said them countless times thirty years before. She started to put her hands on Vernon's for a moment, to show him she was not incapable of response, but he started back, really frightened, and she left it, for the time, at a smile.

"Well, I'm a terror, Vernon, as you may already have noticed," she said. "That's twice today that I've smashed into you without much compunction—the first time was in my car, of course. Not many people can stand me. You seem to be in an agony of fidgets, dear, and I suspect it's because you spend so much time cramped up in this car. Wouldn't you like to get out and walk around my back yard with me for a bit while the light is so lovely? I almost always walk around my back yard this time of day, and I wouldn't think the exercise would hurt you."

Vernon looked at the house and tried to imagine getting out and walking around it, but he couldn't. He was too shaken, although it was beginning to seem that life might go on a little longer—Mrs. Greenway was smiling at him and no longer seemed to be at all downcast. The thought occurred to him that she might not have heard what he said. If she had heard it maybe she wouldn't be smiling. The minute the thought occurred to him he became intolerably anxious. In the new scheme of things, waiting was impossible, and so was uncertainty. He had to know, and he had to know immediately.

"I tell you, I don't know what to do next, Mrs. Greenway," he said. "I don't know if you even heard me. If you was to think I didn't mean it I don't know what I'd do."

"Oh, I heard you, Vernon," Aurora said. "You expressed yourself quite memorably, and I don't believe I have any doubts about your sincerity. Why are you frowning?"

"Don't know," Vernon said, gripping the steering wheel. "I guess I wish we wasn't strangers."

Aurora looked away, at her pines, touched by his words. She had been about to say something light and it got stuck in her throat.

Vernon didn't notice. "I know I spoke out too quick," he said, still in an agony of fidgets. "I mean, you may think 'cause I'm a bachelor and got a few mil and a fancy car that I'm some kind of playboy or somethin', but that ain't true. I was never in nothin' like love in my whole life, Mrs. Greenway—not till just now."

Aurora quickly recovered her power of speech. "I certainly don't think I'd characterize you as a playboy, Vernon," she said. "If you were a playboy I imagine you'd have been able to realize that I wasn't thinking badly of you. The truth is I'm not at my most clear-headed right now, and I think if we got out and walked around my back yard it might be good for both of us. If you're not anxious to rush right off and leave me, perhaps after we've had our little walk you'll allow me to cook you a meal to make up for all I've put you through today."

Vernon was still not sure he could manage the actions of mundane life, but when he got out to open Aurora's door for her his legs worked at least.

Aurora took his arm for a second as they were going across her lawn, and he seemed to be shaking. "I imagine you don't eat well, Vernon," she said. "Since you live in that car all the time it's hard to see how you could."

"Well, I got an icebox," Vernon said humbly.

"Yes, but a stove is necessary too, for some of the healthier things," Aurora said, pausing for a moment to look back at the long white Lincoln sitting in her driveway. Its lines were at least the equal to those of her Cadillac. From a distance it looked quite magnificent.

"Goodness," she said. "Look how well that matches my white house. I wonder if anyone will think I've bought a new car."

2.

THE TWO of them had barely stepped into the kitchen so Aurora could lay down her handbag and kick off her shoes when they were confronted with an example of mundane life at its most woeful. Rosie was sitting at the kitchen table, awash in tears, holding a dishcloth full of ice cubes against the side of her head. She had found one of Aurora's old movie magazines and was crying all over it.

"What's the matter with you?" Aurora asked, in a panic at the sight. "Don't tell me there's been a robbery. What did you let them take?"

"Aw, no," Rosie said. "It was just Royce. I went too far."

Aurora set her purse on the cabinet and considered the scene for a moment. Vernon seemed slightly puzzled, but it was no time to worry about him.

"I see," she said. "He finally had enough, did he? What did he hit you with?"

"A doubled-up fist," Rosie said, sniffing. "He come in an' heard me talkin' to F.V. on the phone. It was just about helping him fix that stinkin' old Packard, but Royce jumped to conclusions. It made me madder'n a wet hen. If I was to start runnin' around it sure wouldn't be with F. V. d'Arch. I was never sweet on nobody from Bossier City in my entire life."

"Well, why didn't you explain that to Royce frankly, and put his mind at ease?" Aurora asked.

"Tryin' to explain something to Royce is like talkin' to a brick," Rosie said. "I was too mad. I accused him of shacking up with one of them sluts he delivers to. Boy did I pour it on him."

She paused to wipe her eyes on the back of her hand.

"So then what happened?" Aurora said. It annoyed her a little to have been gone on the one day when high drama occurred in her kitchen.

"The sonofabitch owned up to it," Rosie said, sliding rapidly downhill now that she had someone to commiserate with. "Oh, Aurora . . ." she said. "Now my marriage is a total wreck."

"Wait a minute!" Aurora said sternly. "Don't you cry until you've finished your story. What precisely did Royce own up to?"

"Every day for five years it's been goin' on," Rosie said. "She works up in some honky-tonk on Washington Avenue. All I know is her name is Shirley. He'd come here an' eat an' then he'd go right off there. Oh, gawd."

Unable to contain herself any longer, Rosie put her head in the crook of her elbow and sobbed.

Aurora looked at Vernon. He seemed to have calmed somewhat at the sight of Rosie's distress.

"Vernon, this seems to be my day for leading you into scenes," she said. "I can offer you a drink if you need fortification." She opened the liquor cabinet so he'd know where it was if he felt like helping himself, and then she went over and gave Rosie a few pats on the back.

"Well, dear, what a mess," she said. "At least we can all thank our lucky stars that you weren't pregnant again."

"That's right," Rosie said. "I don't want no more kids by that lowlife bastard."

"Nor anyone else, I hope," Aurora said. "My, you do have a knot on your temple. It's a very bad thing, hitting people on the temple. It doesn't seem like Royce at all. If he had admitted his guilt why was it necessary for him to hit you?"

"Because I was trying to stab him, I reckon," Rosie said. "I took a run at him with the butcher knife. I guess if he hadn't got a lick in first he'd be laying there dead right this minute."

"Good God," Aurora said. The thought of Royce lying lifeless on her kitchen floor, three steps from where he'd eaten so much good food, was almost more than she could handle. Rosie began to dry her eyes and soon was a little calmer.

"Well, my afternoon has not been entirely without adventure, either," Aurora said. "This poor creature is Rosalyn Dunlup, Vernon—Rosie, this is Vernon Dalhart."

"Just call me Rosie," Rosie said valiantly and dried her tear-drenched hands so Vernon could shake one.

"Rosie, I think you might have a little bourbon to calm your nerves," Aurora said. "Hector Scott behaved very badly and caused me to wreck my car. After that he behaved even worse and I left him sitting. We must call F.V. at once."

"Well, I can't," Rosie said. "Royce went down an' give him hell, an' now he's scairt to talk to me."

"Oh, well, I'll call him," Aurora said. "I just hope you remember the number of that road, Vernon. I'm afraid I don't have a very precise idea of where we left Hector."

"Highway Six right where Fourteen thirty-one comes into it," Vernon said at once.

Both women were amazed. "Fourteen thirty-one?" Aurora said. "I had no idea there were that many little roads. No wonder I'm always lost."

"Uh, it's just a farm-to-market road," Vernon said.

"I don't think Hector's been sitting long enough anyway," Aurora said. "What do you propose to do, Rosie?"

"Royce has gone off on a drunk, I guess," Rosie said. "I made my sister go get the kids, so he wouldn't come home an' beat up on 'em. I guess I'll go back over there afterwhile, if I can get up my nerve. I ain't leavin' no empty house for him to take no slut to, I can tell you that. Possession is nine tenths of the law where I come from."

"Where do you think Royce is now?" Vernon asked.

"Drinkin' with that slut," Rosie said. "Where else would the sonofabitch be?"

"An' how many kids you all got?"

"Seven," Rosie said.

"Why don't I go talk to him," Vernon said. "I bet I can straighten all this out."

Aurora was surprised. "Vernon, you don't even know him," she said. "You don't even know us. Besides, Royce is quite large, I assure you. What could you do?"

"Talk sense," Vernon said. "I got six hundred men workin' for me, more or less. They're always havin' these little fracases. They ain't too serious, usually. I bet I could snap ol' Royce out of it if I could find him."

The phone rang. Aurora picked it up. It was Royce.

"Aw," he said when he heard Aurora's voice. "Rosie there?"

"Why yes, would you like to speak to her, Royce?" Aurora said, thinking a rapprochement was in the offing.

"No," Royce said and hung up.

Instantly the phone rang again. It was Emma.

"I'm ready to hear about your car wreck," she said. "I'm dying to hear what you said to General Scott."

"I've not got a single moment for you right now, Emma," Aurora said. "Royce has beaten up Rosie and we're all in a state. If you want to do something useful get yourself over here."

"I can't," Emma said. "I have to cook supper for my husband."

"Oh, that's right, you're a slave, aren't you?" Aurora said. "How stupid of me to think you might be free to assist your own mother. I'm very glad I wasn't seriously injured. I wouldn't have wanted to do anything that might have disrupted your domestic routine."

"All right, forget it," Emma said. "Goodbye."

Aurora pushed the button down for a second, and then called F.V., who answered instantly.

"Goodness," she said. "Everyone seems to be hovering near their phones this evening. I suppose you recognize my voice, don't you, F.V.?"

"Oh, yeah, Miz Greenway," F.V. said. "How's Rosie?"

"Battered but unbowed," Aurora said. "However, that is not what I called to talk to you about. General Scott and I had a car wreck and also a small disagreement and I'm afraid I left him for you to go fetch. He's sitting in my car, on Highway Six near a farm-to-market road. I imagine he's furious, and the longer you wait to get him the worse things may go for you. Maybe you ought to zip right on out."

F.V. was horrified. "How long's he been sittin' there?" he asked.

"Quite a while," Aurora said blithely. "I have to tend to Rosie now, but I wish you the best of luck. Please remind the General that I don't wish to speak to him again. He may have forgotten that."

"Wait!" F.V. said. "Where'd you say to go? I ain't got nothin' to go in but a jeep."

"That's even better," Aurora said. "Highway Six. I'm sure you'll recognize my car. Good luck now."

"If we aren't going to drink I don't see why we can't at least have some tea," she said after hanging up. "Could you make us some, Rosie. It will take your mind off your troubles."

Then a horrible thought crossed her mind. "Oh, dear," she said. "I didn't lock my car. I was too offended. Suppose someone steals it tonight?"

"No problem," Vernon said. He began to pull at his ear, and he avoided her eye.

"Why there is too," Aurora said. "Unlocked cars are stolen every day."

"Oh, I took care of it," Vernon said.

"How?" Aurora asked. "You don't have a key to my car."

Vernon looked very abashed. His face got red. "Own a garage," he said. "Over on Harrisburg. It ain't no fun bein' afoot in this town. I just called my garage an' told 'em to get a tow truck out there. They work night an' day over there. They can smooth that fender out tonight an' get her back to you tomorrow."

Once again both women were amazed.

"It's more convenient, if you don't mind," Vernon said, pacing around. From time to time he acted like he might sit down, but he couldn't quite bring himself to.

"Fine," Aurora said. "That's very thoughtful. You won't find me looking many gift horses in the mouth, Vernon. Of course I'd like to pay whatever's required."

"Only thing is I never took the General into account," Vernon said. "I figured you'd ease up an' let him ride in with us. They may have towed him in too. I'll just get on the radio an' find out. You wouldn't want that fellow to go off on a wild goose chase."

Before Aurora could answer he was out the back door. "Radio's in my car," he said as he departed.

"Who's he, some kind of millionaire?" Rosie asked when he was out.

"I guess he is," Aurora said. "He's handy, isn't he? Imagine getting my car fixed so quickly."

"You must have struck like lightnin' this time," Rosie said. "Here I spend the day gettin' my head bashed in an' you go out and get a millionaire sweet on you. I was born under an unlucky star if anybody ever was."

"Oh, well, Vernon and I have barely met," Aurora said, shrugging. "I have enough worries in that line and I really don't think I ought to victimize a perfectly nice man like him. Besides, he's going to Canada tomorrow. In view of all he's done for me I thought I might at least make him a decent dinner. I'm not sure he's ever had one."

"He don't look like your type," Rosie said.

Before Aurora could answer Vernon popped back in. "The General rode in with a cop," he said. "I stopped F.V., though. Seen him gettin' in the jeep an' flagged him down."

Aurora immediately began to scratch her head. "Oh, dear," she said. "Now I've really got something to worry about. He's a most vindictive man, Hector Scott. There's no telling what he'll tell them about me. If he can think of a way to get me arrested I'm sure he will."

"Yep, you crossed the wrong man, this time," Rosie agreed. "We both ort to have been nuns, you an' me. That man'll have us both in the pen tomorrow if there's any way he can work it."

"Well, at least I'm not a Communist," Aurora said. "What did we decide to do about Royce?"

"What's there to do about a mean drunk?" Rosie said. "Run from him, that's all. I wouldn't be surprised if he barged in here."

"I would," Aurora said. "Royce wouldn't be ungentlemanly in my presence, no matter how aggravating you've been. You see, the chickens are coming home to roost, Rosie. I told you to be nicer to him."

"Yeah, an' I told you not to screw around with General Scott," Rosie said. "Ain't it a pity we never took one another's advice?"

Aurora looked at Vernon, who was pacing again. It seemed to suit him, and as long as he kept moving he didn't look so short.

"What was your plan for Royce, Vernon?" she asked.

"Don't matter. It won't work if I don't know where to find him," Vernon said.

"If you really want to find him look in a bar called the Storm-cellar," Rosie said. "It's over on Washington Avenue somewhere. I was in there many a time in the old days, when me an' Royce was happy."

"I'm gone," Vernon said, heading for the door again. "The sooner I get over there the less soberin' up he'll take."

He stopped and looked back at Aurora. "I don't want to miss out on supper," he said.

"Goodness, you won't miss out on supper," Aurora said. "I've just started digesting lunch."

Vernon disappeared. "He does come and go, doesn't he?" she said, dialing her daughter straightaway.

"You certainly were rude to me," Emma said.

"Yes, I'm very selfish," Aurora said. "To be frank, I've never liked playing second fiddle to Thomas. I don't suppose the two of you would like to come here for dinner? A rather interesting party seems to be shaping up."

Emma considered. "I'd like to, but I don't think he will," she said.

"Probably not. He doesn't like being outshone by me," Aurora said.

"Shoot, he'd be outshone by a twenty-watt bulb," Rosie said. "Poor Emma, she was the nicest baby."

"Momma, why are you being so mean?" Emma said. "Can't you stop it?"

Aurora sighed. "It just comes out whenever I think of him," she said. "Bad things always seem to happen to me on the day I try to pay my bills. Vernon's been the only bright spot—that's the man I hit. Rosie, I wish you weren't eavesdropping."

"All right, I'll go out an' rake the flowerbeds," Rosie said. "I done know about you an' Vernon, anyway. I seen it in his eyes."

"Oh, well, I guess you did," Aurora said. "Stay, I don't care. I feel quite chaotic just now."

She did too. She had passed through parts of the day without really feeling them, and now those parts were catching up with her. She had begun to feel them all, and they were contradictory and ambiguous, but with Emma on the phone and Rosie in the kitchen she was at least feeling them within familiar human boundaries. She felt strange, but not quite lost.

"What about this Vernon?" Emma asked.

"He's fallen in love with me," Aurora said quietly. "It took him about an hour. Actually I more or less made him, but he did it rather nicely and in his own way."

"Momma, you're crazy," Emma said. "That's just nonsense. You know that's all a myth."

"What is, dear?" Aurora asked. "I'm not following you, I'm afraid."

"Love at first sight," Emma said. "You certainly didn't fall in love with him at first sight, did you?"

"No, I'm not so fortunate," Aurora said.

"That's silly," Emma said.

"Well, you've always been a cautious child," Aurora said, sipping a little tea.

"I have not," Emma said, remembering Danny.

"Of course you have. Look at who you married. Any more caution and you'd be paralytic."

144

"God, you're awful," Emma said. "You're just awful! I wish I had somebody else for a mother."

"Who would you like?" Aurora asked.

"Rosie," Emma said. "She appreciates me at least."

Aurora rapped on the table and held out the phone to Rosie. "My daughter prefers you," she said. "She also denies that there is such a thing as love at first sight."

"She ain't seen Vernon," Rosie said, seating herself on the end of the table. "Hello, honey."

"Be my mother," Emma said. "I don't want my child to have a grandmother like Mother."

"Drop ever'thing an' come over here an' see your ma's new beau," Rosie said. "He's got millions."

"She forgot to mention that, but so what," Emma said. "Her yachtsman's got millions too."

"Yeah, but this one ain't fancy," Rosie said. "He's just a plain old country boy. I wouldn't mind marryin' him myself, now that I'm single agin."

"Royce didn't really beat you, did he?"

"Yeah, he boxed me right on the head before I could stab him, the lying bastard," Rosie said. "I just hope you never get into nothin' like this, honey. Here I been takin' time off to fix him lunch all these years and come to find out the sonofabitch has been running right off to that slut before he even gets 'em digested. You think that don't hit you where it hurts?

"The lowlife sonofabitch," she added, on reflection. "He ain't gettin' the kids, I can tell him that."

"Stop swearing, and don't start feeling sorry for yourself," Aurora put in. "If either of us starts feeling sorry for herself we're lost. Just give my cautious daughter your views on love at first sight."

"What's Momma saying?" Emma asked.

"Something about you being precautious," Rosie said. "I don't know what she thinks is wrong with it. If I'd been a little more precautious I wouldn't have so many mouths to feed now that I been deserted."

"Maybe it's not all that serious," Emma said. "Don't you think you might forgive him if he promises to behave?"

"Hold on a second, honey," Rosie said. She took the receiver away from her ear and looked out the back window on the darkening yard. The question Emma had asked was the very question she had been turning over and over in her mind all afternoon, without arriving at any conclusion. She looked down at Aurora.

"I ortn't to be talkin' to our girl about such as this," she said. "You think I'd be wrong to run him off? You think I oughta just . . . forgive an' forget?"

Aurora shook her head. "You're not likely to forget, I'm sure," she said. "I can't advise you about the other."

Just as she thought she was back in control, Rosie found herself losing control worse than ever. Before she could get the phone back to her ear her lungs seemed to fill up, only with resentment and anger rather than air. It was the memory of how smug he'd been that did it. Having another woman was one thing, but being so smug about it, right to his own wife's face, was something she'd never expected from Royce. If anything was unforgivable it was the look on his face when he told her— At the memory of it her throat began to jerk and she sat up straighter and went, "Uh . . . uh . . . uh . . ." as if she were trying to prevent hiccups. It was an effort not to cry, but it failed. She could only sit up so straight, and the resentment welled up out of her lungs into her throat and she was helpless. She handed the phone back to Aurora, got off the table, and went off, doubled over, to cry it out in the bathroom.

"Well, Rosie's had to go and cry," Aurora said. "Men have not improved, despite what you read. Hector Scott tried to blackmail me into going to Tahiti with him. He took a very nasty tone too."

"What do you plan to do about Rosie?" Emma asked.

Aurora sipped her tea. She never liked to answer her daughter too hastily.

"Naturally Rosie is welcome to whatever she needs, if I have it," she said. "I may propose that she stay here until Royce comes to his senses. My impression is that Royce is far too lazy to do without her very long. I expect he'll try and make amends before very long. Vernon has gone to see to him now, in fact.

146

"I certainly hope Rosie will insist on lots of amends," she added. "If I were in her shoes my demands would be extensive, I can tell you that."

Emma snorted. "Flap says there are two things we'll never be finished with," she said. "Your demands and the national debt."

"Oh, that's a witticism, I suppose," Aurora said. "I'll remember who made it, if I can."

"Why don't you all come over here to eat?" Emma said. "I could manage that."

"No thank you," Aurora said. "Small as that place is we'd have to eat in our cars. Vernon has an ice box in his, did I tell you? Also a television."

"You're awfully flippant about that man," Emma said. "I think that's very unbecoming."

Aurora set down her teacup. It was exactly the criticism her mother would have made, had her mother been privy to all that had been said. Unfortunately, there was no denying that it was just. She remembered Vernon's contortions.

"Yes, I'm afraid you're right about me," she said after a pause. "I've always been frivolous that way. I don't start out to speak ill of people, I'm just unable to resist my little flippancies. I hope Vernon never finds out. He's having my car fixed for me too."

"He's beginning to sound like Howard Hughes," Emma said.

"Oh, no, he's much shorter," Aurora said. "He's about level with my bosom."

"Cecil misses you," Emma said.

"Yes, I'm sure I have to rouse myself and do my annual duty by him," Aurora said. Her annual duty was a dinner for Cecil and the young marrieds. Everyone dreaded it, and with good reason.

"Let's do it next week," she added. "I've begun to feel it hanging over me. If you don't mind, I'm hanging up now. I don't feel quite myself, for some reason, and I don't want us having a fight while I'm defenseless."

She did hang up after saying good night, and then she went around the kitchen turning on the lights and inspecting her food-stocks. Usually she had enough food on hand for several interesting dinners, but when the need for one actually arose it was always necessary for her to do a certain amount of checking. When she was fully reassured about her meats and wines and vegetables she put all thought of dinner aside and went out into the back yard to walk slowly around in the dusk for a while, hoping her feeling of strangeness would go away.

Part of the strangeness was not really strange—it was the usual feeling of panic about money that came on her when it was time to pay her bills. Rudyard had not really left her secure financially, though she and everyone else continued to pretend that he had. There was so much income and no more. She really ought to sell her house and take an apartment somewhere, but she could never fool herself into thinking she meant to do it one day sooner than she had to. It would mean firing Rosie and pulling in her sails, and something in her resisted. As far as her sails went, it had taken her long enough to spread them, as it was; she was not inclined to pull them in until she had to. For four years she had gone along from month to month and bill to bill, hoping something would happen before matters got desperate.

The house was too lovely, too comfortable, too much hers—her furniture, her kitchen, her yard and her flowers and her birds, her patio and her window nook. Without them she would not merely have to change, she would have to find another person to be, and it seemed to her that the only person left for her to be, besides the person she was, was a very old lady. Not Aurora Greenway, but simply Mrs. Greenway. When the day came when everyone who knew her called her Mrs. Greenway, then perhaps it wouldn't matter so much about the house. By then, if she were not dead, she would have dignity enough to manage anywhere—as her mother had managed in her last years.

But she was not ready. She wanted to manage right where she was. She could, if worst came to worst, sell the Klee. It would be a disloyalty to her mother, of course, but then her mother had committed a disloyalty to her in buying it with money that would soon have been hers. It would also be a disloyalty to Emma, because Emma loved it, but then Emma would someday get the Renoir and if she had any sort of life would come to love the Renoir more—far more—Aurora thought.

There was a new part to the strangeness, though—something

more than panic about money—and it was the new part that she seemed to feel increasingly. It was not just loneliness, though there was that; nor yet just sexlessness, though there was that too: a few nights before, to her amusement, she had had a dream in which she opened a can of tunafish, only to have a penis pop out. It had actually been a charming dream, rather inventive, she thought, and her chief frustration in regard to it was that there was no one with whom she felt quite right about sharing it. Everyone she might have shared it with, her daughter included, would only have taken it to mean that she was considerably more fevered than she was.

In any case the strangeness was different from fever—it was more an off-centeredness, a feeling of distortion, as if already, years before her time, she was slipping away, losing touch, either falling behind or, perhaps worse, moving too far ahead. She had the feeling that everyone who knew her only saw her outward motions—the motions of a woman who constantly complained and wheedled affection. Her inward motions no one seemed to see. What frightened her was the knowledge of how much she had already learned not to count on, how much she could do without. If her inward motion was not checked she had the feeling that she would soon find herself beyond everyone, and that was the cause of the strangeness, which seemed to have chosen a physical place inside her, behind her breastbone. She could press hard against her chest and feel it, like a lump almost, a lump that sometimes nothing seemed to loosen.

While she was walking, hoping her back yard would set her right, she heard voices from the kitchen. Hurrying in, she found Rosie and Vernon standing by the sink in earnest conversation.

"He's worked a miracle," Rosie said. "Royce has decided he wants me back."

"What did you do?" Aurora asked.

"My little secret," Vernon said.

Rosie had collected her purse and was obviously ready to go home.

"I'll worm it out of Royce," she said. "Royce never kept no secret in his life.

"At least no nice secret," she added, remembering something.

149

"Sure you don't want me to run you home now?" Vernon asked.

"He's a regular taxi service, ain't he?" Rosie said. "It wouldn't look too good in the neighborhood if I was to come ridin' up in a big white Lincoln. I'll just hop on down an' catch my bus."

"I find this all rather bewildering," Aurora said. "Why are you rushing right back to a cad like Royce? You could sleep here tonight, you know. If I were you I'd let him cool his heels for twenty-four hours at least."

"Just 'cause I'm going back don't mean I plan on callin' things even," Rosie said. "I ain't forgettin' nothin'. Don't you worry."

They all stood silently for a minute.

"Well, good luck, dear," Aurora said. "I'll cook Vernon a dinner and you go home and see what comes out in the wash."

"Many thanks, Mr. Dalhart," Rosie said at the door.

"Don't you take any chances," Aurora said. "If he shows any violent tendencies get a cab and come back here."

"God didn't build me to be no punchin' bag," Rosie said. "I ain't too proud to run."

"What did you do?" Aurora demanded as soon as Rosie was out the door.

Vernon fidgeted. "Offered him a better job," he said reluctantly. "You'd be surprised what a raise and a good new job will do for a man like Royce."

Aurora was astonished. "You hired my maid's husband?" she said. "That's almost presumptuous. What did Royce do to deserve a new job, may I ask? Were you offering a reward for wife beating?"

Vernon looked discomfited. "Them delivery routes gets old," he said. "If a man goes on driving the same one year after year the monotony's bound to get to him sometime. That's how messes get started."

"Quite true," Aurora said. "However, Rosie's work isn't very exciting, and she hasn't started any messes that I've observed. Not for lack of opportunity, either—there's opportunity right down at the end of the street."

She took her midget TV off the cabinet where it lived and set it on the table. Every day, in the hope of crushing the poor little machine—or so Aurora felt—Rosie wound its cord around and around it so tightly that usually the news was half over before she could get it unwound. Vernon leapt to assist her, and she noted with pleasure that it took him as long to get it unwound as it usually took her. He was mortal at least.

"What did you hire Royce to do exactly?" she asked, chopping up some mushrooms.

"Deliver for me," Vernon said. "I got nine or ten little businesses around here an' nobody to deliver things to any of 'em. I been needin' a good full-time delivery man."

"I hope so," she said. It seemed to her that she had cost him an awful lot of money, in one day or less, and she didn't even know the man. It didn't seem quite ethical, but then she knew herself well enough to know that she couldn't cook and resolve ethical dilemmas at the same time; since she was beginning to feel distinctly hungry she let the ethical matters ride and cooked an elemental dinner: a nice little steak, smothered in mushrooms, with some asparagus on the side, and plenty of cheese, much of which she herself ate while she was fixing the meal.

Vernon controlled his fidgets to the point of being able to sit down and eat, and at table he proved an excellent listener. The first thing to be done with anyone new, Aurora felt, was to exchange life stories, and she told hers first, starting with her childhood in New Haven and sometimes Boston. Vernon consumed his steak before she had gotten herself out of the nursery, storywise. She had never seen food disappear quite so rapidly, unless her son-in-law was eating it, and she watched Vernon closely.

"I suppose eating fast is a logical extension of your fidgets," she said. "I think we must take up the question of a doctor for you, Vernon. I don't know when I've seen such a nervous man. You're tapping your foot at this very moment. I can hear the vibrations quite distinctly."

"Uh-oh," Vernon said. He stopped tapping his foot and began to tap his fingers on the table. Aurora let it pass and ate a leisurely meal, talking while he tapped. On the patio after dinner she noticed that his boots were extremely sharp-toed. They were on the patio because she had insisted that he have brandy with her, and she had insisted on that in order not to feel guilty about drinking some herself. Drinking brandy often made her tipsy, and once or twice her daughter had called and caught her in a tipsy state. Such a state would be easier to explain if she had a guest to blame it on.

"Perhaps boots are your problem," she said. "I imagine your toes are in constant pain. Why don't you take them off for a while? I'd like to see what you're like when you aren't fidgeting."

Vernon looked embarrassed at the thought. "Aw, no," he said. "No tellin' what my old feet smell like."

"I'm not squeamish," Aurora said. "You can keep your socks on, you know."

Vernon remained embarrassed, and she let him alone about his feet. "What time are you setting off for Canada?" she asked.

"Ain't goin' for a while," Vernon said. "Put it off."

"I was afraid of that," Aurora said, looking him in the eye. "May I ask why?"

"Because I met you," Vernon said.

Aurora sipped some brandy and waited for him to say more, but he didn't. "You know, you're rather like my late husband when it comes to comment," she said. "He made do with a minimum, and so do you. Have you ever postponed a trip because of a lady before?"

"Lord no," Vernon said. "I never knowed a lady before, not to talk to."

"You haven't been talking to this one," Aurora said. "You've just been hiring people and fixing cars and putting off trips, all on the basis of our rather slim acquaintance. I don't quite know that I want to be responsible for all that. I've known married couples to live together for years without incurring that much responsibility for one another."

"Aw, you mean you don't want me around?" Vernon said. He put his hands on the arm of his chair as if he were about to get up and leave at once.

"Now, now," Aurora said. "You must learn to be very careful about twisting my words. I usually try to say precisely what I mean. Those of you who are in oil have to go find it, I'm told. I have a very bad character, as you should already know. I've never been particularly loath to have people do things for me, if

152

they appear to want to, but that doesn't mean I want you to suffer business reverses just in order to pursue our acquaintance."

Vernon leaned forward and put his elbows on his knees; it made him look very short.

"Aurora, it's all I can do to call you Aurora," he said. "I don't know how to talk like you do—that's the plain truth. I ain't ignorant exactly, but I just ain't had no practice. If you want me around that's one thing, and if you don't then I can always go on up to Alberta an' make a few more mil."

"Oh, dear," Aurora said. "I wish you hadn't said that last word. I don't know my wishes well enough to weigh them against millions of dollars."

Vernon seemed in an agony of worry. He was squinting strangely, as if he were afraid to open his eyes all the way. His eyes were the best thing about his face, and she didn't like him squinting them shut.

"You weren't planning to live in Canada the rest of your life, were you?" Aurora said. "You were intending to return to Houston someday, weren't you?"

"Oh, yeah," Vernon said.

"Well, I intend to go on living here," Aurora said. "So far as I know I will still be living here when you get back. You could come see me then, if you wished, and you won't have lost any millions. Hadn't that ever occurred to you?"

"No, I think it's do or die," Vernon said at once. "If I was to go off now who knows but what you'll marry before I get back."

"*I* know, for God's sake," Aurora said. "I'm not interested in matrimony, and in any case my suitors are a mixed bag. Some of them are worse than others and the nicer ones seem to be the hopeless ones, for some reason. This is an extremely theoretical conversation, you know. We just met today."

"Yeah, but I'm changed," Vernon said.

"Fine. I'm not," Aurora said. "I don't wish to marry."

"Aw, but you do," Vernon said. "It sticks out all over you."

"It most certainly does not!" Aurora said, outraged. "Nobody's ever said anything like that to me in my life. What do you know about it anyway? You admit you never met a lady until you met me, and you may live to regret meeting me."

"Well, however it turns out, meetin' you took the fun outa makin' money," Vernon said.

Aurora had begun to wish she had taken the General's advice and turned the first time she came to the road home. As it was, she had managed to create another complication for herself—and the complication was still fidgeting.

"You've not explained to me why you now feel it unwise to go to Canada, Vernon," she said. "You need a better reason than any you've given."

"Look at me," Vernon said. "I ain't got your kind of style. I can't talk like you do. I look funny and we just barely met. If I run off now you'll just start thinkin' how dumb and funny-lookin' I am and when I come back you ain't gonna know me from Adam an' you ain't gonna want to. That's the reason."

"An astute point," Aurora said, looking at him closely.

They both fell silent for several minutes. It was a soft spring night, and despite Vernon's fidgets Aurora felt rather content. Life continued to be interesting, which was something. Vernon began to wiggle the toe of his boot. For an essentially pleasant man he had more irritating physical mannerisms than anyone she had ever known, and after watching him for a while she spoke up and told him just that. After all, he himself had pointed out that subtleties were lost on him.

"Vernon, you have a great many irritating physical mannerisms," she said. "I hope you mean to try and whittle those down. I'm sorry, but I'm afraid I've always felt free to criticize people immediately. I don't see that it can hurt to try and improve someone. I've never quite been able to improve anyone up to the point where I could accept them, but I do fancy that I've improved a few men enough to make them palatable to others."

She yawned, and Vernon stood up. "You're sleepy," he said. "I'll just give you a handshake and see you tomorrow, if that's all right."

"Oh," Aurora said, accepting the handshake. It seemed strange to be receiving it on her patio. He had a small rough hand. They walked through the darkened house and she stepped out in her front yard with him for a moment. She considered inviting him to breakfast, just to see what he looked like in the morning, but before she could frame the invitation he had nodded to her and turned away. The abruptness of the departure left her feeling a little melancholy. The day had had too much of Cinderella in it, she feared, though she was sorrier for Vernon than she was for herself. He was friendly and had nice lights in his brown eyes, yet in all likelihood, even without a time lag in Canada, the future would reduce him just as he had predicted, to someone fidgety and funny-looking, whose style was hopelessly foreign to her own. It had been a little too dramatic, too full of golden coaches. She went upstairs and looked long at her Renoir as she undressed, all too aware that she would probably awaken feeling that the world was pumpkins after all.

CHAPTER VIII

1.

VERNON HAD often heard it said that human nature was a mystery, but the truth of the statement had not struck home to him until that afternoon, when Aurora had looked at him seriously for the first time. The human natures he encountered in the oil business were nothing like that mysterious, he was sure. His employees and his competitors might make him mad on occasion, but none of them had ever *troubled* him, seriously—not as he began to be troubled when he looked back from his Lincoln and saw that Aurora was still standing on the lawn. The fact that she was still standing there seemed to suggest that she considered the evening not finished, in which case she might have interpreted his leaving as being a sign that he didn't like her, or something like that. It was a horrible thought to have to live with all night, and Vernon soon found it intolerable. After driving fifteen or twenty blocks he turned around and went back to Aurora's street to see if she was still standing there. She wasn't, which left him with nothing to do but turn around again and drive to his garage.

He hadn't told Aurora, but one of the several businesses he owned was a parking garage in downtown Houston—the newest, tallest, and best parking garage in the city. It was twenty-four stories high and equipped not only with ramps but with a super-quick carlift made in Germany. It would hold several thousand cars, and often had; but by the time Vernon got there, full of his new worries, the garage was almost empty.

He drove straight up to the top, the twenty-fourth story, and parked the Lincoln in a little niche he had cut out in the west wall. The wall was still high enough to keep him from accidentally driving off, but it was cut low enough that he could see over it without getting out of his car.

At night no one but him was allowed to park on the twenty-fourth floor. It was where he slept—more than that, it was his home, the one thing money had bought him that he loved completely and never tired of. The garage was only three years old; it was just by accident one night that he had driven up there to see what the view was like. From then on it had been his place. On a few clear nights in the fall he had been able to look southeast and see Galveston, but that was unusual. He always got out of the Lincoln after he parked and walked around the edge of the building for a while, just looking. Off to the east were the strange orange and pink glows of the great clusters of refineries along the Ship Channel—glows that never dimmed.

From his building he could see every road that ran out of Houston, all of which he had driven many times. To the north, whitely lit, were several great interchanges—out of one of them ran the road to Dallas, Oklahoma City, Kansas, and Nebraska. There were roads running east, into the pines of East Texas, or the bayous of Louisiana, or New Orleans, and roads south, to the border, or west to San Antonio, El Paso, and California. The view from the roof was always different, depending on how the weather went. On clear nights there were hundreds of thousands of lights spread out below him, each one distinct; but then there were the foggy, rumbling nights of Houston, with the fog hovering way down below him, somewhere about the twelfth floor, and the mass of lights beneath it orange and green and indistinct.

Then sometimes it was clear below and the clouds hung just above his head, up where the thirtieth story would have been if there had been one; the lights from below lit up the clouds. Sometimes there were northers; at other times the Gulf sent gales from the south, blowing mountainous gray clouds past him and rocking the Lincoln. One night the winds off the Gulf blew so hard that it scared him, and he had had concrete stanchions built to stand on either side of the car, so he could get out and chain it securely in place if the winds got too high.

Often, in his walks about the edge of the building, Vernon would stop and watch the strings of evening jets ease down toward the airport, their wing lights winking. They were like great birds coming in to feed. Despite his ear problems he had flown enough to know most of the flights and their pilots, crews, and stewardesses. He could spot the Braniff coming in from Chicago, or the late evening Pan Am from Guatemala City, both flights he had flown many times.

Usually, by the time the planes were all in, he was ready to do a little business. If he was dirty he might get in the elevator and go down and walk the three blocks to the Rice Hotel for a bath and a change of clothes, but he always came right back to the roof and settled himself in the back seat of the Lincoln and began to put in his nightly calls. The nice thing about being so high up was that he could see so far, literally, that in his mind's eye he could often see the places he was calling: Amarillo or Midland, the Gulf shore, Caracas or Bogota. He had interest in a dozen places, and he knew his crews in each place and seldom let a night pass without calling all of them to find out what was happening.

Once the calls were over, if it wasn't too late, he lay back in the Lincoln with the front door open to let in a little breeze and watched television. The reception was wonderful, up so high. Sometimes there would be lightning storms, with the lightning breaking just over his head, and if that happened he switched the television off, out of a feeling that it wasn't safe. His father had been killed by lightning while sitting on the running board of a tractor, and Vernon hated it.

If he was restless or hungry he could always go down to the fourth floor, where there was a refreshment room with fifteen different machines in it, a kind of small automat. Old Schweppes, the night watchman, was generally settled down for the night in his little cubbyhole next to the refreshment room, but he was too arthritic to sleep well in such humid weather and if Vernon so much as put a quarter in one of the machines the old man would hear it and come hobbling out in hopes of a little conversation. Old Schweppes's whole family—a wife and four children—had been wiped out in a trailer-house fire thirty years before, and he had not recovered from it, nor even tried. He had lived out thirty more years of life as a night watchman, and he didn't talk to many; but somehow the vestiges that remained of the gregarious man he had once been asserted themselves when Vernon appeared, and once that happened it was not easy to shake free of the old man.

Often, so as not to be too abrupt and hurt Old Schweppes's feelings, Vernon would start walking with him up the ramps, the old man always meaning to go just a level or two but never able to stop once he got started. The two of them might take an hour or more winding upward higher and higher above the Gulf Coast, Old Schweppes rambling on and on about baseball, his last love, or about his Navy days in World War I, or about almost anything, until, to his surprise, the two of them emerged onto the roof. Then, embarrassed at the thought of how much he had talked, the old man quickly took an elevator back down to his cubbyhole.

Vernon was not a long sleeper—four hours at a stretch had always been plenty—and the seats of the Lincoln suited him well as a bed. He always woke as the lights of the city were beginning to shine more faintly with the coming of dawn. The cloud of fog over the bays and inlets to the east would be pink underneath, and then white underneath and orange on top as the sun rose through them and shone over the Gulf and the coastal plain. The noise of traffic, which had died out altogether about two o'clock, resumed, and by seven was constant, like the sound of a river. The Lincoln would be beaded with moisture, and Vernon would get a ginger ale out of the icebox to freshen his mouth and then begin his calls again, out to his rigs in West Texas, to see how the night towers had gone.

But Aurora had broken his pattern. This night was different. He got out and walked around the edge of the building several times, but he took no interest in the view. He placed a call to Guatemala, and then canceled it five minutes later. He went out and stood by the wall awhile, popping his knuckles rapidly to make up for all the time he had restrained himself. Two or three planes went over, but he scarcely noticed them. He looked down at the city and after some study was able to figure out almost exactly where her house was. River Oaks was mostly just a patch of darkness because the tall thick trees hid the streetlights, but he knew its perimeters and worked himself north from Westheimer until he located where he thought Aurora must be. He heard the phone ringing in the Lincoln but didn't answer it.

Old Schweppes came to mind, and without hesitating or even pretending to himself that he wanted a packaged sandwich, he took the elevator to the fourth floor and hurried to the old man's cubbyhole. Schweppes was a tall, skinny fellow, six four and thin as a reed, with long tangled gray hair and deep hollows in his cheeks. He wore his uniforms about two months between washings, and he was squinting his way through a coverless issue of *Sports Illustrated* when Vernon appeared, his hands in his pockets.

"Schweppes, how are you?" Vernon asked.

"Worse," Schweppes said. "What in hell's the matter with you? The cops after you?"

"Nothin' like that," Vernon said. "I'm fine and dandy."

"Well, the goddamn cops will get us all, one by one," Schweppes said. "They'll have to look hard to find me, I can tell you. I'd go to Mexico if I had to, to stay out of jail."

"Uh, want to walk up the ramp a little ways?" Vernon asked. His need to talk was too bald to be disguised.

Old Schweppes was so surprised he dropped his magazine. It was the first direct invitation he had ever received from Vernon.

Their conversations normally came about through elaborate indirection. For a minute he didn't know what to say.

"The cops ain't after me," Vernon said, to reassure him. Old Schweppes had nursed a lifelong paranoia about the police, stemming, apparently, from the fact that he had once been arrested at a cockfight in Ardmore, Oklahoma, and had spent a night in the same jail cell with a Negro.

"Yeah, I guess a little walk wouldn't hurt," Schweppes said, heaving himself up. "You got the fidgets the worst I ever seen, Vernon. If it ain't the cops, then it must be some big gambler. I told you about that, didn't I? You keep on skinnin' them big boys an' sooner or later one of 'em gonna skin you back."

Schweppes had other paranoias too, and Vernon decided he had better talk first if he was going to talk at all.

"Schweppes, you was married," he said. "What do you do about women?"

Old Schweppes stopped and looked at Vernon, his mouth open. No question could have taken him more unawares.

"What happened?" Schweppes said, taking his old raincoat off its hook. It was often blowy on the ramps, and his joints ached even when it wasn't.

"I met a real lady," Vernon said. "She run into my car, was what actually happened. Then I took her home an' that started it."

Old Schweppes got an amused gleam in his eye. "Started it, hum?" he said, noncommittally.

He worked himself into his raincoat as Vernon stood on one foot and then the other, and they started up the ramp toward the fifth floor.

"Ask the question agin," the old man said.

"Well," Vernon said, "here I am fifty years old an' I don't know nothin' about women. That's the gist of it, Schweppes."

"Except that now you met this one you kinda wish you knew somethin', ain't that right?" the old man said. "That's the real gist of the matter. That's there's the nitty-gritty."

"That's about the size of it," Vernon said. "This here's all new to me. I know I ought to have done more courtin' when I was

161

younger, but it just never hit me, you know. There's probably eighteen-year-old kids walkin' around who've got more experience at such things than I have."

"Well, you come to the right man this time," Schweppes said. "I was woman crazy half my life—course it was the first half. Somethin' changed after I lost my family. I ain't forgot women, though. I got as good a memory as the next man. Blonde or brunette?"

Vernon was slow to pick up on the question, and Schweppes looked at him silently.

"Uh, brown," he said. "Is that important?"

"Fat or skinny?" Schweppes said. "You just let me ask the questions. At your age you ain't got no margin of error. You ain't gonna survive no mistake, gettin' the woman bug this late in life."

"She's largish," Vernon said, properly docile.

"Where's she from?"

"Boston," Vernon said.

Old Schweppes sucked in his breath. "Good God a'mighty!" he said. "Boston, Mass. Let me walk on that for a while."

They walked, Vernon with his hands in his pockets. Old Schweppes was usually a non-stop talker, and the fact that he had fallen silent at the mention of Boston was a little upsetting. Not a word was said on the sixth and seventh levels; when they got to the eighth Old Schweppes walked to the edge of the building and looked down.

"She's a widow then," he said. "Don't take no Sherlock Holmes to figure that out. She wouldn't come off down here by herself, not if she's from Boston, Mass." He sighed heavily and started walking upward again. "Not a young widow, I don't guess?" he asked.

"She ain't fifty," Vernon said. "At least I'm older than she is."

"Naw, widows mostly marry down, age-wise," Schweppes said. "That's a fact I've observed. They don't want to have to get used to somebody else if they're just apt to die. Havin' to watch one husband play out's enough for most women. Course you're as fresh as a pullet. That's some advantage. It means you'll be easy to outsmart, once the warfare starts. Also means you ain't got nobody to compare them with. It ain't often a fifty-year-old woman gets a chance to be first on the scene. I think that's your biggest advantage."

"She done knows I ain't got no experience," Vernon said. "I never made no bones about that."

Schweppes began to shake his head. "You ever think about night school?" he said. "The oil business is one thing and ladies from Boston, Mass., they're something else. They're particular about speech up in that part of the country. You can get away with just so much of that old country-boy talk, an' then they're gonna let you know it's gettin' old. Right there's one problem."

Vernon began to feel downhearted. He began to wish he'd left Old Schweppes to *Sports Illustrated*. It was all beginning to sound like a lawsuit, and one that was going against him. For every advantage he had, Old Schweppes was finding two disadvantages.

"She's already jumped on me about that," he said. "Schweppes, I can't go to night school. I'd feel plumb ridiculous."

"Well, if you've reached the stage where you've got to have a woman, you're going to feel ridiculous the big part of the time anyway," Schweppes said. "I was never mixed up with nobody from further east than Little Rock neither. I never said more than howdy to a smart woman in my life, and I still went around feeling dumb half the time. They're smarter than us—that's what it boils down to.

"Not as ornery, just smarter," he added.

Then he fell totally silent, and they walked up and up. A late night fog had risen, and they gradually rose above it. Old Schweppes began to belch and clear his throat. "Vernon, you're a lot like me," he said. "You ain't ever gonna be a drinkin' man, or a dopey. I know you gamble, but that ain't serious. Gamblin's only serious if a poor man does it. I guess a woman's about the only chance you got to stay human, if you come right down to it. I guess a fat brunette from Boston, Mass., is as good a place to start as you're gonna get. I'd hate to see you get any crazier than you are, if you want the truth of the matter."

"Me?" Vernon said. "I ain't crazy, Schweppes. I ain't even been sick in the last fifteen years."

"Well, you ain't dangerous crazy, but you're crazy anyhow," Schweppes said, looking Vernon over as he said it. "Normal people sleep in beds, you know—beds with other people in them, if they can manage to. Normal people don't bed down for the night in Lincoln Continentals on the top of parking garages. That's a sign of craziness in my book. You're just a crazy person that ain't lost his ability to make money in the oil business—at least you ain't lost it yet."

Vernon didn't know what to say. It seemed to him that Old Schweppes was a lot like Aurora when it came to speaking out. He had never spoken out that way to anybody in his life. He couldn't think of anything to say in his defense, so he said nothing. They were up eighteen floors and he had the impulse to go over to the elevator and shoot up the last six. He had tried company and it hadn't worked out.

Then, just when Vernon was feeling darkest, Old Schweppes patted him on the shoulder. "Buy her a present," he said. "Women and politicians ain't got much in common, but they can't neither one of 'em totally resist bribes."

"All right," Vernon said, brightening a little. "Then what?"

"Buy her another present," Schweppes said. "You're a rich man. My grandmother was a Yankee and she couldn't get enough of nothing. A woman that don't like presents is bound to have a mean streak in her."

When they reached the twenty-fourth floor Old Schweppes walked over and peered in the Lincoln. He shook his head and sucked in his breath again, making the deep hollows in his cheeks appear even deeper.

"Only a crazy man would own a television set anyway," he said. "You got one in your car—that makes you double crazy. I hear they give out X-rays. You ain't gonna win no widow from Boston, Mass., if you soak up too many of them X-rays."

He reached out and shook Vernon's hand and immediately began to hobble off. "It wouldn't hurt you to try to get used to sleeping in houses," he said, leaving his boss in as much of a quandary as ever.

2.

VERNON MADE his seat down into a bed and lay on it, but when
the sky became gray he still couldn't claim to have slept. He had
thought about the things Aurora had said, and about the things
Old Schweppes had pointed out, and it was clear to him that Old
Schweppes must be right: he was crazy. Twenty years back,
when he was in his thirties, he had thought so himself for a time,
but he kept so busy he forgot about it. Of course it was crazy to
sleep in a car on a roof; no lady would like that, and Aurora
seemed to be more particular than most ladies, besides. So it was
all hopeless and he had been foolish to speak out so absurdly,
and there was nothing to do but give up. Still, he had told her he
would come back and see her, and he thought he could allow
himself that pleasure at least once more.

He started the Lincoln, coasted slowly down the twenty-four
levels of ramp, and drove out South Main to a little all-night cafe
he was fond of near the Astrodome. The Dome was a ghostly
sight in the morning mist; from a certain distance away it looked
like the moon suddenly come to rest on the earth.

The cafe where Vernon customarily ate his breakfast was
called the Silver Slipper, for no good reason at all. It was not
silver, and no one who had worn a silver slipper had ever been
inside it, so far as anyone knew. It was run by a husband and
wife team named Babe and Bobby, who made it their life. They
had a tiny house trailer hitched to the back wall like a Shetland
pony, and whichever one of them was tiredest slept in it while
the other cooked. It was really an antique one-man trailer dating
from the 1930s, and they had taken it in payment for two hundred dollars' worth of cheeseburgers owed them by a one-time
friend named Reno, who had lived for a while in the smelly little
trailer camp a few yards up the street. Reno had eventually
found life in the trailer camp too stable and had moved downtown to the Trailways bus station, where he became a wino. The

bed in the trailer was the width of a narrow shelf, and Babe and Bobby had never figured out a way to sleep in it side by side, though they could copulate in it fairly well if they were careful. It didn't really matter, since they couldn't both leave the cafe long enough to sleep together. Their help was sporadic and they were proud of their ability to do it all themselves.

"Scrapin' by" was what whichever one of them was up said every morning when Vernon came in for his sausages and eggs and asked how they were doing. He had offered to buy them out many times so they could afford some help and maybe a better trailer, but Babe and Bobby were too independent to cotton to such talk. Babe was a fat redhead who thought Vernon was cute as a button, and she teased him about his intentions every time he offered to buy them out.

"I know you, Vernon," she said. "Soon as you got me on the payroll you'd get ideas. I get enough guys in here with ideas in the course of a day. I'm gettin' too old to worry about all you boys and your ideas."

Vernon could not help but be embarrassed by such talk. "Aw, I'm too old," he said usually.

Babe and Bobby were both sitting at the counter stirring their coffee when Vernon walked in. Nobody else was in the Silver Slipper.

"Mornin'," Vernon said.

Bobby kept on stirring his coffee and said nothing—more and more he was prone to lapses. Babe got up and got Vernon some coffee.

"Thank God for a customer," she said. "Me an' Bobby was fallin' asleep in all this quiet. You look like you got the jumps today. About to make another million?"

"Not today," Vernon said. He had been brooding on the matter of a present for Aurora, and it occurred to him that maybe Babe might have an idea.

"Let me ask you a question," he said, fidgeting on his stool. "I met this lady, you know, an' she was right nice to me. What if I was to get her some kind of present, you know, sort of to pay her back?"

Bobby came out of his lapse suddenly and slapped Vernon on the back. "Well, what'ya know, Babe," he said. "Think about that. You mean you finally done went an' got laid?"

Vernon blushed and Babe leapt to his defense.

"Shut your dirty mouth, Bobby," she said. "Vernon wasn't raised that way and you know it. All these years I been feedin' him he ain't never even had an idea, that I could tell. You just shut up an' let Vernon do the talkin' now."

Vernon had done the talking, though. He had no more to say. "She fixed me dinner, was what it was," he said. "I been thinkin' a present would be the right thing to do, but I don't know what to get."

"How about a diament ring," Babe said. "I been wantin' one all my life. Course if you give her a diament ring she's gonna think you got ideas."

"Well, if you never got laid I ain't interested," Bobby said, stirring his coffee some more. "You an' Babe work it out."

Babe was cooking Vernon's traditional sausages and smiling, briefly enjoying the fantasy that she herself was going to receive a wonderful gift from Vernon.

"Well, there's diament rings an' fur coats an' candy and flowers," she said. "Mums is pretty. Chocolate-covered cherries. Bobby even bought me some of them one time in a weak moment."

"Is she fancy?" Bobby asked, more interested than he cared to let on. "Why don't you bring her in an' let us have a look at her? Me an' Babe can tell you in a minute if she's good enough for you."

"Aw, she is," Vernon said.

"You got as much business courtin' a fancy woman as I got ownin' a Cadillac automobile," Bobby said, getting up and leaving. "I'm takin' a nap."

Babe was still musing on the question of the present. "How about a pet of some kind?" she said. "I've always wanted a pet, but Bobby's too sorry to let me have one. How about a goat? A feller over in the trailer camp's got the sweetest little goat you ever saw, and he wants to sell it too. It'd be unusual. Ever' woman's got a problem of what to do with scraps, an' a goat would sure take care of that."

Vernon liked the idea immediately. The nicest thing about it was that the present was handy. He could buy it and take it right over. He gave Babe a dollar tip, more because she helped him solve his problem than because the sausage was anything special.

"You're gonna spoil me yet, Vernon," Babe said, looking at the dollar. "Bobby thinks I'm sweet on you now, if you want the truth. I guess it's a good thing you finally dug you up a girl friend. I'm too old to have Bobby beatin' on me like he used to whenever somebody happened to give me a dollar tip."

Vernon walked around amid the house trailers until he found one with a goat tied outside. It was a small brown and white goat, and a sleepy lady in a pink bathrobe sold it to him for thirty dollars, without really even waking up. By seven o'clock the Lincoln was parked in front of Aurora's house, with the goat and Vernon both in the front seat. Vernon was fidgeting badly. The hopelessness of it all seemed more obvious the longer he thought about it, and he had also begun to have second thoughts about the goat, which kept trying to nibble his maroon seat covers.

While he was fidgeting Aurora stepped out her front door. She was barefooted and wore a bright blue dressing gown. She was evidently in search of her morning paper, and she got halfway across her wet lawn before she noticed the Lincoln sitting at the curb. The sight didn't seem to surprise her. She smiled in a way that Vernon had never seen anyone smile, at least not at the sight of him.

"Why there you are, Vernon," she said. "What an active man you are. Is that little goat for me by any chance?"

"You don't have to take it," Vernon said, abashed that she had spotted it so quickly.

"Now, now," Aurora said. "There's no reason for you to act apologetic about such a charming goat. I don't think you ought to keep it cooped up in that car. Let it see how it likes my lawn."

She stretched out her hands and Vernon handed it out the window to her. Aurora set it on the lawn. The little goat stood stock still in the wet grass, as if it might fall off the world if it took a single step. Aurora spotted her newspaper and walked over to pick it up, and the goat tiptoed after her.

Aurora opened her paper to the comics and scanned them quickly to see if anything crucial was happening. Since nothing was, she picked up the little goat and started for the house.

"Are you coming, Vernon?" she said. "Or did you spend the night having second thoughts? I bet that's it. You probably just ran by to fob this goat off on me before you set out for Alberta, or wherever it was."

"I ain't going nowhere," Vernon said, getting out of the car. How she had figured out that the goat was a farewell present was beyond his understanding. Her eyes were flashing, though thirty seconds before she had been smiling as if she didn't have a care in the world.

"Excuse me, but you're not being very convincing," Aurora said. "Obviously you've come to regret your words. It's quite all right, I'm sure. You needn't look so hangdog. As I said quite frankly yesterday, I'm a terror. You practical men soon get enough of me. Evidently I do something to your little brains that interferes with the making of money, or whatever you do. I can't say I'm not somewhat disappointed, though. You sounded for a time like a man who stood behind his statements, and I hadn't expected you to be ready to scamper away quite so soon."

Vernon felt the same thing happening that had happened in the car the day before. Confusion and fear filled him. "I ain't backing out," he said. "I ain't going to Canada. I meant ever'thing."

Aurora looked at him silently, and he felt that she could see everything that he was thinking; it was as if she were in the process of translating his thoughts into her kind of English the instant they formed in his brain, though it didn't feel like anything was forming in his brain anymore but in some center of pressure somewhere in his chest.

"I mean I am," he said. "Just like yesterday. I still am."

Aurora nodded thoughtfully. "Yes, but you're poised to retreat at the slightest setback, aren't you?" she said. "I'm afraid that makes me rather scornful, Vernon. You've spent the night deciding there's no hope, if I'm not mistaken. Retreats and apologies are hardly the sort of actions that make a woman feel wanted. If you're not going to take the trouble to believe in yourself for a few days, then you might as well go on hiding in your car. No harm can come to you there. I'm not likely to crawl into your car and try to make you speak good English, am I? Nor can I see to it that you stop hunkering over your food like a crab when you eat, if you're going to eat out of the back end of a Lincoln. Your habits are a little disgusting, if you want the truth, and I was ready to expend some energy helping you replace them with something resembling healthy behavior, but if you've no more enthusiasm for me than you've exhibited this morning, then I don't suppose I'll get the chance."

She stopped and looked at him, waiting. Vernon had a feeling she was going to wait all day, until he spoke.

"If we was better acquainted I'd do things better," he said. "I ain't had no time to learn. Don't that make sense?"

To his great relief Aurora smiled, almost as gaily and mysteriously as she had smiled at him when she first saw him sitting at the curb. Another storm appeared to have passed.

"Yes, that makes a certain sense," she said. "What did you have in mind for us to do today?"

Vernon had nothing in mind. "Eat breakfast," he said, though he had just eaten one.

"Of course, breakfast can be assumed," Aurora said. "That will hardly be sufficient for a day's amusement, though. I take a great deal of amusing, I can tell you that."

"Well, I know a lot of card games," Vernon said. "I don't guess you like to play cards?"

To his astonishment Aurora took him by the arm and began to shake him vigorously. He didn't know whether to resist or not, and looked very puzzled. Still shaking, she began to laugh, and then took his arm and tucked it into hers and began to walk across the lawn. The lawn had been mowed the day before and her bare feet were covered with wet pieces of grass.

"I see I'll just have to shake you out of these diffident spells," she said. "For a woman of my temperament they're quite unendurable. Fortunately for you, I'm excessively fond of cards. If you'll really stay and play cards with me I'm quite likely to forgive you everything."

"That's my plan for the day," Vernon said, although it hadn't been two minutes before.

"Then I'm very nearly ecstatic," Aurora said. His arm still tucked in hers, she led him into the house.

CHAPTER IX

1.

AT SEVEN-THIRTY that morning Emma's phone rang, but as she was getting out of bed to go answer it, or, in other words, to go see what her mother wanted, Flap grabbed her ankle and wouldn't turn loose.

"You're not going," he said, though his eyes were still shut.

"Why not?" she asked.

"You're just not," he said, keeping a tight grip on her ankle. She had one foot off the bed and got tired of being spraddled, so she eased back in bed. Flap turned loose of her ankle and put his arm tightly around her waist. The phone rang ten or twelve times and stopped, and then after a pause rang ten or twelve more times and stopped again.

"I wish you were a little less gutless," he said. "You don't have to pop up every morning at dawn, you know."

"Well, you've found out how to keep me from it," Emma said.

"I'd rather lie in bed and be criticized than to stand in the kitchen and be criticized."

"If you'd tell her to fuck off once or twice you could lie in bed and not be criticized," he said.

"Sure," Emma said. "I haven't heard you tell Cecil that when he wants you to do some little errand for him. If you'll start doing it I'll start doing it."

Flap ignored her retort, but he kept his arm around her. "If you're not going to let me talk to Mother, then you ought to wake up and talk to me," she said.

Instead of commenting, Flap went back to sleep. It was a warm, still morning and she slipped back into drowsiness herself. She had sat up until two-thirty reading *Adam Bede*—a book she had begun because Flap said she had to read something by George Eliot and it had looked, at first glance, shorter than *Middlemarch*. It could not have been shorter by much, she decided, because even by reading until two-thirty two nights in a row she hadn't been able to finish it.

"I like it but I don't know why I'm reading it right now," she said at about the halfway point. "Why couldn't I have saved George Eliot for my old age?"

"Read her so we can talk about her," Flap said. "We're running out of things to talk about, after only two years. You have to read more so our marriage won't flag."

Before the day got really hot she awakened from her drowse to find her husband on top of her. Emma was just as glad; the morning had seldom dawned when she wouldn't have rather made love than cook breakfast.

It was only some while after they had that Emma felt a little strange. Something had changed. Sex was happening a lot oftener, and she didn't know why. She told herself she was a fool to question God's plenty, now that she had it, but she couldn't help wondering what was working on Flap to make him want her so often.

It seemed to her to have started after he read Danny's book. "I'm intimidated," he said when he finished it. "Because it's good?" she asked. "Even if it wasn't good I'd be intimidated," he said. "At least he *did* it." Then he walked off to the library and didn't say another word about Danny. She had told him Danny came by—she had to, since her mother knew—and he didn't say much about that either, or ask much, which was strange. His and Danny's friendship had always been rich in mutual curiosity. Perhaps it didn't tie into sex—she didn't know—but the part that was slightly worrisome was that oftener and longer didn't seem to add up to happier, at least not for Flap. It didn't leave him looking as pleased as it had, and she felt that their balance was tipping just a little. Life was getting different and she was not one to sit quietly and let it get different without her knowing why.

"How come I'm suddenly getting all this nice attention?" she said, tapping on his back with her fingernails.

Flap pretended to be in a deep post-coital slumber, but she knew better. He had never been a post-coital slumberer.

"Come on," she said. "No playing possum. Tell me."

Flap suddenly got up and walked off to the bathroom. "You always want to talk about everything," he said, glancing back at her. "Can't you ever let anything just happen?"

Emma sighed and got up and divided what was left of her bedside glass of water between two flowerpots. Some mothers gave their daughters cast-off clothes, but her mother gave her cast-off flowers instead, though usually only petunias or begonias or flowers that didn't require very complex attention. She had been promised a wonderful geranium that her mother had been coddling for years, but that promise, like the promise of the Klee, seemed to depend upon them living somewhere they couldn't afford to live. When Flap came back in the bedroom she was feeling angry.

"You didn't need to put me down that hard," she said. "We are married, aren't we? I have a right to be curious about changes in our life."

"Stop trying to put me on the defensive," he said. "I hate to feel defensive on an empty stomach."

"Oh, for God's sake," she said. "I just asked a simple question."

"You know what I think?" Flap said, putting on his shirt.

"What?"

"I think you majored in the wrong thing," he said. "I think you should have majored in psychology. I think you should be a psychiatrist, in fact. Then you'd have answers for everything. Whenever I changed some little habit you could get out your notebook and write down the Freudian explanation and the Jungian explanation and the Gestaltist explanation, and then you could take your pick, like a multiple-choice examination."

Emma's fat paperback of *Adam Bede* was lying handy and she grabbed it and threw it at him. He wasn't looking at her, hadn't looked at her since he had come back in the room, and he didn't see her throw the book. It was a perfect throw and hit him on the neck. Flap turned, his eyes full of hate, and jumped across the bed at her. He grabbed her arms and shoved her at the open window so hard that her bare behind split the screen almost out of its frame, all the way around. When she felt the frame give Emma thought she was going to be shoved right out the window. "Stop it. Have you gone mad?" she said, squirming out of the window desperately.

While her mouth was open Flap punched her and she felt something jolt against her teeth. She fell backwards onto her couch, and before she could get her senses about her he grabbed her and started trying to drag her to the window again. She saw that he did mean to shove her out, and she wiggled free and fell back on the couch and began to sob, holding on to her end. One of Flap's hands was red. He fell on top of her, apparently meaning to hit her again, but he didn't. He just lay on top of her, his face a few inches from hers, and they stared at one another in surprise, panting and gasping for breath. Neither spoke, because neither had any breath to speak with.

As they were panting, calming a little, Emma suddenly noticed that one of his hands was bleeding all over the couch. She began to try and squirm free. "Get off a minute; you can kill me later," she said and went across the room and grabbed a handful of Kleenex. When she came back Flap was holding his hand up indecisively, apparently trying to decide whether to drip on the couch or drip on the floor. "Drip on the floor, dummy," she said. "The floor can be mopped."

The hatred had gone out of his eyes and he looked friendly

and fond of her again. "I got to respect you," he said. "You're hard to throw out a window."

Emma gave him some Kleenex and used the rest to soak up the worst of the blood on the couch. "Boy I'm really going to get fat now," she said. "If I was my mother's size nobody would ever be able to throw me out a window."

"Don't you know you're not supposed to talk in the middle of a fight?" Flap said. "It's easier to get your jaw broken if you have your mouth open. If you hadn't been talking I wouldn't have cut my hand."

Before Emma could reply someone knocked on the door. They both jumped. Flap was dressed from the waist up and she wasn't dressed at all.

"It's either Patsy or your mother," Flap said. "One of them always arrives when we're having a crisis."

"Who's there?" Emma asked.

"It's Patsy," a cheerful voice said. "Let's go shopping."

"You see," Flap said, though actually Patsy's visits always pleased him.

"Give us two minutes," Emma said, springing up. "Flap's not quite dressed."

In the time it took Flap to put on his undershorts and a pair of trousers she got herself decent, made the bed, and, with the expenditure of a good many washrags and paper towels got rid of most of the blood. Flap was barefooted and looked rather plaintive, probably because his hand was still bleeding.

"You must file your front teeth," he whispered. "I'm cut to the bone. What are we going to tell her?"

"Why should I lie to my friend?" Emma whispered. "She may get married someday. Let's give her a glimpse of what it's like."

"I don't think that's a good idea," Flap said.

"Go run some water on your hand," Emma said. "She's my friend and I'll handle it."

He snuck into the bathroom, still plaintive, and Emma opened the front door. Her friend Patsy Clark stood on the landing in a beautiful brown and white dress reading the Hortons' paper. She was a slim girl, with long black hair—beautiful anyway, and even more so in such a dress.

"I don't think I want to let you in," Emma said, holding the screen shut. "You look too good. I wish you'd stop dressing up when you come over here. You're worse than my mother. Both of you make me feel more squalid than I am."

"If she'd just turn loose of a little of her money you could buy yourself some clothes," Patsy said. "I've always thought it was awful of her to criticize the way you dress when she won't give you money to buy clothes with."

"Let's call her and tell her that," Emma said. "Maybe she'll give me some today. Otherwise I can't go shopping with you."

She held the door open and Patsy swept in, smelling nice and looking wonderful, cheerful and happy. Their bedroom was also their living room, and the minute Patsy stepped into it she said, "I smell blood." The next minute she noticed the smashed-out window screen and she immediately looked keenly at Emma and narrowed her black eyes.

"Did someone try to throw someone out a window?" she asked, slightly puckishly.

Emma opened her mouth and pointed at her own front teeth. "Yes, and someone cut his hand on my front teeth too," she said. Patsy had the same genius her mother had for seeming to perceive the truth of the matter instantly. Emma's secret opinion was that the reason Patsy and her mother couldn't stand one another was because they were exactly alike. No one but her mother could be as totally self-absorbed as Patsy was, and yet, like her mother, she was usually interesting to have around. She was quick-minded, active, and incessantly curious about every aspect of Emma's life. The only difference between the two women that Emma could see was that her mother had had a great deal more practice at being who she was. She was better at everything than Patsy, and she never ceased to press her advantage when the two of them were together.

Patsy looked with a certain fascination at Emma's tooth. "I always knew they were all brutes," she said. "Why didn't it crack it? None of them better ever hit me, boy." She went over and peered through the damaged window screen. "It's not too far down," she said. "I guess you would have lived."

Emma felt better about life than she had in several days. Her husband seemed to have gotten something out of his system, and her friend was there to help her make her day. She yawned and flopped down on the couch to read the paper Patsy had brought in.

"You can read that later," Patsy said, walking restlessly around the room and inspecting things. "Call your mother and see if you can get some money."

"No, we have to wait until Flap leaves," Emma said. "Don't be so restless. We haven't even eaten breakfast yet."

At that moment Flap emerged, a washrag wrapped around his hand. He looked his most most sheepish, which was also his most appealing. Emma was completely won by the way he looked and forgave him everything, but Patsy was not about to be so softhearted.

"I used to think you were nice," she said, giving him a genuinely cold look.

It only made Flap look doubly sheepish, because Flap adored Patsy and would have given almost anything to seduce her. Her attraction for him was so obvious that Emma took it as one of the givens of life, and yet Patsy had never been an awkwardness in her marriage, like Danny was. Whatever she and Danny felt for one another was mutual, whereas Patsy obviously didn't feel the slightest attraction to Flap and was more or less in agreement with her mother that she had been a fool to marry him. Emma sometimes picked at him about Patsy, when she had nothing else to pick at him about, but Patsy's disinterest was so emphatic, in its way, that instead of feeling jealous she felt smugly amused. All Flap would get for his desire was a lot of torment, and that, she felt, was punishment enough.

"These things have two sides," Flap said.

"Not in my book they don't," Patsy said.

"Well, you single people don't understand the provocations," he said.

"I don't understand them either," Emma said, turning to the want ads. "I think I will call Momma."

"Why, for God's sake?" Flap asked.

"I don't know. I thought maybe we could all go over there for breakfast," Emma said. "I don't feel very inspired. Maybe she's having a beau in and would like us to come and help entertain him."

Once or twice a week her mother had one of her suitors in for breakfast, and the breakfasts that sometimes resulted were among her most wonderful and certainly most baroque productions—omelettes with various herbs and cheeses, special spicy sausages that she bought from a strange old woman who lived in the Heights and did nothing but make sausages, pineapples covered in brown sugar and brandy, a porridge she ordered from Scotland and ate with three kinds of honey, and sometimes a crispy kind of potato pancake that nobody but her could make. All her mother's most closely guarded recipes emerged and were called into play for her suitors' breakfasts, which often ran on until the middle of the afternoon, at least.

"You mean it might be breakfast day?" Patsy said. She forgot about Flap and her eyes lit up with the special eager light that always came into them when she thought she might be about to get something especially good to eat. She couldn't stand Emma's mother and lost no chance to ridicule her, but nobody was all bad, and cooking was the one area where she was willing to give Mrs. Greenway her due. Patsy was particularly fond of breakfast, and Mrs. Greenway's were the best she had ever eaten. Also, going there to breakfast gave her a good chance to snoop. Mrs. Greenway was always too busy cooking and flirting with her suitor of the day to bother about her, and Patsy could wander around the house and admire all the wonderful objects Mrs. Greenway had somehow accumulated. The paintings, the carpets, the furniture, and the objects were all more or less exactly what she wanted for her own house, if she ever had one, and she loved to sneak away and examine them and dream.

Emma noted the look in her friend's eye and got up to go to the telephone.

"Well, you two can go over there if you want to," Flap said. "I'm not. Do you think I want to face your mother after I just tried to throw you out a window? What do you think she'd have to say about the fact that my finger's half bitten off?"

"I don't know, but I'd love to hear," Patsy said. "I think she's got the right idea about you after all."

Emma stopped on the way to the phone and hugged her husband to show him that she at least was still a fan.

"Quick, quick, call," Patsy said. "Now that you mentioned food I'm starving."

Emma called and Rosie answered. In the background Emma heard her mother's voice singing an aria. "What's going on over there?" she asked.

"Cookin'," Rosie said, but at once the phone was snatched from her hand.

"Well," Aurora said, abruptly breaking off the aria. "Calling to make your apologies, I hope. And where were you this morning when I needed to consult you?"

"I was very sleepy," Emma said. "I sat up late reading a serious novel. I'm trying to improve my mind."

"I suppose that's admirable," Aurora said. "What do you want now?"

"I wondered if you were cooking breakfast, and if so, who for?"

"For whom," Aurora said. "Why don't you let your mind go and just try improving your grammar. I don't like it that you deliberately ignored my call. I might have been in dire straits."

"I apologize," Emma said cheerfully.

"Don't apologize!" Flap and Patsy said in unison.

"Hum," Aurora said. "Do you have a Greek chorus living with you at the moment? Ask it why you shouldn't apologize to your own mother."

"I don't know why everyone in the world but me is so difficult," Emma said. "Actually Patsy and I wondered if we could come over for breakfast."

"Oh, that little snippet," Aurora said. "Miss Clark. Yes, by all means bring her. It always pleases me to see a young lady of such high principles stuffing herself with my food. Wouldn't Thomas like to come too?"

"No, he cut his hand," Emma said, making a face at him. "He has to go get a stitch."

"He hasn't exposed himself to me in some time, you know," Aurora said. "He can't hide forever. Vernon's brought me a goat, by the way. Unfortunately I don't think I can keep him, since he

eats flowers, but it was a nice thought anyway. You two hurry.
I'm just putting my sausages in."

2.

EMMA SPRUCED herself up a little and she and Patsy zipped off
in Patsy's blue Mustang.

"You haven't told me about your fight," Patsy reminded her. "I
want to know all you can tell me about marriage, so I can weigh
the odds."

"It's a waste of time telling you about marriage," Emma said.
"No two sets of odds are the same. Look, there's the General."

They had just pulled into her mother's street, and General
Scott, in a charcoal gray pullover and immaculate slacks, was
standing in his driveway looking irritable. He had his binoculars
around his neck, and F.V. stood behind him in his undershirt, a
spade in one hand. The General was flanked by his Dalmatians,
both of them as erect as he was.

Just as they drove past, the General put his binoculars to his
eyes and started to focus them on Aurora Greenway's house.
Patsy was so disconcerted at the sight that she didn't know
whether to speed up or slow down.

"That's creepy," she said. "If I were your mother I wouldn't go
out with him anymore."

"Look at that car," Emma said, pointing at the long white
Lincoln. "No wonder Momma hit it."

Patsy parked behind it and they got out and looked in the
windows. "How can you talk on two telephones and drive?"
Emma asked. They looked up the street and saw that General
Scott was still planted on the sidewalk, the binoculars pointed
straight at them.

"The nerve of him," Patsy said. "Let's do something risqué
while he's watching."

"Okay," Emma said. "I think he deserves something for his
persistence."

Both girls lifted their skirts and did a rapid sideways dance up the driveway. They danced faster and faster and lifted their skirts higher and higher, finishing with a can-can kick just before they ran in the side door. Both were giggling when they burst into the kitchen.

Aurora and Rosie and Vernon—much smaller and more red-faced than the girls had expected him to be—were sitting at the kitchen table feasting on an array of curried eggs and sausages, with honeydew melons on the side. A small brown and white goat wandered around the kitchen, bleating plaintively.

"Oh, I want that goat," Patsy said. "It just matches my dress."

Vernon popped to his feet immediately. Aurora merely raised an eyebrow at Patsy and went on dishing up sausages.

"That's you, as usual, Patsy," she said. "You invariably want whatever I have. Vernon Dalhart, I'd like you to meet my daughter, Emma Horton, and her friend Miss Patsy Clark."

The phone rang just as Vernon was shaking hands. Rosie got it. "'Lo, General," she said. "You been banished, you know."

"The nerve of such a man," Aurora said. "You girls sit down and eat. I was feeling rather Asian this morning so I resorted to curried eggs."

"Mr. Dalhart, that's the most charming goat I've ever seen," Patsy said, helping herself to the eggs.

"Sit back down, Vernon," Aurora said. "No need to stand on formality with these girls. Their manners are not all a person of our generation might expect."

Rosie was apparently getting an earful from the General. She had her mouth opened to speak, but had not been able to get in a word and finally closed it. "You better talk to him a minute," she said, handing the phone to Aurora. "I think he's gone bee-serk. He says the girls walked up the driveway naked, or something."

"I knew he wouldn't let bygones be bygones," Aurora said, covering the phone with her hand.

"Hector, I think I recall rescinding your privileges," she said, uncovering it. "If you must remonstrate with me, be brief. I have a number of guests and we're right in the middle of breakfast.

"It won't get you anywhere either," she added.

"Look at my knot," Rosie said, leaning over and pulling back her hair so the girls could see. She had a sizable lump on her temple.

Across the table, Aurora's eyes had begun to flash. They flashed in silence for a few moments, and then she took the receiver away from her mouth. General Scott's scratchy voice could be plainly heard.

"He seems to think you two young ladies exposed yourself indecently," she said, looking at them coolly. "What substance is there to that?"

"Oh, well, he was out there with his binoculars," Patsy said. "We did a little dance."

"Let's show her," Emma said, and they got up and did their dance again, or did it until they noticed that Vernon was blushing. They omitted the can-can kick. Aurora watched them without expression and turned her attention back to the phone.

"Their dance was hardly as scandalous as you make it sound, Hector," she said. "I've just seen it. We've had quite enough of you and your binoculars up at this end of the street."

She was about to hang up, but the General said something that evidently caused her to change her mind. She listened for a moment, and the cheerful devil-may-care expression left her face. She looked over everyone's head, evidently somewhat concerned.

"Hector, there's no point," she said. "I'm in the midst of a crowd. There's really no point. Goodbye now."

She glanced at Vernon and then looked down at her eggs. After a moment she straightened up and resumed her cheerful manner. "Well, nobody's all bad," she said.

"These eggs are wonderful," Patsy said.

"Lookit, he almost made her cry," Rosie whispered to Emma. "I never knowed her to enjoy losin' a beau, did you?"

"What business are you in, Mr. Dalhart?" Emma asked, to change the subject.

"I guess the oil business," Vernon said. "That's what keeps me run ragged leastways."

"Vernon has locutions that go right back to Appalachia, if not to the Scots ballads," Aurora said, forcing herself to speak crisply. She would not have thought Hector Scott could affect her so.

"Are you one of the giants of the oil industry?" Patsy asked Vernon. "I've heard that the real giants go about incognito."

"What a naïve question," Aurora said. "If Vernon were a giant of anything he wouldn't be having breakfast with me at this hour of the day. Giants don't waste their time."

"Naw, I ain't a giant of nothin'," Vernon added.

Emma watched him closely. She was always surprised by any sign of versatility in her mother, and Vernon was such a sign. He looked more suitable to Rosie than to her mother, though actually he didn't look suitable to anybody. The little goat wandered over to her, bleating, and she gave it a piece of rind off her melon.

"You girls haven't told me what brings you out so early," Aurora said. "Are you off to do social work perhaps?"

"Ha," Patsy said. "We're off to go shopping."

The breakfast went on and the talk veered this way and that. As soon as it was polite Patsy left the table and wandered off to snoop. It was very irritating to her that Mrs. Greenway had such good taste.

Rosie commenced trying to get the dishes off the table, no easy task with Aurora still there. Everyone else yielded theirs up, but she kept hers and continued to find tidbits on various platters, little bites that her guests had overlooked. Vernon sat and watched as if he had never seen a woman eat before.

"She'll eat all day if you don't keep after her," Rosie said. Emma scraped the plates and drew Rosie off to the patio as soon as she could to hear about the trouble with Royce. They passed Patsy, who was in the downstairs study poring over a Viking amulet that Aurora had picked up in Stockholm.

"I never find things like this or I'd buy them," Patsy said.

"Did you ever wake up and feel like you was stranglin'?" Rosie asked.

"Not really," Emma said.

"I never either, until last night," Rosie said, a pinched look on her freckled face. "I guess I went home too quick. Your momma tried to stop me, but I guess I figured if I was gonna go home at all I better get with it."

"Was Royce mad at you?" Emma asked.

"Aw, no, he was happy as a lark, all six minutes that he stayed awake," Rosie said bitterly. "Beat me over the head yesterday and told me about his carryin' on an' all, an' then just because Vernon was nice enough to offer him a new job he thought it was all settled an' forgotten. I don't know why I even let Vernon send him home. There I went home—to do my best to forgive him—an' the sonofabitch never even stayed awake long enough to rub my back."

"Aw," Emma said. "Want me to rub it?"

"Would you?" Rosie said, turning around immediately. "You was always the best child. At least the best one I knowed. Rub hard. I been tight as a wire for two weeks now. I guess I must have knowed it was coming on."

"I don't understand," Emma said. "Royce has always seemed so docile. I wouldn't have thought he would dare do anything to make you mad."

"Maybe he finally seen through me," Rosie said. "Maybe he finally realized I ain't as mean as I sound."

They paused to think about it, and Emma kneaded her thin, hard back.

"You didn't tell me about the strangling feeling," Emma said.

"Just came on me," Rosie said. "Royce wasn't hog drunk, but he wasn't sober neither. I had some things I needed to talk to him about, but he flopped down an' went right off to sleep like nothin' had happened. I got in bed an' turned off the light an' first thing I knowed I was shakin' like a leaf. I couldn't get him an' that slut off my mind. I ain't an angel of the lord or nothin', but at least I been a good wife an' done most of the child raisin' an' all. But then I ain't been too accommodating to Royce lately, if you know what I mean—sometimes I am but most times I ain't. Anyway, the more I thought about it the more I got to feelin' it was my fault and not his, so I cried over that for a while, and Royce just kept laying there, snoring and snoring, and I finally started getting this choking feeling, like my throat closed up."

She put a hand to her throat, remembering, and reached around with her other hand and pointed to a spot below her shoulder blade that was particularly sore.

"It ain't that Royce is bad so much," she said. "It's just that he

ain't that good, and I ain't either, you know, and I got to thinkin',
here we've muddled along for twenty-seven years an' brought
seven kids into the world, and what's it all amount to if he can lie
there snorin' when I'm shakin' like a leaf and chokin' to death?
Half the time he don't no more know what I'm feelin' than the
man in the moon. The more I thought about it the more I was
panting and heaving and strugglin' to get my breath, an' there
wasn't a soul to care, so finally I thought, Rosie, it's get up now or
die before mornin'. It was that serious. So I got up and drug the
kids out of bed an' got a cab, like your momma said to, and took
the kids to my sister's an' come on here."

"Why didn't you just stay at your sister's?"

"An' let her think I was leavin' my husband?" Rosie said. "Religious as she is, I'd never hear the end of that. I just told her your
ma was sick. She wasn't even surprised to see me—said she
knowed there wasn't no use in my goin' home. First thing she
did this mornin' was get mad at Vernon for bein' too generous
with Royce."

"What'd he do that was too generous?"

"Give Vernon his first week off, thinkin' we might want to take
a vacation. Shoot, I don't want to go nowhere an' have to be
alone with Royce right now. We never had a vacation farther
away than Conroe anyway that I can remember."

Patsy wandered out just then, looking faintly irritated. "Your
mother certainly sounds happy as a lark," she said.

"I know, it's irritating," Emma said. "She's like a balloon. Any
nice puff of air and she's floating."

"Aw, hush," Rosie said. "You girls just don't know how to have
fun. Your ma took me in in my time of trial and ain't nobody
gonna talk bad about her today unless it's me."

She stood up and picked up a broom that she had laid down
when they started talking, but she seemed in no hurry to leave.
"Lord I'm old," she said, looking down at Emma. "Now you're
having a baby. Who would have thought it would happen so
soon?"

"It's not so soon," Emma said. "I've been married two years."

Rosie tried to smile but wanted to cry. Seeing Emma sitting

there, so trusting and goodhearted, such a happy-looking young woman, filled her with memory suddenly, until she felt too full. She had come to the Greenway house two months before Emma was born, and it was all so strange, the way life went on and seemed the same even though it was always changing. It never quite slowed down so you could catch it, except by thinking back, and it left some people more important than others as it changed.

She had had her children and loved them as much as she could, and she had six grandchildren already, and more to come, and yet somehow Emma had always been her special child, more hers than any of her own—always bright-eyed, always hoping to please, always running to her for hugs and kisses and help of all kinds, watching solemnly while Band-Aids were put on, holding her breath and squeezing her eyes shut while she waited for iodine to sting, racing her tricycle along the front walk as fast as she could go while Rosie pretended to be trying to spray her with the garden hose.

"Two years isn't too soon," Emma said again.

"Naw, precious, that wasn't the kind of soon I mean," Rosie said. "So soon since you was one yourself, that's all I meant." She shook her head to clear it of memories and took her broom and went in.

Patsy had observed more of the scene than Emma had, for Emma was looking at the yard and wondering if Flap would still be in a good mood when she got home.

"I don't know what Rosie would do without you to adore," Patsy said. "Come on, go talk to your mother while she feels good. Maybe she'll let you by a dress."

When they went back in they discovered that Aurora and Vernon were no longer in the kitchen—they were in Vernon's car.

"Look at her," Patsy said.

Aurora was in the back seat watching television. "I made Vernon let me do it," she said gaily. "For the novelty."

"I'd like to get in and see," Patsy said. "I've never done it either."

"Come ahead," Aurora said. "I'd better extract myself, anyway. If I lie here long I'll go right to sleep and there's no telling where Vernon will drive me away to."

While Vernon was showing Patsy the wonders of his car Emma and her mother went back in the house and up to the bedroom, where, to Emma's surprise, her mother sat down and wrote her out a check for a hundred and fifty dollars.

"What have I done to deserve this?" Emma asked.

"I don't know that you do deserve it," Aurora said. "As it happens, I had forgotten how well Miss Clark dresses. It's certainly a mark in her favor—perhaps the only mark in her favor. I think I deserve a daughter who dresses at least as well, which is why I'm giving you this."

Emma felt slightly embarrassed. "How are you?" she asked.

Aurora went over and sat down in her window nook, from which she could look down on the lawn and the street. Vernon was just handing Patsy a Coke from his refrigerator.

"Honestly," Aurora said, flopping on her pillows, "she's just finished one of my better breakfasts and now she's drinking a Coke."

"Pick, pick, pick," Emma said. "Why do you always pick?"

"Oh, I don't know," Aurora said. "I've never been particularly passive."

"So how are you?" Emma asked again.

"How am I?" Aurora said, looking down at the scene below intently, to see if she could pick up the drift of whatever conversation was passing between Patsy and Vernon.

"Why I'm fine," she said. "No one has been obnoxious to me in almost twenty-four hours, and that always brings my spirits up. If only people won't be obnoxious to me my spirits do quite well."

"I like Vernon," Emma said, going to her mother's dressing table. She tried on the newly rediscovered amber necklace. Aurora eyed her watchfully.

"It's a wonder I have a piece of jewelry left, the way people make free with it," she said. "What did you say about Vernon?"

"I said I liked him," Emma said.

Aurora snorted. "That's as noncommittal as Cream of Wheat,"

she said. "Obviously nobody could dislike Vernon. In point of fact you're as puzzled as I am as to why he's here. He's supposed to be in Canada today, not ruining Miss Clark's teeth with beverages she can't possibly need."

"Why *is* he here?" Emma asked.

"As you can see, he hasn't chosen to leave, so he's here," Aurora said. "He's reputed to be quite a good cardplayer, and we're planning to play some cards afterwhile."

"You're leaving matters in his hands, I take it," Emma said, keeping the necklace on so she could enjoy her mother's mild anxiety about it.

"Oh, well," Aurora said. "I don't see that you need worry about Vernon. He's a self-made man and those are always the most resilient. If he doesn't want to be bothered with me he doesn't have to, that I can see."

Emma took off the necklace and Aurora turned her attention back to the scene on the lawn. It was hard to tell who was the more fidgety, Vernon or Patsy. Both seemed to be talking at once.

"That girl rattles on worse than I do," Aurora said. "She's not letting him get a word in edgewise. It's high time she married, you know." She got up suddenly and started for the stairs.

"Where are you going so soon?" Emma asked, trailing along.

"I don't see that he needs to spend the whole morning talking to your rattly little friend," Aurora said. "You two need to be on your way."

"This must be a case of opposites attracting," Emma said.

Aurora didn't look around. "You got your check, be off with you," she said. "Your witticisms are beginning to grate on my ears. My experience is considerably more extensive than yours and I have found cases of opposites attracting to be far more uncommon than everyone supposes. When it does happen, the attraction is usually short-lived. In point of fact opposites usually bore one another. All my opposites certainly bore me."

"Then what about Vernon?" Emma said.

"Vernon and I just met," Aurora said. "All I want is a simple game of cards and a little friendship, for pity's sake." She stopped at the foot of the stairs and looked at her daughter indignantly.

189

"All right," Emma said. "You were the one who said he was in love with you."

"Oh, well, that was yesterday afternoon," Aurora said. "I wouldn't know about him today. I gave him a severe lecture about Royce. A vacation is the last thing a married man like Royce needs right now."

"Poor Royce," Emma said. "I think Vernon is right. Much as I love Rosie, I think somebody needs to be on Royce's side."

"Fine, you be in charge of Royce's morale," Aurora said, peeking out a window. "I don't know what good it will do him, since you're a little too toothsome to venture into that part of town."

As they walked toward the kitchen Emma put her arm around her mother's waist for a second. "Contrary as I am, I do want to thank you for the check," she said. Aurora turned and hugged her, though perfunctorily. Her mind was elsewhere.

"I think if I were a man and met you I'd be terrified," Emma said.

"Sweet little me?" Aurora said. "What's to be terrified of?"

They stepped into the kitchen just as Patsy and Vernon came through the door. The little goat was nibbling timidly on one of Aurora's blue pillows. Aurora hurried over and picked him up.

"Vernon, I hope you've brought your cards," she said.

Vernon had a pack in his hand. "We could play four-handed," he said, nodding at the girls.

Aurora immediately vetoed the suggestion with a shake of her head. "I'm afraid you don't know these girls very well," she said. "They're both very high-minded and much too intellectual to sit around playing cards with the likes of us. Their lives are not devoted to play—they're very serious young women. I imagine they're going to go right off to some library and spend the morning reading serious novels—*Ulysses* or somesuch.

"In any case," she added, "there's no reason why Rosie and I should have to share you with the young. Little enough in the way of diversion comes our way these days."

As the girls went out the door Vernon was just beginning to shuffle the cards. "You're too soft on everybody," Patsy said, poking her friend. "Your husband beats you and your mother bullies you. I guess I even bully you. You know perfectly well she's deliberately rude to me—why don't you ever argue with her about it? What kind of friend are you?"

"A confused kind," Emma said. "She gave me a hundred and fifty dollars without my even asking, just so I can keep up with you."

Patsy was combing her hair and turning the car around at the same time. "One of these days she's going to go too far," she said. "I can't see what she sees in that man either. I'm sure he's nice, but she couldn't live with a cowboy. Or an oil man. I don't know what she thinks she's doing."

When Emma was broke she was always thinking of things she wanted to buy, but with money in her hand she couldn't think of a thing she really wanted.

"I'm not a good consumer," she said. "I can't think of anything I want, except a new gown. Maybe I'll just keep the money and buy something the next time I'm depressed."

"Look at those ridiculous dogs," Patsy said as they passed the General's house. "Do you suppose he makes them stand there all day?"

Pershing and Marshal Ney were standing exactly where they had been on the General's lawn. They looked as if they were waiting for him to come out and stand between them again. Both of them were staring straight ahead like soldiers on a drill field. Nearby, F.V. was unenergetically clipping a hedge.

Patsy shook her head. "You certainly grew up on a creepy street," she said. "No wonder you're timid."

"Is that what I am?" Emma asked.

"Yes," Patsy said. She looked over and saw that her friend was quietly folding and unfolding her mother's check. Emma didn't speak, and Patsy regretted what she had just said. When her friend didn't speak it was usually because her feelings were hurt. "Never mind, Emma," she said. "I just meant you weren't rude, like your mother and me."

"Oh, hush," Emma said. "I'm not that touchy. I was just thinking about Flap."

"What about him?"

"Oh, nothing, I was just thinking," Emma said.

CHAPTER X

1.

LESS THAN two weeks after the advent of Vernon, Rosie came in one morning to find once again that all the phones in the house were off the hook. She was upset anyway, and the sight of the dangling receivers was more than she could stand. She marched upstairs to demand a reckoning and found Aurora barricaded into the snuggest corner of her window nook, with almost every pillow she owned piled around her. She looked almost as tense as Rosie felt.

"What's wrong with you?" Aurora said at once at the sight of her maid.

"What's wrong with *you*, you mean," Rosie said.

"No, I asked first. Don't play games," Aurora said. "I know you. Out with it."

"Royce has left for good," Rosie said. "That's all that's wrong with me."

"Oh, what an idiot," Aurora said. "What's wrong with him, then?"

"He found out he don't have to live with me," Rosie said. "It's as simple as that. Can I put the phones back on the hook, in case he calls and changes his mind?"

"No, you cannot," Aurora said. "I'll instill some feminine pride in you if it's the last thing I do."

"I don't know what I'd do with it at my age," Rosie said.

"Did he beat you again?" Aurora asked.

"Naw," Rosie said. "He just threw his house key across the street and said he wanted his freedom. Imagine Royce wanting his freedom. He never even knew there was such a word two weeks ago. That slut must have taught it to him."

Aurora looked her sternest. "Well, he'll find it's not the answer to everything," she said. "See that he gets about a year of it and he'll sing a different tune."

"So that's my troubles," Rosie said, feeling better for having told them. "Vernon just wasted his money trying to patch us up. What's wrong with you?"

"Nothing very serious," Aurora said. "Nothing I wish to discuss, either. Go clean the house."

Rosie knew that it seldom took Aurora more than five minutes to get around to discussing things she didn't wish to discuss, so she sat and looked out the window for five minutes. Aurora was staring at the wall and seemed to have forgotten her existence.

"Now tell me," Rosie said when she considered that she had waited long enough.

"I've been given an ultimatum. Over the phone too, which is the worst possible way to receive ultimatums. There's no one to hit. I don't know what men think I am, but whatever it is it's not what I am."

"Uh-oh," Rosie said. "Who from?"

"Trevor," Aurora said. "The best-dressed man in my life. I might have known I'd never get to keep anyone well dressed."

"So you told him to go jump in the lake forever, hum?" Rosie asked.

"No, though I should have," Aurora said. "It would certainly be easy enough for Trevor to do; he'd only have to step off his yacht. Nothing surprises me very much, but I can't think what's got into Trevor. I've known him thirty years and he's never behaved this way."

She sighed. "Every time I think life is going to run smoothly for a while, something like this happens. I don't believe life has any intention of running smoothly."

"Well, it's sure runnin' bumpy over on Lyons Avenue," Rosie said. "Reckon it's the Lord callin' down his wrath upon us?"

Aurora tried to swat her, but not very hard. "Hush and go mop," she said. "This is the idiocy of men, not the wrath of God. I have a very hard day ahead of me and I don't need any of your backwoods theology. We're not taking any calls from your husband, just remember that."

"What's gonna happen?" Rosie asked, more alarmed than she liked to admit. Ordinary things seemed to be slipping away, one by one—pretty soon so many of them would be gone that life just wouldn't be life as she knew it, and the prospect of life being completely unfamiliar was very upsetting.

Aurora said nothing, which was disturbing too. "What's gonna happen?" Rosie said again. This time Aurora caught the note of distress in her voice and looked up.

"I don't know if that's a general question or a specific question," she said. "If it's general, I can't answer it. Specifically, in my case, I can be a little more precise. Trevor is having me to dinner. If it's going to rain it might as well pour. Tomorrow, as you know, is my dinner party for Emma and Flap and Cecil, and Vernon is coming. That's as far ahead as I care to think."

"What does Vernon think of all this?" Rosie asked.

"All what?" Aurora said, looking at her critically.

"All this rigamarole," Rosie said.

Aurora shrugged. "Vernon doesn't know a thing about it," she said. "He's insecure enough as it is. I certainly don't plan to burden him with tales of my difficulties with other men."

"It's too bad Vernon ain't educated, ain't it?" Rosie said, hoping to get a hint of which way her boss's feelings were inclining. "He's a nice feller to play cards with."

"Yes, too bad," Aurora said, looking rather vague.

"Yep, a real pity," Rosie said, unsatisfied.

"Oh, get out of here. You haven't done a lick of work today," Aurora snapped suddenly. "What you mean is if he were educated I might think about marrying him, which is plainly insulting. I'm not such a snob as all that. If I wanted him I'd educate him myself. Vernon is far too sweet for me to consider inflicting myself on him permanently. You know very well he wouldn't stand a chance around the likes of me. I haven't got past Trevor yet, so just leave Vernon out of it."

"He's gonna be heartbroken," Rosie said. "You know that, don't you? I never seen a feller fall so deep in love so fast. I'm gonna take up for him while there's still a chance of getting him out alive."

Aurora began to kick her pillows out toward the center of the room, one by one. It was a day when she found it difficult to feel right about anything. Life might be many things, but it would never be anywhere near perfect, not hers at least, and the problem of what to do about the innocent fifty-year-old heart she had so ruthlessly captured was undeniably a serious one. The heart had been there to take and she had taken it, an action as natural to her as taking a bite from a plate. She had never been inclined to pass over accessible hearts, if the person carrying them seemed somewhat palatable.

Self-denial of almost any kind was a mode of behavior she had always rejected—instinctively at the moment when something lay at hand to be grabbed, consciously later on when she had time to think about it. In an imperfect, frequently unsatisfactory life, self-denial seemed the stupidest of procedures. She didn't leave palatable bites on plates, either; and yet, committed as she was, both by instinct and reflection, to having what she could get, she recognized quite clearly that hearts were not much like bites, and the thought of breaking Vernon's, or anyone's, was a very troubling thought. At moments she deplored her greed, but those were rare moments; restraint was not something she expected of herself. Since Vernon had not been passed over, a way would have to be found to take care of him.

It was just that at the moment she could not imagine what that way might be. The thought of him caused her to sigh.

"Well, I wouldn't have thought any fifty-year-old would have been so incautious, to tell you the truth," she said to Rosie. "Vernon has no self-protective instinct at all. I have only one way of proceeding where men are concerned: I try to be worth their while as I go along, one way or another. If I'm not, then they better scram, to use a crude word. I've never been able to vouch for tomorrow, not even with Rudyard."

"Does that mean you never know what you might do next?" Rosie said. "I'm the same way. Wonder why we stayed married so long?"

"Oh, that has nothing to do with vouching for tomorrow," Aurora said. "Who likes to break a habit?"

She got to her feet and wandered about the room distractedly, her dinner date on her mind. "I wish I had time to go buy a dress," she said. "If I'm to be given an ultimatum I don't see why I shouldn't have a new dress."

"Just keep in mind I'm on Vernon's side," Rosie said. "If you don't do right by him I'm quittin'. I ain't gonna sit by an' see that man hurt."

Aurora stopped and put her hands on her hips. "Don't hector me," she said. "I have Hector for that—or at least I did. Of course Vernon's likely to be hurt, somewhat. Let's just get some good food in him first. Do you think a man who waits fifty years to get involved with women and then picks me to try and get involved with is going to come out unscathed. It's partly his own fault, for waiting so long. Meanwhile I hope you'll allow me to take my problems one at a time. My immediate problem is Mr. Trevor Waugh."

"Okay, okay," Rosie said. "If you want me to iron something you better pick it out quick. I'm washing the windows today."

"I guess you can hang up the phones," Aurora said, hanging up hers.

2.

"THERE YOU are, Trevor . . . aren't you?" Aurora said when she stepped into the darkness at the restaurant he had chosen for their dinner date. It was his custom to choose the darkest possible restaurants, for the most obvious possible reasons, and she wasn't surprised by the kind of place she found herself in, only by the degree of the darkness, which was almost total. The maitre 'd had disappeared ahead of her into pitch blackness.

Her confusion lasted only a moment, however; then a familiar figure loomed in the gloom, smelling of tweed, the sea, and good cologne. The figure enveloped her in an embrace.

"More beautiful than ever—you're still the woman I love," a familiar voice said in accents as clearly Philadelphian as they had been thirty years before. The accents were being delivered less than an inch from her ear, and had moved down toward her neck before the last word was out, dispelling whatever doubt she might have had about the identity of the man who was embracing her.

"That's you, Trevor. I believe I sense it," she said. "Get your head out of my collar. I thought I was to be the guest, not the meal."

"Ah, but what a meal you'd be!" Trevor Waugh said, not relinquishing his brief advantage. "A dish for the gods, Aurora, as Byron said."

At that Aurora began to squirm in earnest. "That's you, Trevor," she said. "You've spoiled yet another romantic moment with a misquotation. Lead me to my seat please, if you can find it."

She began to fumble her way along what seemed to be an aisle, with Trevor beside her, fumbling his way along as much of her as he could reach. In a moment she stumbled into the maitre d', who had been waiting a discreet distance ahead, and he led them around a corner into a room with a fireplace and great deep booths covered in maroon leather. The place they were in was a hunt club; wherever Trevor went, and he went everywhere, he managed to find great dim hunt clubs with trophy heads and mounted fish on the walls, fireplaces and rum and booths covered in maroon leather.

When they were seated Aurora allowed herself to look at him and saw that he was much the same, handsome and tanned, with white hair, his old smell of tweed and rum and good barbers, his pipe in his coat pocket, his cheeks full of color, his shoulders still broad and his teeth as even and white as they had been thirty years before, when the two of them had fumbled their youthful way around the dance floors of Boston, Philadelphia, and New York. He was, when all was said and done, the most enduring of her suitors. In the wake of her eventual rejection he had married three times, prominently but unsuccessfully, and had spent his life sailing the seven seas, pursuing the game and fish of the world, pausing now and then to seduce unlikely ballerinas and youthful actresses, ladies of society, and, whenever possible, their daughters as well; but always, once or twice a year, he found some excuse to sail his boat to wherever she was and renew a suit that in his eyes had never really been interrupted. It was flattering, and it had gone on a very long time; and since he had chosen such a discreet booth she let him take her hand under the table.

"Trevor, I've been missing you," she said. "You've waited quite a long time to come see me this year. Who'd you have out there with you on the seven seas?"

"Oh, Maggie Whitney's daughter," Trevor said. "You knew Maggie, didn't you? From Connecticut?"

"I don't know why I tolerate your behavior with the young," Aurora said. "It's inconsistent of me, I must say. I recently disposed of a man for doing far less than you do in the course of your sails. I suppose you'd go sailing with my daughter if she were single."

"Well, I'd rather have the mothers, but I guess I'm slipping," Trevor said. "I can't seem to get the mothers, and I have to have somebody. I can't sleep a wink alone."

"I don't think we need talk about it," Aurora said. It was true that Trevor Waugh was the one man she was hopelessly tolerant of. There had never seemed any harm in him, somehow; he had never been known to be unkind to any woman, young or old. All his wives and ladies and their daughters and all his actresses and ballerinas left him after a while, carrying with them many fine presents and Trevor's love and fond regards; and he remained tender and fond toward all of them. He had in some small way enhanced every woman he had met and never hurt one, and yet not a one had ever returned to him, not even momentarily, that she knew of. The very fact of all those daughters, which in another man would have seemed monstrous, seemed only touching and rather sweet in Trevor—a way, almost, of giving continuity to the love he bore their mothers.

His affairs had never left scars, unless on him, and of course to expect Trevor Waugh not to be physical would have been like expecting the sun not to shine. He and she had not been lovers for almost thirty years—she had been his first romance and he her second—and in the years afterward she had had no urge to go back to his bed, yet when she saw him she made no effort to deny him his hugs and fumblings; indeed, she would have known he was sick if he hadn't hugged and fumbled. Trevor could not be without, no one had ever wished him to, and it was a fortunate thing that the world contained as many mothers and daughters as it did to keep him in good spirits.

"Trevor, I assume you've ordered whatever's best," she said.

"Depend on it," Trevor said, nodding at a waiter, who almost instantly came forward with a wonderful crab salad. Where gustatory pleasures were concerned, his tastes were almost irreproachable, though, sportsman that he was, he was slightly more prone to order game of some sort than she would have been. She allowed him to pat her a bit, as a reward for his excellent crab, and decided that life on the sea did something nice for a man's smell. Trevor had always smelled better than any man she had known. His smell seemed to be a mixture of salt, leather, and spice, and she leaned toward him and sniffed a time or two to see if it was still the same. Trevor took it as a sign of encouragement and got right down to business.

"I guess I surprised you, didn't I?" he said. "I bet you didn't expect me to call up and demand a yes or no after all these years."

"Yes, it was a rude shock, dear," Aurora said. "Only my long-standing fondness for you kept me from hanging up. What put such a thought in your head, if I may ask?"

"I've always thought we were meant for one another," Trevor said. "I've never known why you married Rudyard. I've never known why you wouldn't leave him."

"Why, Trevor," she said. "I got along with Rudyard perfectly well. Or imperfectly well, to be more accurate. At least he was not always off with ballerinas and schoolgirls."

"But that was only because you wouldn't marry me," Trevor said, a pained look on his handsome face. His hair had been an aristocratic white almost from the time he left Princeton, and it went awfully well with his face and his clothes.

"I've never understood it," he said, squeezing her hand. "I've just never understood it."

"Dear, so few things can be understood," Aurora said. "Eat your crab and have a little more wine and don't look so pained. If you'll tell me what it is you've never understood perhaps I can be helpful."

"Why you stopped sleeping with me, to be frank," Trevor said. "I thought everything was all right. Then we took that sail from Maine to the Chesapeake and I still thought everything was all right and you got off the boat and married Rudyard. Wasn't everything all right?"

"Trevor, you ask me that every time we dine together," Aurora said, giving him a little squeeze in consolation. "If I'd known you were going to take it so seriously I might well have married you and spared you all that brooding. Do stop taking it so seriously."

"But why?" Trevor said. "Why? I keep thinking it must have been my fault."

"Yes, your modesty or whatever it is," Aurora said, having a little of his crab, which in the course of his brood he was neglecting. She had immediately finished off hers.

"I really don't wish your modesty to turn into insecurity, Trevor—not over something that happened thirty years ago. I've told you as much hundreds of times, I'm sure. No young woman could have had a better lover than you were, but you see I was just a young woman then, and exceptionally vacant. I expected your eye might rove, I suppose, or else mine might. I can't recall the circumstances too precisely, but I seemed to get the feeling that if I kept sailing around on that boat with you some carelessness might occur. Forgive me, dear, but I've never quite seen you as a family man. Though I don't know that that was it, either. Perhaps you were a little lax in your pursuit, I can't seem to remember. At any rate, the fact that I wandered off and married Rudyard didn't mean that everything we did wasn't 'all right,' as you put it. I do think, considering the life you've led, you'd have stopped worrying about being all right by now."

"I always worry about it," Trevor said. "What else have I got to worry about? I've got plenty of money. Maggie's daughter didn't think I was very all right. I want you to marry me before I slip any farther. You and I wouldn't have any trouble. What if the day comes when I can't even get actresses? You don't want that to happen to me, do you?"

"Of course not," Aurora said. "I'm sure we've had this very conversation before, Trevor. I'm feeling a great deal of déjà vu and I don't see why we're having to wait for the second course. Food might help dispel my déjà vu. I only seem to suffer from it in your company, I might add. You have an unfortunate way of trying to get me to remember things I've forgotten. I never can, you know—all I can remember is this conversation. I really haven't the faintest idea why I married Rudyard instead of you. I'm hardly a psychiatrist, and I do hope the day comes when you let me alone about it."

"All right, marry me and I'll never bring it up again," Trevor said. "I'm sorry if I'm being ungentlemanly about it, but something's come over me lately. Nothing seems to satisfy me. I guess it's age."

"No, it's your preoccupation with sport," Aurora said. "You have something of a mind, dear, and you can't expect it to remain content with the little you seem to want to offer it. I think you've sailed too many boats, caught too many fish, and shot too many animals. Not to mention what you may have done with too many women."

"Yep, now the chickens are coming home to roost," Trevor said, the same look of pain on his face. "You're the only person left who could satisfy me, Aurora. You always have been. You've got to marry me this time. If you get away again there'll be nothing left to hope for. I might as well sail off into the sunset and never come back."

Aurora was examining the lobster that had just arrived and, in a discreet way, smacking her lips. "Trevor, you know me," she said. "I have a hard time concentrating on romance when there's food before me. I do think you ought to avoid images like that, though—as well as misquotations. A dish for the gods is Shakespeare, not Byron, and a threat to sail into the sunset, however sincere and practical, is not apt to sway me. After all, you've spent most of your life in the sunset, for all I know. I think far better of your wines than I do of your imagery."

"Aurora, I mean it," Trevor said, taking her hand in both of his. Aurora immediately jerked her hand away and grabbed a fork with it.

"Trevor, propose to me as much as you like, but don't try to hold hands with me while I'm handling silverware," she said.

"Without you I have no hope," Trevor said, a good deal of his soul in his eyes. Aurora looked over, noticed the soul, and gave him a bite of her lobster, since he had so far ignored his own.

"I think you're being a little shortsighted, dear," Aurora said. "It's the fact that I won't marry you that preserves your hopes. If I did marry you I'd just be your wife. There's nothing very hopeful in that, that I can see. But as long as I remain free, then you can remain perpetually hopeful and I can get the pleasure of your company once in a while, when I need it, and we can go right on, year after year, with our romance."

"But I worry," Trevor said. "I get off at sea with some woman or other and I begin to worry. I think, What if I come back and Aurora's married? It even throws off my aim. I was missing grouse in Scotland the last time I was there, and I never miss grouse. For some reason every time one flew up I had a vision of you in a marriage ceremony. Couldn't hit a thing."

"Oh, dear," Aurora said. "You're the first person whose aim I've thrown off. If it will help any I can assure you I have no intention of marrying. I'd miss our little romance if I did, and I don't like missing things."

"That doesn't help any," Trevor said. "You married Rudyard and that didn't interrupt us. We were already interrupted. Nothing will make me stop worrying."

Aurora shrugged. The lobster was wonderful. "Worry, then," she said.

Trevor began to eat. "Actually, there is one thing that might stop my worrying," he said.

"I was sure there was," Aurora said. He handled a knife and fork with grace—he always had—and the sight made her reflective, or at least as reflective as it was possible for her to be, while she was eating. It did seem strange in retrospect that she had left such a well-bred fun-loving man as Trevor for a person such as Rud, who could have eaten pimento cheese sandwiches every night of his life and not complained. Rud knew about good food, he knew where to get it and what it should taste like, but, except in the brief period of their courtship, he had never made much of an effort to secure it. Trevor's appetites were clearly more of a match for hers, and always had been, and it was not a little odd that she had felt no urge, then or ever, to marry him.

"We'll talk about all that later," Trevor said, reaching under the table to give her leg a friendly squeeze. "I want you to see the way I've fixed up my boat."

"Describe it to me," Aurora said. "It isn't likely I'll be able to risk a boat ride after eating so much. Besides, you've not told me about your women of the year. You're the only man I know who leads an interesting life, and I don't know why you want to thwart my curiosity this way."

With her other suitors she had never been able to tolerate even the mention of other women, but Trevor was the grand exception. He assured her constantly that she was his only real love, and she believed him and derived a great deal of pleasure from hearing about the women he made do with. Trevor sighed, but somehow he always felt better after he had told Aurora about his little loves, so he told her about a Polish actress and a California horsewoman and a couple of nice mothers and daughters from Connecticut. It carried them through the lobster and dessert and into brandy. Aurora was stuffed and content and let him hold her hand while they talked.

"Now you see," she said, "if I hadn't been so good at leading you a merry chase none of that would have happened to you, and some of it must have been merry at least."

"It was all merry," Trevor said. "That's the point, Aurora. Every romance I've had for thirty years has been merry. Maybe that's why I only want you. You're the only one who makes me unhappy."

"Oh, Trevor, don't say that, dear," Aurora said. "You know I can't stand to feel that I've been cruel to you. Here you've just provided me with such a nice meal."

"I don't blame you," Trevor said. "It's just that I like being unhappy about you better than I like being happy about most of the women I know."

"Dear, you're far too nice," Aurora said. "I seem to recall that I was quite cruel to you on one or two occasions in the past and you never worked up anything like enough indignation to suit me. If you had, who knows but what I'd have come to heel."

"*I* know," Trevor said. "I may look big and dumb but I'm not a dope. If I had done that you'd have stopped having anything to do with me."

Aurora chuckled. Her old flame had his endearing aspects still. "True, I can't stand people who presume to blame me," she said. "I've considered the right to blame as my prerogative. What's going to become of us, Trevor?"

"Two lobsters a year, I guess," Trevor said. "Maybe a pheasant now and then. Unless you marry me. If you'll just marry me this time I'll promise to change. We could move to Philadelphia. There's the family business, you know. I'd even sell my boat if you wanted me to."

Aurora quickly patted his hand. She dropped her eyes and something inside her dropped a little bit too.

"Darling, you must never sell your boat," she said after a moment. "I'm flattered that you love me more, and I do believe you, but since I refused to be your life I certainly have no right to ask that of you now. Besides, you cut such a dashing figure on your boat. You don't know how often through the years I've thought of how dashing you were in the days when we sailed around like we did. I really don't know what I'd do for romantic thoughts if I didn't know you were always on your boat . . . looking dashing . . . and that you'd come and see me by and by."

Trevor was silent. So was she.

"You weren't meant for Philadelphia and the family business," Aurora said. "No more was I meant for the sea. I don't know that anything works if one person has to give up too much. I've never been able to do anything about myself, I'm afraid, Trevor, and that being the case, I've always been glad that you loved the sea as much as you do."

"So am I," Trevor said. "It's a good second best."

He thought for a moment. "I don't suppose everyone has that good a second best," he said. "They have a combo here, you know. I don't know why we're sitting here. We'll just get sleepy. Would you like to go upstairs and dance?"

"Why, Trevor, of course," Aurora said, folding her napkin. "Why are we sitting here? You've hit upon the one thing it would never occur to me to refuse you. Let's dance at once."

3.

THEY DANCED at once. "Goodness, how I've missed it," Aurora said.

"How I've missed you," Trevor said. He danced as well as he handled a knife and fork. Then, just as it seemed to both of them that they were hitting their stride, the combo stopped playing and the musicians began packing their instruments. Unfortunately they had had the bad judgment to close with a waltz, and waltzes threw Trevor into such a depth of nostalgia for their waltzing days in the east that the whole blithe balance of the evening was very nearly destroyed.

"Dawn always found us on our feet, remember?" he said, embracing Aurora, who had been airing herself for a moment by an open window. "Let's go to that Mexican place you know. Dawn could find us on our feet again. I'm not too old."

"Very well," Aurora said, since he had been nice and hadn't brought up his ultimatum at all.

Then, in the taxicab, life stopped being a romantic memory and became a muddle again. Trevor was more or less all over her, of course, but she was looking out the window, watching Houston go by, and wasn't taking a great deal of notice.

"Dawn always found us on our feet," Trevor said again. He had grown fond of the line.

"Well, I must say, Trevor, you're the only man I know who realizes dancing ought to be a regular part of life," Aurora said, rather happily.

"Of course, like sex," Trevor said. "I've got to kiss you."

Perhaps because she was having a sleepy moment, or perhaps because his gallantry in pursuing her to so little reward for thirty years always touched her, or perhaps because he still smelled better than any man she knew, Aurora let him, thinking who knows?—though she knew well enough, really. She had had similar impulses, for similar reasons, over the years with Trevor and the results, disappointingly for them both, were never more than bland. Still, little harm was ever done, and none would have been in this case had not Trevor, in a wild, momentary burst of hope, thrust a hand into her brassiere. Just as he did, Aurora broke the kiss, sat up straighter, and took a deep breath, meaning to clear her head and regain her senses, though it was really only pretending to suppose that she had lost them. Trevor had had to turn his wrist at a rather sharp angle to get his hand into the brassiere and when Aurora chose to fill her lungs it not only trapped his hand against her breast but caused a horrible pain to shoot through his twisted wrist.

"Oow, God," he said. "Bend over, please. Bend over!"

"Oh, Trevor, for goodness' sake, we're almost there," Aurora said, misinterpreting the note of urgency in his voice and sitting up all the straighter.

"Oow! God! Please, you're breaking my wrist," Trevor said. He had been forced to slide partially onto the floorboards in order to keep from screaming loudly, and he was sure he had heard a small crack the second time Aurora moved.

Aurora had been politely ignoring his little foray, which was the only sound practice where Trevor was concerned, but she finally realized from the look on his face that something was amiss, and bent forward. Gingerly he removed his hand and held it haplessly before her eyes.

"Why does it dangle like that?" she asked.

"I think it's the first wrist ever to have been broken by a breast," he said, feeling it carefully. He had a feeling that bone ends might be protruding, but could find none, and after Aurora had rubbed it for a while he was forced to conclude that probably it was only sprained.

"I wish it was broken," he said. "Wouldn't that be romantic? Then you'd have to let me stay with you for a while so you could take care of me."

Aurora smiled and rubbed it for him. "It was all that talk about dawn finding us on our feet," she said. "You invariably exaggerate, dear. Dawn usually found us on a couch in the lobby of the Plaza, as I recall."

"It's going to find us on our feet this morning," Trevor said determinedly.

Instead it found them sitting at a red table in the small open courtyard of a place called the Last Concert, with Trevor drinking a bottle of Mexican beer. The Last Concert was only a small Mexican bar, with a jukebox and a tiny dance floor, but of the few after-hours places in Houston it was the one Aurora preferred. It was on an obscure street in North Houston, near the railroad yards, and she could hear, not far away, the sound of boxcars bumping into one another. Her old flame sipped his beer. There was no one there but themselves and an old, old Mexican woman, nodding inside behind the bar, and a large gray rat in one corner of the courtyard.

"I wish I had my pistol," Trevor said. "I'd try a shot at that rat."

The rat was eating a scrap of day-old tortilla, and seemed unperturbed by the presence of two elegantly dressed humans. As the sky above them lightened, the contrast between their dress and the bare shabbiness of the table and the little courtyard became more stark, but Aurora was feeling calmly tired and didn't mind. Trevor spent half his life in the Caribbean or in South America and was wonderful at Latin dances; for once she had been given her fill of rhumbas and sambas, cha-chas and various wilder dances that Trevor had seemed to be improvising on the spot, to the great delight of five or six middle-aged Mexicans who had stayed to drink beer and watch them until almost six in the morning.

The light got better still, and she could see that there were more lines than she would have thought in her old flame's face.

"Trevor, dear, you never let me see your real face," she said. "You always hide it away in the darkest restaurants possible. How do you know but what I'd like it if I got to see it once in a while?"

Trevor sighed. "Let's get on with this ultimatum," he said.

"Must we, dear?" she said, faintly amused.

"We must, we must," Trevor said. "I can't afford to let another ten years slip by. I can't stand having to worry about you marrying. Please say yes."

Aurora watched the rat carry its scrap of tortilla along the fence until it came to a hole. It went through the hole but then evidently stopped to eat some more of the tortilla, because its tail remained in the courtyard.

"You're going off into the sunset and will never see me again if I say no, isn't that right?" she asked quietly.

"That's absolutely right," Trevor said. He slapped the table lightly with his palm to emphasize the point and drained his beer to show her he was capable of finishing things finally and absolutely, absolutely and finally. He looked her right in the eye while he did it.

Aurora got up and went around and seated herself in his lap. She gave him a lavish hug and a nice kiss on the cheek and smelled around a little for good measure, enough to last her for approximately six months.

"Regrettably, my answer is no," she said. "However, I hope you'll help me get a cab before you leave. You've entertained me quite royally and I had planned to have you to my house for breakfast, but now that we're quits forever I suppose you'll have to rush off to look for a sunset, even though it's only dawn and you aren't likely to find one for a number of hours."

Trevor laid his cheek wistfully against the breast that had almost broken his wrist.

"Oh, well, I didn't mean it," he said. "I was just hoping to convince you I meant it. It was the only thing left to try."

Aurora went on holding him. He had always been quite comfortable to hold, and, when all was said and done, he was such an innocent, such a child.

"You couldn't ultimatum your way out of a paper bag," she said. "It's a gift you don't have—not your true character at all. If I were you I wouldn't try it, except with me. We've had all these years in which to mellow together, and I appreciate such little gestures, but I'm not sure a younger woman would."

Trevor chuckled, more or less into her bosom. "No, they massacre me," he said. "You know, it's a strange thing, Aurora. I only feel mellow when I'm with you."

"I'm touched," Aurora said. "How do you feel the rest of the time?"

Trevor looked up at her, but didn't answer at once. The first true rays of sunlight slipped into the courtyard through a crack in the board fence, and the old, old Mexican woman came out with a broom and began to sweep up the scraps of tortilla that the rat had missed. She seemed no more interested than the rat had been in the fact that two well-dressed middle-aged Americans were sitting on the same chair, hugging one another at seven in the morning.

"I guess I feel a little desperate," Trevor said finally. "No one seems to understand what I say, you know. I don't really say much—I know that—but it would still be nice if someone understood me once in a while. But they don't, and I try to explain it, and then they don't understand the explanations either, and that's when I begin to worry that you'll get married, Aurora. Do you know what I mean?"

Aurora sighed and hugged him a little closer. "I know what you mean," she said. "I think you must come to my house and have a little breakfast."

CHAPTER XI

1.

At three that afternoon Emma and Rosie began to lose their nerve. Aurora's annual dinner party for Cecil was due to begin in only five hours, and nothing had been done. Trevor had been given breakfast and had gone away at ten, back to his yacht, and Aurora had disappeared into her bedroom for a nap. She had disappeared merrily, it seemed to Rosie, and had promised to reappear at one, but Emma had shown up at one to help, and the two of them had waited together for two hours, hearing no sound at all from upstairs.

"If she danced all night she's probably just tired," Emma said several times. "If I danced all night I'd be tired, and I'm young enough to be her daughter."

The wit, such as it was, was lost on Rosie, who was chewing a hangnail. She shook her head.

"You don't know your ma like I do, honey," Rosie said. "Dancin' just peps her up. That woman's got energy to spare, I can tell you that. She ain't asleep—she's up there mopin'. That's why I always hate to see Mr. Waugh come to town. She has a good time while he's here, but the minute he leaves things go bad. I never seen such sinking spells as she has after Mr. Waugh leaves. She's up there having one right now."

"How do you know? I think she's just asleep." Emma was trying to be optimistic.

Rosie continued to nibble at her cuticle. "I know," she said. "I don't get this nervous for nothing."

When three o'clock came around both of them knew something had to be done. Aurora would be madder at them for not intervening in time than she would be for having her nap interrupted, Emma reasoned. Rosie gave the nap theory no credence, but she agreed that action was called for and reluctantly followed Emma upstairs. The door to the bedroom was closed. At the sight of it they both lost their nerve and stood stupidly in front of it for two minutes, until the spectacle of their own cowardice became intolerable. Emma knocked softly, and when there was no answer timidly pushed the door inward.

They both saw at once that Aurora was up. She was sitting at her dressing table, in her blue dressing gown, with her back to the door, and she gave no indication at all that she had heard it open. She was staring at the mirror, and her hair was in wild disarray.

"We got the bull by the horns now, honey," Rosie said. Mostly out of a desire to protect Emma she hurried into the room as if nothing was wrong and went straight over to her boss. The look in Aurora's eyes was the look Rosie most dreaded—a look of clear, unfocused hopelessness. Her face was composed, but it was not the face of the gay woman who had had such a good time at breakfast, only a few hours before.

"All right, quit mopin'" Rosie said quickly.

"Momma, please," Emma said. "Don't stare at the mirror that way. What's wrong?"

"Quit mopin', I said," Rosie repeated. "Get up from there. You got a dinner to cook, if you ain't forgotten. Don't sit there feelin' sorry for yourself. That ain't gonna get your dinner cooked."

Aurora turned her head briefly and met her maid's eye. Her own were completely without feeling.

"You think I'm feeling sorry for myself, do you?" she said. "I suppose you'd like a raise for supplying me with that little diagnosis."

She glanced at Emma before turning her gaze back to the mirror. "I suppose that's what you think too, Emma," she said.

"For God's sake, I don't know what's wrong," Emma said. "Neither of us know what's wrong. What *is* wrong?"

Aurora shrugged but didn't answer.

"Momma, please answer," Emma said. "I hate it when you won't tell me what's wrong."

"Ask Mrs. Dunlup," Aurora said. "I'm sure she knows me better than I know myself anyway. The truth is I was not prepared to have the two of you enter my bedroom. I do not wish to be visited—that should be plain enough. I would consider it a kindness if the two of you would take yourselves and your opinions away. I might begin to feel vicious at any moment, and for your own sakes I'd rather we didn't risk a confrontation right now. Two people I know might not survive it."

"Go ahead an' get mad," Rosie said, hardly able to breathe she was so tense.

Aurora said nothing. She picked up a hairbrush and idly hit her palm with it a few times. Her eyes were still focused on nothing.

"We don't know what to do about dinner," Emma said. "Please talk. Can't you just give us some instructions?"

Aurora lifted the brush and gave her hair a few hopeless strokes. "All right, Emma," she said, not turning around. "I do not like inflicting myself on people when I am in my present mood, but I see you aren't going to give me any choice. Evidently I no longer have the privilege of deciding when I'm to have company and when I'm not."

"That's right," Rosie said, her voice a little hollow from the bluff she was trying to pull. "We're gonna barge right in on you whenever we feel like it from now on."

Aurora turned on her. "You listen, Rosie," she said. "Talk as much as you like, but you better have another job lined up if you choose to accuse me of self-pity again. I don't like it."

"Shoot, I feel sorry for myself all the time," Rosie said retreating. "Don't ever'body?"

"No," Aurora said.

"A lot of people do," Emma said nervously, trying to help Rosie out.

Aurora whirled on her. "I was not addressing you, and you have very little knowledge of what you're talking about," she said. "There are times when one is ashamed to be seen, and I was in the midst of such a time when the two of you barged in. It was most thoughtless of you. Evidently the two of you concluded that I am so weak or so feeble-minded that I would forget my own dinner party, so you came up to prompt me. I wish you hadn't. I have been giving dinner parties for a great many years and I am quite capable of preparing a dinner in considerably less time than I have left. I had no intention of shirking my duties as a hostess, which is apparently what you both assumed I was about to do."

"Don't go jumpin' on me," Rosie said, on the verge of tears. "I'm half crazy anyway."

"Yes, you're getting much less than you deserve out of this life," Aurora said. "I happen to have the opposite problem. I happen to be getting better than I deserve. Trevor Waugh never fails to bring that home to me. Why that happens to be so I don't know, but even if I could figure it out it wouldn't be any of your business, that I can see.

"Nor yours," she said hotly, turning back to Emma. She stopped, her bosom heaving, and considered herself in the mirror for a moment. "It's odd," she said. "My lower lip seems fuller when I'm unhappy."

Emma and Rosie exchanged hopeful looks, but their optimism was premature. Aurora was staring again, and once her chest stopped heaving she seemed even more drained of energy and spirit than she had before her little outburst.

"All right," Emma said. "I'm sorry we came in without warning you. We'll go away and leave you alone."

Aurora looked straight ahead. A tear had leaked out of one eye. It made its way down one cheek, but no more followed.

"No need for you to go now," she said. "You've seen me at my worst."

She looked around at Rosie, sighed, then tightened her lips and drew back her fist in a weak mockery of anger. "I'll self-pity you," she said tiredly. "Would you please make me some tea?"

"Make you a bucketful," Rosie said, so glad the tension was finally broken that she sniffled a little as she went out.

"We're dreadfully sorry," Emma said, squatting down by her mother's chair.

Aurora looked at her and nodded. "Yes, that's you, Emma," she said. "You've apologized three or four times now for doing something that was perfectly natural. In fact, you may have been right. I might have sat right there and let my dinner party collapse. I'm afraid you're just going to apologize your way through life, and you'll be sorry if you do."

"What was I supposed to do?" Emma asked. "Kick you while you were down?"

Aurora began to brush her hair in something like earnest. "If you had any instinct you would have," she said. "It's certainly the only chance you'll get to kick me."

"Your lower lip *is* fuller when you're unhappy," Emma said to change the subject.

Aurora considered it. "Yes, I'm afraid it makes me look a good deal more passionate than I am," she said. "I've never quite lived up to my lower lip."

"How was old Trevor?" Emma asked.

Aurora looked down at her with a touch of hauteur. "Old Trevor is no older than I," she said. "You might keep that in mind. Old Trevor and old Aurora had a very nice evening, thank you, and in point of fact old Trevor is very nearly ideal. What do you think made me so gloomy? Unfortunately he timed our whole life wrong. I didn't need him when I had him and now I need him and don't want him. He even offered to take an apartment in New York this time. Considering that he loathes it there, that was extremely sweet of him. I'd have Bloomingdale's and

Bendel's, and the Met and the Metropolitan, and a decent Sunday newspaper for a change. I'd also have a nice warm loving man like Trevor. That's practically everything my nature craves."

"Do it then," Emma said. "Go marry him."

Aurora looked her over thoughtfully. "Yes, you have a good deal more of your grandmother's nature than you have of mine," she said. "She was a great advocate of half measures too."

She got up and wandered over to the window to see how her back yard looked. Life was beginning to return to her in little stages. She tried singing and found that she was in good voice. It made her feel even better, and she looked down at her daughter tauntingly.

"Was Daddy a half measure?" Emma asked. "You never tell me anything important. How much of your life was he? I need to know."

Aurora came back to the dressing table and began to brush her hair vigorously. "Thirty to thirty-five percent," she said crisply. "Somewhere in that range."

"Poor Daddy," Emma said. "That's not very much."

"No, but it was steady," Aurora said.

"I wasn't sympathizing with you, I was sympathizing with Daddy," Emma said.

"Oh, naturally. I'm sure you prefer to think I made your father miserable, but in fact I didn't. His life was quite agreeable to him—a good deal more so than mine has been to me."

"I wish you'd tell me about your wicked past," Emma said. "Sometimes I don't feel that I know you well."

Aurora laughed. She was enjoying brushing her hair. It had the kind of lights it should have, which pleased her. She got up and went to her closet to begin thinking about what to wear.

"I have no time to reveal myself just now," she said. "If I had any time to spare I'd run out and buy a new dress. Unfortunately I do not have time. I'm having a rather exotic goulash tonight—this will be a real test. If Cecil comes up with a dry plate we'll know he's superhuman."

"Why were you so blue?" Emma asked.

"Because I ought to marry Trevor and make him happy and in

the process lead the life I was meant to lead," Aurora said. "Unfortunately I don't think I'm going to achieve the life I was meant to lead. At the moment the line of my life seems to be pointed off into nowhere. Trevor seems to be having trouble with his women, and he's only going to have more as he gets older. It's rather disgusting that I don't care enough about him to haul him out of his stews, but evidently I don't. There are times when I find myself an unrewarding person. It's not a feeling I enjoy, and Trevor almost always causes it."

She reflected for a moment, twisting her rings. "It's a good thing my hair still looks nice," she said.

"It's also a good thing you're in a better mood," Emma said. "I never know how we get through this dinner party anyway. I never know why we even try."

"I think that's quite plain," Aurora said. "It's a social necessity you forced upon us by marrying Thomas. If you hadn't, it's certainly not likely that I'd be entertaining Cecil, though actually I suppose he's a decent sort."

At that moment Rosie came in with the tea, and the phone rang. Aurora nodded for Rosie to take it. Rosie said hello and immediately handed the phone to Aurora.

"Hello, Vernon. When were you planning to come over here?" Aurora asked. She listened a moment, lifting her eyebrows.

"Vernon, if I expected you to be in the way I would hardly have asked you," she said. "I don't have time just now to deal with your self-doubts. If you're afraid to risk yourself in my company perhaps you ought to huddle in your car making phone calls for the rest of your life. That's certainly safe enough, though it's rather ridiculous behavior. You come along whenever you've got your nerve up."

"All right, remember what I told you," Rosie said when Aurora put down the phone. "I got loyalties to that man. You better not mistreat him."

"Don't be silly. I was just trying to make him feel wanted," Aurora said, going rapidly to her closet. "I wish to have my tea in private, if no one minds, and then I assure you we're going to get cracking on our little party. Cecil Horton is going to get a goulash the like of which he's never reckoned with before."

Before Emma and Rosie could get out of the room she had thrown off her dressing gown and pulled a half dozen dresses out of her closet, strewing some on her bed, some on her sofa, and some in the window nook, all the while continuing to brush her shining hair.

2.

EMMA'S EVENING started with a fight—par for the course on the evening of her mother's annual dinner for Cecil. The ostensible cause of the fight was a new tie, which she-had bought Flap on her way home that afternoon. She had bought it in a nice men's shop in the River Oaks shopping center, and it had cost nine dollars. That was extravagant and she knew it, but she still had most of the money her mother had given her to buy clothes with, so it was really her mother's extravagance, not hers. Besides, it was a wonderful tie, black with deep red lines in it, and she would probably have bought it even if she had been spending their own money.

Flap, in a bad mood anyway, took offense at the very sight of the tie and refused to consider even putting it on so Emma could see how nice he looked in it.

"I won't wear it," he said flatly. "You just bought it hoping it would make me look good in the eyes of your mother. I know you. You're a coward to the end. You're just a Quisling where your mother is concerned. You're always trying to make me appear to be what she wants me to be. If you were loyal to me you wouldn't care what I wore."

He said it so meanly and looked at the nice tie so contemptuously that Emma was stung to tears, though she was ashamed of letting such meanness affect her and tried to hold them back. All that did was make her eyes sting and her chest feel tight.

"It isn't just for this one dinner," she said. "We'll probably go to other dinner parties in our lives, you know. You haven't bought a new tie since I've known you. It's horrible to be mean to somebody when they've just given you a present, don't you know that?"

"Well, I don't like your motives," he said.

"My motives are better than your manners," she said, getting angry. You like to spoil things just to prove you can. That's the tackiest thing about you. Also it's so predictable. You always do it. Every time I feel really happy you try to spoil it."

"Come on," he said. "Don't tell me buying a new tie made you feel really happy."

"Of course it did," Emma said. "You don't understand me. I felt really happy thinking how nice it would look with your blue suit. You're too dumb to understand that kind of happiness."

"Just watch who you're calling dumb," Flap said. "I don't happen to be dumb."

"I wish I wasn't pregnant," Emma said in a shaking voice. "I don't like being pregnant by someone little and mean and tacky."

She went off to the bathroom and stifled her tears. It stopped up her head but it was worth it not to give him the satisfaction of making her cry. When she came out Flap was crying, which shocked her.

"I'm sorry," he said. "I was horrible. The thought of your mother makes me irrational. I'll wear the tie, but please tell me you didn't mean what you said about wishing you weren't pregnant."

"Oh, for God's sake," she said, relaxing at once. "Of course I didn't mean it. I was just trying to hold my own. Go wash your face."

He emerged from the bathroom looking friendly again, but both of them were in a shaky state when they dressed. "I don't know why we do this to ourselves," he said.

"It'll be all right once we get there," Emma said. "It's just thinking about it that makes me nervous. It's sort of like going to the dentist."

"That's true," Flap said. "It's like going to the dentist. My point is that going to a dinner party oughtn't to feel like going to the dentist. And furthermore, going to the dentist almost always hurts."

"My hair has no shine," Emma said, contemplating it with

annoyance. At the last minute she decided to change dresses, and Flap, forgetting that he had promised to wear the new tie, forgetting even that he had a new tie, put on an old one. Cecil arrived just as Emma was trying to decide whether it was worth it to risk another scene to remind Flap about the new tie. She was also trying to hook her dress.

"Hi, Toots," Cecil said, patting her shoulder and squeezing her arm. He was wearing an ancient three-piece suit, his traditional garb for going to Aurora's house. The minute he walked in he spotted the new tie lying on the couch, took a fancy to it, and asked if he could wear it, since nobody else was. Flap was embarrassed. Cecil said he thought it was the best-looking tie he'd ever seen.

"Yeah, I wish I'd hung myself with it," Emma said, to Cecil's mystification. She gave up on the evening and went to the bathroom to finish hooking her dress. When she came out Cecil was wearing the new tie and looking highly pleased, and Flap managed to whisper that he'd make it up to her somehow.

"That's all right," Emma said. "I'd just as soon have it to hold against you."

Cecil drove them, whistling as he drove. Emma and Flap were in a state of great tension, and Emma thought she might eventually scream if Cecil didn't stop whistling. When they were about halfway there he stopped and said, "Oh, boy."

"Oh, boy what?" Emma asked.

"I always look forward to your mother's cooking," Cecil said. "I never know what I'm eatin' but you can't beat it for tasty."

Aurora greeted them at the door. She was wearing a splendid long green gown that she thought might be Hungarian. She also wore a good deal of silver jewelry.

"Yes, it's high time you got here," she said, smiling. "Cecil, there you are and your tie is little short of magnificent. I've never seen anything so becoming. You ought to buy yourself a tie like that some time, Thomas."

"Can I help with the drinks?" Flap asked, keeping his eyes on the floor.

"That's considerate of you," Aurora said, looking him over. "However, it's so rarely that I get to see you that I don't think I'll let you rush off just yet. My friend Vernon is bringing us some margaritas any minute now."

She tucked her arm in Cecil's and led him off toward the patio, Emma and Flap trailing far in their wake.

"I've ruined everything, right?" Flap said.

"Not if you shut up and stop being defensive," Emma said. "If you had worn it she wouldn't have said a word about it."

Rosie burst through the door at that moment carrying a tray of glasses. "What's wrong with you?" she asked, looking at Flap as if she had caught him stealing something.

Before Flap could answer Vernon came out of the kitchen carrying a pitcher of drinks. "Howdy, howdy," he said, shaking hands. Emma found herself wanting to giggle. She had never expected to see a little person who said howdy emerge from her mother's kitchen.

They found Aurora on the patio plying Cecil with pâté, and also with compliments, most of them about his health.

"Yes, it's quite wonderful the way men improve with age," she said. "I do believe your circulation is the best I've ever seen it, Cecil. It's a wonder some woman hasn't snatched you right up."

Cecil proved her point about his circulation by turning beet red. The sight seemed to embarrass Vernon, who turned red himself—for a minute the two of them were of a matching shade. "Well, the gang's all here and that's fine with me," Rosie said cryptically and hurried off to the kitchen.

Aurora was in a state of such high brilliance that Emma could hardly believe it. She bore almost no resemblance to the woman who had been staring lifelessly at her mirror only five hours earlier. She turned her full presence on Cecil, dazzling him just short of speechlessness. Emma munched her way through some excellent hors d'oeuvres and settled back to watch. Flap kept the hors d'oeuvres circulating and began to get drunk. He was so much more tense than anyone else that he was half drunk before he noticed that his mother-in-law was in a pleasant mood for once. She didn't seem to be trying to cut him off at the knees. Once he noticed, his relief was so great that in the process of loosening up he drank several more margaritas. By the time dinner was served he was so drunk he could hardly walk to the table. It occurred to him then that the reason Emma had been digging him with her elbow all evening was because he was drinking too much, but the realization came several margaritas too late.

By the time they got to the table Cecil was so red with pleasure that he couldn't have remembered who was President first, Eisenhower or Kennedy. Aurora was unrelenting. She filled his plate with such an enormous helping of goulash that even Cecil, in his bedazzlement, was momentarily taken aback.

"Good gracious, Aurora," he said. "I don't know if I can eat that much."

"Nonsense, Cecil, you're the guest of honor," Aurora said, smiling at him teasingly. "Besides, you know the Serbs."

In his drunkenness the remark amused Flap so much that he began to laugh, only to realize in the midst of a wild fit of laughter that it was going to cause him to vomit. He managed to excuse himself and dashed frantically down the hall.

Rosie watched from the kitchen doorway like an avenging angel. "I knew you was sick all along," she said.

Emma felt rather detached from it all—so much so that she was able to lose herself in enjoyment of her mother's food. She decided she didn't care to watch her mother be brilliant, so she watched Vernon instead. He never took his eyes off Aurora, except when he sensed, as he did from time to time, that someone was watching him watch her, at which times he stared earnestly at his food for a little while until he felt it was safe to watch again. While she was watching Vernon, Flap returned looking pale but no less drunk, and Aurora paused for a second from a story she was telling Cecil and took a long look at him.

"Thomas, you poor thing, you've obviously been immersed in your studies again," she said. "I suppose you worry too. Cerebral people have so much more to worry about than the likes of you and I, Cecil. Wouldn't you agree?" She settled her chin comfortably on one palm and began to watch Cecil attempt to cope with what was left of his goulash.

Cecil had become so relaxed that he gave Aurora a pat on the shoulder before continuing to eat. With the help of a good deal of wine he had managed to wash down most of the goulash, and what remained posed no problem for him. Aurora had for a time wavered between goulash and bouillabaisse, and evidence of her wavering remained, in the shape of a number of prawns. The prawns, and a quantity of rice which he had reserved, were the means by which Cecil intended to see that everything came out even, as it should; and he went about the last stages of his work with the skill of an instinctive tactician, marshaling the remaining rice in such a way as to utilize to the fullest its absorbent properties. Using the prawns as pushers, he pushed up little mounds of rice and moved them around in the soupy remains of the goulash until they had absorbed as much of the liquid as possible. Once the rice was gone he used the prawns to swab up what remained of the soup. Aurora watched raptly.

"Virtuosity has to be admired," she mumbled, winking at Emma.

Once the soup was gone Cecil coolly moved a leaf of lettuce from his salad plate and used it to clean his plate until it was shining and dry. Then he put his knife and fork across the top of the plate, and the whole service looked clean enough to be used in a *New Yorker* ad.

"Well, *salud,* Cecil," Aurora said, downing what was left of her wine. Emma downed what was left of hers too and then drank another glass. Soon she quietly followed Flap into drunkenness. For about five minutes she felt gay and high, and made what she considered a witty attempt to turn the conversation to political topics. Her mother merely waggled a spoon at her and proceeded to serve a rich dessert. By the time it was finished Emma had passed through the gay phase of her drunkenness and went into a sleepy phase that didn't really end until an hour and a half later, back home on her couch, when she noticed that her husband had revived and was determined to seduce her in her good clothes. That was fine, except that the liquor upset her timing, particularly when her timing was given no warning, and thanks to the element of surprise or something she had a small premature orgasm; before she could manage to have the one she really wanted, Flap withdrew.

"Idiot," she said. "I wasn't through."

Flap was, however. "I thought you were," he said.

"No," Emma said, really annoyed.

Flap's mind was elsewhere. "I wonder if I said good night to Dad," he said. "I can't remember."

"Call him and say good night now," Emma said. "There's not going to be anything else to do this evening. You never seem to realize that things are different when I'm drunk. Why do you always seduce me when I can't concentrate? I think it's becoming a pattern."

"Don't talk to me about patterns when I'm happy," he said. "The worst evening of the year is over. The relief is wonderful."

"Great, so I get eight seconds of sex," Emma said, not pleasantly. She knew what she had wanted, and with a little more help she could have gotten it; the fact that Flap hadn't noticed made the whole evening seem stupid. Everything was in-between. She wasn't dissatisfied enough to have a real fight, nor satisfied enough to go to sleep. Flap was in bed and asleep before she got her party clothes hung up. While she was sitting in front of their bookcase in her nightgown trying to spot something she might want to read, the phone rang.

"You weren't asleep?" Aurora said.

"No," Emma said, surprised.

"I was thinking of you," Aurora said. "I was thinking you might want to wish me good night. I believe you said it once, but I wouldn't mind hearing it again."

"Did Cecil upset you?" Emma asked.

"Of course not," Aurora said. "If the worst a man can do is clean his plate with his food there's not much harm in him. Vernon's helping Rosie do the dishes. There's not much harm in him, either. I suppose I'm keeping you away from your husband."

"No, he's asleep. He drank too much."

"I noticed," Aurora said. "It's one of the things I like about Thomas. He's capable of getting drunk. It's a human trait, at least."

"It's a little too human for my purposes," Emma said.

"You're mumbling," Aurora said. "Thomas is not without instinct. If he hadn't rendered himself helpless I might have attacked him."

"You never call me at night," Emma said. "What's wrong? Are you scared of Vernon?"

"You've seen him twice," Aurora said. "Do you really think anyone need be scared of him?"

"No," Emma said. "What are you scared of then?"

Aurora thought of her daughter, young and pregnant, innocent of so much, only twenty-two, and she smiled to herself. Picturing Emma, probably in her nightgown, probably reading, tipped back some inner balance that she had felt herself about to lose. She straightened her back and picked up her hairbrush.

"Oh, it's naught, it's naught," she said. "One of my little sinking spells—that's all. You've fixed me already. It's just that I sometimes get the feeling that nothing will ever change."

"I know that feeling," Emma said. "I have it all the time."

"It's not appropriate to you," Aurora said. "You're young. Life is sure to change every five minutes for you."

"No, it goes right on the same for me. You're the spontaneous one, remember. I thought it changed every five minutes for *you*."

"It did, up until a week or two ago," Aurora said. "Now it feels like it's never going to change anymore. You know how impatient I am. If it doesn't change soon I'll become hysterical."

"Maybe Vernon will change it," Emma said.

"He better try. Otherwise I'll have wrecked my car for nothing. I've left him down there with Rosie. Wouldn't it be horrible if she took him away from me? No one's ever taken a man away from me before."

"Thinking of marrying him?" Emma asked.

"Of course not," Aurora said.

"Despite the fact that I'm pregnant you still seem to have plenty of suitors," Emma said.

"I don't call it plenty," Aurora said. "I've been forced to banish two in recent weeks. For practical purposes I'm down to Alberto and Vernon, neither of whom are altogether suitable."

"They're both sweeties, though," Emma said.

"Yes, if one doesn't care to put too fine a point on it," Aurora said. "The brutal fact is that they're both old, short, and afraid of me. If I stacked them one on top of the other they might be tall enough, but they'd still be old and afraid of me."

"Everybody's afraid of you. Why don't you try being gentle for a change?"

"I do try—it's just that I seem to be prone to exasperation," Aurora said. "Rosie is here by her own choice, in case you were wondering. Royce has left home, and I expect she finds it more cheerful here."

"Poor Rosie," Emma said. "Maybe you should let her have Vernon, if she wants him. They speak the same language at least."

"Vernon and I speak the same language, I believe," Aurora said. "I speak it well and he speaks it badly, that's all. In fact he hardly ever speaks at all, in any language, so your suggestion is invalid. Besides, the fact that Rosie speaks English as poorly as he does doesn't mean they'd be happy together. For a mother-to-be you're not getting much less naïve, Emma, I must say."

"I just mentioned it because I know you don't want him yourself," Emma said. "I thought he might be nice for Rosie. What's wrong with you?"

"I don't know," Aurora said. "I used to only feel desperate just before my periods, but now it's apt to happen anytime."

"That's ridiculous," Emma said. "Desperate about what? You're perfectly fine."

"I don't know why I'm talking to you," Aurora said. "There you sit, on the threshold of life, as I believe they say. I bet you're in your little nightgown, reading some little book or other. Don't tell me I'm all right when I'm not. While you're sitting there on the threshold I'm looking out the back door, and I don't like what I see. Who knows when my last chance might slip by?"

"Last chance for what?" Emma said.

"For someone!" Aurora said. "Just someone. Or do you think I ought to give up in deference to your father's memory and dig in my garden for the next thirty years? It's far from a simple problem. Only a saint could live with me, and I can't live with a saint. Older men aren't up to me and younger men aren't interested. No matter how brilliant a child you manage to have, I'm hardly the sort to content myself with being a grandmother. I don't know what's going to happen."

"Go grab Vernon then," Emma said, yawning. The wine was coming back on her.

"I can't," Aurora said. "I don't think Vernon took the slightest notice of women before he met me. What's one to do about a man who's waited fifty years to notice women?"

"You mean you smashed your car into a fifty-year-old virgin?" Emma said.

"If such a thing is possible, I've done it," Aurora said.

"Oil millionaires usually have girls tucked away somewhere," Emma said.

"Oh, if only Vernon had one," Aurora said. "That would be perfect. Then I could have the thrill of taking him away from her. But I've sniffed around thoroughly and there's not a trace of a girl. I think that Lincoln is my only competition."

"All this is very reassuring," Emma said. "Your life is as much of a mess as mine. Experience must not be everything."

"Hardly," Aurora said. "Now I've brushed my hair and filed my nails, only my hair was already brushed and my nails already filed. I've been doing a great deal that's superfluous lately. That can't be a good sign."

"Vernon's probably biting his," Emma said. "We've been talking fifteen minutes."

"What a boor your husband is to go to sleep so early," Aurora said. "He didn't make a single witty remark all evening, and his tie was dull. I can't understand why you married someone so unenergetic. Energy is the very least one should be able to expect from a man. There's no visible evidence that Thomas does you any good at all. Your hair is dull, and he evidently expects you to raise a child in a garage."

"We don't plan to live here forever," Emma said. "I hope you'll be careful with Vernon. He may be a tender plant."

"What can I do, with you and Rosie protecting him?" Aurora said. "He has no business being a tender plant at his age, but you don't have to worry. I may be impossible, but I'm not a lawn mower."

3.

AURORA HUNG up, sighed, and went downstairs to find Vernon and Rosie sitting rather somberly at the kitchen table. The kitchen was spotless. Rosie had her raincoat on and her purse in her hands, but she did not seem eager to leave. Vernon was nervously shuffling a deck of cards.

"You two are hardly encouraging," Aurora said. "Why are you so quiet?"

"I'm plumb talked out," Rosie said, although she had said almost nothing all evening. Her face looked a little sunken. When Aurora sat down, she got up to leave.

"I better get going," she said. "I don't want to miss that last bus."

Aurora got up again and walked with her to the door. "Thank you for staying," she said. "I won't make a habit of keeping you this late."

"You didn't keep me," Rosie said. "I was just purely too lonesome to leave. Emma looked a little peaked, I thought."

Aurora nodded, but didn't comment. Rosie loved to speculate about Emma's unhappiness, and it was not something she wanted to get into a conversation about just then. She said good night. The sidewalk was pale in the moonlight and she stood in the doorway and watched Rosie walk along it, past the Lincoln, toward the bus stop at the corner. The sound of her heels on the concrete was quite distinct in the still night.

She glanced at Vernon and saw that he was still fiddling with his deck of cards. For some reason, or no reason, the hopefulness in her, which had pulsed quite strongly for part of the evening, began to fade and grow faint, in time, almost, with her maid's fading footsteps. To stop it from going out altogether she shut the door and turned back to the table.

"Ort to have driven her home, I guess," Vernon said.

Aurora had picked up a teapot, thinking to make them some tea, but something, some nervousness or uncertainty in his tone,

227

irritated her. She left the teapot where it was and went at once to the table.

"Why?" she asked. "Why ought you to have taken her home? I fail to see that you have any obligation of that sort at all. Rosie stayed here by her own choice, and she is quite habituated to riding the bus. It isn't raining and she isn't a hardship case, despite her present circumstances. She's a grown adult who's rather more accustomed than most to fending for herself. If you don't mind, I wish you'd explain to me why you made that remark."

Vernon looked up and saw that she was pale with anger. He was horrified—he couldn't think what he had done that was so bad.

"Don't know," he said honestly. "She looked lonesome, an' her house ain't much out of my way."

"Thank you," Aurora said. "Why don't you leave, then? You can probably catch her at the bus stop, and if not you can chase down the bus. I doubt that any bus can outrun a fancy car like yours. If you don't mind my saying so, that car of yours is more suited to someone in the heroin traffic than to a respectable businessman."

It suddenly occurred to her that she knew almost nothing about the man sitting at her table. "Are you in the heroin traffic?" she asked.

Vernon was having trouble with his lungs. "I didn't mean nothin' wrong," he said.

Aurora watched him, her teeth clenched. Then she stopped watching him and stared at the wall. "Yes, go on, apologize five or six times," she said. "It doesn't matter now."

"But what?" Vernon asked. "But what?"

"Oh, shut up," Aurora said. "I don't want to talk. It doesn't matter now. I suppose I should be grateful you bothered to stay as long as you did. No doubt it was very foolish of me to suppose the evening might not be quite at an end. Of course it was also foolish of me not to notice what a fancy you've taken to Rosie."

Vernon stared at her, trying to understand. He was hearing a language he had never heard before—a language not so much of

228

words, but of emotions. He didn't understand it at all—he just knew that everything depended on his being able to set things right.

"I ain't a fancy," he began desperately. "That ain't what. It's just . . . I was being polite."

The pain in his voice was compelling enough to cause Aurora to look at him again. "Yes, you're much too polite, I know that," she said. "It's a pity I'm not, but it doesn't matter now. It happens that you were my guest tonight, and Rosie is not the only woman in the world who is sometimes lonely. I have no claim on you and I certainly don't want any now, but it would have been only mannerly of you to sit and drink a cup of tea with me before you rush off to huddle in your car again. However, I'm sure that's much too much to ask of a busy man like you. You were ready to seize any excuse to rush off, weren't you?"

Her eyes held his, and Vernon knew there was no point in denying it.

"Maybe so, but you don't understand," he said.

"I understand you didn't really want to stay," Aurora said. "Nothing is more basic than that. Either you were scared to or you just didn't want to. The first explanation isn't very flattering to you, and the second isn't at all flattering to me."

"Scairt, yeah," Vernon said. "I don't know. I never met nobody like you, nor been in nothin' like this. Why wouldn't I be scairt?"

Aurora turned so livid with fury that she felt her skin might split. A sense of wrongness overwhelmed her and she hit the table with both hands. The sight of Vernon, honest, nervous, and maddeningly meek, was unendurable. When she hit the table he jumped.

"I don't want you to be scared!" she yelled. "I'm just a human being! I just wanted you to sit and drink some tea . . . with me . . . and be my companion for a few minutes. I'm not going to pour the tea on you unless you drive me completely out of my wits with your reticence, or your stupid inarticulateness. I'm not scary! Don't tell me I'm scary! There's nothing frightening about me. You're just all cowards!"

She sank into a chair and hit the table several more times

before the energy began to go out of her. Vernon stayed in his chair; he didn't try to move. Aurora was panting from her outrage.

"Why don't I make the tea?" Vernon said after a minute. "You're all upset about something."

He said it without the slightest sense of irony. Aurora shook her head in acquiescence and waved him toward the stove.

"Certainly. I'm glad to see that terror hasn't paralyzed you," she said. "Good God. What a useless . . . stupid . . ." She shook her head again and left the sentence unfinished.

She watched Vernon without much interest as he made the tea. He did know how, which was something, but by the time he brought the two cups to the table both anger and energy had left her and she was as she had been that afternoon—spiritless, convinced of nothing except that there was not much point in trying to make things right. Things would never be right.

"Thank you, Vernon," she said, taking her cup. He sat down opposite her. With a teacup in his hands he seemed to feel more secure.

"If I could just talk like you do it'd be an improvement," he said.

"Oh, Vernon, don't bother about me," Aurora said, noting that he actually was the nice little man she had thought him to be— only it didn't matter.

"I was not mad at you because of the way you talk," she said. "I was mad because you were scared when you had no reason to be and because you were all set to rush off and leave me with no one to drink tea with. That's one of the only things I look forward to about an evening like this, you know—someone to drink tea with at the end of it. For all I know, the whole point of civilization is to provide one with someone to drink tea with at the end of an evening. Otherwise you have no one with whom to talk over whatever may have happened during the evening. Dinner parties are often more fun to talk about than they are to attend— at least they aren't complete until they've been discussed."

She stopped, aware that she was making no sense to Vernon.

"In any case, I would like to apologize for my outburst," she said. "I'm sorry I accused you of designs on Rosie. You saw a chance to escape and be polite at the same time, that's all. It doesn't matter now."

The fact that she kept saying that it didn't matter made Vernon very uneasy. "How am I gonna learn if I don't make mistakes?" he said.

"You aren't going to learn," Aurora said. "Not from me. You'd be dead before you got to the third lesson. It was very wrong of me to encourage you—I'm sorry I did. We're worlds apart, or light-years, or however you want to measure it. I'm entirely to blame, as usual. I'm a very ill-tempered, disagreeable woman."

"I thought it was my fault," Vernon said.

"Sure, like the car wreck," Aurora said. "You can't get away with that here, Vernon. I'm harder to fool than that young patrolman."

"It's just ignorance," Vernon said. "That's my trouble."

"Of course. It's hard to learn much if you live your life inside a car," Aurora said. "That Lincoln is like a big egg, you know. Frankly, I don't think you want to hatch."

"Didn't much care until I met you," he said.

"Please don't leave off your pronouns," she said. "You've no idea how it irritates me to hear people chop their sentences that way. I really meant to bring you out and show you a bit of my world, but now you've discouraged me."

"I can still take a run at it, can't I?" Vernon asked.

"No," Aurora said, determined to strip him of every shred of hope. "Go on to Alberta, where you were going to begin with. You'll be more comfortable, I'm sure."

"You'd make a poker player," Vernon said, trying a smile. "It's hard to tell when you're bluffin'."

"Wrong," Aurora said. "Ladies never bluff. They may change their minds, but that's a different matter."

"Folks is right," Vernon said. "Love means trouble."

"Oh, hush," Aurora said. "I made you fall in love with me, if that's what you did. It was my whimsey, and certainly none of your doings."

She found that she had stopped wanting to talk about anything. She wished very much that Trevor were back, because he would have hugged her, if he had been there, and to be hugged was what she wanted most. She could have forgiven almost any-thing for a nice hug. She looked longingly at Vernon, but he didn't know the meaning of the look. What she felt was too subtle for him.

His instinct was not completely passive, though. He could tell that she needed something, so he brought the teapot and care-fully poured her some more tea.

"There you are," he said hopefully, starting to go back to his side of the table.

Aurora reached out with a foot and dragged a chair from one end of the table around to her side. "I do think you could at least sit on the same side of the table with me," she said.

Vernon sat down, a little nervously, in profile to her. His profile was only a couple of bumps, and Aurora recovered a touch of her good humor in contemplating it. When she had had enough she reached down and caught the leg of his chair and with a grunt or two managed to twist it so he was more or less facing her.

"There, now we're having tea, Vernon," she said prettily. "You're on my side of the table, you're more or less facing me, I can see your eyes instead of just your chin and the end of your nose, and you're close enough that I can hit you if you irritate me. This is almost civilized procedure."

Vernon's breast was all confusion. Aurora was smiling at him, which didn't fit with all the terrible things she had just said. She seemed exuberant again, and seemed to have forgiven him for all the wrong things he had done, but he knew he might do more wrong things at any moment. He jittered and tapped his fingers rapidly on his knees, hoping very much that he could manage not to do anything wrong. Generally when there was a woman around she was a waitress and there was a counter in between them, but there certainly wasn't a counter between him and Aurora.

"Jitter, jitter, jitter," she said. "Stop tapping your fingers."

Actually, watching him twitch had reminded her of the first small man in her life—a tiny dean from Harvard who had been her first lover and whose memory had remained surprisingly fresh after quite a number of years. His name was Fifoot, Dean Fifoot, so small and ugly, so energetic and competitive and intense—compensating constantly in every possible way—that neither her scruples nor her maidenhood had stood the slightest chance; she had lost both at the same time and never really recovered even the scruples, it seemed to her. If there had really been anything wrong with Trevor it had been that he was mild and lazy and tall and confident and had the bad fortune to follow upon a man with gigantic energies and ambitions and a small body. Trevor could never have imagined such hunger as her little dean had; she herself was only to encounter its like again, briefly, in Alberto, when he was flush with his first great success as a singer. For that matter, Trevor would never have got the chance to sail her around on his boat if Dean Fifoot hadn't suddenly married a rich unattractive woman. Aurora could not recall that she had been precisely heartbroken—her heart had never had time to get focused exactly—but for several years thereafter she did feel that life was a comedown in some respects. And now there was another small man, in her very own kitchen, rattling his teacup against his saucer, worth six million dollars by his own admission, energies to burn, the need to compensate sticking out all over him, and yet without a speck of savoir-faire.

"It's just my luck," she said.

"What is?"

"You," she said. "Here I need a man of the world and I get a man of the oil fields."

Vernon looked puzzled.

"You're a very unrewarding person, in my view," Aurora went on. "You wait fifty years to fall in love for the first time, and then you pick me. I'm fiendishly difficult, as you've already discovered. Only years of experience could prepare any man to deal with me. You have the nerve to present yourself to me without a shred of experience, just when I need a lot of love and skillful handling. In short, you're a washout."

She sat back happily to watch him make what he could of *that* speech.

"How'd I know I was gonna meet you?" Vernon asked. "Chances was one in a million."

"What a ridiculous defense," Aurora said. "The point of my criticism was that you've lived fifty years and made no effort to meet anybody, that I can see. You're a perfectly nice, competent, efficient, friendly man, and you might have made some woman very happy, yet you've made no effort to use yourself at all. You've made no one really happy, not even yourself, and now you're so set in your ridiculous ways that you wouldn't know how to begin to relate to another person. It's shameful, really. You're a wasted resource. Furthermore, you're a resource I might have wanted."

"Ought to be ashamed of myself, I guess," Vernon said.

"Shame never made anybody happy," Aurora said. "It's one of those perfectly useless emotions, like regret. Meanwhile all around you people are starving."

"Well, I got half my life left, if nothing don't fall on me," Vernon said. "Maybe I can learn something."

"I doubt it," Aurora said. "The day we met you showed some promise, but I don't know where it went. You've allowed me to cow you. I guess you were just a flash in the pan."

Vernon stood up suddenly. He knew things were hopeless, but he couldn't stand to hear Aurora say it so cheerfully. "No, I'm just an ignorant fool," he said.

Aurora was on the point of telling him his remark contained a redundancy, but she noted just in time that she had tripped along too far and hurt his feelings.

"Now, now," she said. "Of course I apologize. Don't you have any sense of play at all? I was speaking in a spirit of fun. I just like to see how you react. Pay attention to the tone of my voice once in a while, for goodness' sake. I can't be serious all the time, can I? Are you trying to leave again just because I twitted you a little?"

Vernon sat back down. "I'm in a pickle," he said, thinking out loud. "I don't know whether I'm going or coming," he added, blushing.

Aurora accepted the blush as a sign of emotion, and decided she'd better be satisfied with that. She spent the last twenty minutes of the evening trying not to do anything that might upset him, but when he asked if he could come for breakfast she shook her head.

"I don't think you should bother, Vernon," she said. "I don't even think you really want to. We're a bigger puzzle to one another than we were the day we met. I'm glad you wanted me for your first sweetheart, but I'm a little too formidable for a first sweetheart. I might have made a nice last romance, but you haven't had your first one yet, have you?"

"Well, this," Vernon said.

When he got in his car to drive away, Aurora shook her head, in criticism of herself, and without another word turned and went back to her house.

Vernon drove away feeling so confused he was almost sick at his stomach.

4.

SOMETIME IN the night Aurora awoke. She hated to awake in the night and tried to will herself to stay asleep, but it didn't work. She woke into a state of deep *tristesse*—helpless and wordless. It was happening more and more often, and it was something she never told anyone about. It was too deep. She usually made a special effort to be gay after such nights; if anyone noticed anything out of the ordinary, it was Rosie, and Rosie held her peace.

When she knew she was awake, with the sadness upon her again, she got up and took her pillows and her comforter to the window nook and sat looking out the window. There was a moon, and the trees in her back yard cast deep shadows. It was a thoughtless state, a formless sadness; she could not even say whether what she missed was someone to want, or someone to want her, but the ache behind her breastbone was so pronounced that she occasionally hit herself, hoping that would make it loosen and go away. But the feeling that made the ache was too strong; her little blows didn't affect it. It was her old off-centeredness, or uncenteredness, a sense that something was stopping that hadn't ought to stop.

She had made every effort to remain active, to keep open to life, and yet life was beginning to resist her in unexpected ways. Men, some of them decent and good, seemed to march through her life almost daily, and yet they caused so little to stir within her that she had begun to be afraid—not just that nothing would ever stir again, but that she would stop wanting it to, cease caring whether it did or not, or even come to prefer that it didn't.

It was that fear, finally, that left her awake and tearless at her window late at night. She wasn't falling behind, slipping into some sort of widow's stupor; she was moving ahead, beyond reach. Her own daughter had suddenly made her realize it by quietly usurping her right to have a child. It was Emma's turn to have children, but what was it *her* turn to do? It had taken her daughter's pregnancy to make her realize how nearly impregnable she herself had become—impregnable in a variety of ways. Let her get a little stronger, a little older, a little more set in her ways, with a few more barricades of habit and routine, and no one would ever break in. Her ways would be her house and her garden and Rosie and one or two old friends, and Emma and the children she would have. Her delights would be conversation and concerts, the trees and the sky, her meals and her house, and perhaps a trip or two now and then to the places she liked best in the world.

Such things were all very well, yet the thought that such things were going to be her life for as far ahead as she could see made her sad and restless—almost as restless as Vernon, except that her fidgets were mostly internal and seldom caused her to do anything more compulsive than twisting her rings. As she sat at the window, looking out, her sense of the wrongness of it was deep as bone. It was not just wrong to go on so, it was killing. Her energies, it seemed to her, had always flowed from a capacity for expectation, a kind of hopefulness that had persisted year after year, in defiance of all difficulties. It was hopefulness, the expectation that something nice was bound to happen to her, that got her going in the morning and brought her contentedly to bed at night. For almost fifty years some secret spring inside her had kept feeding hopefulness into her bloodstream, and she had gone through her days expectantly, always eager for surprises and always finding them.

Now the stream seemed dry—probably there would be no more real surprises. Men had taken to fleeing before her, and soon her own daughter would have a child. She had always lived close to people; now, thanks to her own strength or her own particularity and the various quirks of fate, she was living at an intermediate distance from everybody, in her heart. It was wrong; she didn't want it to go on. She was forgetting too much—soon she would be unable to remember what she was missing. Even sex, she knew, would eventually relocate itself and become an appetite of the spirit. Perhaps it had already happened, but if it hadn't it soon would.

The worst of the sadness passed, but when it did she felt so wakeful that she knew she wouldn't sleep for the rest of the night. She went down, made tea, and got some cookies. Then she returned to her window nook and drank and ate, considering her options. So far as men went, all of the ones she knew were wrong, quite wrong. She had stopped feeling desperate, but she knew that unless something changed and changed soon she was going to do something sad—give up on herself in some way. She didn't sigh or flounce at the thought; she looked out her window at the dim yard and the cold facts. The cold facts seemed to be that unless she wanted to live alone for the rest of her life, in a general and rather quiescent way, she would have to hack her way into the best relationship she could get.

What seemed to be required was a somewhat cold blooded decision, and hot blood had been the way of her life. What was obvious was that if she were to wait for hot blood to take her any farther she would probably wait in vain. Miracles did happen, but there was no counting on them. Nothing would ever be right, but it was four in the morning and she was in her fiftieth year. She didn't want to surrender to everything middling, placid, empty. Better pride be let to fall, if pride was what it was that was reducing her spirit day by day.

She thought of the nice little man in the white car whose love she had idly called into being. It would probably be a very decent love, and it might even be possible to teach him to express it; but the thought of his decency didn't cause her to lift the phone. Instead, when her ship's clock told her it was five o'clock she lifted it and called her neighbor, General Hector Scott.

"Yes, General Scott here," he said, briskly and scratchily, as wide awake as if it were noon.

"Of course you're up, Hector," she said. "You've not let down your standards. I must admit that's something. However, I've decided to sue you."

"Sue *me?*" General Scott said, momentarily incredulous. "You're calling me at five A.M. to tell me you're going to sue me? That's the goddamnedst gall I've ever encountered, I can tell you that."

"Well, I'm not likely to relent now that my mind's made up," she said.

"Aurora, what in the hell's got into you?" he asked. "This is arrant nonsense. You can't sue me."

"Oh, I believe I'm well within my rights, Hector," she said. "I believe your whole position in regard to our car wreck was highly illegal. However, I like to think I'm a fair woman. I'm willing to invite you to breakfast, to give you a chance to plead your case. I don't see how anyone could be fairer than that."

"Yes, well, I'd like to give you a punch in the goddamn nose while we're talking of fair," the General said, his temper flaring at the memory of how coolly she had walked off and left him in the Cadillac.

"Hector, you're far too old to punch anyone," Aurora said. "Anything you got you can be sure you deserved, if you're speaking of inconvenience. Are you coming to breakfast or are you just going to stand there mouthing ineffectual threats?"

"What's become of your little gambler?" he asked.

"That is a matter that doesn't concern you at all," she said. "Are you coming over here or are you going to go run around with those silly dogs?"

"They are not silly, and of course I intend to run," the General said. "I invariably run. Then I'm coming over there and punch you right in the nose."

"Oh, sticks and stones, Hector," Aurora said. "How will you take your eggs?"

"Poached," the General said.

"All right," Aurora said. "Try not to exhaust yourself on your ridiculous little run, please. We have our lawsuit to discuss, and I won't have you flagging."

She hung up before he could utter another word. Three minutes later, not entirely to her surprise, someone began to bang on her front door. She put the phone back in its place and belted her robe. The banging stopped but the doorbell began to ring. Aurora put on her robe, got a hairbrush, and sauntered slowly downstairs, brushing her hair. She opened the front door and met the eye of a very angry red-faced general. He had on the gray sweat suit he wore to run in.

"I'll punch you in the nose, God damn you, and then I'll do my run," he said.

Aurora lifted her chin. "Un-uh," she said.

The General could scarcely see, he was so angry; but even in his fury he could detect a look of cool, rather careless challenge in Aurora's eyes. She had not even stopped brushing her hair.

"I want you to know that you're the most intolerable, arrogant bitch I've ever encountered in my life, and I've encountered a great many," the General said. He didn't hit her, but he could not refrain from giving her a good hard shove.

Aurora noted that he had nice firm, rather delicate hands, the hands of a far younger man. There was something to be said for men who kept themselves in trim. She caught herself just short of her stairway, and saw that his chest was heaving and his face very red.

"You think I'm a coward, don't you?" he said. "All these years I've loved you and what it comes down to is that you think I'm a goddamn coward."

"How long have you loved me, Hector?" she asked in a friendly tone.

"Years . . . years," he said heavily. "Since the forties. You know that. Since that party you gave us before I was sent to Midway. You remember that. Your baby had just been born and you were still nursing her. I remember the dress you wore."

Aurora smiled. "What amazing memories men have," she said. "I can barely remember that war, much less that party or that dress. Let me have your hand."

The General held it out. To his amazement she seemed to want to examine it. "Well, it was around then," he said. "I thought about you a lot while I was overseas.

"Pacific theater," he said, to help her memory.

Aurora linked her arm companionably in his and kept his hand. "I'm sure there were any number of sentimental scenes I'd enjoy remembering, if I could," she said. "You men have such patience too."

"How's that?" he asked.

"Never mind, dear," Aurora said. "I suppose I'm just feeling rather ashamed. In all these years I've never shown you my Renoir. You might come and take a look at it now, if you aren't in too great a hurry to get to your run. I think that's the least I can do for someone who's loved me twenty years."

General Scott instantly freed the hand she held, but only in order to grasp her more firmly in both his hands. The agitation of anger gave way to another, equally powerful agitation, and that increased when it became apparent that finally, finally, after all those years, Aurora had stopped being reluctant to be grasped.

"Aurora, I'm not interested in your art, I'm only interested in you," the General managed to say before passion choked him completely.

Aurora heard a new resonance in the familiar scratchy voice. She smiled, but ducked her head, so the smile was only for herself.

"Oh, well," she said, "never mind about it, Hector. My Renoir is not likely to walk away. We'll save it until all else fails."

She looked up and met his eye. The General felt a fool, an old frightened fool, but not so frightened or such a graceless fool as to question miracles. Amiably, rather merrily, and with a great deal more conversation, Aurora led him upstairs, to a place he had long since ceased to expect to go.

CHAPTER XII

1.

Rosie, that same morning, awoke to find that her hot water heater was on the blink. Little Buster, her baby, fell down and split his lip trying to take a toy duck away from his big sister Lou Ann, and Lou Ann made matters worse by laughing at him. Little Buster's lip bled so profusely it looked like his throat was cut, and all either child could think about was when their daddy was coming home. When that might be, or where their daddy was, Rosie had no idea. There had not been a sound out of Royce in three weeks. Every day she went home expecting to find him there, lonely and repentant, and every day she found nothing but an empty house and two disagreeable children. It was almost too much, and by the time she got Little Buster cleaned up and shuttled the two of them down the street to the neighbor who kept them during the day, she was feeling desperate. She boarded her morning bus almost in tears and rode across Houston with her eyes closed, so tired of the world that she just didn't want to look at it anymore.

When she opened her eyes again one of the first things she saw was F. V. d'Arch sitting on the curb near her bus stop. That was the first time that had ever happened, and Rosie was mildly intrigued. F.V. looked like the bottom had fallen out, but then so far as she knew the bottom had always been out where F.V. was concerned. It was only the fact that he was sitting on the curb that surprised her. He had on his chauffeur pants and his undershirt.

"What's the matter, you get fired?" she asked.

F.V. shook his head. "Worrit sick," he said.

"Yeah, me too," Rosie said. "I don't know if Royce is alive or dead. I don't know what he thinks I'm supposed to tell the kids. I never would have married him if I'd known it was going to end up in a mess like this."

"Guess where the General's at, an' you'll know why I'm worrit sick," F.V. said.

"Where is he, off somewhere buyin' a tank?"

"Naw, he's up at Miz Greenway's," F.V. said. "Ran up there two hours ago. Never even took his run. Them dogs is about to scratch the door down."

"Uh-oh," Rosie said, looking up the street.

"There ain't no light in the kitchen, either," F.V. said. "There ain't no light in the whole house, if you want the truth."

"Uh-oh," Rosie said again. She sat down on the curb beside F.V. and both of them stared at Mrs. Greenway's house. The sun was up and it was a fine bright day, but somehow the house seemed dark and ominous.

"What are you thinkin' about?" Rosie asked.

F.V. shrugged an expressive Cajun shrug, signifying general calamity. Rosie accepted the fact of calamity but wanted something more precise.

"This is awful," she said. "I wish Royce would come home."

"I was gonna tell you about somethin'," F.V. said. "I was plannin' to mention it to you, but now all this happened."

"What, what?" Rosie asked, thinking he had news of Royce.

"Dance," F.V. said. "It's tonight, out at the J-Bar Korral. You know, that place on McCarty Street."

"Aw, yeah," Rosie said. "What about it?"

F.V. pulled on his mustache for a while. A minute passed, but he seemed unable to bring himself to speak.

"F.V., I can't stand no more suspense," Rosie said. "What about the dance?"

"Wanta go?" F.V. managed to utter.

Rosie stared at him as if he was crazy. In fact, it seemed to her the whole world was crazy. Royce had disappeared into nowhere, and General Scott had disappeared into Aurora's house. Now F. V. d'Arch had just asked her for a date.

"You oughta get out more," F.V. mumbled, staring at his shoelaces.

"I guess it's the truth," Rosie said vaguely. "I oughta get out more. Little Buster's driving me crazy."

F.V. fell hopelessly silent, waiting for Rosie to rule on his invitation.

"Aw, well, what's the use," Rosie said. "If Royce don't like it he can lump it."

F.V. decided that meant she would go, but he wasn't entirely sure.

Rosie looked up the street. "If he ain't killed her that means they're involved," she said. Involved was a word she had picked up from Aurora's soap operas. "It's gonna break poor Vernon's heart."

"We still goin' to the dance?" F.V. asked. The fact that his boss was involved with Mrs. Greenway faded into insignificance beside the fact that he almost had a date with Rosie.

Before Rosie could say a word Vernon's white Lincoln pulled into the street.

"Oh, my God," Rosie said and rushed out to stop it. Vernon saw her and pulled over. He had spent a sleepless night pacing his garage and had finally decided to ignore what seemed to be his orders and return for breakfast.

"Stop right there!" Rosie yelled dramatically. Vernon looked at her questioningly, at which point Rosie suddenly found herself at a loss for words. She turned around and looked at F.V. to see if he had any inspiration. F.V. had stood up and was carefully balancing himself on the edge of the curb as if it were a tall building. After a moment or two of euphoria he was beginning to have intimations of calamity again. He had nothing at all to say.

Fortunately just at that moment one of the phones rang in Vernon's car. The fact that he was on the phone gave Rosie time to gather her wits.

"I'll take him to Emma's," she said. "Maybe she can help me break the news."

"What about the dance?" F.V. asked.

Rosie felt very annoyed. It was just like someone from Bossier City to try and pin her down at a time when she didn't know her own mind two minutes in a row.

"Aw, honey, let me call you about it later," she said. "Right now I don't know up from down."

F.V. looked so gloomy that she reached out and gave his hand a little squeeze. After all, they had spent many happy hours together tinkering with the General's Packard. Then she ran out and jumped in the Lincoln.

"Turn around," she said as soon as Vernon hung up the phone. The order came too late: Vernon was staring down the street. Rosie stared too. General Hector Scott, in one of Aurora's bathrobes, was walking briskly across Aurora's lawn. He found the paper, walked briskly back into the house, and shut the door behind him.

Vernon put the Lincoln in reverse and took his foot off the brake. The big white car began to ease slowly backward. F.V. appeared in front of them in his gray pants and his undershirt, still balanced on the edge of the curb. He didn't wave.

"I don't know what come over her," Rosie said.

Vernon let the Lincoln continue to drift backward until it had drifted around a curve—Aurora's house was hidden from view. They had drifted some distance before it dawned on him that Rosie was still in the car.

"Here I am taking you out of your way," he said.

"Well, I ain't had breakfast," Rosie said. "Wanta go see if Emma's up?"

Vernon found that his arms were tired. It was so much easier to back than to turn around. He would have liked to go on as he was, just drifting back down some quiet street, across some carless country, no more trying to go forward. But they were in Houston, whose traffic wouldn't admit such easeful defeat. The wiry little woman sitting across from him wouldn't admit it, either.

A few minutes later Emma answered a knock and looked out with surprise to see the two of them on her landing.

"Good morning," she said. "Are you two eloping?" She had not been awake very long and could not think of any other reason why they would be standing on her landing.

"You might say we're at loose ends," Rosie said. "We're inviting ourselves to breakfast."

Rosie at once threw herself into making breakfast, as if there were an army to be fed. Instead there were only three confused people, none of whom were hungry.

Vernon meekly took a seat and watched. He had foolishly put himself in the path of larger forces, it seemed to him, and he felt deprived of will.

"Vernon's just been shot out of the saddle by General Scott," Rosie said bluntly. "How many eggs, Vernon? We got to face facts."

"Two," Vernon said.

"General Scott?" Emma said. "General Scott's been banished. He's the last man she'd have anything to do with."

Vernon and Rosie were silent. Rosie deftly cracked eggs.

"I wonder what made her change her mind." Emma said after a while. At that point Flap appeared in the kitchen doorway in his pajamas. Vernon got up and shook hands.

"I must have an unusual hangover," Flap said. "Did we have a slumber party?"

"We're taking counsel with one another," Emma said. "There's a rumor afoot that Momma's taken up with General Scott."

"Perfect," Flap said, sitting down. Emma was annoyed.

"It's not perfect and don't sit there making tactless remarks," Emma said.

Flap immediately rose. "Okay," he said. "I'll go back to bed. Then I won't slip up and make tactless remarks."

"Thank you," Emma said.

"I done put his eggs on," Rosie said. "Better let him stay."

"You heard her, I've been banished," Flap said. "Put those eggs back in their shells." He left the room, looking insolent. Emma didn't care.

"Maybe you misinterpreted something," Emma said. "Maybe she's just settling a score with the General, or something. She loves to settle scores."

"Look at it this way, it ain't none of our business," Vernon said.

Both women looked at him quickly. Rosie broke a yellow and shook her head at her own carelessness and the world's intractability.

"Oh, well, if you don't care no more than that why'd you drag me over here?" she said. "I could have had the kitchen floor mopped by this time."

Vernon was silent. It had become clearer and clearer to him that he spoke one language and women another. The words might be the same but the meanings were different. The language was so different from his that he had become afraid to try and say the simplest thing, like asking for a drink of water. He said nothing and ate his eggs under the malevolent eye of Rosie.

While he ate, Rosie's mind drifted back to her own problem, which was what to do about F.V. and the dance. "Vernon, I got the perfect solution," she said suddenly, her face brightening. "Even if you ain't heartbroken you're bound to mope—I know. I've lived with a moper twenty-seven years, and what's it got me?"

"A big family," Emma said. "How's Little Buster?"

"Split his lip," Rosie said indifferently. Her mind was elsewhere.

"Dancin' beats mopin' any old day," she said, and got up and did a step or two.

"Can't dance," Vernon said.

246

"Then it's time to learn," Rosie said. "Me an' F. V. d'Arch have got a date to go dancin' tonight, and I just know F.V. would be glad for you to come along. We could go in your car an' it'd cheer you up a whole lot."

Vernon didn't think so. He thought sitting on his building and watching the evening planes come in would cheer him more, but he didn't say so. He looked across at Emma, who was smiling nicely at him—smiling as if she understood it all.

"Well, you're out of the frying pan, Vernon," she said. "You know what that leaves."

They left a little later, and Emma went into the bedroom. Flap was sitting on the bed reading the paper. He looked at her balefully. "I have a bone to pick with you," he said.

"You'll have to wait," Emma said. "I'm not going to fight with you until I've called Momma. I want to know what's happening."

"You were awfully arrogant this morning," he said.

"You were awfully insensitive to Vernon's feelings," Emma said. "I think we're even."

"I only said one word and that was ambiguous," he said. "I could have meant it sarcastically, you know. You didn't have to insult me in front of company."

"All right, I apologize," Emma said. "I was jumpy."

Flap didn't say anything. He looked at the paper intently.

"Oh, to hell with you," Emma said. "I've apologized. It wasn't that big an incident."

"No, but it reminded me of a lot of other things you've done that I haven't liked," he said.

Emma looked up the want ads and began to read them. Of late she had found herself particularly engrossed by the want ads. Flap suddenly tried to snatch them from her. He began one of his blitzkrieg passes, but Emma held on to the want ads. There was a lot of crinkling of paper. Flap tried to wrestle her down, but Emma was disgruntled and didn't allow herself to be kissed. She used the newspaper to shield all vital areas.

"Stop," she said. "I want to call Momma."

"Our sex life has priority," he said.

"Lay off me, I mean it," she said.

When he saw that she really did mean it he began to tear the want ads into shreds. Emma gave up and watched him tear them into dozens of strips and fling them on the floor.

"There," he said. "I may not get to screw you but at least I won't have to watch you read the goddamn want ads for three hours."

Emma felt annoyed with herself for having stepped into the bedroom in the first place. "I never seem to learn," she said. Flap didn't respond, and she went to the kitchen and called her mother.

"Yes," Aurora said at once.

"What are you doing?" Emma asked, taken aback that the phone had been answered so quickly.

"Why do you ask?"

"Because you startled me," Emma said.

"What a strange girl you are," Aurora said. "You must be trying to hide something, or you wouldn't have called me. Your young writer's returned, I suppose."

"You sound like my husband," Emma said. "You're both snide. I guess you know your maid and your former boy friend were over here for breakfast?"

There was a moment of silence on the other end. "Which former boy friend?" Aurora asked, rather absently.

"Vernon, of course," Emma said. "I hear you've made up with the General."

"Oh, well, you know me," Aurora said. "I'm not one to hold grudges. I acquire so many of them that some have to be discarded. Hector and I have had a modest rapprochement. In fact, we were thinking of taking ourselves to the beach this morning, if you ever get off the phone."

"I'm sorry," Emma said. "I didn't know he was there."

"He's not," Aurora said. "He's gone to mollify his wretched dogs. I believe I will continue to bear my grudge against those dogs."

There was another silence. "Is that all you're going to tell me?" Emma asked.

"Well, Vernon said it was none of our business," she said when her mother didn't answer.

"Yes, Vernon's a champ," Aurora said. "Also a chump, unfortunately. Well, it was sweet of you to call me, dear, even if scandal was your object. However, right now I'm going to go look for my bathing suit. It's disappeared just when I finally need it. Perhaps we'll speak this evening."

Aurora hung up and immediately padded downstairs and cornered Rosie, who had come in without announcing herself. She was vacuuming the living room.

"Taking him to Emma's was a brilliant stroke," Aurora said. "I thank you. Is he all right?"

"Hard to say," Rosie said. "He ain't normal anyway. What about the General?"

"Oh, well," Aurora said. "He's considerably better than nothing."

"Yeah, an' I got a date with F.V. tonight," Rosie said. "Vernon's comin', I think. Vernon needs to loosen up," she added.

"Everybody needs to loosen up," Aurora said. "I wish Vernon only the best, but frankly I'm not sure that chaperoning your dates with F.V. is likely to do much for him. Relations on this block are certainly getting soap-opera-ish. Hector and I are due to leave for the beach any minute."

"Then why are you still in your bathrobe?"

"Oh, well," Aurora said. "There's no point in getting ready until Hector shows up. I don't want him to think he can change my ways."

The doorbell rang. General Scott, in immaculate white ducks, stood on the doorstep. His car was at the curb.

"Hector, you look spanking," Aurora said. "Come in and have some tea, why don't you?"

"I don't see that I have much goddamn choice," the General said.

He waved irritably at F.V., who killed the Packard's motor. "Now it probably won't start again," the General said.

Rosie could not restrain a giggle. The General looked at her sternly, but it had no effect.

"Armies have to be on time or wars would never get won," the General said loudly.

Aurora yawned. "I seem to have stayed up all night," she said. "Why don't you sit down and have some tea while I get dressed?"

"No," the General said. "I'll wait in the car. You may come or you may not, but at least I'll be in my own car." He turned to leave, then stopped and looked back.

"You don't click your heels, like you used to, you know, Hector," Aurora said. "I thought it was rather sexy, I must say. It's certainly not every man can click his heels."

Aurora was idly looking out a window at her flowers, but for a moment General Scott had the illusion that he had her in the palm of his hand. He saluted and clicked his heels. Then he did it twice more. On the third try he produced what he considered to be an excellent click.

"How's that?" he asked.

Aurora inclined her head first one way then another, considering the click. "Somehow it seems to lack the old arrogance," she said, and then suddenly threw out her arms and emitted a burst of song. It was quite a loud burst. The song was from some opera or other, the General didn't know which, and the mere fact that she would sit there singing it irritated him enormously. It was always irritating to him when Aurora sang, because it meant that she was, for the moment, perfectly happy, and therefore quite oblivious of him. There was no effective way to handle a woman who sat right in front of you singing. The sight of Aurora merrily warbling in Italian reminded him of how grateful he was that his wife had been tone deaf. Unfortunately she had also been inaudible as well, so that he had always had to ask her to repeat her statements three times; in retrospect, it had come to seem a charming trait.

"It's a pity you aren't more musical, Hector," Aurora said when she was through singing. "It would be nice if we could sing some duets. I don't suppose you'd consider taking lessons, would you?"

"Singing lessons?" the General said. He looked at his watch sternly. The notion of singing lessons discomfited him a good deal.

"Aurora, for God's sake," he said. "I thought we were going to the beach. I'd look like an utter fool, taking singing lessons at my age."

Aurora strolled to the stairs but didn't go up them. She stood on the bottom step, looking happy and rather reflective. The General was afraid she was going to burst into song again, as was Rosie, who hurried out. The General couldn't help noticing that Aurora looked wonderful. Her hair was filled with lights. She was all he had hoped for in a woman, and his admiration, or maybe it was even love, got the better of him and he walked up behind her and put his arms around her.

"I hardly thought you'd be such a brute as to refuse my first request," she said. "All I want is someone to sing duets with."

"Oh, well, maybe I will then," the General said. Emboldened, he tried to kiss her, but she skipped up several stairs.

"If I were you I'd go get that unreliable car started," she said. "I intend to be ready in five minutes and I'd like to depart immediately."

Aurora ran upstairs and the General turned to go to the door, only to find Rosie blocking his way. She looked accusatory.

"Tell F.V. not to get stung by no jellyfish," she said. "Me an' him's gonna shake a leg tonight."

"What's that?" the General said. "You women are both crazy. Shake a leg? Why would F.V. want to do that?"

"Dancin'," Rosie said. "We're going dancin'."

"Oh, shake a leg in that sense," the General said. "Can F.V. actually dance?" He opened the door and waved F.V. a command to start the car.

"He better can, he asked me," Rosie said. "You better go out there and tell him to stop pumping on that foot feed. If he floods that old thing it won't dry out for a week."

"F.V., stop pumping," the General roared, sticking his head out the door.

For his part, F.V. stared straight ahead and pretended not to hear the demand. He felt he had the engine primed just to the point where it would have to start, and he was reluctant to give up his advantage.

"He's still pumping," Rosie said, looking out. "I can tell by the way he's starin' straight ahead. F.V.'s got a one-track mind."

"F.V., stop pumping!" the General yelled again.

"If he gets it down to Galveston and floods it out when Aurora's just got a fresh sunburn, you're gonna wish you was back in the war," Rosie said grimly.

The General had just been thinking the same thing. "Maybe it would be better if I got a new car."

"Yeah," Rosie said. "Too bad you can't go buy one while she's getting dressed. It might save you a lot of agony.

"The Lord only knows where all this will end," she added somberly, turning to go to the kitchen. "Course there's some things don't never seem to end at all, but if any of this here ever ends the Lord only knows where I'll be at the time."

"That's the damn truth, it's hard to judge," the General said.

CHAPTER XIII

1.

ROYCE DUNLUP was lying in bed with a cold can of beer balanced on his stomach. The phone by the bed began to ring and he reached over and picked the receiver up without disturbing the can of beer. He had a big stomach, and it was no real trick to balance a can of beer on it, but in this instance the can was sitting precisely over his navel, and keeping it there while talking on the phone was at least a little bit of a trick.

Since leaving Rosie and taking up, more or less formally, with his girl friend Shirley Sawyer, Royce had learned a lot of new tricks. For one thing, Royce had learned to have sex lying flat on his back, something he had never done in all his conservative years with Rosie. Nobody had ever tried to teach Royce anything like that before, and at first he made a nervous pupil, but Shirl soon broke him in. While she was in the process of breaking him in she talked to him about something called fantasy, a concept she had picked up in her one year of junior college in Winkelburg, Arizona. Fantasy, as Shirley explained it, meant thinking about things you really couldn't do, and her own favorite fantasy involved having sex with a fountain. In particular, Shirley wanted to have it with Houston's new Mecom fountain, a splendid new gusher of water right in front of the equally splendid Warwick Hotel. At night the Mecom fountain was lit up with orange lights, and Shirley insisted that she couldn't think of anything better than seating herself right on top of a great spurt of orange water, right there in front of the Warwick Hotel.

That wasn't possible, of course, so Shirley had to make do with the next best, which was seating herself every night or two on what she primly referred to as Royce's "old thing." About all that was required of Royce at such times was to keep still, while Shirley jiggled around and made little spurting sounds in imitation of the fountain she imagined herself to be sitting on. Royce's only worry was that someday Shirley might lose her balance and fall backwards, in which case his old thing was bound to suffer, but so far it hadn't happened and Royce had never been one to look too far ahead.

His own favorite fantasy was simpler, and involved sitting the beer can on his navel. What Royce liked to pretend was that the beer can had a little hole in its bottom and his navel a secret hole in its top, so that when he put the can of beer over his navel a nice stream of cold beer squirted right down into his stomach with no effort on his part at all. That way the two pleasantest things in life, sex and beer drinking, could be accomplished without so much as lifting a hand.

Shirley evidently liked sitting on his old thing so much that she was willing to support him to keep it handy, so Royce had become a man of substantial leisure. His memory had never been very keen, and in three weeks he managed to forget Rosie and his seven children almost completely. Now and then longings for his darling Little Buster would come over him, but before they got too strong Shirley would come home and set a cold beer on his navel and the memory would subside. Shirley lived in a three-room house on Harrisburg, right next door to a used-tire center, and Royce spent much of his day staring happily out the window at a mountain of some 20,000 worn-out tires. For activity he could walk two blocks down Harrisburg to a 7-Eleven and buy some more beer, or, if he was especially energetic, walk another block and spend an afternoon happily playing shuffleboard at a bar called the Tired-Out Lounge, the principal hangout of his old friend Mitch McDonald.

Mitch was a retired roustabout who had had a hand pinched off in an oil field accident years before. It had been him, in fact, who had introduced Royce to Shirley. She had been Mitch's girl friend for years, but they had had a falling out that started (Shirley later told Royce) because Mitch's old thing acquired the bad habit of falling out of Shirley just at the wrong time. Despite this, Mitch and Shirley had decided to stay friends, and in a moment of lethargy Mitch handed his friend Shirley over to his friend Royce. He himself regarded Royce as being far too crude for Shirley, and he was very upset when they happened to hit it off. It was his own doings, however, and he managed to keep quiet about how wrong it all was, except to Hubbard Junior, the nervous little manager of the Tired-Out Lounge. Mitch frequently pointed out to Hubbard Junior that Royce and Shirley couldn't last, and Hubbard Junior, a very neat man who had the bad luck to own a bar that was only two blocks from a tire factory, always agreed, as he did with everybody, no matter what they said.

Still, on the surface, Royce and Mitch were still buddies, and it was no great surprise to Royce that it was Mitch who rang him up on the phone.

"What's up, good buddy?" Mitch asked when Royce said hello.

"Restin'," Royce said. "Havin' a few beers."

"You're gonna need something stronger than that when you hear what I got to say," Mitch said. "I'm over here at the J-Bar Korral."

"Aw, yeah?" Royce said, not much interested.

"It's this here East-Tex Hoedown," Mitch went on. "They have it ever' Friday night, unescorted ladies free. The pussy that walks around loose over here ain't to be believed."

"Aw, yeah?" Royce repeated.

"Anyhow, guess who just come in," Mitch said.

"John F. Kennedy," Royce guessed, feeling humorous. "Or is it old LBJ?"

"Nope," Mitch said. "Guess again."

Royce racked his brain. He could think of nobody they both knew who might be likely to turn up at the East-Tex Hoedown. In fact, in his relaxed state, he could not even think of anybody they both knew.

"Too tired to guess," Royce said.

"All right, I'll give you a hint," Mitch said. "Her name starts with an R."

Mitch expected that crucial initial to burst like a bombshell in Royce's consciousness, but once again he had miscalculated.

"Don't know nobody whose name starts with an R," Royce said. "Nobody 'cept me, an' I ain't hardly even got out of bed today."

"Rosie, you dumb shit," Mitch said, exasperated by his friend's obtuseness. "Rosie, Rosie, Rosie."

"Rosie who?" Royce said automatically, all thought of his wife still far from his mind.

"Rosie Dunlup!" Mitch yelled. "Your wife Rosie, ever hear of her?"

"Oh, Rosie," Royce said. "Ask her how Little Buster's doin', will you?"

Then the bombshell finally burst. Royce sat up abruptly, spilling the can of beer off his navel. He didn't notice it until the cold liquid began to leak underneath him. Then, since when he sat up his stomach hid the can, he thought the sudden shock must have caused him to wet the bed.

"Rosie?" he said. "You don't mean Rosie?"

"Rosie," Mitch said quietly, savoring the moment.

"Go tell her I said to go home," Royce said. "What's she think she's doin' over there at a dance with all them sluts?

"She oughtn't to be out by herself," he added.

"She ain't out by herself," Mitch said. It was another moment to savor.

Royce stuck his finger in the puddle he was sitting in, and then smelled the finger. It smelled like beer rather than piss, so at least he was rid of one anxiety. Dim memories of his married life began to stir in him, but only vaguely, and when Mitch dropped his second bombshell the room of Royce's memory went black.

"Whut?" he asked.

Mitch adopted a flat, informative tone and informed Royce that Rosie had arrived with two short men, one of whom wore a mustache. The other was a well-known oil man who drove a white Lincoln.

There was silence on the line while Royce absorbed the information. "Fuck a turkey," he said finally, running his fingers through his hair.

"Yeah, don't that beat all?" Mitch said. "I guess what they say is true: While the cat's away, the mouse will play."

"Why, what does she mean, goin' off an' leavin' the kids?" Royce said. A sense of indignation was rising in him.

"She's a married woman," he added forcefully.

"She sure ain't actin' like one tonight," Mitch said. "Her an' that Cajun's dancin' up a storm."

"Don't tell me no more. You're just makin' it hard for me to think," Royce said. He was trying to keep in mind a paramount fact: Rosie was his wife, and she was in the process of betraying him.

"You comin' over?" Mitch asked.

In his agitation, Royce hung up the phone before he answered. "You goddamn right I'm coming over," he said to no one. Problems lay in his way, however. One of his shoes was lost. Shirley had a scroungy little mongrel named Barstow, after her home town, and Barstow was always dragging Royce's shoes off into corners so he could nibble at the shoestrings. Royce found one shoe in the kitchen, but the other one was completely lost. While he was looking for it, though, he found a bottle of Scotch he had forgot they had, a good deal of which he gulped down while he was looking for the shoe. The shoe refused to turn up, and Royce, tormented by the thought of what his wife was getting away with, grew more and more frantic. He turned the bed upside down, thinking it might be under there. Then he turned the couch upside down. Then he stepped outside to kick the shit out of Barstow, who had vanished as neatly as the shoe.

As the minutes ticked by, Royce's desperation increased, and his fury with it. Finally he decided the shoe was nonessential; he could do what he had to do with one shoe on. He rushed out into the street and jumped into his delivery truck, but unfortunately, thanks to a month of inactivity, the truck's battery was dead. Royce felt like turning the truck over, as he had the bed and the couch, but sanity prevailed. After trying vainly to flag down a couple of passing cars he hobbled rapidly up to the Tired-Out Lounge. Everybody got a good laugh at the sight of him with one shoe on and one shoe off, but Royce scarcely heard the uproar.

"Shirley's damn turd hound stole it," he said to silence speculation. "Got an emergency. I need somebody to come help me jump-start my truck."

Nothing wins friends in a bar like someone else's emergency, and in no time Royce was getting a jump-start from a '58 Mercury, his shoe problem forgotten. Five or six tire experts from the used-tire center stood around idly kicking at the tires of Royce's truck while the jump-start took place. Several of them tried not too subtly to find out what the emergency was. After all, they had left their drinking to participate in it and had done so with the expectation—always a reasonable one on Harrisburg—of gunshots, screaming women, and flowing blood. A used potato chip truck with a rundown battery was a poor substitute, and they let Royce know it.

"What the fuck, Dunlup," one said. "Your old lady's house ain't even on fire."

Royce was not about to admit the humiliating truth, that his wife was out honky-tonking with other men. He silenced all queries by slamming his hood down and roaring away, although the hood popped up again before he had gone a block, mainly because in his haste he had neglected to remove the battery cables and had slammed it down on them.

The men who had helped him watched him go with a certain rancor. "The son of a bitch is too ignorant even to put on both shoes," one of them said. They were hoping maybe he'd have a car wreck before he got out of sight, but he didn't and they were left to straggle back to the bar without even a story to tell.

"Dumb bastard," another tire whanger said. "I wouldn't help him next time if a snappin' turtle had a holt of his cock."

OVER AT the J-Bar Korral, meanwhile, a colorful evening was in progress. A group called the Tyler Troubadours was flailing away at a medley of Hank Snow favorites, and the customers had divided themselves roughly into three equivalent groups: those who came to drink, those who came to dance, and those who hoped to accomplish a little of both. Brylcream and Vitalis gleamed on the heads of those men who bothered to take their Stetsons off, and the women's hair was mostly upward coiffed, as if God had dressed it himself by standing over them with a comb in one omnipotent hand and a powerful vacuum cleaner in the other.

Everybody was happy and nearly everybody was drunk. One of the few exceptions to both categories was Vernon, who sat at a table smiling uncomfortably. He was not sober on purpose, but then neither was he unhappy on purpose. Both states appeared to belong to him, which was just as well, since as near as he could tell nobody else wanted them.

Certainly Rosie didn't. She had immediately flung herself into dancing, figuring that was the easiest way to keep her mind off the fact that she was out on a date with F.V. d'Arch. It was very clear to her that it was a date, since at the last minute she had let him pay for her ticket; beyond that, her imagination refused to take her. She had more or less forgotten why she had been so determined to drag poor Vernon along, but she was glad that she had, anyway, just in case problems arose with F.V.

Fortunately, though, F.V. had shown himself to be a model of comportment. He flung himself into dancing just as eagerly as Rosie had, mostly to keep his mind off the fact that he couldn't think of anything to say to Rosie. For years the two staples of their conversation had been Bossier City, Louisiana, and Packard engines, and neither seemed quite the right thing to talk about on their first date.

Also, looming in both their minds was the specter of Royce Dunlup. Despite the fact that he had not been heard from in weeks, and might be in Canada, or even California, both Rosie and F.V. secretly assumed that somehow he would find them out and turn up at the dance. They also secretly assumed that by their being there together they were guilty—probably in the eyes of God and certainly in the eyes of Royce—of something close to adultery, although they had as yet to exchange even a handshake. Both were sweaty before they had danced a step, from guilt and nervousness, and the dancing proved to an enormous relief. At first F.V. danced with great Cajun suavity, from the hips down, never moving his upper body at all, which struck Rosie as slightly absurd. She was used to lots of rocking and dipping and hugging when she danced, and while she didn't especially want F.V. to try any hugging she did expect him to at least turn his head once in a while. Right away she poked him in the ribs to make her point.

"Loosen up there, F.V.," she said. "We ain't standin' in no boat, you know. You're gonna be a dead loss when they play one of them jitterbugs if you can't twist no better'n that."

Fortunately a little practice and five or six beers and the fact that there was no sign of Royce did wonders for F.V.'s confidence, and Rosie had no more cause for complaint. F.V. had her on the floor for every dance and they were only cut in on twice, both times by the same massive drunk, who couldn't seem to get over the fact that Rosie was as short as she was. "Ma'am, you're plumb *tiny*," he said several times.

"That's right. Be careful you don't fall on me. I'd just be a smear on the floor if you was to," Rosie said, charitable in her happiness at finding out she could go about in the world and dance with various men without any lightning bolts striking her dead.

In her happiness, and because the inside of the J-Bar Korral was roughly the temperature of a bread oven, she began to drink beer rapidly during the intermissions. F.V. drank beer rapidly too, and Vernon bought beer as rapidly as they drank it. The top of their table was a puddle from all the moisture that had dripped off the bottles, and Vernon amused himself while they danced by soaking up the puddle with napkins.

"F.V., we ort to of been doing this years ago," Rosie said during one intermission. She was feeling more and more generous toward F.V. The fact that he had gotten up the nerve to mumble, "Wanta go?" that morning was the beginning of her liberation.

"We ort, we ort," F.V. said. "Wanta come next week?"

"Oh, well," Rosie said, fanning herself with a napkin. The "oh, well" was a delaying tactic she had picked up from listening to Aurora.

"They have these dances ever' week," F.V. said. He paused. "Ever' week on the dot," he added, in case Rosie doubted it.

"That's sweet," Rosie said vaguely, looking around the room in such a way as to leave in question as much as possible. It was rather vulgar of F.V. to rush her so, she felt, and the thought of having to commit herself to something a whole week away was scary.

"It's the same band all the time," F.V. persisted.

"Vernon, you ought to try a dance or two," Rosie said, hoping to slip quietly off the spot she was on.

"I was raised Church of Christ," Vernon explained. "They ain't partial to dancing."

Vernon was not going to be any help, Rosie saw. He was merely waiting politely for the evening to be over. Meanwhile, F.V.'s dark Cajun eyes were shining and he was waiting to find out if he had a date for next week.

"Well, if Little Buster ain't been kidnapped, or the sky don't fall . . ." Rosie said and let her sentence trail off.

That was enough for F.V. Anything less crushing than blank refusal had always been enough for F.V. He leaned back and drank beer while Vernon ate pretzels.

Vernon felt like he was still in a state of backward drift. Old Schweppes, the baseball fan, would have said that life had thrown him a curve, the curve being Aurora, but to Vernon it felt more like the road of his life had just suddenly forked, giving him no time to turn. He had left the old straight road of his life, probably forever, on the impulse of an instant, yet it did not surprise him very much that the fork had so quickly led him into the sand. He did not expect to get back on the old road, and to him the sweat and the roar of the J-Bar were just part of the sand. He watched and ate his pretzels rather disconnectedly, mild in his dullness, not thinking of much.

None of them knew that outside in the far reaches of the J-Bar parking lot a baby blue delivery truck was revving up. Royce Dunlup had arrived and was preparing his vengeance.

He had not, however, parked his truck. On the way over he had had the feeling that a few beers might clear his head, so he had stopped at an all-night grocery and bought two six-packs of Pearl. To his annoyance, everyone in the store had laughed at him because he had on only one shoe. It was beginning to seem to Royce that he must be the first person in the history of the world to have a shoe carried off by a girl friend's dog.

The cashier at the grocery store, no more than a pimply kid, had felt obliged to crack a joke about it. "What happened, hoss?" he asked. "Did you forget to put the other one on, or forget to take this one off?"

Royce had taken his six-packs and limped to his truck, followed by the rude jeers of several onlookers. The incident set him to brooding. People seemed to assume that he was some kind of nut, a kind who only liked to wear one shoe. If he went limping into a big dance like the East-Tex Hoedown wearing only one shoe hundreds of people would probably laugh at him; his whole position would be automatically undermined. For all he knew, Rosie could have him committed to an insane asylum if he showed up at a dance with only one shoe on.

It was a thorny problem, and Royce sat in his truck at the far end of the J-Bar parking lot and drank his way rapidly through a six-pack of beer. It occurred to him that if he waited patiently enough some drunk was sure to stagger out and collapse somewhere in the parking lot, in which case it would be no trouble to steal a shoe. The only risky part about such a plan was that Rosie and her escorts might leave before he could find a collapsed drunk. In light of the seriousness of it all, the matter of the missing shoe was a terrible irritation, and Royce made up his mind to strangle Barstow the next time he came home, Shirley or no Shirley. He drank the second six-pack even more rapidly than the first. Drinking helped keep him in a decisive mood. The J-Bar was only a cheap prefabricated dance hall, and Royce could hear the music plainly through the open doors. The thought that his own wife of twenty-seven years was in there dancing with a low-class Cajun put him in a stomping mood, but unfortunately he had nothing but a sock on his best stomping foot.

Then, just as he was finishing his twelfth beer, a solution to the whole problem accidentally presented itself. Royce had about decided to wait in the truck and try to run over Rosie and F.V. when they came out to leave. He killed his motor and prepared to lie in wait, and just as he did the solution appeared in the form of two men and a woman, all of whom seemed to be very happy. When they stepped out of the door of the J-Bar they had their arms around one another and were singing about crawfish pie, but by the time they had managed to stagger the length of the building the party mood had soured. One of the men was large and the other small, and the first sign of animosity Royce noticed came when the big man picked up the little man by his belt and abruptly flung him at the rear wall of the J-Bar Korral.

"Keep your fuckin' slop bucket mouth shut around my fiancée, you little turd you," the big man said, just about the time the little man's head hit the wall of the J-Bar Korral. Royce couldn't tell if the little man heard the command or not. Instead of answering he began to writhe around on the concrete, groaning out indistinct words.

The woman paused briefly to look down at the small writhing man. "Darrell, you never need to done that," she said calmly. "I've heard the word 'titty' before anyway. I got two of 'em, even if they ain't the biggest ones in the world."

The big man evidently didn't think her comment deserved an answer, because he grabbed her arm and stuffed her into a blue Pontiac without further ado. The two of them sat in the Pontiac for a while watching the little man writhe; then, somewhat to Royce's surprise, the big man started the car and drove away, without bothering to run over the little man. The little man finally managed to get one foot under himself. The other foot evidently wouldn't go under him, because he hopped on one leg right past Royce's potato chip truck and on into the darkness of the parking lot.

Royce scarcely gave him a glance. He had just had an inspiration. When the little man struck the building, it seemed to Royce that the building had crunched. He had distinctly heard a crunching sound. Obviously the building was flimsy; it was probably only made of plywood and tarpaper. There was no reason for him to wait half the night so as to run over Rosie and F.V. in the parking lot. A building that would crunch under the impact of a small dirty-mouthed man wouldn't stand a chance against a six-year-old potato chip truck in excellent condition. He could drive right through the wall and run over Rosie and F.V. while they were actually dancing together.

Without further contemplation, Royce acted. He drove his truck up parallel to the rear wall and leaned out and punched the wall a time or two with his fist. It felt like plywood and tarpaper to him, and that was all he needed. He chose as his point of entry a spot right in the center of the rear wall, backed up so as to give himself about a twenty-yard run at it, revved his engine for all it was worth, and, with blood in his eye, drove straight into the wall.

The J-Bar Korral was a big place, and at first only those customers who happened to be drinking or dancing at the south end of the building noticed that a potato chip truck was in the process of forcing its way into the dance. The first impact splintered the wall and made a hole big enough for the nose of the truck, but it was not big enough for all the truck and Royce was forced to back up and take another run at it. A couple from Conroe were celebrating their first wedding anniversary at a table only a few yards from where the nose of the truck broke through, and the young couple and their friends, while mildly surprised to see the wall cave in and the nose of a truck appear, took a very mature attitude toward the whole thing.

"Look at that," the husband said. "Some sorry son of a bitch missed his turn an' hit the wall."

Everybody turned and watched, curious to see whether the truck was going to break on through. "I hope it ain't a nigger,"

the young wife said. "I'd hate to see a nigger while we're cele-
bratin', wouldn't you, Goose?" Goose was her pet name for her
husband. He didn't like for her to use it in company, but the
sight of the truck caused her to forget that temporarily. Her first
name was Beth-Morris and that's what everybody called her,
including her husband's best friend, Big Tony, who happened to
be sitting right next to her at the table, helping her celebrate her
first anniversary. No sooner had she uttered the forbidden nick-
name than Big Tony gave her a best-friendly hug and began to
make goose talk right in her little white ear. "Shit, your husband's
already too drunk to cut the mustard. Let's you an' me sneak out
to the car and play a little goosey-gander," Big Tony said.

Before Beth-Morris could take a firm stance Royce and his
truck burst right into the J-Bar Korral. Annoyed at being stopped
the first time, Royce had backed halfway across the parking lot
for his second run. Beth-Morris looked up just in time to see a
potato chip truck bearing right down on their table. She
screamed like a banshee, spoiling everyone's anniversary mood.
Big Tony instantly had all thoughts of goosey-gander driven from
his mind. He had just time to fling his beer at Royce's windshield
before the edge of the front bumper hit his chair and knocked
him under the table.

For a brief moment there was a lull. The people in the south
end of the dance hall stared at Royce and his truck, unwilling to
believe what they were seeing. Royce turned on his windshield
wipers, to get Big Tony's beer off his windshield, at which point
people began to scream and push back their chairs. Royce knew
he had no time to lose. Rosie and F.V. might escape him in the
confusion. He let out his clutch and roared right out on the dance
floor, scattering tables like matchsticks.

Of the people Royce sought, F.V. was the first to see him. He
and Rosie were dancing near the bandstand. They had both
heard the first screams, but screams were not uncommon at a big
dance, and they didn't immediately stop dancing. At the sound of
gunfire they would have stopped dancing, but screams ordinarily
just meant a fist fight, and fist fights were not worth stopping
for.

Thus it was a severe shock to F.V. to complete what he

thought was a nicely executed step and look up to see Royce Dunlup's potato chip truck driving straight toward the bandstand. If shocks really froze blood, his circulatory system would have achieved a state of immediate deep freeze. As it was, except for a couple of involuntary jerks, he managed to control himself rather well.

"Don't look now," he said to Rosie. "Royce is here. Don't look now."

Rosie felt instantly weak. It was not a surprise, though; the only thing surprising was that she seemed to hear the sound of a truck. It was bound to be her imagination, however, and F.V.'s tone had more or less convinced her that her life depended on keeping her head down, so she did. She assumed Royce was stalking through the dancers, probably with a gun in his hand; since she had nowhere else to put it, she reposed her trust in F.V. Perhaps he could steer them out the door so they could make a run for it.

But F.V. had stopped dancing and stood stock still, and the sound of a truck got louder; then the sound of screams got far too loud to be the result of a fist fight, and the musicians suddenly lost the beat. "My gawd," the vocalist said, and Rosie looked up just in time to see her husband driving past in his familiar baby blue delivery truck.

For a moment Rosie suddenly felt deeply happy. There was Royce in his delivery truck, driving with both hands on the wheel, just like he always did. Probably all that had happened had been a dream. Probably she was not at a dance but home in bed; the dream would be over any minute and she would be back in the life she had always lived.

A happy relief swelled in her as she stood there expecting to wake up. Then, instead of her waking up, Royce's truck hit the bandstand, flinging musicians left and right. The drummer's drums all fell on top of him, and the vocalist was knocked completely off the platform into the crowd. To make matters worse, Royce backed the truck up and went at the bandstand again. The drummer, who had just managed to get to his feet, was once again knocked sprawling into his drums. The second crash did something bad to the electrical system. It spluttered and flashed a very white light, and the electric guitar, which was lying off by itself in a corner, suddenly emitted a horrible scream, frightening everyone in the place so badly that all the women screamed too. All the musicians picked themselves up and fled except one, the bull fiddle player, a tall gangly fellow from Port Arthur who preferred death to cowardice. He leapt over the fallen drummer and smashed at the potato chip truck with his bull fiddle. "Son of a bitch bastard!" the bull fiddle player yelled, raising the fiddle on high.

Royce was mildly surprised at the stance the bull fiddle player took, but he was far from daunted. He backed up a few feet and went at the bandstand a third time. The gallant from Port Arthur got in one tremendous swing before being flung backward into the drums and the drummer. The fight was not gone from him, though; he rose to his knees and flung a cymbal at the truck, cracking Royce's windshield.

"Security, security, where's the goddamn security?" the vocalist yelled from the midst of the crowd.

As to that, no one knew, least of all the two owners of the J-Bar, Bobby and John Dave, who had run out of their office to watch the destruction of their place of business. They were both middle-aged businessmen, long accustomed to dealing with rowdiness, but the spectacle that confronted them was more than they had bargained for.

"How'd that get in here, John Dave?" Bobby asked, astonished. "We never ordered no potato chips."

Before John Dave could answer, Royce was off again. He was largely satisfied with the destruction of the bandstand, and whirled the truck around to face the crowd. He began a fast trip around the perimeter of the dance hall, honking as loud as he could in order to scatter the many bunches of people. It worked too; the people scattered, hopping around like grasshoppers over the many fallen chairs. In order to block the exit Royce then began to use his truck like a bulldozer, pushing chairs and tables into the one door and then smashing them into a kind of mountain of nails and splinters.

Vernon, ever a cool head in an emergency, had rushed to Rosie's side as soon as he figured out what was happening, and the two of them were concentrating on trying to keep F.V. from panicking, which might give their position away. The fact that they were all short gave them some advantage, though it didn't seem so to F.V. "Good as dead, good as dead," he kept saying.

"Damn the luck," he added mournfully.

"It ain't luck, it's justice," Rosie said grimly. She was not especially calm, but she was a long way from panic. She had not lived with Royce twenty-seven years without learning how to take care of herself when he was mad.

Vernon watched the little blue truck chug around the room smashing what few tables it hadn't already smashed. The three of them had taken refuge behind the huge man who had danced with Rosie; fortunately he was with his equally huge wife. The two of them seemed to be enjoying the spectacle enormously.

"That's a pretty little blue truck," the huge lady said. "Whyn't we get one of them to haul the kids in?"

At that very moment the pretty little blue truck veered their way. "Here's what you do. You two run for the ladies' room," Vernon said. "Run, run!"

Rosie and F.V. broke for it and the moment they did Royce spotted them. He braked in order to get an angle on where they were going, and while he was slowed down six drunks rushed out of the crowd and grabbed his rear bumper. The huge man decided to get in on the sport and ran right over Vernon, who had just moved in front of him to try and get in the truck. Royce jerked the truck into reverse and flung off all but two of the drunks; then he shot forward again and the last two let go. As the truck went by, the huge man threw a table at it, but the table only hit one of the drunks.

F.V. outran Rosie to the ladies' room, only to remember at the last second that he wasn't a lady. He stopped and Rosie ran into him.

"Ooops, where's the men's room?" F.V. asked.

Rosie looked around and saw that the crowd had parted and that Royce was bearing down on them. There was no time for commentary. She shoved F.V. through the swinging door and squeezed in behind him about two seconds before the truck hit the wall.

The part of the J-Bar where the rest rooms were had once been the projection area when the J-Bar had been a drive-in theater rather than a dance hall. It had cinderblock walls. Royce had expected to plow right through into the ladies' john, but instead he was stopped cold. He even bumped his head on his own windshield.

His confusion at finding a wall he couldn't drive through was nothing, however, to the confusion inside the rest room. Most of the women who had been using it were blissfully ignorant of what was going on out on the dance floor. They had heard some screaming, but they had just assumed it was a bigger than usual fight and more or less resolved to stay where they were until it was over. Several were in the process of combing their hair upwards, one or two were regluing false eyelashes, and one, a large redhead named Gretchen who had just finished getting laid out in the parking lot, had one leg propped up over a lavatory and was douching.

"Lord knows the trouble it saves," she remarked, to general agreement, and the conversation, such as it was, was largely concerned with the question of unwanted pregnancies. A woman who was sitting in one of the toilets was regaling everyone with a story about unwanted triplets when with no warning at all a small male Cajun popped through the door and right into their midst. The appearance of F.V. was so startling that no one noticed the small frightened-looking redhead who was right on his heels; but the shock that followed when the truck hit the wall was nothing anyone could miss. Gretchen fell right off the lavatory, and a blonde named Darlene opened her mouth to scream and dropped a false eyelash in it. F.V., off balance to begin with, had the bad fortune to fall right on top of Gretchen.

"It's a monster, get him away," Gretchen screamed. She assumed she was about to be raped and rolled on her belly and kept screaming. A couple of women rolled out from under the doors of the toilet stalls. They assumed a tornado had struck, but when they saw F.V. they began to scream for the police. Rosie had her ear to the door, and could hear the wheels of the truck spinning on the slick dance floor. When she looked around she saw that F.V. was in real trouble. Five or six women had leaped on him to keep him from raping Gretchen, and a particularly tough-looking young brunette was trying to strangle him with a tubular syringe.

"Naw, naw," Rosie said. "He ain't out to hurt nobody. He just run in here to hide. My husband tried to run over him in a truck."

"He dove at me," Gretchen said.

"You mean there's a truck loose in this dance?" the young brunette said. "That's the dumbest thing I ever heard of."

She hurried over and peeked out the door. "Aw," she said, "it's just a little truck. I thought you meant a cattle truck, or something like that. Anyway, it's driving off."

Gretchen was still looking at F.V. with burning eyes. The news that a truck was loose in the dance hall seemed to mean nothing to her at all. "I still think he's an ol' sex fiend," she said, looking at F.V. "A man that waits till he's right between my legs to fall down may fool you, honey, but he ain't fooling me."

F.V. decided Royce was the lesser of two evils. He ran out the door, with Rosie close behind him. On the dance floor a scene of pandemonium reigned. Royce had a headache from bumping his windshield, and had decided to go back to his original plan, which had been to run over the two sinners in the parking lot. To make that work he had to get back to the parking lot, and it wasn't proving easy. The patrons of the J-Bar had had time to size up the situation, and a number of the drunkest and most belligerent began to throw things at the truck—beer bottles particularly. The outraged vocalist had managed to locate the two security policemen, both of whom had been taking lengthy craps when the trouble started. The two policemen rushed onto the dance floor with guns drawn, only to discover that the criminal was in retreat.

Royce ignored the rain of beer bottles and plowed on across the dance floor, honking from time to time. The two policemen, plus Bobby and John Dave and the vocalist, began to chase the truck. Neither of the policemen was the sort to enjoy having a crap interrupted, though, and they weren't running their best.

When a small man jumped out at them and yelled "Stop!" they stopped.

"Don't stop," the vocalist yelled, very annoyed.

Rosie joined Vernon. "It's all right, it's all right," she assured the policemen. "It's my husband. He's crazed with jealousy, that's all."

"I knowed it, Billy," one of the policemen said. "Just another goddamn family fight. We could have stayed where we was."

"Family fight, my Lord in heaven," John Dave said. "Lookit this dance hall! Hurricane Carla never done us this much damage."

"No problem, no problem," Vernon said quickly, pulling out his money clip. He peeled off several hundred dollars. "The man's my employee and I'll make good your damages," he assured them.

At that moment there was the sound of a car wreck. Despite the bottles and an occasional chair, Royce had managed to drive more or less calmly down the length of the dance floor and out the hole he had made coming in. It was just after he got out that the wreck occurred. The large man in the blue Pontiac had thought it all over and decided to come back and throw the little man against the wall again, and he was driving along slowly, looking for him, when Royce drove through his hole. Darrell, the large man, was not expecting anyone to drive out of the wall of the dance hall and was caught cold. The impact threw Royce out the door of his truck and onto the asphalt of the parking lot.

The next thing Royce knew he was looking up at a lot of people he didn't know, all of whom were looking down at him. The surprising thing was that there was one person in the crowd he did know, namely his wife Rosie. The events of the evening, particularly the unexpected car wreck, had confused Royce a good deal, and he had for the moment completely forgotten why it was he had come to the J-Bar Korral in the first place.

"Royce, just keep still now," Rosie said. "Your ankle's broken."

"Aw," Royce said, looking at it curiously. It was the ankle belonging to the foot on which he had no shoe, and the sight of his sock, which wasn't even particularly clean, made him feel deeply embarrassed.

"I never meant to come with just one shoe on, Rosie," he said, doing his best to meet his wife's eye. "The reason is Shirley's damn old dog carried the other one off."

"That's all right, Royce," Rosie said. She saw that Royce had forgotten her little indiscretion for the moment; he just looked tired, drunk, and befuddled, as he often did on Friday night, and squatting down beside him in the parking lot, with hundreds of excited people around, was indeed a little bit like waking up from a bad dream, since the man before her was so much like the same old Royce instead of the strange new hostile Royce she had been imagining for several weeks.

Royce, however, felt a little desperate. It seemed very important to him that Rosie understand he had not deliberately set out to embarrass her. Long ago his own mother, a stickler for cleanliness, had assured him that if he didn't change his underwear at least twice a week he was sure to be killed in a car wreck someday wearing dirty underwear, a fact that would lead inevitably to the disgrace of his whole family. A dirty sock and one shoe was maybe not so bad as dirty underwear, but Royce still felt that his mother's prophecy had finally been fulfilled, and he needed to do what he could to assure Rosie it hadn't really been his fault.

"Looked ever'where for it," he said morosely, hoping Rosie would understand.

Rosie was plain touched. "That's all right, Royce, quit worryin' about that shoe," she said. "Your ankle's broke an' you wouldn't be able to wear it anyhow. We got to get you to a hospital."

Then, to Royce's great surprise, Rosie put her arm around him. "Little Buster asked about you, hon," she said softly.

"Aw, Little Buster," Royce said, before relief, embarrassment, fatigue, and beer overwhelmed him. Soon, though, he was completely overwhelmed. He put his head on his wife's familiar slate-hard breastbone and began to sob.

In that he was not alone for long. Many of the women and even a few of the men who had gathered around forgot that they had come out to tear Royce limb from limb. At the sight of such a fine and fitting reunion the urge for vengeance died out in the crowd's collective breast. A number of women began to sob too, wishing they could have some kind of reunion. Darrell, the owner of the ill-fated Pontiac, decided to forgive Royce instead of stomping him, and went off with his girl friend to continue the argument they were having over whether "titty" was an okay word. Bobby and John Dave shook their heads and accepted ten of Vernon's one-hundred-dollar bills as collateral against whatever the damages might total up to be. They realized that, once again, the East-Tex Hoedown had been a big success. The two policemen went back to their bowel movements, Vernon started an unsuccessful search for F.V., and Mitch McDonald, Royce's best buddy, immediately went to a phone booth to call Shirley and tell her Royce had gone back to his wife. He made it clear that he had nothing but forgiveness in his heart, and hinted rather broadly that his own, very own, old thing was aching to have Shirley come and sit on it again. To which Shirley, who was filling beer pitchers with her free hand at the time, said, "Sit on it yourself, you little tattletale. I got better things to do if you don't mind."

Rosie knelt by her husband, gratefully receiving the warm sentiments of the crowd. Many a woman leaned down to tell her how happy she was that she and her husband had got it all straightened out. Royce had cried himself to sleep against her breast. Soon an ambulance with a siren and a revolving red light screamed up and took Royce and Rosie away, and then two big white wreckers came and got the Pontiac and the potato chip truck. Some of the crowd straggled back through the hole in the wall to talk things over, others drifted off home, and many stayed where they were—all of them happy to have witnessed for once, such passion and compassion. Then, when all was peaceful, a spongy raft of clouds blew in from the Gulf, hiding the high wet Houston moon, and the clouds began to drop a soft, lulling midnight drizzle on the parking lot, the cars, and the happy, placidly milling crowd.

CHAPTER XIV

1.

THE NEXT morning Aurora was downstairs early, merrily making her way toward breakfast. She was not so much making it as compiling it from a number of exotic leftovers and a new omelette recipe she intended to try. She was watching the *Today* show with one eye and thinking to herself what a good idea it had been to reduce her load of suitors, since it meant she didn't have to attend to such a confusing battery of morning calls. Without the calls she was able to make much better breakfasts, and she could not remember anything that had been said on any of the calls that could compete with food.

Just as she was tasting some plum jelly to see if it was holding its flavor the General came through the back door and slammed it resoundingly.

"Hector, it's hardly the door of a tank," Aurora said mildly. "It's not made of plated steel. How are you this morning?"

"You'll find out," the General said. He immediately poured himself some coffee.

"Where's the paper?" Aurora asked, switching off the *Today* show to watch him a minute.

"It's in the goddamn yard, if it's been delivered," the General said. "I'm not in the mood for it just now."

"No, I can see that you're in a snit," Aurora said. "Naturally you would decide to be in a snit on a brilliant morning when I happen to be in a wonderful mood and could be talked into almost anything. There's not a bit of telling what I could be talked into if only I had a cheerful man for five minutes."

"Well, you don't," the General said succinctly.

"Tsk, tsk, what a waste," Aurora said. "Go back and get the paper then."

"I told you once I wasn't in the mood for it," the General said, taking his place at the table.

"I heard you once and your mood is quite irrelevant to the issue at hand," Aurora said. "It's my paper and one of your little obligations under the terms of our new arrangement is that you bring it in to me in the morning. I am always in the mood for it, since there seems to be little else to do with you around."

"I'm sick of your sexual innuendos," the General said. "What do you think life is?"

"It could be very nearly a pure pleasure if men weren't such spoilsports," Aurora said. "I refuse to take this bad mood of yours seriously, Hector. Just go get me the paper, please, and I'll make you a delicious omelette and we'll start over on the day once we've eaten."

"I won't get you the paper," the General said. "If I get it you'll sit there and read it for two hours, singing opera. I don't sing opera when I read the paper and I don't see why you should. You shouldn't read and sing at the same time. I particularly don't want to watch you read and listen to you sing right now, because I'm very annoyed and I want some answers."

"My God, what a pill you are," Aurora said. "I'm beginning to wish I had some of my other suitors back."

Without further ado she went out the back door and got the

paper. The sun was high and the grass was shining with water from the midnight rain. A gray squirrel was sitting on her lawn, very erect and evidently not at all discomfited by the wet grass. He was often on her lawn in the mornings, and Aurora sometimes said a word or two to him before going back in.

"Well, you're a pleasing sight," she said. "If you were only a little tamer you could come in and have breakfast with me. I have lots of nuts."

She picked a few flowers, wet though they were, and went back to the kitchen, hoping the General's mood had improved in her absence.

"I was talking to a squirrel, Hector," she said. "If you took more interest in animal life you might be a jollier man. The only animals you ever see are those spotted dogs you're so fond of. Frankly, those dogs are not terribly well behaved."

"They are perfectly behaved around me," the General said. "They are wonderful animals, I do not want any others, and I do not want to be a jollier man."

"Oh, Hector, what do you want then," Aurora said, flinging down her paper. His scratchy tone was beginning to irritate her exceedingly.

"Tell me," she said. "I must confess it's more than I can figure out. I'm wearing my new red robe and it's a wonderful morning and I had a nice breakfast planned. I was quite prepared to go to unusual lengths to please you today, just to see if we could get through one day without you being surly, but now I see it's hopeless. If you're going to be surly you might at least tell me what you fancy you have to be surly about."

"F.V. never came home," the General said. "He wasn't there this morning. I had no one to drive my car, so I couldn't go on my run. I've been waiting for him for two hours. The dogs are frantic. They get very upset when they don't get their exercise."

"My goodness, Hector, you could just turn them loose," Aurora said. "They could just run around like normal dogs. I wouldn't think it would hurt you to miss your run now and then. You're too skinny as it is. Much as I admire you for keeping up your standards, I do think you could lower them a bit now that you have me to entertain you.

"As for F.V.," she added, "I don't see why you should worry. F.V. will turn up."

"I don't think so," the General said darkly. "F.V.'s always there. He knows what's expected of him. He's worked for me six years and he's never been late before."

"Hector you have two legs," Aurora said. "If you were so desperate to run why didn't you just run? You've been doing it for years. It seems very unlikely you would choose just this morning in which to have a heart attack."

"There are times when I despise the way you speak," the General said. "You choose your words too well. I could never trust you."

"What's that got to do with anything?" Aurora asked. "You seem to be a churning mass of non sequiturs today, Hector. Obviously you intend to blame me for everything that's gone wrong in your life, so why don't you just go on and blame me and then we can have breakfast. I don't like to eat while I'm being criticized."

"All right then, it's Rosie," the General said. "I think she's responsible for the disappearance of my chauffeur. She took F.V. to the dance last night and now he's not here."

Aurora opened the paper to the society page and scanned it hastily to see if any interesting parties had taken place, or if the daughters of any of her friends had gotten engaged.

"Now I understand," she said. "You think Rosie's seduced F.V.—that's what you've decided is my fault. What remarkable gall you have, Hector. Rosie's never displayed the slightest interest in F.V."

"Where is she then?" the General said. "It's time she was at work, isn't it? Where is she?"

Aurora turned to the financial page and peered at it closely to see if any of her stocks had risen or fallen. The fact that the print was so small made it very hard to tell, but she found one that seemed to have risen and she took that as a good sign.

"You don't care," the General said. "You'd rather read the paper. You don't really love me, do you Aurora?"

"How am I supposed to know?" Aurora said. "You haven't even mentioned me so far this morning. I was feeling very attractive for a while and now I hardly know what to make of anything. You men have an unfortunate tendency to muddle me, if you want the truth. I don't think I particularly want to love anyone who's only intent on muddling me."

"You see, you've avoided my question," the General said.

Then, abruptly, he noticed again how beautiful she was, and he forgot about his annoyance with F.V. and quickly scooted his chair around to her side of the table. Her color was high and the General decided his run had been well lost. He saw there was no hope of resisting her and buried his face in her hair, since it concealed most of the neck he suddenly felt compelled to kiss.

"Ah, *mon petite*," he said, nuzzling. He had always understood that French was the language of love.

"It's amazing how often passion merely tickles," Aurora said, wrinkling her nose in slight dismay and going on with her reading. She looked down at the top of the General's bald head and felt life to be more ridiculous than ever. Why was such a head trying to kiss her neck?

"Also, Hector, you really would do better to address me in English," she said, hunching one shoulder to relieve the tickling sensation. "Your French is rudimentary at best, and you should remember what a stickler I am for having matters put well. A man with a really elegant command of the French language, or any language for that matter, could no doubt seduce me in an instant, but I am afraid you will have to depend on something other than eloquence. A man who sounds like he's sawing wood in his voice box does just as well to keep silent.

"And don't start talking about time's winged chariots, either," she said when the General drew back a moment and opened his mouth to speak. "Just because you read one poem doesn't mean I have to respond to it, does it? Come to think of it, where is Rosie? She's so harassed these days, you know. One of her children could have had an accident. I think I ought to call."

"Don't call," the General said. "I can't resist you. Think of all those lost years." He did his best to crowd onto the chair Aurora was sitting on, but it was only a kitchen chair and he ended up half on hers and half on his.

"What lost years?" Aurora said. "I certainly didn't lose any. I've had a perfectly good time every year of my life. Just because you waited until the age of sixty-seven to learn how to enjoy yourself doesn't give you the right to accuse me of losing years."

"You were so friendly when I first came in," the General said. "Now I'm not hungry and I can't wait."

Aurora looked him in the eye and laughed heartily. "Pooh," she said. "I admit I enticed you but now I think I prefer to save you for the evening. I'm not exactly dealing with a stripling, am I?"

Then, seeing that he was too confused to defend himself properly, she was forced to relent. She laid down her paper and gave him a few nice squeezes. "This will teach you not to be surly with me when I'm feeling flirtatious," she said. "At this late hour nothing takes precedence over breakfast. Why don't you go run some cold water over yourself while I cook. Missing your run seems to have overheated you."

The phone rang, and the General flinched. "We never get to have breakfast without the phone ringing," he said. He flinched because the sound of the phone was all it took to remind him of how attractive Aurora was, and how many other men wanted her. Even though she had assured him she was giving them all up now that she had him, the General felt he had good reason to hate the phone.

"What are you talking about, Hector?" Aurora said. "This is only the second morning we've had breakfast together, and thanks to your sulks we haven't even had it yet. It's not the phone's fault."

She answered it, watching him closely. Obviously he thought it was a rival calling, when in fact it was only Rosie.

"Why hello, you old darling," she said, as if she were speaking to a man. The top of the General's head grew red, and Rosie grew silent, at which point Aurora laughed merrily again. At least having the General in her life made for a few laughs.

"Well, now that I've had my little joke how are you, Rosie?" she asked.

"You never called me darlin' before," Rosie said.

"Why aren't you at work?"

"Because of Royce," Rosie said. "Ain't you read the paper?"

"No, I've not been allowed to," Aurora said. "Don't tell me I've missed something."

"Yep," Rosie said. "Royce found out about me an F.V. goin' to the dance. He drove his truck through the wall of the dance floor, trying to get at us. He smashed up the place good and then had a wreck an' broke his ankle. We was at the hospital half the night. Vernon paid for it all. It's all on page fourteen, down near the bottom."

"Oh, no," Aurora said. "Poor Vernon. I must have cost him almost a million by now, directly or indirectly. I certainly wasn't worth it, either."

"Ask her what happened to F.V.," the General said. He didn't want the conversation to linger on Vernon.

"You hush," Aurora said. "Where is Royce now?"

"He's in bed, playin' with Little Buster," Rosie said. "That child sure favors his daddy.'

"So you've taken him back," Aurora said.

"I don't know if I have or not," Rosie said. "We ain't talked about it. Royce just woke up. I thought if you didn't need me real early I'd maybe try to find out what's on his mind."

"Oh, by all means, take your time," Aurora said. "Your marriage comes first, and anyway Hector and I have done nothing but fuss at one another all morning. I don't know when we'll get around to eating. I'm fainting from starvation now. Where's Vernon?"

"Where's F.V., you mean," the General said. "I've asked you twice to find out about F.V."

"What a pest," Aurora said. "General Scott insists on knowing what you've done with his chauffeur. Do you have his chauffeur or don't you? F.V. seems to be more essential to his life than I am, so it would oblige me very much if you could give us a clue to his whereabouts."

"My God, what did become of him?" Rosie said. "I guess I just forgot about him." Then she remembered that her husband was right in the next room, and she became embarrassed.

"She just forgot him," Aurora said to the General. "Evidently there was something of a fracas. You can read about it on page fourteen of the paper, near the bottom."

"I bet he left town," Rosie whispered. "I can't talk, on account of Royce."

"Correction—she now believes F.V. has left town. Goodbye, Rosie. Come over and tell me what's happened when you can. In all likelihood Hector and I will still be sitting here bickering."

"I don't like to hear you mention that man's name," the General said when she hung up.

"I can't think why you should care," Aurora said. "After all, I never slept with him."

"I know, but he's still around," the General said.

Aurora lowered her paper and looked all around the kitchen, turning her head slowly, like a searchlight. "Where?" she said. "I don't seem to see him."

"I mean he's still in Houston," the General said.

"Yes, it's his home," Aurora said. "Do you want me to drive the poor man from his home just to please you?"

"You never say poor Hector," the General countered.

"All right, that's it," Aurora said, getting up. "Now I'm going to cook and I'm going to sing, and when I've finished we can go on with this, if we must. You sit there and read the paper like a normal male and after breakfast we'll see if you're feeling any nicer."

"While you cook I'm just going to run back home and see if F.V.'s there," the General said.

"Go on, then. It's amazing what lengths you'll go to to avoid hearing me sing."

The General started for the door, expecting to hear a great burst of opera. None came, and just before he went out he glanced back over his shoulder. Aurora was standing at the sink with her hands on her hips, smiling at him. Abruptly the General did an about-face and marched back toward her. He had heard her say several times how much she liked surprises; perhaps it was just the right time to kiss her.

"That's not the way to your house," Aurora said happily. She reached behind her and turned on her water faucet, which had a

281

hose-and-nozzle attachment for washing dishes. Just as the General reached out to grab her shoulders she sidestepped and squirted him with quite a lot of water.

"Gotcha," she said, and laughed loudly for the third time that morning.

"Now you don't look so neat," she added.

The General was absolutely dripping. Aurora was swishing the nozzle back and forth, getting her kitchen floor quite wet. At that moment, as if to mock him, she let out the burst of opera he had been expecting.

"Shut up!" he yelled. "Don't sing!" No one that he could remember had ever taken him less seriously than she did. She seemed to have no concept of order at all. The look in her eye suggested that if he tried to come any closer she wouldn't hesitate to use her little nozzle again; but his pride was challenged and with no more hesitation he rushed in and after a brief struggle wrested the nozzle from her and squirted it at her to make her stop singing.

Aurora kept singing anyway, despite the soaking that she was getting, indifferent to his dignity and her own. Still, the General wouldn't relent. She had to be shown. While he was showing her she reached back and shut off the water, reducing the squirt to a drip. They were both quite wet, despite which Aurora had somehow managed to retain a certain magnificence. The General quite forgot that he was on his way home; he quite forgot his missing driver.

"What's the meaning of this? What's the meaning?" he said. "Let's go — I want to see your Renoir."

"Ho, ho, I bet you do," Aurora said. "Why this euphemism?" She flipped a little water at him. Her hair seemed filled with dew, and she was clearly about to laugh at him again.

"What?" he said, made suddenly cautious by the realization that he was standing on a slick floor.

"Yes, you prude," Aurora said, flicking more drops of water at him. She shook a bit of the water out of her hair. Then she shook the nozzle at him, rather suggestively. She even made it balance upright for a moment, but then it fell and dangled from her hand.

282

"Goodness, I hope this isn't a portent, Hector," she said with a wicked gleam in her eye. "But then with your great interest in art I don't suppose it would matter much to you. Show me your Renoir indeed!"

"But that's what you said the other time," the General said. His anger was gone, his passion confused, and he was beginning to feel helpless, in the main.

"Yes, but I'm well known for my flare for metaphor," Aurora said. "I know how sensitive you military men are. I'm careful not to put things crudely. You won't find me calling a nozzle a nozzle, I can tell you that."

"Stop it!" the General said. "Stop talking! I wish you lived in Tunisia!"

"That's the most original thing you've said all day, Hector," Aurora said. "It's amazing the things that pop out when your back is against the wall. Keep yelling. You've almost succeeded in reawakening my interest."

"No," the General said. "You don't mean a word you say. You just mock me."

"Well, another nice thing about you is that your face isn't flabby," Aurora said. "It's too bad you chose to stop making advances just at the moment when my interests were beginning their recovery."

"It's because of the goddamn floor," the General said. "You've wet it. You know how I hate wet floors. I could fall down and break my hip. You know how easily hips break at my age."

Aurora shrugged lightly and gave him a friendly, taunting smile. "I never said we had to stand here," she said. "I no longer feel like an omelette." She picked up the large tray of fruits and exotic leftovers that she had already prepared and, looking him in the eye, walked straight across the wettest part of the floor, making loud squishy splats with her bare feet. She went right on out of the kitchen, without once looking back. She didn't ask the General to follow, nor did she forbid it.

In a minute, not very confidently, the General followed.

CHAPTER XV

1.

THE MORNING after the General had his annual checkup was, from Aurora's point of view, much like any other morning, only better. It was sunny and warm, but then it was usually sunny and warm. What made it better was that the General's man from Brooks Brothers was in town. That meant that the General had to spend the morning getting fitted for new suits and new shirts. With much difficulty Aurora had got him to promise to branch out a little from his beloved charcoal gray. Since the General was tied up downtown, Aurora found herself with a whole morning free, a state of things that had become increasingly rare since the change in their lives.

She meant to take full advantage of the luxury and spend the morning as she had once spent all mornings, lying in her window nook talking on the phone, paying bills, and reading the array of magazines she had managed to accumulate. She rushed the General so that he scalded his tongue on his coffee and went off in a grumpy mood. Aurora didn't care. All she wanted was a little peace and quiet, a few hours to herself.

"It's amazing how omnipresent men become," she said when Rosie came in to begin to clean the bedroom. Since Royce's return Rosie had worn a pinched look, and she was moving nervously around the bedroom looking more pinched than ever.

"How what?" she asked.

"Omnipresent," Aurora said, looking up from her *Vogue*. "You know, once you give them the slightest privilege they always seem to be around."

"That's the God's truth," Rosie said. "That's just what's driving me crazy. You ought to have one with a broke ankle sometime."

"I don't think I'd live with one who had anything broken," Aurora said. "I've always kept myself in working order, and I don't see why they shouldn't. How is Royce?"

"Worst and worst," Rosie said. "It's getting to me, bad. All he does is lie on his back and drink beer and think up dirtiness to bother me with."

"Dirtiness?"

"It ain't fit to talk about," Rosie said. "That slut's made a prevert out of my husband, that's all."

Rosie was staring into the bedroom closet, as if she thought General Scott might be hiding in it. She had a disgusted expression on her face.

"The General's not in there, if that's what you're worrying about," Aurora said. "I got rid of him for once."

"I know the General better than to think he'd hide in a closet," Rosie said.

"Well, it's pervert, not prevert and I don't see how Royce could be one," Aurora said. "Not if I follow what you're referring to."

"I may not know how to pronounce it, but I know it when I see it waved in my face," Rosie said fiercely, turning an accusatory eye on her boss.

"Don't glare at me. I'm merely trying to help. It doesn't do to bottle these things up, you know. I never bottle things up and I'm certainly a lot happier than you seem to be."

"Talk's cheap," Rosie said.

"Some talk. It can also be quite valuable. If you won't talk to me I'd like to know who you expect to talk to."

"Nobody," Rosie said. Tight-lipped, she began to strip the bed.

"That's a foolish attitude," Aurora said. "I know you're under a strain and I'd like to help, but I don't see what I can do unless you give me some clue as to what the trouble is."

Rosie continued to strip the bed.

Aurora sighed. "Look," she said. "You're not the first woman in the world to have such problems. Millions of men take mistresses, you know. The fact that your husband took one for a while is not quite the end of the world, that I can see. Men have never distinguished themselves for sexual fidelity. The poor things have short attention spans."

"Your husband never took up with no slut," Rosie said. "You was married a long time too."

"True, but mine had very little initiative," Aurora said. "Probably he just never happened to meet a woman who cared to supply it. I don't kid myself that it was my undying charms that kept him home."

"It sure wasn't," Rosie said. "He'd have taken up with a slut too, if he hadn't been so timid."

"Oh, Rud wasn't especially timid. He was just lazy, like me. Both of us had a healthy capacity for idleness. We happened to like to stay in bed. If you were a little lazier you might not have the problems you're having now."

"Some people have to work," Rosie said hotly. "Don't lay there an' tell me I ought to have been lazy! You know I could never afford it."

"You work compulsively," Aurora said. "You always have, and in my opinion you'd work compulsively if you were a million-airess. It's all you want to do, you know. You didn't even particularly like raising your children. All I've ever seen you do is pick on Royce, and now you're accusing him of perversity. Probably his mistress was somewhat less strait-laced than you are, that's all. Probably she didn't pick on him. Maybe all he wanted was a little peaceful sex."

"Yeah, the dirty kind," Rosie said bitterly.

"No kind is exactly impeccable," Aurora said. "What are you talking about?"

"She sits on it," Rosie mumbled. "On Royce, I mean."

"I know what you mean," Aurora said.

"I don't know what I'm living for anymore, to tell the honest truth," Rosie said. "Royce has got it into his head I oughta be like her, and now my daughter's husband has taken up with a slut. He thinks if Royce can get away with it he can too. He drove right past Elfrida's house with her, not three days ago."

"Elfrida should never have married that boy, and we both know it," Aurora said. "She should divorce him at once, in my opinion. Royce has had twenty-seven years in which to get restless and that boy's only had about five. Frankly I'm surprised he isn't in jail by now. Don't you go mixing Elfrida's troubles up with your own. That won't help. Go wash my sheets and let me think about all this. Maybe I'll have something helpful to say afterwhile."

Unfortunately, Rosie was more wrought up than either of them knew. Without suspecting she was near it, Rosie suddenly reached her breaking point. Thirty years of confusion were pressing her down. She tried to remember when somebody had been really good to her, but she couldn't. Her life, it seemed to her, was nothing but work, disappointment, and constant combat—it was too unfair. She would have liked to let go and beat everybody in it, particularly Royce, particularly Shirley, and maybe even Little Buster, who thought his daddy was so wonderful; but they were all elsewhere. The only person around was Aurora, smiling, buxom, and happy, as she had always been, it seemed to Rosie.

It was too much. Pain swelled in her breast like a balloon, until she couldn't breathe, and she flung the armful of bedclothes at Aurora's dressing table. Aurora looked up just in time to see a great wad of sheets and spreads strike her dressing table, knocking bottles and sprays every which way.

"Stop it," she yelled, and the next thing she knew Rosie came charging around the bed like a berserk person and began to beat at her with a pillow.

"It's your fault, it's your fault!" Rosie cried. "It's your fault."

"What?" Aurora said, completely confused as to what she might have done. Before she could scoot back into the depths of the window nook or get to her feet or even ask a question, Rosie hit at her again with the pillow. Aurora was wide-eyed with surprise at the attack, and the tip of the pillow hit her right in the eye. The eye watered instantly, and she moaned and clasped her hand to it.

"Stop it!" she said. "Stop, you hit me in the eye."

But Rosie was far too wrought up to stop. She didn't hear Aurora, didn't notice that she had hit her in the eye. In her own mind's eye all she saw was Royce sitting in Aurora's kitchen pretending to eat, when all he was really doing was watching Aurora drift around.

"Your fault!" she said, striking again. "Your fault. You was the one that got him thinkin', in the first place . . . All these years . . ."

She stopped, not knowing what she wanted to say or do, but still filled with pain. She lost her breath again, thinking about the sorry mess she was in.

"All right," Aurora said. "All right, just stop. I can't see . . ." Though even with one eye she could see the fury in Rosie's face.

"All right, I give up," she added. "You can go, you're fired, whatever you want. Anything. Just get away from me."

"You ain't firing me, 'cause I quit," Rosie said, throwing the pillow at the dressing table. "I double quit! I wisht I'd never seen this house. I wisht I'd never done none of it. Maybe something in my life would be right."

"I don't know why you think so," Aurora said, but Rosie had already stalked out of the bedroom. She stalked straight out of the house. Aurora looked out the window with her one good eye and watched her walk along the sidewalk to the bus stop. Rosie did not look up. She took her place stiffly at the bus stop, and before she had been there thirty seconds a bus came up, as if by prearrangement. A few more seconds and Rosie was gone.

Aurora hobbled over and got a mirror in order to look at her stinging eye. Then she crawled back into her window nook and waited, touching her eyelid now and then with a fingertip. It caused a flood of tears to flow down one cheek. She found, though, that she was quite calm. Indeed, everything was quite calm. The house was silent, no vacuum cleaner going, no General grumping around; and except for the twitter of a bird and the occasional sound of an insect bumping into the window screen, nature was silent too. The morning had no sound, only a feel— the feel of heat slowly gathering in the air. In contrast to that feel the coolness of the bedroom was even more delightful, but the fact remained that she had just been in a dreadful scene and had fired her maid.

After a time she called Emma. "Rosie and I have had a dreadful fracas," she said. "She went rather crazy all of a sudden. She smashed my dressing table and hit me in the eye with a pillow. I'm not hurt, but I'm afraid in the confusion I fired her."

"That's terrible," Emma said.

"I didn't mean it, of course," Aurora said. "I was just trying to get her to stop beating me. Our old friend Rosie is not happy just now, you know."

"What are you going to do?"

"Nothing, until this afternoon. By then she'll have calmed down, if she's ever going to. Perhaps she'll agree to a truce. She seems to feel it's all my fault."

"Oh, because you used to flirt with Royce," Emma said.

Aurora looked out the window. Her idle morning had not worked out as planned.

"Yes," she said. "To tell the truth, I can scarcely remember Royce. I flirt with everybody. It's been my way of life. What's a girl to do? Royce has never spoken a whole sentence in my presence in all the years I've known him. I suppose I ought to take the veil, or something. I never meant anything with Royce. I don't even mean anything with Hector, to tell you the truth.

"Why, after all these years, do people still think I mean anything?" she asked. "I never have, and I no longer expect to get to. I just like a little pleasant banter. Would you please call Rosie this afternoon and assure her I want her back?"

"Sure," Emma said. "Maybe everything will be calmer by the afternoon."

2.

By the time she got on the bus, Rosie knew she had been hasty. Quitting a job to make a point was one thing, but what it really meant was that she had to go home and cope with Royce and Little Buster. She felt rather sorry for having hit Aurora, since it wasn't Aurora's fault that she was buxom and happy rather than skinny and miserable. She started to get off at the next bus stop and walk back, but she saw F.V. watering the General's lawn and the sight was enough to keep her on the bus. If there was any trouble she didn't need, it was trouble with F.V.

She rode across Houston feeling blank. The only thing about life that was still normal was the weather, which was hot. Everything else was askew, and when she stepped off the bus onto the sidewalks of Lyons Avenue nothing seemed right. She was supposed to step off the bus there in the late afternoon, when the asphalt was beginning to cool and when jukebox music could be heard through the open door of every bar. Now it was so early that the asphalt wasn't even very hot, and most of the bars still had their doors closed.

She walked down Lyons Avenue listlessly, not particularly wanting to walk, but not particularly wanting to get home either. On the way she passed Pioneer Drive-In Number 16 and noticed a sign saying "Carhop Wanted." The Pioneer Number 16 was one of the roughest places in Houston, catering, as it did nightly, to Negroes, Mexicans, and rednecks; but seeing the sign reminded Rosie that she had a husband who was both crippled and unemployed, and children to feed and clothe. In short, she had a living to earn.

A fat woman in a blond wig was inside the shell of the drive-in cleaning out the Dixie-cream machine. Her name was Kate, and Rosie knew her slightly from having bought Little Buster a good number of milkshakes and Lou Ann a great number of corndogs—a food she particularly loved.

"What are you lookin' so draggy for?" Kate asked when she saw Rosie leaning on the counter.

"I ain't draggy," Rosie said.

"What have you done with that little boy of mine?" Kate asked. "I can't hardly get through the day without some sugar from Little Buster."

"Maybe I can bring him later," Rosie said. "Your carhop job still open?"

"More open than ever," Kate said. "We had another elopement last night."

"Aw," Rosie said.

"Yep," Kate said. "Girls these days just don't know how to keep their pants on, seems like."

"Well, I'm applyin' for the job," Rosie said.

Kate was startled, but after looking Rosie over she decided not to ask any questions. "You got it, honey," she said. "You want the day shift or the night shift?"

"I'll work both if you want me to," Rosie said. "We got bills to pay, and I never was one to sit around the house."

"Honey, I know you're tough, but you ain't workin' both," Kate said.

"I guess the night shift then," Rosie said, trying to decide which would be the worst time to be around the house. She thanked Kate for the job and walked on up the street feeling a little more chipper. It was something, being employable—not much, maybe, but something.

3.

WHILE ROSIE was getting hired, Royce was having his midmorning conversation with Shirley. He had fallen into the habit of calling her frequently, to relieve the monotony of his day. Despite his husbandlike behavior in regard to Rosie, despite his hasty action and his broken ankle, Shirley still seemed to want him. Royce didn't know it, but the main reason Shirley wanted him was because he was so easy to manage. Shirley considered herself a busy woman, and it was necessary for her to have a man who followed orders without complaint. Royce did just that, and Shirley spent an hour or two on the phone with him each day, priming him for a return to the comforts of her apartment on Harrisburg. She told him about a number of novel plans she had for his old thing, once she got it back within her jurisdiction, and Royce listened raptly, his old thing not much less hard than the cast on his ankle.

He was lying on the bed in his underwear, watching his old thing stick up and trying to imagine some of the novel things Shirley was even at that moment whispering about in his ear, when with no warning whatever his wife Rosie walked through the bedroom door.

"You're at work," Royce said, in his shock.

"Naw, but I got to go in about five minutes, sugarpuss," Shirley said in his ear, thinking the statement was meant for her.

"Well, I ain't, Royce, you can see that," Rosie said.

"It's about that time agin," Shirley said, yawning. She meant work time.

"Who's on the phone?" Rosie asked. "If it's Aurora, let me talk to her." On the walk home the joys of being employable had begun to fade and she was hoping Aurora would call so they could go about making up.

She assumed it was Aurora, in fact, and held out her hand for the phone. Royce was so taken aback by her sudden appearance that once again his sense of reality deserted him, and instead of hanging up the phone he simply handed it to his wife.

"Well, how's your eye, you pore thing?" Rosie asked, growing remorseful at the memory of how startled her boss had been when she attacked her.

"Royce? Operator?" Shirley said, thinking there had suddenly been a break in the connection.

"What?" Rosie said. Poor Aurora had never been able to stand to be hated, or even disliked, or, for that matter, even mildly disapproved of, and remembering suddenly all the kindnesses Aurora had done her over the years, Rosie had begun to feel that her own actions constituted a kind of Pearl Harbor in their relationship. She had struck without warning, and she wanted to be forgiven so badly that she didn't even hear Shirley's reply.

"I don't know, I guess I just went out of my head," she said, before Shirley broke in.

"Royce, can you hear me?" Shirley said. "Somebody else is on this line."

Then Rosie heard. She looked at Royce, thunderstruck, and dropped the phone as if it had been a cobra. The receiver dangled an inch above the floor, and Royce looked down at it in order to avoid Rosie's eye.

"Royce, I'm gonna hang up and call you right back," Shirley said. "Don't you call me, I'll call you. Just hang up."

Royce looked intently at the dangling receiver, but he didn't reach down to hang it up.

"That was *her*, wasn't it?" Rosie said. "You was talkin' to *her*."

"Uh, Shirley," Royce admitted. "Called about my broke ankle."

Then he happened to notice the member Shirley had really called about. Not realizing what trouble Royce was in, it had continued to maintain itself as it had been when Shirley was talking. That was embarrassing, but fortunately Rosie stalked out of the bedroom without seeming to notice. Then, before Royce could even hang up the phone, she marched back in carrying the garden shears. Before Royce could so much as move she bent over and neatly snipped the cord that held the receiver. It had begun to buzz, but when Rosie snipped the cord it fell to the bedroom floor and became silent.

Rosie's only regret was that snipping the cord had been so quick and easy. She would have liked to snip telephone cords for an hour or two, but there was only the one to snip and once she had done it she became confused. She sat down on the bedroom floor.

"Hell, you cut the phone," Royce said, the import of it just beginning to penetrate. "Why'd you cut the phone?"

"So you can't lay there talkin' to that slut. Why'd you think?" Rosie said. "I go off and work myself ragged and you lay there talkin' to a slut. Whyn't you go on back an' live with her if you like her that much?"

"Can I?" Royce asked.

Rosie began to jab the point of the garden shears into the bedroom floor. So far, she realized, she had spent the whole morning making matters worse for herself. With the phone out of commission there was not even any way Aurora could call and hire her back. Now Royce was talking of leaving again. That too had been at her suggestion.

"I could take the bus," Royce said. "You could have the truck, in case you wanted to drive the kids around. Take 'em to the zoo. You know how Little Buster loves the zoo."

"Royce, the truck don't run," Rosie said. "We ain't had the money to get it fixed since you had the wreck."

She continued to jab the shears into the bedroom floor, which worried Royce a little. Rosie had unpredictable ways, and he would have been happier if she had left the shears outside or taken them back when she had finished cutting the phone. There was no telling where she might decide to jab them next.

"All right, go on. Go back to her," Rosie said. "I give up. It seems to me after twenty-seven years we ought to be able to find a few blessings to count, but I guess you don't think so, do you Royce?"

Royce was unable to think of any blessings.

"Are we supposed to get a divorce, or what's the deal?" Rosie asked.

Shirley had raised the question of divorce a few times too, but Royce had never really got around to grappling with the concept. Living with Shirley had been task enough; divorcing Rosie was a little too much to think about.

"Naw. You can still be my wife," Royce said earnestly. "I wouldn't wanta make you go through that."

"I don't know," Rosie said. "If you're gonna live with a slut maybe I oughta get divorced and marry some decent feller. I done got a job carhoppin'—I'll probably meet a decent feller some night if I keep my eyes open."

"Carhoppin'?" Royce said. "What about Miz Greenway?"

"We had a fight," Rosie said. "I got fired. I beat her up with a pillow."

"Hit Miz Greenway?" Royce said unbelievingly.

"Yeah, Miz Greenway, that you been making me jealous with

for twenty years," Rosie said. "She was your idea of heaven until this slut come along."

In recent months Royce had all but forgotten Aurora Greenway. Suddenly a vision of her in a dressing gown swam before his inner eye.

"She ain't marrit yet, is she?" he asked, remembering that she had always been the woman of his dreams.

"What's it to you?" Rosie asked. "You'll never see Aurora agin, now that I'm fired an' you're goin' off to live with Shirley."

Royce's head was in a spin. Too many things were happening at once. Now that he had learned about fantasy, he would have preferred to lie in bed and have a fantasy about Mrs. Greenway, who, he remembered, smelled awfully good. Rosie was comparatively smell-less, and Shirley usually smelled as if she kept an onion in each armpit. Royce didn't consider himself finicky, but the memory of Aurora, so talkative and fragrant, was hard to put down. His erection had gone away while Rosie was jabbing the shears into the floor, but at the memory of Aurora it came back.

Rosie noticed and got to her feet. "If you're just gonna lie there an' point your old jigger at me I'm leavin'," she said. "I'll go visit my sister until you can get your things packed."

Then, hardly knowing what to think, she went over to her bureau and buried her head in her arms. She was not crying; she just didn't want to look at anything for a while. What there was to look at wasn't very cheerful. Unrewarding as Royce was, she didn't want him to leave, because the house didn't feel right with him gone. It left her with nothing but two argumentative kids and what few material possessions the other five kids hadn't broken as they were growing up. She had just lost her nice job and had nothing to look forward to workwise except long evenings of carrying hamburgers and fried shrimp to carloads of teenagers. She rested with her head in her arms for a few minutes, doing her best not to think about it all.

Then, with a sigh, she turned around to start getting on with the process of separation, only to find that Royce, exhausted by the complex developments of the morning, had fallen asleep, one hand under his underwear. Rosie tiptoed over for a closer look. In repose Royce and his youngest son, sweet Little Buster, looked exactly alike, except that Royce hadn't shaved in a couple of days and had a large sagging belly and bowlegs. Even flat on his back his legs looked bowed. Lou Ann had drawn a kitty cat and some flowers on his cast, and Little Buster, unable to master kitty cats and flowers, had covered most of the rest with swirls and scribbles.

Rosie looked down at her sleeping husband for a minute or two, unable to get clear in her head exactly why she wanted to keep him. Nothing visible to the eye was anything a sensible woman would want, and she did consider herself a sensible woman. It seemed to her it would be a good deal pleasanter to have a nice little man like Vernon around—someone neat and small, like herself. All her married life she had been slightly bothered by the fear that Royce might accidentally roll on top of her and suffocate her some night.

Even so, she reached down and took Royce's hand out his underwear. It would be more seemly in case the kids should suddenly come back. Just as she did it, someone began knocking on the front door. She hurried in and saw that it was her oldest daughter, Elfrida, who was supposed to be at her job, which was checking at Woolworth's.

"What in the world?" Rosie said. "Why ain't you at work, honey?"

Elfrida, a tiny thin blonde, burst into tears. "Aw, Momma," she said. "Gene took our savings. All our savings. He come in drunk an' demanded 'em. Said he give a hot check, but I bet he never. I bet he just took 'em to buy somethin' for *her*. I know it was *her* put him up to it."

She flung herself into her mother's arms, sobbing bitterly. Rosie led her daughter to the couch and let her cry it out, stroking her back in comfort. "How much was your savings, Elfrida?" she asked.

"A hunnert an' eighty dollars," Elfrida sobbed. "We was gonna get a rug. We'd planned! I know it was her!"

"A hunnert an' eighty dollars ain't the end of the world, hon," Rosie said.

"But we'd *planned!*" Elfrida sobbed, cruelly betrayed. "And he took it anyway."

"You should have told me you needed a rug, hon," Rosie said. "Your daddy and I would of got you one. We don't want you to be without. That ain't no big deal."

"I know . . . but our savings . . . it was ours," Elfrida sobbed. "What am I gonna do?"

Rosie looked out the door. The asphalt on Lyons Avenue was heating up, and the traffic was heavy. "I ain't right sure, Elfrida," she said, letting her daughter sob. "Right now I ain't right sure."

CHAPTER XVI

1.

AURORA HELD her peace until four in the afternoon; then she began calling Rosie. A fight was a fight, and so far as she was concerned that one was over with. Upon reflection she had concluded that perhaps she had been a bit too exuberant in some of her little exchanges with Royce, if exchanges was a fair word for any conversation involving Royce; and, aware of the strain that Rosie had been under, she was prepared to go to unusual lengths to humble herself and be apologetic.

Then, to her intense annoyance, the only response she·could get from Rosie's telephone was a busy signal. After an hour and a half of the busy signal her apologetic mood was beginning to sour. Nothing was more frustrating than to be willing to bring herself to her knees and then not have the gesture appreciated. Besides, she was quite sure there was no one Rosie had any business talking to for an hour and a half, unless it was her.

After another hour she began to feel paranoid. Perhaps it was

Emma she was talking to. Perhaps the two of them were talking about what an awful, selfish person she was.

Immediately she called Emma, who denied having heard from Rosie.

"I don't hear you denying that I'm an awful, selfish person," Aurora said.

"That would be pointless," Emma said. "Maybe Rosie's phone's broken."

"There are lots of pay phones where she lives," Aurora said. "She should have understood that I'd be frantic by now."

"If you'd flirted with my husband for twenty years I'd let you sweat a few hours, I think."

"It would be hard to flirt for eight seconds with your husband," Aurora said. "He's not good flirting material. Your friend Patsy can flirt with him if she likes. They're ideal for one another—neither of them have any manners. Perhaps they'll run off together and spare you a life of academic boredom."

"I don't think the academic life is boring," Emma said. "What an insulting thing to say."

"Perhaps it isn't at Harvard, but few places are Harvard," Aurora said, winking her eye to see if her eyelid still worked.

"Snob," Emma said.

"Oh, hush," Aurora said. "You're a very young person. You haven't lived the academic life. What you've lived is the student life. Wait until you've been a faculty wife for ten years and then tell me it isn't boring. They're the dreariest women in America, faculty wives. They have no taste and they couldn't afford it if they had it. Most of them don't have the sense to realize that all men aren't as dull as their husbands. The ones that realize it go crazy in a few years, or else devote themselves to good works."

"What's so bad about good works?" Emma asked. "Somebody has to do them."

"Sure, fine," Aurora said. "Don't bother me with them. I've not lost interest quite to that extent."

"I hope I never become arrogant, like you," Emma said. "You dismiss whole classes with a wave of your hand. At least academic people take time to discriminate."

"Take time? Why, what else do they have to do, dear? I've

noticed that mediocre people always pride themselves on their discrimination. It's a vastly overrated ability, I can assure you. One creditable lover is worth a ton of discrimination, more or less. I discriminate instinctively, as it happens."

"Arrogantly, like I said," Emma said.

"Uh-huh, well, just be grateful that you're grown," Aurora said. "You're spared the pains of living with me. I'm going to hang up and call Rosie."

She did and called Rosie, only to get the same busy signal. She called the phone company, who informed her that Rosie's phone was out of order. She considered the information for a moment and called Emma.

"She's broken her phone," she said. "That's very inconvenient. I know how her mind works. She won't call me because she'll assume I'm still mad at her. That means this impasse will continue until I actually go over there. It's quite intolerable that it should continue, so I shall have to go over there at once."

"Your logic is relentless," Emma said dryly.

"The timing is most unfortunate," Aurora said. "Hector will be returning any moment now, expecting a lot of praise and admiration for doing what any normal person would do as a matter of course. He's going to be in a snit if I'm not here, but then that's his lookout. I would like it if you would accompany me, just in case Rosie is in a mood to be difficult."

"Sure," Emma said. "I haven't seen Little Buster lately. My husband won't like it, though. He's due home too."

"So what. He's not a general," Aurora said. "He can open his own beer for once. Tell him your mother needed you."

"Surprisingly enough, he thinks his needs take precedence over yours."

"Goodbye. I'm hurrying," Aurora said.

2.

AT SIX-THIRTY, when they arrived at Rosie's door, most of the evening traffic had subsided, but Lyons Avenue was still choked with beat-up pickups and cars with crumpled fenders, many of them honking and competing recklessly for position.

"Amazing," Aurora said, watching a few of them go by. A mauve Cadillac with a little antenna on top flashed by, driven by a thin Negro in a huge pink hat.

"Now where'd he get that?" Aurora asked, fanning herself.

"By trafficking in human flesh," Emma said. "If he sees us he may come back and try to traffic in us."

"It's amazing that Rosie's survived, isn't it?" Aurora said, surveying the street. A Mexican dance hall was a few doors down from Rosie's house, and a Negro liquor store right across the street. They got out and went to Rosie's door, but their knocks brought no response.

"She's probably over at her sister's, telling her what a bitch you are," Emma said.

"Royce had a broken ankle," Aurora said. "Do you suppose that man has hobbled off to a bar?"

The house key was under an old washpot in the back yard. A large colony of bugs was also under the pot in a circle of bleached grass. The back yard also contained two broken tricycles and the motor of a Nash Rambler Royce had owned many years before.

Once they were inside, it took only seconds to determine that the Dunlups had vanished. Three of the four rooms bore the stamp of Rosie's orderliness: the dishes were washed in the kitchen, the toys neatly stacked in the children's room. Only the bedroom showed signs of activity. The bed wasn't made, the bureau drawers were open, and, most mysterious of all, the telephone receiver was lying on top of the bureau.

"That's rather drastic, don't you think?" Aurora said. "If she wasn't in the mood to talk she could have stuck it under a pillow. I didn't think she'd be this mad at me."

"It could be Royce," Emma said. "Maybe they broke up again." They went back out and dropped the key back amid the bugs.

"Most inconvenient," Aurora said two or three times.

They got in the car and started back down Lyons Avenue, but they had not gone three blocks before Emma, glancing casually at a drive-in and wishing she could have a milkshake, spotted the very person they were looking for carrying a large tray of food to one of the parked cars.

"Stop, Momma!" she said. "There she is at the drive-in."

Instead of stopping Aurora executed a majestic turn, narrowly missing a pickup full of Mexicans, all of whom began to curse her in spirited terms. When she did finally stop it was in the middle of a side street that ran by the drive-in—the street, as it happened, that the pickup full of Mexicans had been meaning to drive down. They began to honk, but Aurora was not to be hurried. She peered calmly across the parking lot, trying to ascertain if Rosie was actually there.

"I don't see why those men didn't pass me when they had the chance," she said. Then she coughed, almost overcome by exhaust fumes as the old pickup roared by. A number of brown fists were shaken at her.

"I'm glad I don't live in a Latin country," she said. "I'm sure I'd have a great deal of trouble if I did." She did another majestic turn and brought the Cadillac to rest midway between two convertibles, both of them full of raucous white boys with long sideburns.

"You're taking up two spaces," Emma said. "Maybe three."

"That's fine," Aurora said. "I don't like our neighbors. I'm sure they're saying very profane things. I'd rather your young ears weren't sullied."

Emma giggled at the idea, and as she did Rosie walked out toward them. Her head was down and she was not noticing much. She had only been working an hour, but she had already learned that it was better to keep her head down and not notice much. Before she had been at work ten minutes a heavy equipment operator with a little bulldozer tattooed on his arm had hinted that he might like to marry her if, as he put it, they "hit it off."

When she looked up to take an order and found herself looking into the apparently uninjured eye of her former employer, the shock was almost too much. It rendered her speechless.

"Yes," Aurora said. "There you are, aren't you? You've already secured employment. I suppose I'm to be given no chance to ask to be forgiven, though I would have thought you might offer me that chance after all our years together."

"Aw, Aurora," Rosie said.

"Hello, over there," Emma said.

Rosie couldn't answer. She was about to cry. All she could do was stand and look at her boss and her favorite girl. Their appearance at the Pioneer Number 16 seemed nothing short of a miracle.

"Why did you cut that phone?" Aurora asked. "I only waited a reasonable interval before I called you."

Rosie shook her head, then leaned it against the car door. "Honey, it wasn't over you," she said. "I come home an' caught Royce talkin' to his girl friend. I don't know, I just got the shears and cut it before I even thought."

"I see," Aurora said. "I should have guessed. That was perfectly sensible, only you might have called me first so I would have known what was happening."

"I thought of it two seconds too late," Rosie said. "Y'all want anything to cat?"

"Milkshake," Emma said. "Chocolate."

"I'll be back in a minute," Rosie said.

They watched silently as she delivered two large trays of food to the adjacent convertibles. "Look at her," Aurora said. "She acts like she's been doing it for years.

"Go take off that uniform and get in the car," she said when Rosie came back. "I take it back about firing you."

"That's a big relief," Rosie said. "I'll be there in the morning. I can't walk off the job just when they're busiest. Did Royce tell you where to find me?"

"No, Royce was not about. My eagle-eyed daughter spotted you."

Rosie heaved a deep sigh and without a word walked off shaking her head. Two or three cars had begun to honk for service. It was several minutes before she got time to stop at the Cadillac again.

"That means he's gone back to her," she said. "I guess that's that. I ain't takin' him back no second time."

"We'll talk about this tomorrow," Aurora said, but Rosie had already taken their tray and gone.

3.

"Do you ever hear from Vernon?" Emma asked as they were riding back. The moon had risen early, and it hung above the buildings of downtown Houston.

Aurora didn't answer.

"I think you might have made something of Vernon if you'd tried," Emma said.

"I'm not an educator. Enjoy that nice moon and mind your own business. When I was younger it was sometimes amusing to draw people out and give them polish, if they needed it, but it's been my lot to know quite a number of people who are already polished, and I suppose they've pampered me."

"Are you and the General thinking of marrying?" Emma asked timidly.

"Hector is thinking of it," Aurora said. "I am not. I thought I told you to mind your own business."

"I'd just like to find out what makes you tick," Emma said. "I don't care what it is, I'd just like to know."

"Yes, that's your academic bias showing," Aurora said. "In this case you made a bad choice of metaphor, since clocks tick and I am not a clock. If you're interested in the source of clicks you will have to study clocks. Horology, I believe it's called. You'll never know much about me, I'm afraid. Half the time I'm a mystery to myself, and I've always been a mystery to the men who think they know me. Happily, I enjoy surprises. I'm always happiest when I manage to surprise myself."

"I wish I'd never brought it up," Emma said.

"Since you are my daughter, I'll tell you something," Aurora said. "Understanding is overrated and mystery is underrated. Keep that in mind and you'll have a livelier life."

When she stopped at Emma's apartment, they could both see Flap. He was sitting on the steps that led up to the apartment. They both sat and looked at him through the deep twilight.

"He isn't running out to embrace you, is he?" Aurora said.

"Is the General going to run out and embrace you when you get home?"

"Well, at the very least he's going to be pacing the floor," Aurora said. "Thank you for accompanying me. I trust you'll give your old mother a call when you sense that you're about to give birth."

"Sure. Give my best to the General."

"Thank you, I shall. I always do anyway, but it was nice of you to say it. This time it can be legitimate."

"Why do you always say it?" Emma asked, waving vaguely at Flap in reassurance.

"The General's fond of believing that he's widely loved and adored," Aurora said. "In fact he's hardly loved or adored at all, but since I seem to have taken him under my wing I have to do my best to conceal that from him. The slightest whiff of disapproval casts him down."

"You mean you become an approving person when you're not around me? I'd like to see that sometime."

"It's quite a sight, I admit," Aurora said, waving as she drove away.

4.

THE MINUTE she turned into her driveway Aurora knew there was trouble ahead, because Alberto's disreputable old Lincoln was parked where her Cadillac was supposed to sit. Alberto was not in the Lincoln, which meant that he was probably in the house somewhere. There had been no light on in the General's house when she had passed it, so it was not unlikely that he too was in her house. She managed to squeeze the Cadillac in past the Lincoln, wondering how in the world Alberto had managed to squeeze in past Hector.

She sat and thought about the whole matter for perhaps a minute, and decided that the more leisurely her entrance the better, if only because it would save her breath. A lot of breath was going to be necessary, she felt sure. Despite several lengthy telephone calls on the subject, Alberto evidently refused to accept that the General had become a serious part of her life; the General, for his part, had never accepted that Alberto was a member of the civilized orders. It seemed likely to be an interesting evening, so she brushed her hair for a while before getting out of the car.

She opened her back door a crack and listened for the sound of angry male voices, but she heard nothing. The house was intimidatingly quiet—so quiet, in fact, that she allowed the situation to intimidate her briefly. She eased the door shut and took a short walk along the sidewalk, trying to work out in her mind what her position ought to be relative to the two men. They had been rivals for a good twenty-five years, and matters would require some delicacy, she knew. Alberto had had his success early, and the General was having his late—the twain between the successful and the disappointed was not likely to meet. All she really hoped to accomplish was to get Alberto out alive. He had always been the least self-protective of men, and she lingered a while on the sidewalk in the hope that perhaps he would emerge on an errand, or in disgust, or something, so she could have a moment or two alone with him before the storm broke.

But Alberto did not emerge and Aurora went back and opened the back door wide. "Yoo hoo," she said. "Are you boys in there?"

"Of course we're in here," the General said. "Where have you been?"

Aurora stepped into the kitchen and saw that the two of them were sitting at the kitchen table, one at each end. A vast profusion of flowers were ranged along the cabinets. Alberto wore a familiar much-injured look and a shabby brown suit. The General was glaring at her with his usual fierceness.

"Why, I've been out," she said. "Why do you ask?"

"Aurora, I won't have you answering questions with questions," the General said. He seemed about to say more, but then abruptly he stopped.

"Alberto, what a surprise," she said, giving him a pat. She set her purse on the table and looked both men over.

"You've raided the flower shops again, I see," she said.

"Well, I buy a few flowers . . . for old times' sake," Alberto said. "You know me, I have to buy some flowers."

"I'd like to know why," the General said. "Look at those things. It's ridiculous. I haven't bought that many flowers in the last twenty years. I don't expect to have that many flowers at my goddamn funeral."

"Oh, stop grumping, Hector," Aurora said. "Alberto has always had a weak spot for flowers, that's all. It's his Italian heritage. You've been in Italy surely. You can appreciate that."

"I don't appreciate anything," the General said hotly. "I find all this very goddamn mysterious. I find it irritating too, I might say. What does he think he's doing here?"

"What is you doing here!" Alberto said, growing suddenly red in the face. He pointed a finger at the General.

Aurora slapped his hand lightly. "Come on, put your finger away, Alberto," she said. She looked around to see that the General was silently shaking his fist.

"Stop shaking your fist, Hector," she said. "May I remind both of you that none of us met yesterday. Whether either of you like to admit it or not, I've known both of you for a very long time. We're products of a rather lengthy acquaintanceship, and I think the less finger pointing and fist shaking we have the more we'll all enjoy the evening."

"What do you mean, enjoy the evening?" the General said. "I certainly don't intend to enjoy any evening with *him* around."

Alberto chose that moment to rise and burst into tears. He started for the door, abasing himself as he went.

"I go, I go," he said. "I am the one who is wrong to be here, I see it Aurora. Is nothing. I was just bringing some flowers for old times' sake, and perhaps say hello, but I make a mistake. You can be in peace."

He threw her a tearful kiss, but Aurora raced around the table and caught him by his shabby brown coat sleeve just before he got out the door.

"You come right back here, Alberto," she said. "Nobody's leaving just yet."

"Ha!" the General said. "That's the goddamn Italian heritage that I remember. They're all a bunch of crybabies."

Alberto switched abruptly from tears to rage. Several large veins stood out on his forehead. "You see, he has insult!" he said, waving his left fist. Aurora clung calmly to the right and managed to drag him back to his chair.

"Sit, Alberto," she said. "This is extremely colorful and on the whole flattering to a lady of my years, but my tolerance for colorful behavior is limited, as you both ought to know."

When she saw that Alberto was going to sit, she released him and walked down to the other end of the table. She put a hand on the General's arm—which, despite his pretense of cool, was quivering somewhat—and looked him calmly in the eye.

"Hector, I would like to inform you that I have decided to ask Alberto to take dinner with us," she said.

"Oh, you have, have you?" the General said, faintly intimidated. Being looked directly in the eye had always made him somewhat uncomfortable, and Aurora did not shift her gaze in the slightest.

"I don't see that I need to repeat myself," she said. "Alberto is a friend of long standing and I have been rather negligent lately where he is concerned. Since he's been so considerate as to bring me these nice flowers, I think it's only appropriate to use the occasion to repair my negligence, don't you?"

The General was not about to say yes but did not quite dare say no. He held his silence.

"Besides which," Aurora went on, with a slight smile, "I have always felt that you and Alberto should get to know one another better."

"Like fun we should," the General said grimly.

"Yes, it would be fun," Aurora said, blithely ignoring his meaning. "Don't you think so Alberto?"

She glanced down at the table and fixed Alberto with the same direct gaze. Alberto took refuge in a profound if somewhat exhausted Italian shrug.

"You're being goddamn dictatorial, you know," the General said. "Nobody's going to enjoy this dinner but you, and you know it."

"Far be it from me to dictate to you, Hector," Aurora said. "If you feel this to be the slightest imposition, then of course you know that you're free to leave. Alberto and I would be sorry to lose you, but we've dined alone before, and once more probably wouldn't hurt us."

"Oh, no you don't," the General said. Aurora continued to gaze at him. She seemed to be smiling, but he hadn't the least idea what she was really thinking, so he repeated what he had just said. "Oh, no you don't."

"You've said that twice, Hector," Aurora said. "If it's some kind of military code, would you mind translating? Does that mean you've decided to stay for dinner after all?"

"Of course I'm staying for dinner," the General said. "I was invited properly, I might remind you. I didn't just come driving up with a car full of flowers and force my way in. At least I do these things by the book."

"So you do," Aurora said. "I wouldn't be surprised if that's not why you and I so often find ourselves in disagreement, Hector. My old friend Alberto and I leave a bit more room for impulse in our lives, don't we, Alberto?"

"Sure," Alberto said, yawning despite himself. He was already exhausted from his own emotion. "Anything we can think of, that's what we used to do," he added, once he had completed his yawn.

The General merely glared. It was not to be his last glare, nor Alberto's last yawn either. As soon as she saw that she had command of the situation, Aurora applied herself to it with complete precision. She forced a large rum drink on the General, having found from long experience that rum was the only drink that was likely to cause him to mellow. Alberto she restricted to wine, on the grounds that it was better for his heart. Then she sang a medley of Alberto's favorite songs while she whipped up some pasta, an excellent sauce, and a salad. Alberto's eyes shone briefly. He managed to compliment her twice, and then, quietly, halfway through his third glass of wine, he went to sleep. He went to sleep sitting up, at a tilt, but Aurora got up, removed his plate, lowered him gently until his head rested where his plate had been, and, after thinking a moment, left him his wine glass.

"I've never known Alberto to spill wine," she said. "He might want to drink it when he wakes up."

Before the General could say anything she took his plate, which was empty, and gave him another helping of pasta and what was left of the sauce. She set his plate in front of him sharply, as if she were a military orderly, and then gave him a little rap on the head with her knuckles before sitting down to finish her salad. She glanced for a moment at Alberto, peacefully sleeping, before turning back to the General.

"He's not got quite your vigor, you see," she said. "You were quite foolish to make that scene. What's it to you if Alberto comes over and goes to sleep at my table once in a while?"

Alberto's quick fade left the General mildly abashed, but not so abashed that he lost sight of the main point. "I don't care if he went to sleep," he said. "Look at all those flowers."

"If you make me lose my patience with you you're going to be sorry," Aurora said with a bit of flash in her eye. "Your jealousy is understandable and I understand it. I've put Alberto to sleep and pointed out to you that he's harmless. Sometimes I think you're a waste of good meat sauce. All I want is for him to go to sleep at a friendly table once in a while. His wife is dead and he's lonely—considerably lonelier than you are, since I seem to have taken you in. Nothing that exists between us requires me to drive my old friends from my door, that I can see. Is that what you want? Are you really prepared to be that ungenerous at your age?"

The General ate some pasta. He knew he should leave well enough alone, but despite that he still felt anxious.

Aurora pointed to Alberto. "Does a sight like that make you feel threatened, Hector? Don't you think you might stop and count your blessings before we continue this discussion?"

"All right," the General said. "I suppose there's no harm in a meal. It was those flowers that made me mad."

Aurora took up her fork again. "That's better," she said. "I like flowers in my house. Alberto loves to give them to me, and you don't. There's no point in pretending that you do. I doubt you've smelled two flowers in your life."

"All right, what do you think the man's after?" the General said loudly.

"Sex, probably, since you're too prudish to say it," Aurora said. "Once again you've managed to miss the point by your usual mile, Hector. The fact that most men have the same ultimate motive doesn't mean that they have the same qualities. Desires may not vary that much, but their expressions do. Alberto's little floral offerings show some real appreciation—appreciation of me, appreciation of flowers too. I wouldn't think of denying Alberto that little expression. It would mean that I didn't appreciate him—which I do. I'd be remarkably shallow if I weren't able to appreciate an affection that's persisted as long as his has."

"Mine's persisted as long as his has," the General said.

"Not quite," Aurora said. "It might surprise you to know that Alberto had already won and lost me before I met you. He predates you by four years, if I'm counting right. The fact that he's still around is quite endearing."

"But he was married. You were married," the General said.

Aurora continued her meal.

"Well, at least you admit he's got an ultimate motive," the General said. "I heard you."

Aurora looked over at him. "Well, the bittersweet is not your sphere, Hector," she said. "Perhaps you're better off—I'm not the one to say. However, if I had chosen to remain dependent for appreciation, or kindness either, solely upon those who could achieve their ultimate ends, I'm sure I would have often eaten alone.

"I ate alone enough, anyway," she added, thinking back on her last few years.

They were quiet. The General was not without sense. Aurora poured herself a bit more wine and turned the wine glass slowly in her fingers. She was sitting, he saw, not so much with him as with memory, and he stopped trying to argue about Alberto and switched from wine back to rum. The rum mellowed him, so that when Alberto awoke and managed to fumble his way out to his car he heard himself trying to persuade the tired little man that it would be safer, tired as he was, to spend the night on Aurora's couch. He even heard himself asking him to drop in again sometime, since after all it had been harmless, quite harmless. Alberto, yawning and rumpled, didn't hear him. He backed the Lincoln into a shrub and eventually managed to steer it into the street. Aurora stood on her lawn smiling a little, evidently not at all alarmed by the way Alberto was driving. The General, rather drunk, forgot her until she put her hand on the back of his neck and gave it a hard squeeze.

"What a hard neck," she said. "Nothing bittersweet about you, and that's fine. I must say I'm deeply pleased."

"What?" the General said, still peering after the weaving car.

"Yes, you and Alberto will end friends," she said, walking off a few steps and looking up at the waves of night clouds. "Who knows? Maybe you'll take in old Vernon and old Trevor and a few more of my others before you're done. All of you can sit crying into your drinks at the memory of what a lot of trouble I was."

"What?" the General said. "Where are you going to be?"

"I'll have caught the tide," Aurora said. Her head was tilted back. She was watching the rapid, passing Houston clouds.

CHAPTER XVII

1.

Deep in the fall, with her time at hand and the weather still almost as hot as it had been in July, Emma came home with a cart full of groceries just in time to catch her husband in the midst of a poetic flirtation with her best friend Patsy. Flap was sitting at one end of the couch, and Patsy, slim and lovely as ever, was sitting at the other end blushing.

"Hi, there!" Flap said, a little too enthusiastically.

"Hi, hi," Emma said, dragging the groceries in.

"Thank God," Patsy said. "He was reading me improper verse."

"Whose?" Emma asked dryly.

"I'll help," Patsy said, jumping up. She was very relieved to see her friend. Her own tendency to flirt was an embarrassment to her, yet she could seldom resist. Males were always surprising her with compliments, and she responded with witticisms and blushes, which seemed to bring even more compliments. With Flap Horton a flirtation was the only way around listening to him pontificate about literature, but that was all it was good for. She had always found him slightly repulsive physically and couldn't imagine how her best friend Emma could stand to sleep with him. She went over and gave Emma a big smile so she wouldn't think anything had really been afoot.

"Nobody ever reads improper verses to me," Emma said, casting herself as the unromantic drudge, for the sake of convenience.

Patsy helped her unpack the groceries and they made iced tea and sat at the kitchen table drinking it. After a while Flap got over being embarrassed at having been caught flirting and came and joined them.

"Has your mother got rid of that repulsive old general yet?" Patsy asked.

"Nope," Emma said. "She's caused him to mellow a little."

"Bullshit," Flap said. "They're both just as snobbish and arrogant as they ever were."

For a moment Emma got angry. It always angered her to hear people coolly dismissed. "They're no more snobbish than some other people I could name," she said. "No more arrogant. At least they don't spend all their time fishing, like Cecil."

Flap hated all conflict, but he particularly hated conflict in front of guests. He looked at Emma, large, hot, and hostile, and couldn't see anything about her that he liked.

"Why shouldn't Cecil fish?" he asked. "He wouldn't be any better off if he were out chasing women all the time."

"I didn't say he should chase them all the time," Emma said. "I just don't think he's better off for avoiding them."

"Maybe he was a one-woman man," Flap said.

"Sure, like you," Emma said. She knew she shouldn't be acting that way in front of her friend, but she didn't want to stop. Patsy was part of it, in a way, and would have to take her chances.

Patsy was even less able to bear conflict than Flap. "Oh, cut it out, you two," she said. "I wish I hadn't asked about your mother. I was just popping off."

Flap turned sullen. "Her mother's never had less than three men trailing her around," he said. "That doesn't happen by accident, you know. Men don't trail unless women leave a scent."

314

"I don't particularly like your choice of words, but I'll remember what you're saying," Emma said. She gripped her iced-tea glass tightly, wishing Patsy were gone. If she weren't there, anything might happen. She might fling the glass at him, or ask him for a divorce.

There was a minute of horribly tense silence, in which Flap and Emma held themselves in and Patsy pretended to look out the window. They all pretended to look out the window. In order to have something to do Emma got up and made some more tea, which the others accepted silently. Patsy was wondering if she left a scent. The notion was slightly repellent but slightly sexy. She opened her purse, got a comb, and began to comb her hair. She was imagining marriage, something she often did. In her vision marriage was mostly a house, beautifully furnished and appointed, like Mrs. Greenway's, in which she lived with a neat, polite young man. She could never envision the young man very clearly, but insofar as she saw him at all she saw him as neat, blond, and kind. He certainly wouldn't be a sloppy, sullen, sarcastic person like Flap Horton.

Flap only noticed that Patsy's arms weren't chubby like his wife's.

Emma, well aware that she was everything her husband no longer wanted, was chewing the lemon from her tea and looking at the same hot green lawn she had looked at every day for many months. She had stopped feeling hostile. What she felt was that it would be nice not to be pregnant anymore.

Patsy stopped combing her hair the minute she noticed that Flap was watching her. Actually she felt rather put off by both the Hortons. There was something violent in their attitude toward one another that she didn't like and didn't want to think about. Probably it had to do with sex, something else she didn't want to think about. In her fantasies of marriage sex was seldom more than a flicker on the screen of her mind. It had not happened to her very many times yet, and she was not sure about it at all.

"Why are we all sitting here staring?" Flap asked. Long silences made him uncomfortable.

"Because there's nothing else to do," Emma said. "I interrupted a poetry reading and made everyone uncomfortable."

"Don't apologize," Patsy said.

"I hadn't."

"No, but you were about to. You have a tendency to assume the sins of the world."

"Let her assume them," Flap said. "She commits enough of them."

"I'm leaving," Patsy said. "I don't know why you got her pregnant if you didn't intend to be nice to her."

"These things happen," Flap said.

Patsy was hyperventilating, as she always did when she was upset. "Boy, they're not happening to me," she said. She smiled at Emma and left.

"We made her cry," Flap said the minute she was out of earshot.

"So what?" Emma said. "She cries constantly. She's just the crying sort."

"Unlike you," Flap said. "You would never want to give anyone the satisfaction of having affected you that much."

"No," Emma said. "I'm made of stern stuff. The fact that my husband lusts after my best friend isn't going to get my goat. Maybe if you try real hard you can seduce her while I'm in the hospital having the baby."

"Oh, shut up," Flap said. "I was just reading her poetry. Her mind could stand some improving."

Emma flung the tea glass. It missed Flap and hit the wall behind him. "Would you like a divorce?" she said. "Then you could devote all your time to improving her mind."

Flap stared at her. He had passed from fantasies of escape with Patsy into the strange state of contentment that sometimes came with the realization that he really didn't have to do what he had been fantasizing. Before he could even sort out his wishes a tea glass had sailed past his head and his wife was looking at him out of deep, unfathomable green eyes.

"That was an asshole thing to do," he said. He had a sinking feeling. There was never any knowing what would happen.

"Would you like a divorce?" Emma repeated.

"Of course not. Will you try to be rational for a moment?"

Emma was satisfied. She would have liked to throw the table. "Don't ever talk to me about improving her mind again," she said. "That wasn't what you were thinking about."

"It's fun to talk about literature to someone who listens," Flap said. "You don't listen."

"I don't even like literature anymore," Emma said. "All I'm really interested in is clothes and sex, just like my mother. Unfortunately I can't afford clothes."

"You seem so scornful," Flap said. He stopped trying to argue and just sat not looking at her, presenting an entirely passive surface. Passivity was his only defense at such times. With no anger of his own, he was no match for his wife. Emma saw what he was doing and got up and went and showered. When she came out Flap was sitting on the couch reading the same book he had been reading Patsy. Her tension had drained away; she no longer felt hostile. Flap wore the meek look he often wore when he had been made to feel guilty or had been bested in a fight.

"Stop looking that way," she said. "I'm not mad at you anymore."

"I know, but you're looming over me," he said. "You really are immense."

Emma nodded. Outside, the evening had begun, and the spaces between the trees were already dark. Emma went to latch the screen door. In her mind there was only one certainty: that she would soon have a child. Its weight pulled at her as she stood and watched the shadows in her yard.

2.

ACROSS HOUSTON, in the stinking, oily evening air of Lyons Avenue, Emma's greatest champion, Rosie Dunlup, was standing at her own front door saying goodbye to a life, if it was a life, if it had ever been a life. Rosie wasn't sure. All she planned to carry away of it, though, was what she had in the two cheap suitcases that were sitting on her tiny porch. The children weren't there.

Once again Lou Ann and Little Buster had been dispatched to their aunt's, where there were so many children underfoot that two more wouldn't matter, not for a few days anyway, and in a few days Rosie planned to be settled back in Shreveport, Louisiana, the city of her birth.

She scratched around in her purse and found her housekey but she had no real desire to lock her house and in fact would have liked to walk away and leave it open. The washing machine she had saved so long to buy was about the only thing in it she wanted that she couldn't get in the two suitcases. It was a poor house and most of the furniture was broken; it had never been much good anyway. Leave it to whoever wants it, Rosie thought. Let the Negroes and Mexicans and thieving restless street kids that she had spent twenty years locking out come in and take what they pleased. Let them gut it, for all she cared; she didn't mean to come back and try to make a life amid such cheap objects, not anymore. She was finished with Lyons Avenue and all that went with it, and in fact it would have suited her fine to see someone drive up with a house-moving rig and a few jacks and steal the house itself, leaving nothing but a space and some dirt and a few pieces of junk in the back yard to show where her life had been lived. It had been a junky life anyway, Rosie thought and it would serve Royce right if someone just drove up and stole the house itself.

But habit was strong; even though she didn't want anything that was left in the house and never meant to return to it again, she searched until she found her key and locked the front door. Then she picked up her suitcases and walked over to the bus stop by Pioneer Number 16. Kate was out sweeping up the day's debris to make room for the debris that evening would bring.

"Going on your vacation?" she asked, noticing the suitcases.

"Yeah, permanent," Rosie said.

"Aw," Kate said. "Stood it long enough, have you?"

"That's it," Rosie said.

The news embarrassed Kate, who couldn't think of a thing else to say. It was obviously a momentous event, but as it happened, her mind was really elsewhere—specifically, it was on the fact that her lover wanted her to get a tattoo. Her lover was named Dub. She didn't want a tattoo, but he was being persistent and had even agreed to let her get it on her upper arm instead of her behind, which is where he originally hoped to see it. All it was supposed to say was Hot Momma, inside a heart; Dub's would say Big Daddy, inside another. She had promised him a decision that evening, in fact; and with that on her mind and the drive-in to run, it was hard to work up much of anything to say to Rosie, even if she *was* leaving forever.

"One of these days, after it's done too late, he's gonna wisht he hadn't been such a fool, honey," she said finally, just as Rosie stepped onto her bus.

Kate waved, but Rosie didn't see it. The bus had nobody in it but six tough-looking white kids. They stared at Rosie insolently and she sat behind the small barricade of two cheap suitcases and thought how funny it would be if after twenty-seven years on Lyons Avenue she suddenly got raped and murdered just as she was leaving. Such things often happened, she knew. The fact that she had managed to live so long in such a dangerous neighborhood without being raped was only an indication of how unattractive she was anyway. Plenty of people had been raped right on her own block, including a woman ten years older than her. The youths stared and Rosie looked away.

She got out at the Continental Trailways station, bought a ticket to Shreveport, and then sat silently by her suitcases. A lot of people in the bus station were sitting just as silently as she was. The people who rode buses, it seemed, were mostly like herself—too beaten down to have much to say.

What had beaten Rosie down was another month of Royceless life, during which nothing at all had happened except that Little Buster had at one point managed to wander into a wasp nest. He had been bitten all over and had scratched so badly that half the bites became infected. During the month that he had been gone, Royce had called only once, and that had been to tell her to be careful and not wreck the truck, since, as he put it, he might be needing it. What that meant Rosie didn't know; when she asked him he said, "You'd argue in a sandstorm," and hung up.

Insomnia settled on her, and her nights were filled with nothing more comforting than the sound of Little Buster bumping against his crib and moaning slightly, or of Lou Ann complaining that he'd wet his bed. Rosie tried TV, but anything of a family nature caused her to burst into tears.

She took to lingering at Aurora's longer and longer every day, not because she had anything to do but because she didn't want to go home. Aurora and the General were getting along happily and her house was a jolly place to be, but almost every day, on the bus ride back across Houston from the quiet palaces of River Oaks to the stews of the Fifth Ward, her spirits gradually sank. At night she had so little that she could hardly recognize herself. After keeping her fight for forty-nine years, she had finally lost it. Fortunately Little Buster and Lou Ann had a repertory of only three bedtime stories, and once Rosie had droned through one or two of them she was free to be as spiritless as she felt and to sit on her bed and sip cups of coffee most of the night. It was no life, she thought, night after night, and yet her only options were to take it or leave.

Rosie looked around the dingy bus station, in which forty or fifty people were sitting in separate silences, and reflected that the new thing about her life was that it had become sort of like the bus station—silent. She had always had plenty to say about everything; but suddenly she was finding that though she still had plenty to say she had no one to say it to. Her sister Maybelline was too married and too religious to be much help. All she ever did was quote the Bible and suggest that Rosie think of some way to get Royce to church more often. "Fine, Maybelline. All he's ever done in church his whole life is to go to sleep and snore," Rosie said. Maybelline had been married thirty-four years to her twenty-seven, and to the most stable man in the world, Oliver Newton Dobbs, who managed a shoe polish factory on Little York Road and had never missed a day's work since he left the oil fields in 1932. With a man that steady there was no use talking to Maybelline about marital problems.

Nor could she talk to Aurora, in good conscience, because Aurora had already heard about her problems with Royce fifty times, and had already advised her to divorce him. Rosie agreed that that was what she ought to do, but somehow she never quite got around to calling a lawyer. She had not told Aurora that she was leaving, or why. Aurora didn't understand how it was to bounce across Houston every afternoon to a house on Lyons Avenue that she had never liked anyway and two kids that weren't being raised well. Lou Ann and Little Buster were a constant reproach to her; they just weren't getting the raising the other five kids had had. Kids deserved parents with some enthusiasm, and she no longer had much. That was why she was going home to Shreveport—maybe there, away from all thoughts of Royce and his slut, she could shake off her blues and become the enthusiastic person she had always been. It was home, after all—Shreveport—and home was supposed to count for something.

She stared at the row of telephone booths across from her and wondered if she dared call Aurora, just to let her know. If she wasn't told something she would worry herself into a frenzy, but if she was told too soon she would just try to stop her from going. Then she thought of Emma. She didn't feel strong enough to deal with Aurora, but dealing with Emma was no problem.

"It's me," she said when Emma answered the phone.

"I believe I recognize the voice," Emma said. "What's happening?"

"Oh, honey," Rosie said. "I don't know why I even called you. I'm just scared to call your momma, I guess. I got to get out of here before I go plumb crazy. I'm going home to Shreveport tonight, and I ain't comin' back."

"Oh, dear," Emma said.

"Yeah, I stay too tore up here," Rosie said. "It ain't fair to the kids. Royce ain't comin' back an' there just ain't a whole lot to stay for."

"There's us," Emma said.

"I know, but you and your momma got your own lives to live."

"All right, but you're part of them," Emma said. "How can you leave when I'm finally about to have my baby?"

"Because I'm here at the bus station an' I got my nerve up," Rosie said. "I might not never get it up agin." The very sound of Emma's voice made her want to stay. Part of her felt that it was insane to leave the few people who really cared about her, but another part felt that nothing could be more insane-making than another night on Lyons Avenue.

"I best go on, honey," she said. "Tell your ma I'm sorry I didn't give no proper notice—she'd just have talked me out of it. It ain't that she don't mean well. It's just that . . . well . . . she don't know how I'm livin'."

"All right," Emma said, realizing it was no use.

"Be sweet, honey. I got to go," Rosie said, choking suddenly. She hung up and in a kind of panic of emotion, weeping profusely, managed to get across the station to her suitcases.

She was not the only traveler who was upset, though. The line of people waiting to board her bus, when it was finally called, was long and forlorn. Two teenage lovers were being parted, and they clung to one another miserably. Rosie had managed to compose herself, but just in front of her a family of country people were putting a son on the bus for Fort Dix; a mother, grandmother, and two sisters were all bugging the boy at once and weeping, while the father stood by looking awkward. A family of Mexicans waited stoically, and a peroxided mother with two children kept dragging one of them out from under Rosie's feet as the line shuffled forward.

Finally, though, all were loaded. Rosie sat by a window and played peekaboo with a little boy who sat in the seat in front of her. The bus rose onto a freeway, over the bayou, over the railroad yards, and, in a surprisingly few minutes, was among the dark pine groves of East Texas. Rosie yawned, exhausted by the leaving; the speed and the hum of wheels lulled her past all awareness of trouble. Soon she was asleep, leaving her young friend, full of energy, to play a one-handed game of peekaboo, on past Conroe and Lufkin, far into the night.

3.

AURORA RECEIVED the news of Rosie's departure in silence.

"You're too quiet," Emma said. "Have I called at a bad time?"

"In fact you have called at a terrible time," Aurora said, looking angrily at the General. He was sitting at the foot of her bed glaring at her.

"I'm sorry. I thought you'd like to know right away."

"I would have liked to have known two hours ago," Aurora said. "If I had I would most certainly have stopped her."

"She didn't want to be stopped. That's why she didn't call you. She knew you'd talk her out of it."

Aurora was silent.

"I'm sorry I called at a bad time," Emma said.

"Oh, stop apologizing," Aurora said. "Bad news has a way of coming at awkward times. That's all this is, I suppose: awkward. It may force General Scott to vary his inflexible schedule by a few seconds or so, but perhaps he can live with that."

"Oh, he's there," Emma said. "I'll hang up and you can call me later if you want to."

"Hector is not God, you know," Aurora said. "He just thinks he is. The fact that he is in my house doesn't mean we can't discuss this little catastrophe. In fact Hector is almost always in my house these days, so if we're to talk at all we'll more or less have to talk around him."

"I can goddamn well leave, if that's your attitude," the General said.

Aurora took the receiver away from her ear and covered it with her hand. "Do not swear at me while I'm talking to my daughter," she said. "I won't stand for it. Suppose you just sit silently until I've finished this conversation. Then we can take up where we left off."

"We didn't leave off," the General said. "We didn't even take up."

Aurora looked at him sternly and put the receiver back to her ear. "If she's gone she's gone," she said. "Nothing can be done tonight. Tomorrow we'll just have to set about getting her back. In all likelihood I shall have to go up there. It's what I get for not bringing her over here to live when Royce left the second time."

"Maybe you can talk to her on the phone and coax her back."

"No, she's too stubborn. I can't do anything with such a stubborn person on the phone. You're too pregnant to go with me, so someone else will just have to go. I'll have to go at once. It's not wise to give Rosie time to dig in."

"Sorry to disrupt your evening," Emma said again.

"My evening is just beginning," Aurora said and hung up.

"Go where?" the General asked. "I'd like to know where you're planning to go now?"

"Now?" Aurora said. "I'm not aware of having been anywhere lately."

"You spent all day yesterday shopping," he said. "You're always going somewhere."

"I'm not a plant, Hector," Aurora said. "I know that you would prefer that I never leave my bedroom, or even my bed, but that's your problem. I've never liked being house-bound."

"Anyway, where are you going now?"

"Shreveport. Rosie's left. She's in considerable distress these days. I'll have to go bring her back."

"That's goddamn nonsense," the General said. "Call her on the phone. Besides, she'll come back anyway. F.V. ran away and he came back, didn't he?"

"Hector, I know Rosie better than you do, and I don't think she'll come back," Aurora said. "Don't you think we've argued enough for one evening? Anyway, it won't hurt you to go to Shreveport."

"Who said I was going?" the General asked. "She's your maid."

"I know she's my maid," Aurora said flatly. "You're my lover—God help me. Are you telling me that you're going to be so inconsiderate as to allow me to drive three hundred miles by myself, when not twenty minutes ago, if I'm not mistaken, you were trying to drag me into bed?"

"That has nothing to do with the issue at hand," he said.

"Pardon me, but your behavior *is* the issue at hand, Hector,"

Aurora said with a flash of anger. "I seem to be making an unpleasant discovery about the person I'm sleeping with, namely that he doesn't care enough about me to ride to Shreveport with me and help me retrieve my poor maid."

"Well, I might if it isn't on one of my golfing days," the General said.

"Thank you very much," Aurora said, coloring with fury. "I'll certainly make every effort to see that you don't miss your golf."

The General failed to notice the fury and took her remark at face value, something he was apt to do when his mind was elsewhere. He reached across the bed to take her hand and to his amazement her hand eluded him and slapped him right in the face.

"What's that for?" he said, very startled. "I said I might go."

"Play back your last five statements, General Scott," Aurora said. "I believe you'll find that you just ranked me second to golf."

"But I didn't mean it that way!" he said, noticing the fury at last.

"Of course not. Men never seem to feel that their statements mean what they very clearly do mean."

"But I love you, Aurora," the General said, horrified at the turn things had taken. "I do, remember?"

"Yes, I do remember, Hector," she said. "I remember that you made your usual rather clumsy pass at me at around eight-thirty. You happened to break the band of my wristwatch this time, and also one of my earrings fell behind the bed. I remember those details precisely."

"But you yanked your arm away," the General said. "I didn't mean to break your wristwatch."

"No, and I don't mean to be screwed at eight-thirty so you can be asleep by eight forty-five, or more accurately eight thirty-six, and up for your goddamn run at five," Aurora shouted. "That is not my idea of *amore*, as I've told you countless times. I'm a normal woman and I'm quite capable of staying awake until midnight, or even later. I had rather hoped that in time I'd become more important to you than your golf or your run, or even your dogs, but I see it was a vain hope."

"God damn it, why are you always so much trouble!" the General said. "You *always* are. I do my best."

They looked at one another in angry silence for a moment. Aurora shook her head. "I'd rather you left," she said. "It's just like golf to you, you know, Hector. All that interests you is the shortest route to the hole."

"There's no goddamn short route to yours, that's for sure!" the General yelled. "You've made me a nervous wreck. I can barely get to sleep now anyway."

"Yes, I suspect I'm the most difficult course you ever played, General," she said, looking at him coolly.

"Too difficult," the General said. "Too goddamn difficult."

"Well, my doors are open," Aurora said. "We can go back to being neighbors, you know. You blundered into this, you know, and there's no tank around to protect you."

"Shut up!" he yelled, enraged that she had acquired command of herself when he was still shaking with confusion.

"You just talk to hear yourself talk," he said. "I haven't had a tank for twenty years."

"All right," Aurora said. "I merely wanted you to think seriously about what we're doing. I've gone to quite unusual lengths to be accommodating to you, and we still seem to fight all the time. What's life going to be like if I suddenly decide to be troublesome?"

"You can't be any goddamn worse than you are," the General said.

"Ha ha, little you know," she said. "I've made almost no demands on you. Suppose I decided to make a few."

"Like what?"

"Sensible demands. I might demand that you get rid of that broken-down car, or those two overweening dogs."

"Overwhat?"

"Overweening," Aurora said, amused by the look of astonishment that the General wore.

"I might even demand that you give up golf, as a special test of your seriousness," she said.

"And I might demand that you marry me," the General said. "Two can play at that game."

"Only one can play at it successfully," Aurora said. "I've grown surprisingly fond of you and I'd like to keep you, but don't you bring up marriage again."

"Why not?"

"Because I said not. Unless one of us changes drastically, it's out of the question."

"Then go get your own goddamn maid," the General said, angered beyond endurance. "I don't ride a mile with any woman who talks to me this way. I don't like your goddamn maid anyway."

"No doubt she reminds you of me," Aurora said. "Anything less than a total slave reminds you of me."

The General stood up suddenly. "Neither of you have any goddamn discipline," he said, feeling more and more pressured.

Aurora hadn't moved. "Beg pardon," she said. "I admit to being hopelessly lazy, but the same hardly applies to Rosie. She has discipline enough for both of us."

"Then what's she doing in Shreveport?" he asked. "Why isn't she here where she belongs?"

Aurora shrugged. "The fact that she has problems doesn't mean that she doesn't have discipline," she said. "If you want to do something useful why don't you get my earring out from under the bed? I'm not interested in your opinion of Rosie."

"I just said she should stay where she belonged," he said.

"I'm sure she would have, if her husband had stayed where he belonged. Let's drop the subject and all other subjects. Please get me my earring and we can go watch television."

"You can't talk to me this way," the General said. "To hell with television. Get your own goddamn earring."

He waited for her to apologize, but she merely sat looking at him. Her words were bad enough, but her silence was so infuriating that he couldn't stand it. Without another word he strode out of the bedroom and slammed the door.

Aurora stood up and went to the window. In a minute she heard the front door slam and saw the General stride across her lawn and down the sidewalk toward his own house. His bearing, she observed, was excellent.

She waited for a few minutes, thinking the phone might ring;

but when it didn't she went to the closet, got a clothes hanger, and got down on her hands and knees to rake the lost earring out from under the bed. It was an opal, and she took the other one off, looked at them a moment, and put them in her jewel case. Her house was silent and cool and peaceful. Without another thought for General Scott, she went downstairs, poured herself a glass of wine, and settled contentedly down in front of the television. Tomorrow she would deal with Rosie.

CHAPTER XVIII

1.

THE REASON Royce Dunlup had called his wife and told her to be careful with the truck was because he and Shirley Sawyer had in mind to take a trip in it. Shirley was so delighted to have Royce back with her that she immediately began to take steps that would make him hers forever.

"You ain't never gettin' away from me agin, puddin'," she told him pointedly on the day of his return. Then to drive her point home, as it were, she proceeded to fuck him into a stupor.

For three intense weeks Shirley didn't allow the pace to slacken, either. Every time Royce showed the slightest signs of liveliness Shirley immediately set about wearing him back down. After three weeks Royce was so totally pussywhipped that there was little danger of his ever escaping again, and it was then that Shirley began to make plans for a vacation.

"We could go to Barstow," she said one day after a long bounce.

"Where is Barstow?" Royce said, thinking she meant the dog. He had a vague memory of a grudge against the dog, but in his lethargy he couldn't remember what the grudge was. He drank some more beer.

"You know where Barstow is, honey," Shirley said. Sometimes Royce's bad memory got on her nerves.

"On the porch?" Royce said, opening one eye.

"Aw, not the puppy," Shirley said. "My home town, Barstow, California. I'd like to take you there and show you off." She wiggled his cock a little, out of habit.

"Some day when you're not doin' nothin', whyn't you get your truck?" she said. "I don't see why *she* should get to have it. Whose truck is it anyway?

"If we went home we could stay in a motel," she added, wiggling his cock some more. "That'd be romantic, wouldn't it? I ain't stayed in a motel since I went home in fifty-four."

Royce tried to think about it. At the moment his cock had no more sensation in it than any of the thousands of used tires piled outside the window; but it didn't matter, because sex wasn't what he was thinking about. He was thinking about driving his potato chip truck around California.

"Where's Hollywood at?" he asked, stimulated by the thought.

"A good long way from Barstow," Shirley said. "Just get that out of your mind."

"We could go to Hollywood," Royce said. "Where's Disneyland?"

"I wouldn't mind seeing Disneyland so much, but I'd have to be a rank fool to take you to Hollywood," Shirley said. "One of my sisters works there and she's always said it was full of whores and promiscuous women."

"Pro what?" Royce asked nervously. Shirley's habit of wiggling him was what made him nervous. She was so careless about it that she was always hitting him in the balls with the head of his own cock. Royce couldn't think of a nice way to ask her to be careful, so he drank beer to take his mind off the danger.

"You know, women that do it with anybody," Shirley said. "I ain't taking you into no mess like that. You just remember to go get that truck this week. My vacation starts in ten days."

For the next day or two Shirley entertained herself between bouncings with fantasies of the two of them driving to California in Royce's truck. Royce himself had never been farther west than Navasota, but it all sounded fine to him. He kept thinking every day that he'd get out of bed and go over to Lyons Avenue and get the truck, but every day it occurred to him that he didn't really need to produce it until the day Shirley's vacation started, so he stayed where he was and drank beer.

Rosie took a dim view of Royce's rapprochement with Shirley, but there was one person in Houston who took an even dimmer view. That person was Mitch McDonald. When Rosie had carted Royce home after the accident at the J-Bar Korral, hope had sprung up afresh in Mitch's breast. He knew Rosie, and it never occurred to him that she would be so careless as to let Royce slip away again. He knew Shirley too and was quite positive she wasn't going to want to do without somebody's old thing to sit on—not for very long anyway. He gave her a day or two and then installed himself as a fixture in the bar where she worked. As proof of his gentlemanly intentions he drank two dollars' worth of beer before he even broached the subject of Royce.

"Well, what do you hear from your old friend Royce?" he asked finally as he was starting on this third dollar's worth.

"None of your business, you little cocksucker," Shirley said brutally. In fifteen years as a barmaid she had acquired some vulgar habits of speech.

"Aw, stop it," Mitch said. "Me an' Royce is best buddies."

"Then why are you over here tryin' to put the make on his girl friend?" Shirley asked.

"You wasn't always his girl friend," Mitch said.

"You wasn't always a fuckin' weasel, neither," Shirley said.

"You keep sassin' me an' I'll bust you right in the mouth," Mitch said.

"Lay a finger on me an' I'll have Royce twist your other arm off, you little turd," Shirley said.

Mitch was forced to conclude his first day's courtship on that unpromising note, but he refused to let it discourage him. He decided the gallant approach was best, and the next day he presented Shirley with a box of chocolate-covered cherries.

"To show you my heart's in the right place," Mitch said. "I've learned some new tricks since you an' me was in love."

"What do you mean *new* tricks?" Shirley asked. "You never knew no tricks."

Heartlessly she proceeded to pass out the chocolate-covered cherries to a tableful of truck drivers.

After that humiliation Mitch decided to try the silent treatment. He went to the bar every day and invested a few dollars in beer. He allowed Shirley to see that he was suffering, but suffering humbly, and he expected that any day she would follow him home and pounce on his lap. Instead she flounced in one day and announced that Royce was back.

"Royce?" Mitch said. It was a bolt from the blue.

"Yep, he's getting a divorce, an' me an' him's gettin' married, soon as we get time," Shirley said blithely.

"So that sorry son of a bitch has left his wife and kids agin," Mitch said. "You two-timin' slut. You home-breakin' bitch. You an' him'll be sorry. I'll get you both."

After that Mitch transferred his business to the Tired-Out Lounge. He knew Royce would hobble in sooner or later, and Royce did. In the interim, Mitch had taken to spending his nights with a bottle of bourbon and his days getting in shape for the night's drinking. As soon as Royce hobbled into the bar he announced his intentions.

"I never figured you for a coward, Dunlup," he said, breathing whiskey fumes in his friend's face.

"You been drinkin'," Royce said. Actually he had been getting lonesome lying around Shirley's all day with no one around but Barstow. He was rather glad to see Mitch and ignored his remark.

"Just tell me one thing," Mitch said. "Just tell me one thing. Why'd you steal my girl?"

Royce couldn't remember, so he didn't answer the question. He stared across the bar, waiting for Mitch to change the subject.

"All right then, you dumb shit," Mitch said. "You ain't good enough for that girl. You ain't good enough for nothin'. You wouldn't be good enough for a nigger."

Royce remained silent. He had never been very responsive to

insults, and besides he had Shirley. As long as he had Shirley, there was not much need to talk.

"Wanta beer?" he asked, motioning to Hubert Junior.

"Ain't you heard nothin' I said?" Mitch asked, exasperated. "I just called you ever' name in the book. I ain't just about to drink with you."

Royce took his beer gratefully. Mitch was not turning out to be very good company. "You're drunk, you ol' son bitch," he said.

"Dunlup, you got a brain like a goddamn brick," Mitch said. His fury was beginning to rise at the thought of such a dumb person getting to fuck a sensitive woman like Shirley.

"I guess you think 'cause I'm a cripple I won't fight," he added. "I'll give you two days to get out of Shirley's house, and if you don't I'm gonna kill your ass. Hubert Junior's my witness."

"I don't want to be no witness to no murder oath," Hubert Junior said nervously. Since opening the Tired-Out Lounge, scarcely a day had passed without him overhearing one or more ghastly threats, a fair number of which had actually been carried out. He didn't quite see how Mitch was going to manage to kill anyone as big as Royce, but then Mitch answered the question before he even had time to ask it.

"It don't take but one hand to hold a gun, Dunlup," Mitch said, breathing more whiskey fumes at Royce.

"Kill your ass if you don't let Shirley alone," Royce said in response.

After a few more threats from Mitch, to which Royce didn't reply, the conversation petered out. Mitch went over to his one-room living quarters on Canal Street to get a little drunker, and it occurred to him while walking home that if Shirley ever decided to tell Royce about the chocolate-covered cherries Royce might well try to kill him. It was an ominous prospect, and the more Mitch thought about it the more likely it seemed. That night he found he could barely drink bourbon fast enough to keep the prospect out of his mind, and the next morning, as soon as things opened, he staggered down Canal Street to Son's Surplus store and bought himself a beautiful machete, complete with scabbard, for $4.98. He meant to buy a pistol, but then pistols cost twenty dollars, and it occurred to him that it would be just his luck for a pistol to jam. As Son explained to him, there was no way you could jam a machete. Son even loaned him a whetstone to sharpen it on.

For the next three days Mitch sharpened and drank and sharpened and drank, and as he did, his frame of mind got steadily worse. His hatred of Royce and Shirley increased minute by minute. Jealousy lit his brain like a large hot lightbulb. Somehow the chain that was supposed to turn the bulb off had gotten broken, so the bulb burned on and on. After three days of sharpening and heavy lonely drinking it seemed to Mitch that the only way he could forestall his own murder was to go over and whop Royce's balls off with the machete. With his balls missing, Royce was not likely to be up to killing anyone.

Soon Mitch's waking consciousness was only a haze of jealous thoughts, and he developed a great desire for revenge. After all, Royce and Shirley had insulted his own manhood. Prolonged drinking always made Mitch bitter sooner or later—bitter about his lost arm and lonely life—and one night with no thoughts in his head at all he found himself stumbling down Harrisburg with the machete under his arm. The time had come; hell would be to pay. They'd be sorry they insulted him when they looked up and saw him coming through the door with his machete.

He got to Shirley's house and took his machete out of its scabbard. Barstow was on the porch, and Mitch gave him a pat. Then he let himself into the house with a key he had refused to give back when Shirley kicked him out of the house. When Mitch opened the door Barstow managed to sneak in. Barstow lived in constant hope of being able to get in his mistress's house, where there were always shoes to chew. Mitch kept a good grip on his machete, expecting to have to cut Royce down at any moment, but Barstow made no sound and the whole house was quiet. All Mitch could hear was the soft sound of an electric fan, and that came from the bedroom.

Since no one seemed to be moving around and no immediate action was required, Mitch sat down in a big stuffed chair in the living room to think things over. He pulled out his bourbon bottle and took a few swigs. Before he knew it, being back in old familiar surroundings caused his anger to rise. Shirley's house was the only place he had been happy since losing his arm, and Shirley had been the only person to be nice to him. To be deprived of it all and have to live in a squalid little room on Canal Street was a terrible unfairness, and Royce had caused it—Royce who had had a hardworking wife and a job too.

A pulse began to pound in Mitch's temple. After it had pounded for a while Mitch started to shake. He got out of the chair and stumbled into the bedroom, gripping the machete tightly. The sight that met his eyes was what he had expected—Royce and Shirley were in bed, both mother naked and both sound asleep. Though it was what he might have expected, he hadn't expected it. He had somehow expected Royce to be in his work clothes, the way he had always known him to be, and the sight of him sprawled out on his back with his mouth open was horrible. It was worse than Mitch had thought it would be, and the worst part of it was that Royce took up almost all the bed. Shirley was crowded off on an edge, all scrunched up and about to fall on the floor.

Mitch had more or less expected that Royce would have a huge cock, but instead he seemed to have none at all. Whatever he had was completely hidden under the vast fold of his lower belly. Royce had always had a beer gut, but a few months of doing nothing but drinking beer had caused it to swell to enormous size. It was the hugest, grossest thing Mitch had ever seen. The idea that his little Shirley would have anything to do with such a lard-gut as Royce was intolerable. The lightbulb of his jealousy popped back on, blinding hot, and without otherwise announcing himself Mitch took a poke at Royce's big gut with the machete. Unfortunately, his hand was unsteady, and instead of sticking him in the gut he merely stuck him in the breastbone. That'll wake you up, you fat bastard, Mitch thought as he started to jerk the machete out and get ready for another poke.

Oddly, though, Mitch was wrong. Royce did not wake up—nor did the machete come out. It was well lodged, and Mitch's hand was sweaty. When he jerked, his hand slipped off and he staggered two steps back and stepped on Barstow, who yelped loudly. The yelp woke Shirley, who reached over instinctively to see what state Royce's old thing was in. "Shut up, puppy," she said sleepily, before she noticed that a machete was sticking out of her lover's chest. As soon as she noticed that, she screamed and rolled off the bed in a faint, knocking over the little electric fan as she fell. Stepping on Barstow had caused Mitch to fall down too, and he didn't bother to get up. He crawled out of the house as fast as he could and began to stagger down the street in the direction of the Tired-Out Lounge.

Shirley's scream woke Royce. Automatically he reached over for the can of beer he had set on the bedside table before going to sleep. He took a sip and discovered that it was warm, just as he had feared; still, it was handy, and it was not until his second sip that he got his eyes open enough to notice the machete sticking out of his chest.

"Uh-oh," he said; then his panic accelerated and he screamed loudly. Mitch, more than a block down the street by that time, heard the scream and assumed it was Royce's death cry. He managed to keep stumbling on.

Royce too assumed it was his death cry, although he didn't really hear it. He grabbed the phone but then dropped the receiver and had to pull it slowly up onto the bed.

"Help, they kilt me, cut my guts out!" Royce yelled into the phone, but since he had not remembered to dial, the phone didn't answer.

At that point Shirley began to come out of her faint. She turned over and tried to pull herself back onto the bed, thinking maybe it had all been a nightmare, only it wasn't, because the machete was still sticking out of Royce's chest. The only non-nightmarish thing about it was that Royce was still alive and was trying to talk on the telephone—calling his wife, Shirley concluded.

"Who you calling, Royce?" she asked. For several weeks she had suspected him of sneaking calls to his wife.

Then the sight of it all made her feel weak all over, and she clung to the edge of the bed as if it were a ledge.

"Help, help, help!" Royce cried into the phone. Then he managed to dial the operator and one answered. "Help, 'mergency," Royce yelled.

The operator was not slow to catch the note of desperation. "Just be calm, sir," she said. "Where are you, sir?"

Royce went blank. He knew he was on Harrisburg, but he couldn't have remembered the street number if he had had several weeks, and he knew very well he didn't have any weeks. He handed the phone to Shirley, who released one hand from the ledge she was clinging to and managed to mumble the address.

"Oh, gawd, lady, hurry up with an ambulance," she said. While she was talking Royce passed out.

Mitch, meanwhile, had managed to stumble into the Tired-Out Lounge, and from the look on his face Hubert Junior knew at once that he must, to the best of his ability at least, have fulfilled his oath.

From wanting Royce to suffer, Mitch had very quickly come around to not wanting Royce to die.

"I kilt Dunlup," he said, panting. The statement got him the immediate attention of everyone in the bar. Hubert Junior, used to emergencies, picked up the phone at once and gave the ambulance driver he knew best precise instructions as to where to go. Then he scooped the money out of his cash register in case a robber came wandering in while he was gone. In a matter of seconds he and everyone else in the bar were racing down the street toward Shirley's house, leaving Mitch sitting at a table, aghast and weak, trying to think of how he could begin his story when the police came.

So efficient was Hubert Junior that the police, the ambulance, and all the former customers of the Tired-Out Lounge arrived at Shirley's house almost at once. "Is anybody in there armed?" a young policeman asked.

"Naw, it's just an attempted murder," Hurbert Junior said. Two policemen got up their nerve and opened the door. They weren't convinced it was safe, but the crowd at their back gave them little choice. At the sight of so many people Barstow yelped once and scuttled into the bedroom to hide under the bed. He had never been much of a watchdog.

When the crowd pressed into the bedroom they were given a choice of two sights: a large man lying unconscious on a bed, a machete sticking out of his chest or a large woman sitting naked on the floor. Shirley in her shock had been too weak to try to dress. She sat by the bed in a kind of stupor waiting for Royce to finish dying; the next thing she knew twenty men were in the bedroom.

"Ma'am, we're the police," the young officer said, taking off his hat.

"This is terrible. We wasn't doin' a thang," Shirley said. Then she remembered her nakedness and hurriedly got to her feet and scrambled through the men to the bathroom, holding a brassiere in front of her. Everyone watched silently, aware that they were witnessing the real thing: a crime of passion, naked woman, dying man. Only almost immediately the sight of Royce began to act on their unsteady stomachs. Several rushed to the porch to begin puking. Only the ambulance drivers were blasé. They set about getting Royce on a stretcher, and soon the ambulance raced away. Several of the men stayed around to comfort Shirley, who had come out of her faint and said several times that she wished she was dead. Hubert Junior got in the police car and took the officers back to his bar to get Mitch. He was sitting at a table shaking when they walked in.

"What happened?" he asked. "Did Royce die?"

"They don't know if he's critical," Hubert Junior said gently. An air of solemnity settled over the bar as the officer led Mitch away.

"Pore bastard," one of the men said. "Ruint his life over a woman."

It was their theme—their only theme—and as the patrons began to stumble in they began to worry it, to tell one another for the first time the story, as they variously fancied it, of Royce Dunlup's tragedy—a story they would embellish for many a year.

2.

AURORA RECEIVED the call at three A.M. When the phone rang she assumed it was Emma about to go be delivered of her child. But the voice wasn't Emma's.

"Ma'am, sorry to wake you up," the officer said. "Would you know the whereabouts of Mrs. Rosalyn Dunlup? We understand she works for you."

"Yes of course. What's she done?" Aurora said. The General was beside her, and she began nudging him to wake up.

"It ain't her, it's her husband," the officer said. "It ain't delicate, ma'am, it ain't delicate."

"It isn't delicate for you to keep me in suspense at three in the morning either," Aurora said. "Just tell me."

"Well, he was stabbed, ma'am," the officer said. "I just about upchuck every time I think about it. It was a case of jealousy, we believe."

"I see," Aurora said. "I'll contact Mrs. Dunlup at once. She's not in town, but I'll get her here as soon as I can."

"He's at Ben Taub," the officer said. "The criminal's done confessed, so there ain't nobody to catch. The doctors just think Mr. Dunlup will do better if he's got his wife beside him."

"I quite agree," Aurora said, nudging the General again.

The General opened his eyes, but then he shut them again. It took her several minutes to get him awake, and then he got angry.

"Your servants are nothing but trouble," he said. "F.V.'s never cost me an hour's sleep."

Aurora was pacing the floor, trying to decide how best to proceed. "Hector, must you really cite F.V. to me at this hour of the night?" she said.

She dressed in silence. Annoying as it was, it was clearly an occasion that would require her to be respectable, so she made herself respectable The General lay in the bed and yawned. When she was dressed Aurora sat down on the bed and waited, hoping he would have a suggestion—any suggestion would have been helpful.

"Well, it's damned inconvenient," he said. "I'm sure Rosie's asleep. What was the damn fool doing?"

Aurora looked at him unhappily. "Hector, you were a general," she said. "Why can't you ever act like one when I need it? What I need is someone to help me think of a way to get Rosie back here quick."

"She's unstable," the General said. "If there was ever a time when she needed to be here it's now, and where is she? I don't know why you keep her on." He got up and marched into the bathroom.

When she heard him urinating she got up and followed him. "We aren't married, Hector," she said. "You are not exempt from the practice of ordinary good manners."

"What?" he said, but Aurora slammed the door and took the telephone to her window nook. She had secured a phone number from Rosie's sister and called it. After many rings Rosie answered the phone.

"Sad news, dear," Aurora said. "Royce has gotten himself hurt. I don't know the details, but it's somewhat serious. You'll have to come back at once."

Rosie was silent. "My lord," she said. "Somebody probably shot him over that slut."

"No, they used a knife, not a gun," Aurora said. "Is somebody there who can drive you back?"

"Naw," Rosie said. "June's boy's taken off in the car. I could take a bus back, come morning. Maybe even a plane."

"Wait," Aurora said, remembering someone she had been trying to remember since the time the policeman called. "I just thought of Vernon. He's got planes and pilots. I heard him say so. I'll call him at once."

She hung up. The general strode out of the bathroom. In pajamas he looked quite skinny, his calves particularly. "Who are you calling?" he asked.

Aurora got a busy signal, which filled her with relief. At least he was there. She didn't answer the General.

"I might get a military plane in the morning," the General said.

Aurora got another busy signal. She dialed Rosie again. "I shall have to go down there," she said. "He might be on his phone for hours. You pack and I'll call you as soon as I've arranged something."

"It's that oil man," the General said. "You really love *him*. I knew it anyway."

Aurora shook her head. "Nothing of the sort, sorry to disappoint you," she said. "I just happen to trust his judgment in emergencies. I would be happy to trust yours, but you don't seem to have a judgment, except that F.V. is a better servant than Rosie."

The General looked around with a show of brusqueness. "I'll get dressed and go with you," he said.

"No," Aurora said. "You get back in that bed and go to sleep. It will be time for your run in two hours. This is no proper concern of yours and there's no reason you should disrupt your daily schedule. I'll be back afterwhile, as soon as I've gotten Rosie set."

The General looked at her. She was hastily brushing her hair. "I can go on and sleep here?" he asked just to be sure.

"Why not?" she said. "Where were you thinking of sleeping?"

"I don't know," he said. "I don't know what you mean half the goddamn time. I don't see why you need that goddamn little oil man, though. I kind of like the old Italian."

"He's younger than you," Aurora said. "Vernon happens to own planes, Hector. I'm trying to get Rosie here, not reshuffle my very unromantic romantic life. If you're too thick-skulled to see that, then perhaps I better reshuffle it."

With that she stuffed her hairbrush into her purse and left, leaving the General to climb back into an empty bed, wondering, as he often did, what was going to happen. What was going to happen?

3.

AURORA DROVE her Cadillac through the almost empty streets until she came to the parking garage that Vernon had said was his. She turned in, punched a button, and received a green ticket. She began to drive slowly up the winding ramps, looking down now and then at Houston, orangeish under its lights.

When she got to the fourth floor she was startled to see a tall, gaunt old man step out of a door and hold his hand up at her. She felt a flutter of fear and contemplated trying to back down, but she knew very well she couldn't back down four floors without having several smashups. Better to hold her ground. The man walked toward her and she watched him closely. He was trampy-looking and had shaggy hair and was large enough to have made an excellent assailant, but somehow he looked more like a night watchman. He stopped and looked at her for a considerable time, and then made a rolling motion with his hand. He wanted her to roll her window down. After a moment she rolled it down half-way. The old man made a rolling motion again. Aurora looked at him and decided he was older than she had thought. She rolled the window the rest of the way down.

"Howdy," the old man said. "I'm Schweppes. My guess is you're the widow from Boston, Mass."

"Ha," Aurora said. "He talks about me, does he?"

The old man put his long hands on the door of the car. "He did before you cut his water off," he said.

"Yes, I'm Aurora Greenway," she said. "Is he around?"

"Yep, up on the roof, making them phone calls," Schweppes said. "Gonna marry him this time?"

Aurora shook her head. "Why does everyone think I ought to be married?" she asked.

Old Schweppes looked embarrassed and took his hands off the door. "Pleased to meet you," he said. "Go right on up."

She drove on, upward and upward, until the fear of height began to assert itself, after which she concentrated on the curving ramp in front of her. When she finally came off the ramp on top of the building, there was so much space around her that she gripped the steering wheel tightly. Sure enough, Vernon's white Lincoln was parked near one edge of the building. Aurora drove slowly across the roof. She could see Vernon quite plainly. His car door was open and he held a phone to his ear. When he heard her approach he looked around in amazement. Aurora stopped, set her brake, and got out. Once out of the car, the roof was no longer so frightening. The air was familiarly heavy and moist, and there was no breeze.

Vernon got out of his car and stood by it, clearly amazed, as Aurora walked toward him. His shirt and gabardines were fresh, she noted.

"There you are, Vernon," Aurora said, holding out her hand. "Guess what?"

Vernon, not sure whether he should first answer the question or first shake the hand, awkwardly shook the hand. "My lord, what?" he asked.

"I need a little help, old friend," Aurora said, amused.

Two minutes later Vernon was on the phone to his man in Shreveport, and Aurora had settled herself comfortably in the front seat of the Lincoln to wait her turn to call Rosie and tell her where she would be picked up.

CHAPTER XIX

1.

VERNON, AS usual, was a model of helpfulness and efficiency. Within ten minutes he had arranged for a company man to pick up Rosie and take her to the airport, where a company plane would be waiting to bring her to Houston. In two hours she would be there, which meant that all Vernon had to worry about was what to do with Aurora for two hours. Once the plane had been arranged she no longer seemed in a crisis mood at all.

"It's too bad you got rid of me so quickly, Vernon," she said, examining the numerous gadgets she found in the Lincoln. "I scarcely got time to play with your gadgets, and I'm sure you have a lot more that I don't know about."

Vernon tried to remember what he had done to make her think he had got rid of her, but he couldn't remember a thing.

Aurora found indeed that she was feeling extraordinarily good, for some reason. "I don't see why we don't take a walk on this roof, since it's yours," she said, and they did.

"You know, it feels quite wonderful to be out of my house," she said. It had just begun to seem faintly morninglike, and the night clouds were breaking.

"Of course, being away from home has always made me feel quite gay," she added. "I believe I'm a born gadabout. One of my problems is that I frequently need a change. Are you that way, Vernon?"

"I don't guess," Vernon said. "I pretty much go along the same."

It amused her so much that she gave him a quick shake, to his puzzlement. "I'm irresistibly drawn to shake you, Vernon," she said. "Particularly in my rare moments of buoyancy. You're a little too useful, that's all. If you were more erratic someone would probably take a few pains with you. As it is I have plenty of people to take pains with, and some of them are adept at giving pains back."

"We could have breakfast," Vernon said.

"I accept," Aurora said, getting into the Lincoln at once.

"Why it's a little like driving in Switzerland," she said as Vernon expertly swirled them down twenty-four stories to the street.

"The place I'm taking you to ain't noplace fancy," he said, turning in the direction of the Silver Slipper.

"Good, we'll slum together," Aurora said. "Perhaps we should have regular breakfasts together, fortnightly perhaps. Being taken to breakfast is my idea of romance, you know. Very few people have been willing to entertain the thought of me at the breakfast hour, I can tell you that."

"It's called the Silver Slipper," Vernon said when he parked outside the cafe. The pink stucco walls were beginning to peel, which he hadn't noticed before. In fact, he hadn't noticed how generally ugly and seedy the whole area was. Debris from a nearby drive-in littered the white shale parking area—smashed beer cans and old french fries and paper cups were plentiful.

Babe and Bobby were cooking a grillful of eggs for a half dozen pipecutters when Vernon and Aurora walked in. The sight of Vernon with a woman almost caused them to overcook the whole mess. They were hard put to do anything but stare, and

Vernon, for his part, was hard put to mumble out an introduction.

Aurora smiled when she was introduced, but it didn't help much. Bobby took refuge in professionalism, but Babe tried gallantly to rise to the occasion.

"Honey, any girl of Vernon's is a pleasure for us to meet," she said, not sure if she was striking the right note. She patted her hair a few times and said, "Y'all excuse me while I get this order out."

Aurora had an omelette, and Bobby snuck as many glances as he dared while he was making it.

"I like your night watchman," Aurora said when conversation flagged.

"Aw, Schweppes?" Vernon said.

"Don't say aw," Aurora said. "It's very annoying that you didn't hang in there long enough for me to improve your English."

"I give it my best try," Vernon said.

"I hardly think so. You accepted defeat rather calmly—almost with relief, I would have said. You've obviously discussed me with these people, and with your night watchman. Why didn't you discuss me with me instead of with your various cronies and employees?"

"Babe says I'm a born loner," Vernon said. "She's always said that."

Aurora glanced over her shoulder at Babe. "If you'd rather believe her than me, fine," she said. "It doesn't matter now. I've decided I'd rather have you take me to breakfast once in a while. It will irritate General Scott exceedingly, but that's his lookout."

"Now what do you make of that?" Bobby asked Babe the minute they went out the door.

"I wish I hadn't suggested he give her that goat," Babe said. "I never knowed she was so old. She'd look nice with a diament, an' lord knows he can afford to give her one."

2.

Rosie popped out of the plane the minute its doors opened, at a little airport far out Westheimer. Aurora and Vernon stood watching.

"We bounced around like a boll of cotton," Rosie said, hugging Aurora.

"Shame on you for running away," Aurora said. "You could have come and lived with me."

"Don't like to impose," Rosie said.

"No, I'm the only one who seems to. I'm only sorry there aren't more people willing to be imposed upon." She picked up a car phone and called Emma, who didn't answer.

"I bet she's gone to the hospital," she said, and at once called the General.

"General Scott," General Scott said.

"We know that, Hector," Aurora said. "Has Emma called?"

"Yes, and it's about time you thought to check," the General said. "I don't know what you'd do if I wasn't around to take messages for you."

"Get to the point," Aurora said. "We weren't discussing what I'd do without you. No doubt I'll find that out soon enough. What's my daughter up to?"

"She's having a baby," the General said.

"Thank you, Hector. Have a good day if you can," Aurora said.

"Where are you?" the General asked. "I've been worried."

"On our way to the hospital. Rosie's in quite good spirits."

"Well, I'm not," the General said. "I don't see why I couldn't have come along. There's nothing to do here."

"I guess it's not fair to exclude you from all this excitement," Aurora said. "The baby's being born at Hermann Hospital—make F.V. bring you there. We have to go to Ben Taub first to see to Royce. Try to look commanding when you come. You know how difficult hospital personnel can be.

"As long as it's going to be a party I must invite Alberto," she said when she hung up. "You know how happy babies make him. On the other hand, he's never much good in the morning. Perhaps I'll have everyone to dinner instead."

"This is Emma's baby," Rosie said. "I ain't gonna sit by and watch you take it over like you've taken over every'body else."

"Emma won't care," Aurora said. "She's one of the meek, like Vernon here."

"I ain't one of the meek," Rosie said.

When they got to the ward where Royce was, Shirley Sawyer was there. As Aurora and Rosie and Vernon walked through a long aisle between beds they saw a large woman stand up in confusion. She was by Royce's bed.

"You mean she's that old?" Rosie whispered in astonishment, unprepared for Shirley to be large, ugly, and confused.

"I think she'll leave, if we let her," Aurora said.

Shirley looked at Royce, who was unconscious, and began to tiptoe out. She had to come right past them, and she continued to tiptoe, rather pitifully, Aurora thought.

"Miz Dunlup, I just had to see him," Shirley said plaintively. "I know you hate me—I'm the cause of it all."

She began to cry and went on up the aisle. Rosie didn't speak, though she did nod a kind of acknowledgment. Then they all went and looked at Royce, who was asleep but obviously not dead. He looked pale and unshaven and had several tubes running into his body. "He's breathin', but he ain't snorin'," Rosie said tearfully.

Aurora put her hand on Vernon's arm. Life was such a mystery, and such a drama. She had just seen two grown women moved to tears by the sight of the pale bandaged hulk of Royce Dunlup. Few bodies could have contained less of human grace than Royce's, it seemed to her, and she could find nothing at all to say about his spirit, since in her presence he had never shown any. Royce was as near to being a human zero as she had encountered, and yet her own Rosie, a woman of morality and good sense, was ruining several Kleenex over him as she and Vernon watched.

"I better tell her he can have his job back," Vernon said.

"Oh, be still," Aurora said. "You can't cure all the ills of humankind with your jobs, you know. You'd do better to cure a few of your own and let the rest of us flounder."

Vernon shut up, and, while Rosie was examining the countenance of her husband, Aurora looked about the ward. It seemed to be mostly filled with old, hopeless Negro men and young, hopeless Negro men, some of them grotesquely bandaged, none of them looking at anyone else. Thirty people were sitting around in one room, quite removed from one another, and when Aurora looked at Vernon she too felt removed, and rather personless. Who could she weep for? Not likely Hector, at least not at the moment. Perhaps Trevor. It would be just like Trevor to contract some horrible disease, become beautifully gaunt, and die splendidly, thus breaking at last all those sunny hearts who had so relentlessly melted his own over the years. But that was remote. With a sigh she went over to Rosie.

"Ain't it somethin'," Rosie said. "An old man like Royce havin' the gumption to carry on that way."

"It's something," Aurora said.

"You know, if I'd of known she was that old, I never would have run off," Rosie said. "Royce told me she was nineteen, the liar."

"You never told me that."

"Didn't want to make it look no worse than it was," Rosie said.

"Dear, we'd better get over to Emma," Aurora said. "I'll check on you later, when I can."

Walking out, she found herself pondering what Royce had told Rosie—that his mistress was only nineteen. It struck her as being a remarkably keen piece of invention for a man of Royce's stolidity—the detail most likely to cause Rosie the keenest jealousy, for whatever she might manage to be or do as a wife she would certainly not be able to be nineteen again.

"Human beings have such genius for deception," she said once they were in the car. "I've not been fortunate. I'm far more gifted at deception than any man I've ever known. In my heyday I deceived everyone I knew, and never got caught. I hesitate to think what I might have been capable of if I'd found a man smart enough to deceive me and then let me find it out. I doubt that my admiration would have known any bounds. Unfortunately I was always the more cunning, and I still am."

When they walked up to the other hospital they saw the General's old blue Packard sitting out front, with F.V. in his chauffeur's cap at the wheel. The General got out and stood at attention as they approached.

He had decided, while waiting, to take a businesslike approach to Vernon, and he shook his hand briskly. "What's the situation?" he asked.

"Well, I'm feeling very philosophical, so don't ruffle me," Aurora said. "Talk to Vernon while I calm down. I just remembered that Emma's having a child."

"That must be an antique car," Vernon said, looking at the Packard.

"It's no better than mine," Aurora said, looking in her mirror. She felt a little confused. Inside, nothing seemed certain. Emma had given her the slip, finally, and looking at Vernon and the General trying awkwardly to talk to one another made her realize how strange it was that she should be involved with either of them in whatever way. No sooner did she gain a sense of herself and feel a little authority than it all slipped away. Having nothing to say suddenly, she walked into the hospital, leaving the two men to follow uneasily.

"Is she all right?" the General asked awkwardly. "I never know."

"She ate a good breakfast," Vernon said. "I guess that counts for something."

"No, I don't think so," the General said. "She always eats. She seemed a little out of sorts when she left home."

Aurora heard the sound of male voices behind her and whirled on them. "All right, I feel quite sure you two are discussing me," she said. "I don't see why you can't keep up with me. It would be a good deal nicer if we all walked along together."

"We thought you wanted to be alone to collect your thoughts," the General said hastily.

"Hector, my thoughts have been collected since I was five," Aurora said. "You know I become irritable when I think I'm being discussed. It does seem like you and Vernon could remember that. I'd rather not have a scene right now, if we can help it."

She waited until they caught up and obediently and silently kept pace with her. The nurse at the registration desk had trouble finding Emma's room number, and Aurora was just on the point of an acid remark when she finally found it.

Immediately she went striding off. Vernon and the General tried to anticipate which way she might turn so as not to bump into her. It was obvious to both of them that she was in no mood to tolerate minor awkwardnesses.

Indeed, riding up in the elevator was terrifying to both of them. Aurora had a tigerish look in her eye—she seemed the very contradiction of everything a grandmother ought to be. It was plain that she suddenly felt almost intolerably hostile to both of them, but neither of them knew why. They felt their best course lay in keeping silent, so they kept very silent.

"Well, you're both total failures as conversationalists," Aurora said angrily. Her bosom was heaving; she herself could not remember when she had felt so mixed and so violent.

"Evidently you're only able to talk about me," she said. "You're not at all interested in talking to me. The sight of the two of you makes me wish I was ninety instead of forty-nine. I might as well be ninety, for all the good it's going to do me. In a healthier age I'd still be having babies, you know—in a healthier age I could probably find someone worth having them by."

Fortunately the elevator opened just then, and Aurora strode out, giving them a haughty, rather contemptuous glance.

"I knew she wasn't all right," the General whispered. "I'm getting so I can tell."

Aurora walked rapidly down the long white hall, the two men forgotten. She felt like she might burst into tears or fury at any moment, and she wanted to get away from both men. Then, before she had time to calm down or even to consider why she felt so pent up, she was at Emma's door, Room 611. The door was partially open and she could see her pale, unshaven son-in-law sitting by the bed. Without a glance at the two tag alongs, she opened the door and saw her daughter. Emma lay back amid some pillows, her eyes unusually wide.

"He's a boy," Emma said. "So much for family tradition."

"Oh, well, I'd just like to see for myself," Aurora said. "Where have you put him?"

"He's splendid," Emma said. "You won't be able to resist him."

"Un-huh, and how come you didn't wear that blue gown I bought you—for this very occasion, I seem to remember?"

"Forgot to pack," Emma said. Her voice sounded tired and cracked.

Aurora remembered that she had two men with her and looked around for them. They were standing quietly outside the room.

"I brought Vernon and the General to share your moment of triumph," she said. "I believe they're both too timid to come in."

"Hello, hello," the General said when they had been ushered in. Vernon managed a greeting, and Flap gave them cigars.

"Thank God, someone to give them to," he said.

"I'll leave the four of you to complete these formalities and go have a look at that baby, I believe," Aurora said. She left them all looking vaguely at one another and went down two floors to the nursery. After some prodding, a nurse produced a tiny midge of an infant, who refused to open its eyes. She had wanted especially to see whose eyes it had, but saw she would have to wait. She wandered down the hospital corridor shaking her head and clenching her jaw. Everything was wrong—everything—but she couldn't say what.

When she got back to Emma's room she found conversation at a lull, as it had been when she left. "Thomas, you look quite tired," she said. "Fathers are allowed to rest while the infant is in the hospital, you know, but seldom afterward. If you'd like my advice you ought to go home and go to bed."

"For once I'll take your advice," Flap said. He bent and kissed Emma. "I'll be back," he said.

"All right, gentlemen, I'd like a private word with my daughter," she said, looking at her very uncomfortable suitors. "Perhaps you'd like to wait for me in the lobby. I'm sure you have notes to compare, or something."

"Why are you so itsy?" Emma asked, once the men were gone.

Aurora sighed. She was pacing the room. "Is that what I am?" she asked.

"Well, something," Emma said. "Remember when I told you I was pregnant and you had that fit?"

"Um," Aurora said, sitting down. "Yes, I suppose I need to burst into tears, but neither of those men is man enough to provoke me to it."

Her daughter's eyes were quite luminous, she noticed.

"I would have liked to hear your grandmother's comment on that child," she said. "If your first child wasn't a girl, then your last one is sure to be. I imagine that would have been her comment were she here."

She noted that Emma was quite exhausted. Her fatigue was tinged with a kind of delight, or triumph, but it was fatigue nonetheless. The unusual brightness of her eyes only served to highlight her exhaustion. She felt it incumbent upon herself to stop fretting, if that was what she was doing, and to behave in a motherly and, she supposed, grandmotherly fashion.

"I'm being quite bad, Emma," she said. "You've done everything properly, I can see, aside from forgetting my gown, and I've no excuse for rattling on this way."

"I just want to know why you're itsy," Emma said.

Aurora looked at her directly, and for a long time. "I shall give you the Klee," she said. "Come and get it when you're on your feet."

"All right," Emma said. "I hope you don't mind that we named him Thomas. We would have named it Amelia if it had been a girl."

"It's of no moment," Aurora said and reached over and took her daughter's light, almost lifeless hand.

"You must get your strength back," she said. "You've a lot of safety pins to bend."

"I have time," Emma said.

"Yes, well, I shall keep the Renoir yet a bit," Aurora said.

Emma stopped looking delighted—a look of slight downcastness came into her face. "You don't like being a grandmother, do you?" she said. "You don't accept it as being a natural part of life, or anything like that, do you?"

"No!" Aurora said, so fiercely that Emma jumped.

"Okay, but I hoped you would," Emma said faintly, in the beaten, retreating tones Aurora's own mother, Amelia Starrett, had employed so often and so tellingly when faced with her own daughter's sudden angers.

"I'm stripped . . . don't you see?" Aurora began passionately. But then her heart twisted and she blushed, very ashamed, and took Emma into her arms.

"I'm sorry. Please forgive me," she said. "You've been a perfect and proper daughter and I'm simply crazy . . . just crazy."

Then she seemed to pass out for a while, holding her weak white daughter, and when she looked up she was enough herself to notice that Emma's hair was as awful as ever. She refrained from comment, though, and stood up and walked around the bed.

Emma's eyes had recovered a bit of their shine. "Why did you decide to give me the Klee?" she asked.

Aurora shrugged. "My life is crazy enough without that picture around," she said. "It's probably had an influence on me all these years, you know. It's probably why my lines never meet."

She took out her mirror and looked at herself thoughtfully for a while, neither really calm nor really wrought up.

"How come you brought two men?" Emma asked.

"I've decided to force them down one another's throats," Aurora said. "Those two and Alberto and any others that come along. I'm going to require plenty of attendants from now on, I can tell you that.

"You must consider that I've only been a grandmother as long as you've been a mother," she said. "It's likely I'll come to feel differently about the role, or if not about the role at least about the child."

She noticed that her daughter was smiling shyly. In her fat way, with almost no hair to speak of, she yet managed to be an endearing, even a fetching girl, and nicely mannered, despite her dreadful marriage.

"Count yourself lucky you've got my Boston, my dear," she said. "And don't tell me it was only New Haven. If you just had your father's Charleston I'd not count on you for very much."

She shook her fist at her daughter's shy smile and northern eyes, and turned and left.

3.

IN THE lobby of the hospital the General and Vernon were walking around and around feeling uncomfortable with one another, but less uncomfortable with one another than either of them felt at the prospect of Aurora's return.

"I've felt all day she was somewhat out of sorts," the General said several times. "There's no predicting her moods, you know."

Vernon would have agreed, but before he could she stepped out of the elevator and took them by surprise. "What'd you think of the baby?" she asked at once.

"We didn't go see it," the General said. "You didn't tell us to."

Aurora looked haughty. "You've spent thirty minutes in the same building with my grandchild and haven't even gone to see him," she said. "That shows rather a lack of ambition, or generalship, or something, and that includes you, Vernon. I hope you've at least made friends while I've been busy."

"Of course," Vernon said.

"I bet," Aurora said. "Would you please take me back to the building where my car is? I'm tired. I'll meet you at home quite shortly, Hector, if you don't mind."

The General stood by the Packard and watched them drive off in the Lincoln. F.V. held the door open for him.

"It's true this car's becoming a bit inconvenient, F.V.," the General said. "A Lincoln would be somewhat more convenient, I'll admit."

355

"A Lincoln?" F.V. said in disbelief.

"Well, or something comparable," the General said.

4.

AURORA RODE downtown in silence. Vernon could not decide whether she was happy or unhappy, and he didn't ask. She held her silence until they were eight stories up the garage ramp.

"Up, up, up," she said and yawned.

"Yeah, you been up a while," Vernon offered.

"Not brilliant, but it's conversation," Aurora said and yawned again. She spoke no more until Vernon pulled up beside her Cadillac.

"It doesn't look as classic as it used to," she said. "I've a feeling that one of these days my key is going to refuse to go in the ignition."

"Gimme a buzz if you need me," Vernon said.

"A buzz indeed," she said, collecting her shoes, which she had kicked off. "I'll settle for having you at my door at seven this evening, and bring some cards."

"Seven today?" he asked, noticing her yawn again.

"Seven today," Aurora said. "We're going to have a reckless middle age, the several of us. Maybe I'll win enough money to buy a Lincoln and a beach boy, and then I won't need any of you." She pointed her bent key at him and got in and left.

5.

WHEN SHE got home she found the General sitting at her kitchen table, ramrod straight, eating a bowl of Rice Krispies.

Aurora wasn't fooled. She went over and gave his lean neck a good hard squeeze to see if she could make a dent in it. She didn't make much of a dent, and the General didn't look around.

"All right, why are you looking like Don Quixote?" she asked.

"There's nothing more ridiculous than a General with a mournful countenance. What have I done now?"

The General kept eating, which annoyed her.

"Very well, Hector," she said. "I wouldn't mind being friendly, but if you're going to sit there eating that stupid cereal I don't see why I should bother."

"It isn't stupid," the General said. "You've no goddamn right to criticize my cereal. I've been eating Rice Krispies for years."

"I can believe that—it's why your calves are so skinny, more than likely," Aurora said.

"No, that's because I run," the General said. "I keep in shape."

"What's the point of keeping in shape if you're going to be gloomy every time I'm friendly?" Aurora asked. "I'd rather have you friendly and with a little more meat on your calves. Legs are crucial, you know. In fact, where I'm concerned, little else counts."

The General didn't pursue the argument. He poured some more milk on his cereal and listened to it snap, crackle, and pop, faintly. In the rare intervals when he wasn't chewing he clenched his teeth. He felt like having an angry fit, but was trying to control himself.

Then Aurora gave him a silent, haughty look, as if to say she had never seen anything more ridiculous in her life than him eating Rice Krispies. Exasperated beyond control, he let go his fit. He grabbed the box of Rice Krispies and shook it at her, and then slung it back and forth in great sweeps, scattering Rice Krispies all over the kitchen and even getting some in Aurora's hair, which is what he had really meant to do. He wanted to dump the whole box over her head, in fact, but unfortunately he had been feeling nervous for a couple of days and had been eating Rice Krispies steadily to calm his nerves and there weren't enough left in the box to pour over her head—at last not satisfyingly. When he had slung the box around until it was empty he threw it at her, but it was no very effective throw. Aurora managed to catch the box easily, with one hand, and she strolled over lazily and dropped it in a wastebasket.

"Had your fun, Hector?" she asked.

"You're going to mess up our life with that little oil man," the

General shouted. "I know you. You've already humiliated me with that Italian. How much do you think I'm going to put up with? That's what I want to know."

"Oh, quite a lot," Aurora said. "I'll sketch it in for you after I've had my nap. I think you better come and have one too. After all this excitement you're bound to be exhausted, and I've planned a little party for tonight.

"You can bring your cereal," she added, seeing that he still had half a bowlful. Then she crunched her way across a light skein of Rice Krispies and went up to her bedroom.

6.

SOME HOURS later, in her bedroom, as the evening was commencing, she sat in her window nook with a Scotch in her hand, listening to the General grumble as he tied his tie. It was a red tie she had bought him a few days before; it went beautifully with his accustomed charcoal gray.

"If we're going to play poker, why do you want me in a suit and tie?" he asked. "Alberto and Vernon certainly won't be dressed up."

"I'm glad you're able to call them by their first names," Aurora said, looking down at her darkening yard. "That's a promising beginning."

"It doesn't answer my question," the General said. "Why am I the only one who's required to dress?"

"You aren't," Aurora said. "I intend to dress splendidly, pretty soon. You are the host, Hector—a position I'd think you'd appreciate. Also you look quite attractive in your suits and rather ridiculous in sports clothes. In our new life you will be the one that dresses, if you don't mind."

"So far I don't like a goddamn thing about our new life," the General said. "You seem to think it's going to be pleasant to have three men around."

"Four when Trevor's in town," Aurora said. "Not to mention anyone entertaining I may meet."

"I know my days are numbered," the General said grimly, getting into his coat. Instead of feeling angrily gloomy he had started feeling resigned and nobly gloomy.

"I know you're getting rid of me," he said. "I can tell when I'm being phased out. You don't have to pretend. Old soldiers never die, you know . . . they just fade away. I guess that's my duty now, just to fade away down the street."

"Jesus," Aurora said. "I certainly never thought I'd hear a speech like that in my own bedroom."

"Well, it's true," the General said stoically.

"On the contrary, it's bullshit, if I may make use of a vulgar phrase," Aurora said. "You know perfectly well how reluctant I am to alter my basic arrangements."

"Oh," the General said.

"It won't hurt you to have some friends, Hector, even if they are my other suitors," Aurora said. "You've seen no one but your chauffeur and those dogs for far too long."

"All right, I'll try it," the General said, standing at attention and looking in the mirror. "I just don't know what you're doing, Aurora. I never know what you're doing—I'll never know what you want. It's all a mystery to me."

"Some gaiety," Aurora said, smiling at him. "That, principally— and perhaps another Scotch, after a while."

The General looked at her silently, still at attention.

"Admirable bearing," Aurora said. "Why don't you go down and get out some ice? Our guests will be arriving soon, and I shall be awhile."

Later she looked out her window and saw two cars arriving at once, the old Lincoln and the new. She raised her window a bit higher so she could watch the arrivals and hear whatever was said. Alberto, she could see, had his arms full of flowers. When he saw Vernon beside him and the General at the door, he looked puzzled. His instinct was to bristle, and yet he was not quite certain that he should bristle just then. Vernon had put on a Stetson hat for the occasion. Aurora waited, smiling, and then by peeking over saw the General step out on her porch and extend his hand.

"Come in, gentlemen," he said in his scratchy voice. Vernon took off his Stetson and the gentlemen went in.

Aurora watched the evening for a bit, and then stood up and pitched her dressing gown at the bed. She went to her closet and selected a dress for the evening, and when she had selected it and put it on and found the right necklace to go with it she took her hairbrush and stood for a while in front of her Renoir, brushing and looking at the two gay young women in their yellow hats. It occurred to her, as it often had, that their gaiety seemed a good deal quieter than her own had ever been. Then the young women blurred and the painting became like an open window, the window of memory, and Aurora looked through it and saw her own happiness—with her mother in Paris, with Trevor on his boat, with Rudyard beneath the mosses of Charleston. It seemed to her that it had mostly been all happiness then, before quite so much had been said and done.

After a bit her eyes ceased to swim and the two simple young women smiled once again from their pinks and yellows. Aurora felt quite peaceable. She dried her cheeks, finished dressing, and descended gaily to her fellows, all of whom, all evening, found her to be a high, indeed an inestimable, delight.

BOOK II

Mrs. Greenway's
Daughter
1971–1976

EMMA'S FIRST lover was her banker, a large, lugubrious Iowan named Sam Burns. He had something of the melancholy of a basset, and had been married twenty-six years when the affair started.

"That means you have at least twice the excuse I have," Emma told him. "I've only been married eleven years."

She always talked to Sam while they were undressing, for fear that if she didn't he would change his mind and lumber out of the room. The mention of his marriage was a mistake, however. Any mention of it, ever, only made Sam the more melancholy. The notion that marriage led inevitably to affairs was deeply offensive to him. He was first vice-president of a small but prosperous suburban bank in Des Moines, and he loved his wife, children, and grandchildren very much. He didn't know why he was spending his lunch hours in bed with a client's wife. "I guess the Lord made us all sinners," he said one day; but then it occurred to him that his wife, Dottie, would certainly never sin, or at least not in the manner in which he himself had just finished sinning, and his large brow wrinkled.

"Stop thinking about it, Sam," Emma said. "It's not as bad as you've been told."

"I've been a banker all my life," Sam said wistfully.

"You're still a banker," Emma said. "What are you talking about?"

Sam clutched her silently. What he meant was that in his own thoughts he no longer felt grounded in his profession; what he felt himself to be, all day long sometimes, was an adulterer. He had spent his whole dutiful life maintaining a state of respectability, only to lose it utterly in his fifty-second year—in order to sleep with a client's wife. At least his parents were dead; they would never have to know about it if he were caught and disgraced. His wife and children would have to know about it, though. Sometimes when Jessie and Jinny, his two little granddaughters, were crawling around in his lap the thought of how unworthy his lap really was struck him, and appalled him so that he was close to tears. At such times he laughed too loud, annoying everyone in the house.

"Hush, Grandpa, too loud!" Jessie said, putting her fingers in her ears.

Sam thought of Emma as a client's wife, although for all practical purposes she herself was his client. Flap Horton had long since taken refuge in a pose of academic impracticality; all bills and financial arrangements, such as the loan they needed on a house they wanted to buy, he left to Emma; though the pose didn't prevent him from complaining constantly about her inability to balance a household budget.

Their fights about money were violent and bitter—terrible fights in which all their disappointment with one another came out. Whenever one started, Tommy and Teddy grabbed the nearest basketball or the nearest skateboard and fled the house. Years later, when she and Flap no longer argued, even about money, Emma's strongest memory of Des Moines was of sitting at the kitchen table trying to calm down, and feeling guilty about the boys, whom she could see out the back window: Tommy often lying down on the grass by the driveway, refusing to play,

364

waiting tensely for it to be over so he could come back to his science fiction magazines and his mineralogy set; Teddy, even more forlorn, a little boy so thirsty for love that he gulped it like water, dribbling miserably, shooting his ineffective push shots that usually fell two feet short of the rim of the basket, or else circling in endless lonely circles on his skateboard—all of it under a cold Iowa sky.

Tommy, tense himself, could live with tension. He could climb up on his bunk bed and read, answering no questions and responding to no demands; but not Teddy. Teddy needed arms around him, ears to listen; he needed everyone in the house to be warmly, constantly in love with one another. Emma knew it; her youngest son's yearning for a household filled with love haunted her, as her marriage died. Tommy wanted no illusions; Teddy wanted them all, and his mother was his only hope.

Fortunately for them all, she and Flap had made one another happy for five or six years, when the boys were very young. They had that credit at least. For a time their marriage had some energy, and it got them from Houston to Des Moines and six years into teaching. In the sixth year Flap got tenure, even though he had never quite finished his book on Shelley. They bought a house and had been living in it two years before Emma realized that she wanted to seduce Sam Burns, the man who had got her their mortgage. In the two years, something had slipped. Flap had quietly started to be a failure. He had always expected to fail, and slid into failure easily. In the context of academic life it was as common and as comfortable as his pipe and his slippers, but he hated Emma for letting it happen. It had been up to her to demand success of him; she was supposed to push, nag, bite if necessary. Instead, she left it to him, knowing that he would rather sit and read, or drink coffee and talk literature—or, as it later developed, fuck students.

Emma too knew that it was up to her, but the task of making Flap succeed was more than she could manage while raising two boys. It was a pity, but it was not her nature anyway. Flap had misread her to begin with. She too liked to sit and read; she also liked to sing songs with her boys and discuss life with them, to drink wine, eat chocolate, grow flowers, cook the five or six dishes she could really cook, see movies, watch TV, and get laid now and then—all that in no particular order. Success demanded a particular order. Besides, she found successful academics universally obnoxious; failed academics were at least sometimes a little sweet. She knew how obnoxious Flap would become if he succeeded; what she hoped for was a middle ground that would leave him friendly and relaxed and incline him to stay home a little, spend some time with the boys, and maybe even a little with her.

The Shelley book would have been enough, she thought later. One book would have done it. In his own view he would have been established forever. Yet he finicked too long, kept reading, polished what he had excessively, and never wrote the last two chapters. He published three articles, enough for his tenure, but that was that. Emma was too proud to nag—she was not about to nag. Flap hated her pride and paid her back by attacking her handling of money. Soon what energy was left between them all centered on money; arguments about it constituted their only real form of communication. Everything else, sex included, became perfunctory, impersonal, and mute. Flap went away to the library, the faculty club, his office, saw students and colleagues. He relocated his emotional life. Emma ignored the fact for six or eight months, until she began to ache for love too badly to be proud.

"You've abandoned me!" she cried one day in the midst of a fight about an air conditioner. "It's summer. Why do you stay over there all day?"

"That's where I work," Flap said.

"What work? What work?" Emma said. "It's summer. You could read here."

"Did you realize how anti-intellectual you are?" Flap said. "You really hate colleges. Did you know that?"

"Yes, I know it," Emma said. "Faculties, at least. I hate them because they're all depressed."

"That's arrogant," Flap said, stung. "Who's depressed?"

"Every teacher on that fucking campus," Emma said. "They just don't acknowledge it, that's all. I hate unacknowledged depression. At least I show it when I'm depressed."

"Which is always," he said.

"Not always."

"You might be more attractive if you pretended to a little cheer," he said.

"Who do I have to pretend for?" she said.

"The boys."

"Oh, shut up," she said. "You don't see the boys six minutes a week. I'm not depressed with them. They cheer me up. So could you if you cared to."

"Mine and my colleagues' depression is more civilized than your cheer," Flap said.

"Then keep it, you shitheel," Emma said. "I don't have to be civilized in my own bedroom."

Flap kept it, and left. He retreated into his profession and had fewer fights with his wife. Tommy, with the precociousness of a well-read eleven-year-old, noticed and blamed his mother for his father's remoteness.

"You have a lot of hostility," he told her one morning. "I think you've driven Daddy away."

Emma stopped and looked at him. "How'd you like this pancake in the kisser?" she said.

Tommy held his ground, for the moment at least. "My brother and I live here too," he said. "We have a right to our opinion."

"I'm glad you admit that he's your brother," Emma said. "You don't usually. The way you treat Teddy doesn't leave you a lot of room to talk about hostility—would you agree?"

"Well, there's a difference," Tommy said. Argument fascinated him.

"What?"

"Teddy's too young to leave," he said. "He has to put up with it. Daddy doesn't."

Emma smiled. "You're your grandmother's grandson," she said. "That's a good point. Perhaps we could reach an agreement. You try to be kinder to Teddy, and I'll try to be kinder to your father."

Tommy shook his head. "It won't work," he said. "That kid irritates me too much."

"Then eat your breakfast and don't pick on me," Emma said.

From the first Sam's size and his lugubriousness fascinated her. His large face always brightened when she came into the bank. It had been so long since she had had an active sense of wanting someone that she was a long time in recognizing her own feelings for what they were, and then it was another eight months before she worked up to doing anything about it. She had met his wife, a dumpy, yappy, extremely self-occupied little woman named Dottie who ran half the civic and charitable organizations in Des Moines. She seemed to have little time to spare for Sam, and she was so pleased with herself generally that Emma never felt the least remorse about seducing him. Dottie was obviously not going to miss a few hours of Sam.

During the eight months, Emma flirted with him. She was not so fine a flirt as her mother, but she had nothing else of an emotional or romantic nature to do and she managed to find a great many reasons for going to the bank. Sam Burns had no idea he was being flirted with, but he certainly felt perked up whenever young Mrs. Horton stopped to say hello to him for a minute. His secretary, Angela, was slightly more aware; but she would never have suspected Emma of truly dark designs. "You're the only one makes Mr. Burns blush, honey," she told Emma. "I'm always glad to see you coming. He gets the blues easier than any man I ever saw. I've seen that man so blue he could hardly dictate."

Emma befriended Angela; she was most discreet. Indeed, for a time she didn't expect to succeed in her little flirtation. There seemed no way to lure such a large, sad, respectable man out of his bank office and into an illicit bed. Even if she succeeded in getting him out of the bank, what illicit bed would they use? Emma told herself she wasn't serious, that all she needed was a little attention, someone to perk up when she came into the room. In fact, it wasn't true. Her sex life at home had sunk to what she would have once considered an unbelievable low. Flap had made a happy discovery: that the student generation he was teaching attached no more moral significance to sex than they might attach to a warm bath. Better still—since he was lazy by nature—he discovered that it was not even necessary to seek out students; drably dressed but nubile twenty-year-olds were pleased to seek him out. Often it was only necessary to tag along to their apartments and perhaps listen to a few records and smoke a little grass in order to accomplish a seduction. He quickly formed a student habit and approached his wife less and less often, and then only when drunk or prompted by guilt.

Emma knew Flap had more of a sex drive than he was getting home with, but she didn't inquire. She felt secondary in her own bed, which was humiliating enough; she was not about to make matters worse by acting jealous. In regard to Flap she felt more contemptuous than jealous anyway, but somehow that didn't make her feel the less secondary. A year passed; she knew that inside she felt desperate, half the time, but she covered the desperation with such thick wads of activity that she thought perhaps no one would suspect it. She told herself to be matter-of-fact; she needed a lover. But she was living in a middle-class neighborhood, in a middle-class city, with two boys to raise and a house to take care of. Where was the time for a lover, and how could one be found in such a place? Sam Burns was an absurd fantasy, she realized. There was no way to get him out of his bank, and even if there was she would probably be too scared to do anything. Certainly he would be too scared—no man ever looked less adulterously inclined.

She gave up on her fantasy, then upon all fantasies. Resignation crept in; she told herself she might as well forget the whole business. Then one day in November she was at the bank chatting with Sam and Angela, and Sam Burns shrugged into his overcoat and told her he had to run to inspect a house the bank owned and needed to sell. Emma moved. On the spot she invented a friend who might be moving to Des Moines and who might be needing just such a house. Sam Burns was delighted to take her with him; he had wanted to anyway, but would never have been able to think of an excuse for asking her.

It was very cold and they were both very nervous. The house was empty of furniture. Emma knew from his eyes that he wanted her. She also knew it was up to her. They were walking around the empty house silently, their breaths condensing, now and then bumping into one another awkwardly. She didn't know what to do; Sam was too tall to reach. Then he knelt down to examine a broken baseboard and Emma went over and put her cold hands on his face. His large neck was like a stove. They squatted awkwardly for several minutes, kissing; Emma was afraid to let him stand up, for fear he would flee. They made love in a cold corner, on their overcoats. As Emma had hoped and suspected, it was like being embraced by a large hesitant bear— very satisfying. Driving back to the bank, Sam was in terror, sure that everybody would know; Emma was quiet and at ease and when they got there discussed the house and her imaginary friend with Angela, quite persuasively, until she saw that Sam was over his panic and settled into an afternoon of making loans.

"Honey, you're a tonic for that man," Angela said, blithely noting how much happier her boss looked than he had looked that morning. She had no use for the yappy little Dottie anyway and thought it was sweet that a nice young woman like Mrs. Horton took some interest in her hen-pecked, neglected boss.

"HUMPH, BEARLIKE. Yes, I know the appeal," Aurora said a few weeks later. It had taken only two calls for her to perceive that her daughter was no longer so depressed, and a third for her to worm an admission out of Emma.

"Money may have something to do with it too," she added. "Handling it sometimes gives even rather dull men something of an aura. My goodness. Hector is ill and now I have to adjust to your sinfulness. That's rather a lot to ask of me, isn't it?"

In fact she was not in the least disturbed by Emma's action. She had been waiting for it to happen for several years, but she had nursed the hope that when it did happen it would be some suitable and if possible available man who might take Emma away and give her a marriage that was worthy of her. That, evidently, had not happened.

"You've a penchant for the disadvantageous, my dear," she said. "If you hadn't, you'd not have chosen a grandfather. Obviously the possibilities of this liaison are short-lived."

"What's wrong with the General?" Emma asked, to change the subject.

"Nothing I can't cure," Aurora said. "He inhaled too much pollution on his stupid runs. His runs are little more than crawls these days anyway. Meanwhile Vernon's been gone for a month to Scotland and I'm quite put out about that. If he's going to stay much longer I may require him to have me over. Alberto's quite sunk too. Alfredo's taking over the store. I tell you we're all falling apart down here, and what do you do to help? You seduce a grandfather. I shall have to keep it from Rosie. Since Royce's death the slightest thing upsets her.

"Little Buster's been caught stealing again," she added. "I don't expect that boy to avoid reform school very much longer. Which reminds me to advise you to be careful. I imagine they still stone adulteresses in places like Des Moines."

SAM BURNS took almost that pessimistic a view of their future. He was sure they would be discovered, and that when they were he would have to divorce his wife and marry Emma; then, in order to survive the disgrace, they would have to leave town. He had gone so far as to decide that the move would be to Omaha, where an old army buddy of his was president of a solid little bank.

"Honey, I never got away with nothing in my life," he told Emma, tugging at one of his large ears. "I mean it. I can't scheme worth a damn."

Yet he was adept enough at finding reasons to visit the several empty houses the bank needed to sell. One night while Flap and the boys were gone to a basketball game Emma stuffed an old secondhand mattress in the station wagon and hid it in one of the houses. She told Flap she had donated it to a charity bazaar. For the next year and a half, as the houses slowly sold and were replaced by other houses, the mattress got moved around from one bare development neighborhood to another. All the houses were empty, and always unheated; and once some of the new wore off Sam Burns, Emma began to wonder what it would be like to have a love affair in a warm place, perhaps in a grand and grandly furnished hotel room, or at least in a place with chairs and toilets that flushed.

Once, in fact, they thought they had managed to plan a trip to Chicago, which would have been a nice change, and elegant enough, but Dottie managed to screw it up at the last minute by falling off a parade float and breaking her hip. The fact that he was screwing around while his loyal wife lay in the hospital with her leg in traction increased Sam Burns's guilt to an almost intolerable degree, and Emma decided at several points that she ought to let him go back to the safety of Dottie, Angela, and his work.

She would have let him, out of kindness and affection, had he really wanted to go, for she knew that half the time the affair was a kind of moral torture for him. Yet, for all his suffering, Sam didn't want to go. In his way he had been even more desperate than Emma. Dottie had never been interested in sex anyway, and when she turned forty-five her disinterest quickened, as it were, and became an active dislike. She was not the sort of woman to entertain that which she didn't enjoy either, and Sam's sexual future, insofar as he could imagine it, consisted of occasional call girls at occasional conventions.

Thus, to him, Emma was a miracle. He knew he had been given one last chance to love, and frightening and troubling as it was, he had to have it. He had known no one so kind or so tender as Emma, and he adored her. The empty houses and the odd hours, the cold, the unadornedness of their surroundings made him sad. He wanted to give her all the conventional comforts. Sometimes he even imagined that Dottie had passed honorably away, perhaps of heatstroke at the Jaycees' barbecue, the cooking of which she always supervised all day long in the broiling July sun; if that happened, then he could, as he put it, do right by Emma, take her away from her negligent husband and give her a decent house, nice clothes, a good kitchen, perhaps even a child. It never occurred to him to think that Emma might not want such things, and as it turned out it didn't matter, for Dottie outlived Sam Burns by exactly the length of their marriage—twenty-nine years.

When Emma heard of Sam's death she was pregnant by Flap

and she and her family were living in Kearney, Nebraska, and had been for nine months. Flap had been offered the chairmanship of the English department of a little state college there, and after much indecision had taken it. Emma and the boys had been for staying in Des Moines, but he overruled them; in fact, the dynamic of the family was such by that time that had they wanted to go to Kearney he might well have decided they belonged in Des Moines.

When he was told she was going, Sam Burns was bereft. He sat on the mattress for a long time looking at his huge feet in despair. He would not get to give Emma those comforts. He brought it out haltingly, his most illicit fantasy. Dottie might die; they might marry. He looked at her mournfully, wondering if such a wonderful woman would laugh at the mere notion of marrying him.

Though she would never have married him, Emma didn't laugh. She saw that he did not understand that he had already given her a great comfort. All his life he had been too big, had been treated as a bumbler—and in truth he was a bumbler, had never been expert with her, yet she had enjoyed him deeply.

"Of course, sweetheart," she said. "I'd marry you in a minute," hoping as she said it that Dottie Burns enjoyed a very long life, so she would never have to take it back.

Sam looked at his feet with less despair. His whole large body shook with sorrow the day they parted. "Don't know what I'll do," he said.

"Well, maybe you can improve your golf," Emma said, hugging him. She kissed him and tried to make it a joke, because he hated golf. Shyly, he had admitted it one day. It was on the golf course that he endured the worst ridicule about his bumbling. He only played the game because it was expected of him.

Emma didn't know what she would do, either.

It was Angela, remembering young Mrs. Horton's kindness, and having no one to talk to, who called Kearney and told Emma of Sam's death.

"Oh, not Mr. Burns," Emma said, remembering to be formal even in her shock.

"Yes, he's gone," Angela said. "Had a heart attack right in the middle of the golf course. Naturally he would get out there an' play, hot as it was . . ."

Emma sat at her kitchen table for days, chewing napkins, or else slowly tearing them into little strips. Napkins were her new neurosis. It wasn't just that Sam was dead—it was that she had let him die unhappy. Truth was, her energy had failed for the affair. She had begun to lose the courage for all the hiding, the lies, the empty houses. And another fear had crept in: the fear that Sam was getting too much in love with her. If she fed him much more affection he would start wanting to leave Dottie. It wasn't going to stay nice, or manageable, she knew, and she didn't fight hard for Des Moines when the time came. She thought they had had the best of it, she and Sam, and Kearney was a natural way out.

If he had died in bed, or in an accident, she might not have grieved too deeply, for he didn't understand his life or love it. He had considered himself a Big Fool for fifty-some years, and the fun had gone out of the joke, if there had ever been any fun in it.

It was the fact that he had died on a golf course that haunted her. Maybe he had misunderstood her last remark. He was not a man with an ear for irony. Maybe he had thought she really wanted him to improve his golf game, or even thought she was making little of him at the end.

The heartbreak in that possibility was too much. She chewed napkins and had nightmares in which she saw a large body being dragged off a golf course. Flap and the boys walked well clear of her. He had no idea what was wrong; he told the boys it was pregnancy. Fortunately he had a department to run, which meant that there was always more to do than could be got done. He need never come home, and he seldom did. Tommy took to his upper bunk and his collection of Heinlein. Teddy, desperate, tried to get his mother back to herself. He hugged, he did all his tricks, he told jokes, he played cards, he cleaned up everything, he hung up his clothes, he even offered to make breakfast. Emma couldn't hold out against him. She got up, shook it off, helped him make the breakfast. Then she broke down and told it all while talking to her mother.

374

Aurora listened gravely. "Emma, I have only one word of comfort," she said, "and that is to remind you that men seldom listen to women. Even at the moments when you think they must be listening, they often aren't. I don't know what they're doing—I've often wondered—but it's not listening. I'm sure poor Mr. Burns had better things to remember than your last remark."

"I wish I could be sure," Emma said.

"I'm sure," Aurora said. "You're lucky if you meet one in your life who's really attentive."

"Have you met your one?"

"No, and if I did meet him now, he'd probably be so old he'd be deaf.

"I wish you'd come here to have your baby," she added. "Rosie and I could take care of you both, for a while. Nebraska's no place to have a child. I thought you weren't having any more, by the way. What changed your mind?"

"I don't know," Emma said, "and I don't want to speculate."

INDEED, THERE were times when what she had done seemed almost insane. Things were no better at home, and she thought constantly of divorce as she was growing bigger. It seemed absurd to be pregnant by a man she no longer felt any connection with. Someday she would be a divorcee with three strange children rather than two. It didn't make sense.

Then she had a girl, Melanie, a little creature so immediately happy with herself that it seemed to Emma she had been created just to make everyone feel better.

Emma refused to allow anyone to call her Mellie. From the first she was called Melanie, and she was born with the ability to charm everyone who came near her. Within six months Emma realized that what she had done was to recreate her mother. When she thought about it, in certain ways it was an appalling realization, one more trick life had played on her, for she realized it meant she herself would always be upstaged, if not by her mother, then by her child. Melanie even had gorgeous golden curly hair, so fine that half the light in the room seemed to gather about her head. In another sense the trick was merely amusing, particularly so when grandmother and grandchild got together and attempted to outdo one another in gaiety or willfulness.

The wonder of Melanie, though, at least in her first years, was that she made Teddy happy. Perhaps that was the explanation of her, Emma thought: it was the only thing she could think of to do for Teddy, the only way to bring love back into the house. For a while it seemed to work beautifully. Even Flap couldn't remain aloof from Melanie; for a year or two he came home more often in order to be charmed by his daughter. Tommy never said much about Melanie, but he took a shy, nervous, protective interest in her and was very critical of anyone who let anything bad happen to her—which was usually Teddy, if only because he was with her more than anyone else.

Watching them, Melanie and Teddy, Emma felt rewarded. It was worth a great deal to have two children who loved one another so completely. Indeed, Melanie and Teddy were almost like lovers, constantly lying around in one another's arms. Melanie seemed to live in Teddy's lap—from the time she could toddle she made a beeline for his bed first thing in the morning— and Teddy's behavior was oddly loverlike, for sometimes his very attachment to her seemed to make him perverse. He treated her like a two-year-old girl friend, and when he wasn't smothering her with hugs and affection he was taunting her and teasing her, hiding her toys, driving her to furious heights of anger and pique. Yet always, after storms of tears on Melanie's part, they made it up, they forgave, they forgot, and ended the day in a bunk bed reading one another stories.

Often it was Melanie who did the reading, or at least the telling; for her first vanity was the belief that she could read. When she first began to make words she also began to snatch books from people. "Me can read," she insisted, nodding eagerly, hoping for agreement. Teddy allowed her to think she could, and everyone else, for some reason, denied her her claim. He would listen to her explanations of her picture books for hours, while the rest of the family tried to bully her into being read to. Melanie resented it—she resented seeing people sitting happily with books that had no pictures in them, books that shut her out or forced her to absurd lengths of pretense. When she could she snatched such books and dashed them in the nearest waste-basket. In fact, when no one was watching her, she often went about the house hiding the books people were reading, sliding them under beds or cleverly stuffing them in the backs of closets, where they were not found for months.

She was an extremely clever child, and the spirit of vengeance was strong in her. If she could not get her way she was quite willing to commit her entire energy to seeing that nobody else got their way either, using her great charm shamelessly to divert them from whatever had been in their minds, but resorting to temper instantly if she saw that all else was going to fail.

On visits to Houston she demonstrated a strong preference for Rosie and Vernon, both of whom adored her beyond words. She treated General Scott rather offhandedly, although she liked to poke at his Adam's apple and try to figure out why his voice was so scratchy. He told her he had a frog in his throat and she believed it and was always commanding him to make the frog jump out.

With her grandmother she was generally cool, though now and then the two of them flung themselves into an amorous tussle. Aurora contended at once that Melanie was outrageously spoiled, and she contended it the more vehemently when Melanie rejected her efforts to contribute to the spoiling. She would allow Vernon to trot her on his knee for hours, but the minute Aurora picked her up she became a terrible wiggle-worm. What she loved about her grandmother was the jewelry she wore, and she was always pulling off Aurora's earrings or trying to persuade her to let her wear her necklaces. Sometimes, when the two of them were feeling friendly, they sat on Aurora's bed and Melanie got to try on all her jewels in the jewel box. It amused Aurora to watch her tiny golden-haired grandchild bedeck herself with all the jewels she herself had managed to accumulate, the relics of the passions of her lifetime, or of her own whims—mostly the latter, for, as she frequently lamented, none of her loves had been talented gift givers.

"Me put it on," Melanie said, reaching up for whatever Aurora might be wearing. She loved the amber and silver necklace above all else, and as often as she was allowed traipsed around with it hanging just below her knees. Most of her traipsing was done in pursuit of Rosie, whom she totally adored.

"Lord, it breaks my heart to think of this child growin' up in Nebraska," Rosie said, watching her poke oatmeal in her mouth.

"It breaks mine to consider what will happen to whatever men are around when she grows up," Aurora said.

"She can't be no harder on 'em than you've been," Rosie said.

"Possibly not, but men were tougher in my day. They were brought up to expect difficulty."

"Don't talk," Melanie said, pointing her spoon at Rosie. She was quick to note that people were always talking to her grandmother, and it didn't please her.

"Talk to me," she said a moment later, holding out her dish for more oatmeal.

"Can't be much wrong with a kid that's got an appetite like she has, can there?" Rosie said happily, hurrying to the stove.

Aurora buttered a croissant and Melanie immediately stretched out a hand for it.

"Not much," Aurora said, and ate the croissant herself.

FOR A time after Melanie was born Emma felt free. She had done something right, or so it seemed to her, and she rather contentedly sat back and watched Melanie pull the family together. There were even moments when she felt some solidarity with Flap once again; but they were only moments, and the period of grace didn't last. For one thing, Melanie seemed a finality, in a way. Emma felt that she had delivered what she could deliver. In a few months she began to feel lost again. She told herself it was silly, but at thirty-five she had the persistent feeling that nothing remained for her to do. Everything left was a repeat, and, past a point, she didn't like repeating.

Then there were times when she felt that even had she been happy she would have had to become unhappy in order to live in Kearney. She had become accustomed to the Midwest. The people there were unfailingly courteous, and she had come not to mind their practicality, their gracelessness, their lack of imagination. All that went with the landscape, in a way, yet she could not get across the courtesy into real friendship with anyone. The landscape was meant for loneliness, it seemed. She took long walks along the banks of the Platte in the keen, strong wind—and the wind seemed to her the dominant thing, the eternal thing about where she lived. It was what the plains had instead of beaches, waves, and tides; the wind was her ocean while she lived in Nebraska, and though the natives all complained about it she loved it. She could lean against it almost; she liked to hear it sighing and roaring at night when only she was awake; she didn't mind it. The summer calm and the occasional winter calm were what she minded; then in the stillness she sensed her own lack of balance. When the wind died, she felt herself falling; only the falling was not something taking place in a dream. It was taking place while she was wide awake.

Also in Kearney Flap fell in love. It was prosperous country, relatively speaking; and also it was more remote from the twentieth century than Des Moines. The students there got crushes on him still, but it was not so easy for him to march them off to bed. The town was too small for that, and the girls too inexperienced. One of them would have gotten pregnant, and Flap would have been finished as a department head.

To avoid that danger he began to see a woman only ten years his junior, a young woman who taught drawing. She was liberated, for Kearney; she had studied in San Francisco, had been married and run out on. She was a local girl of good family—indeed, the best family in town—and the community had long ago granted her the right to a mild bohemianism. She painted; she taught the life class. She and Flap were on three faculty committees together which gave them ample reason for meeting. She was intense, didn't talk much, and withheld herself for six months. She had studied modern dance and taught a local Yoga group; her figure was admirable and she moved well. Her name was Janice, and Flap would have left Emma in order to sleep with her, had it been necessary. Janice didn't require that, but she did require that he be in love with her. He told her he had been in love with her for a year, which was as true as not; three weeks after the affair was consummated he was so in love with her that he confessed it to Emma. Melanie was in his lap at the time drawing blue circles on a napkin with one of his felt pens.

"Why are you telling me?" Emma asked quietly.

"But you must know anyway," Flap said. "Can't you tell by the way I act."

"Don't let her draw on the tablecloth, please," Emma said. "You always let her ruin my tablecloths."

"I mean it," Flap said. "Can't you tell by the way I act?"

"No, if you must know," Emma said. "I can tell you don't love me by the way you act. That's not necessarily anything I can hold against you. Maybe you just loved me as long as you could—I don't know. But knowing that you don't love me is not the same as knowing that you love someone else instead of me.

"It's a different hurt," she added, snatching the pen from Melanie just before she started on the tablecloth. Melanie looked darkly at her mother; it was astonishing how dark her eyes became when she was angered. She didn't howl, having learned that it did no good to howl at her mother. She had inherited her grandmother's talent for silences, and she got off her father's lap and marched silently out of the room. Flap was too distracted to notice.

"Well, anyway," he said. He was growing a mustache, to please Janice, and it made Emma feel the more contemptuous of her taste. With a mustache and his bad clothes he looked awfully seedy.

"Tell me what you want," Emma said. "You can be divorced, if you want to. I'm not going to stand in the way of anyone's passion. Go live with her if you want to. Just tell me what you want."

"I don't know," Flap said.

Emma got up and started making hamburgers. The boys were due home soon.

"Well, will you tell me when you decide?" she asked.

"If I can decide," he said.

"You better decide," Emma said. "I'd rather not start hating you, but it might happen. I think I'm going to need a decision."

Flap never made one. In truth, he was more scared of Janice than he was of Emma. She had a capacity for hysteria that

Emma lacked, and he mistook hysteria for conviction. When she screamed that she would kill herself or him if he stopped seeing her, he believed it; and in any case, he had never had any intention of stopping. Janice knew that well enough, but she liked to create scenes. She wasn't in love with Flap and she didn't particularly want him to leave his wife; but she wanted all the rituals of passion, and scenes were necessary. In time their passion became dependent upon her attacks.

In contrast, Emma withdrew. She expected to be left; after a few months she even hoped to be left. If nothing else, it would be nice to have more closet space. But then she realized that Flap wasn't going to leave unless either she or Janice forced him to. He was being very polite and rocking no boats. Emma gave up on him then. She allowed him his house and his children; he didn't want her, so that was no problem. She generally watched the *Late Show* and went to sleep on the couch anyway. She made no scenes. Scenes upset the children too much, and in any case there was nothing left to make a scene about. What had been, for a time, a marriage was lost; the fact that two long-related people were continuing to share a house meant little.

She knew she should probably force him out, but he was so sluggish, so entrenched in the children, so possessive of his habits, that to do so would have taken a major commitment of fury and energy. Emma didn't have it. The kids took all her energy, and she seemed to have no fury. She had exhausted her capacity for disappointment in Des Moines; what Flap was doing seemed cowardly, but it was right in character. She no longer wanted the bother of trying to make him better than he was; she just wasn't that involved.

What she did do was retreat completely from campus activities. She refused all invitations, ignored all functions, spurned all faculty wives. Since she was a department chairman's wife, that made awkwardnesses for Flap, but Emma didn't care. When speakers came to the campus, she didn't go hear them; when teas were held, she didn't attend.

"Go to these parties with your mistress," she said. "It'll titillate people, and God knows they need it here. I hope I never see a plate of goddamn chicken macaroni again."

"What's that got to do with it?" Flap wanted to know.

"Why, it's been the great staple of our social life, honey. Can't you remember?" she said. "Cheap wine, cheap prints, cheap furniture, dull talk, depressed people, tatty clothes, and chicken macaroni."

"What are you saying?" he asked.

"That twelve years as a faculty wife is enough," she said. "You'll just have to forge ahead without me."

In that mood she made a bad mistake. Flap had a colleague who seemed to hate academics as much as she did. His name was Hugh; he was a youthful forty, cynical, a Joycean. He was recently divorced, and Flap brought him home from time to time. He liked to drink and talk about movies, and Emma rediscovered that she too liked to drink and talk about movies. He had a dry wit, and his put-downs of fellow academics and of university life in general were hilarious. When Hugh was around, Emma found it possible to laugh herself out. Some of all that she was holding back got laughed away. It was an immense relief. Hugh had a cold twinkle in his blue eyes and a pouty lower lip; one day he showed up in the middle of Melanie's nap—he was a father himself and had a fine sense of domestic timing—and seduced Emma in Teddy's bunk bed. Emma had suspected it was going to happen, but she was not prepared for the aftermath. Hugh coolly informed her that she hadn't satisfied him.

Emma was very startled. "Not at all?" she asked.

"No," Hugh said. "I think you've forgotten how to fuck." He said it pleasantly while lacing his sneakers. "Let's have a cup of tea," he added.

Instead of throwing him out, Emma fell for it. She took his criticism to heart. After all, how long had it been since she'd given sex any real attention? Flap had been largely indifferent to her for many years, and Sam Burns had been too much in love to require much polish. Besides, she had long been accustomed to repressing both her hopes and her physical feelings; the maintenance of her home life required it.

Still it was a startling criticism; she was very flustered by it.

"Don't let it worry you," Hugh said, still pleasantly. "It's all there. Things will pick up."

The picking up was done at his house, which was only three blocks away and on a perfectly reasonable route for walks. His wife had fled to the east. In time—not much time—Emma knew why. Hugh's eyes never lost their cold twinkle. Emma wanted out almost before she was in, but for a time she was caught. It wasn't right, but it was something. She soon saw that Hugh's contempt for the university was only a pose; he fit in perfectly. Sex was his real study, and the university provided him a comfortable base. His bedroom was a kind of classroom. He trained Emma critically, as if she were a dancer. For a time it seemed rewarding; she accepted the fact of her ignorance and was an eager pupil. Then it stopped seeming rewarding; she felt taken over. Her orgasms were so hard they felt like blows. Hugh often got phone calls from people to whom he was curt. He didn't want Emma listening, and he didn't like it if she lingered past a certain hour. She began to feel shamed. She knew it was masochistic to see a man who had no affection for her, and yet she did it. After a time she felt she was practicing a form of hatred instead of a form of love. Hugh had turned pleasure into humiliation. She didn't know how he had done it, nor how to get away from him either.

Cautiously she attempted to talk to her mother about it.

"Oh, Emma," Aurora said. "How I wish you'd not married Thomas. He's not been adequate. My lovers have not been geniuses, by any means, but at least they've all meant me well. Who is this man?"

"Just a man. A teacher."

"You've got those children to raise, you know," Aurora said. "You just get out of it. Things that are truly wrong never get better. They inevitably get worse. The only way to stop anything is to stop at once. Deciding to stop next month means you haven't decided to stop. Why don't you bring the children and come here?"

"Momma, the boys are in school. I can't come there."

Aurora controlled herself, but not easily. "You're not a balanced person, Emma," she said. "You've always had this self-destructiveness. I don't think you'll get out. Perhaps I ought to come there."

"And do what? Tell the man he has to stop seeing me?"

"I quite well might tell him just that," Aurora said.

Emma realized she quite well might. "No, stay there," she said. "I'll do it."

Emma did get out, but it took another three months. She destroyed it by meeting Hugh's standards sexually—she trumped him with his own card. An equal was not what he wanted, and as her head cleared and her confidence came back she felt less and less need to please him. His response to her became more and more sardonic, more and more contemptuous. He kept himself in perfect shape; his cabinets were full of health foods and vitamins and he scorned Emma because hers weren't. At first he chose an easy target for criticism, namely her figure. He reminded her that her behind was too big, her breasts too small, and her thighs too flabby. Emma shrugged it off. "I'm not a narcissist like you," she said. "Even if I exercised ten hours a day my figure would be indifferent."

She knew he was working his way up to dumping her, and she felt relieved and also quite content to let him do the work. He was waiting to hurt her in some way, she knew, so she was on her guard. It was clear from his eyes that he had every intention of leaving a scar. One day while they were dressing she mentioned something about her children. "God you have ugly brats," Hugh said. Emma was bent over and his large sneaker lay just in front of her hand. She whirled and hit him in the face with it as hard as she could. His nose smashed and blood immediately flooded onto his beard and began to drip down his chest. She threw the sneaker down. Hugh couldn't believe it. "You've broken my nose, you crazy bitch," he said. "What do you mean?"

Emma said nothing.

"You've broken my nose," Hugh repeated as blood continued to flood out. "I have to teach tonight. What do you think I'm supposed to tell people?"

"Tell them your girl friend hit you in the nose with a tennis shoe, you conceited little drip," Emma said. "Don't ever criticize my children."

Hugh began to hit her and she was almost as bloody as he was before she got out, though most of it was his blood. She had to leave her shoes, but fortunately she managed to get into her bathroom without any of the kids seeing her. She lay in the bathtub and soaked out the whole affair. Feeling the sneaker connect had been very satisfying.

For a few weeks after the fight she was able to look at life with a clear eye. It was as if she had been purged, temporarily. Flap, she knew, was of no further use to her. He was too lethargic to change, and Janice had become dependent on him. He would never muster the strength it would take to break off the affair—not that Emma really wanted him to. He had forced her to remove herself from him, and she had. She didn't mind making him breakfast and attending to his laundry; it was far easier than keeping him up to snuff emotionally. She was glad to leave that task to Janice; there would be no problem with Flap unless Janice for some reason decided to dump *him*.

For a time Hugh made himself obnoxious. He hated Emma for breaking his nose, but he hated her even more for breaking off the affair. He had been ready to get rid of her, but it seemed that she had gotten rid of him first, and that was intolerable. It felt like rejection, and he couldn't stand rejection. He wanted her back so he could dump her properly. He began to call and to show up on her doorstep at odd times. Emma refused to let him in, but he succeeded in rattling her. His calls were mean—he was looking to hurt her if he got the chance. It was midwinter, and Hugh's sullen persistence made her claustrophobic. On impulse, she persuaded Flap that she needed to get away, and not to see her mother, for once, but her friend Patsy—now living in Los Angeles and evidently quite happy in her second marriage. Her husband was a successful architect.

Flap agreed, and Emma went. Patsy had become Patsy Fairchild. Her husband was a very good-looking and apparently nice man: tall, tense, hardworking, and witty on the rare occasions when he spoke. Patsy's son by her first marriage was eleven, and she had two lively daughters by her second. She herself looked great, and she had a wonderful modern house in Beverly Hills.

"I knew it would turn out this way," Emma said. "As Momma would be the first to point out, your life is everything mine isn't."

Patsy looked at her shapeless, dowdy friend and didn't bother to deny it. "Yes, I like it here," she said. "I owe it all to Joe Percy—you remember, my friend the screenwriter? He made me come out one time when I was miserable—you remember when I cut my hair? That was when I met Tony."

They talked most of the night, in a splendid room with a slanted roof. The lights of Los Angeles were brilliant below them.

They talked, in fact, for three days as Patsy drove Emma around the city. She took her to the beaches, took her up the coast to San Simeon, and, on the night before Emma was to return to Nebraska, dutifully gave a party for her, complete with movie stars. Anthony Fairchild had built homes for some of them. In party clothes the Fairchilds were a brilliant couple—more brilliant than some of the movie stars. Ryan O'Neal and Ali McGraw were there, and Ali McGraw's husband; there were several men in Levi's who were apparently executives; there was a tiny French actor, and some man who seemed to be a neighbor. He and Anthony Fairchild talked politics while everyone else laughed at one another's jokes. Emma had never been more conscious of her dowdiness, and spent the evening trying not to be seen, which was easy, because no one was looking. Except for the merest politeness, she was assumed to be a non-person and ignored. Peter Bogdanovich and Cybill Shepherd came in late, and Joe Percy, Patsy's old screenwriter friend, got drunk early in the evening and fell asleep in the corner of one of Patsy's vast couches.

When the guests had gone Patsy brought a blanket and covered him up. He mumbled and she sat down and hugged him for a while.

"I don't remember him having such bags under his eyes," Emma said.

"No, he has no judgment," Patsy said. "Women have ruined him. He has a room here, you know. The whole guesthouse, in fact. It's just that pride drives him out once in a while. We're one another's company. You've seen what hours Tony works."

Flying back, Emma got lost in reverie, trying to imagine herself living as Patsy lived, in a grand house that was always clean, with kids that looked like they had been raised on toothpaste and soap. She worried about Hugh, but he stopped being a problem.

He had taken a new girl friend. It was easier than dealing with Emma, who, after all, might only be perverse enough to reject him again.

"How does Patsy look?" Flap asked. He had always been a fan of Patsy's.

"Better than all five of us combined," Emma said, contemplating her shabby small-town brood. Only Melanie was going to make it into Patsy's class, looks-wise; that much was clear.

WITH HUGH no longer a problem, Emma felt more clear-headed than ever. By great good fortune, almost the greatest of her life, a nice person presented himself at her door, in the form of Flap's young graduate assistant, a lanky, gentle boy named Richard. He was from Wyoming, not terribly intelligent but extremely sweet. Also he was very shy and honorable; it took Emma several months to get him in love with her. It was very difficult for Richard to believe that a grownup lady would want to sleep with him in the first place, and very hard to accept that he himself would sleep with somebody's wife. It was a terrible fall from grace, and also, since Emma was Dr. Horton's wife, he felt fairly sure it would result in his failing to get his M.A., which would upset his parents very much.

Emma didn't rush him. She was extremely careful, and waited out his many retreats and hesitations. If there was ever a person she didn't want to hurt, it was Richard. He seemed not terribly older or more grown up than her own boys—in fact, Tommy could outread him—and she was painfully aware that she might not like it if an older woman such as herself suddenly laid hands on one of her own boys.

Yet, for the first time since Sam Burns, she was immediately confident of her capacity to be good for someone. Richard was planning to teach high school in Wyoming. He had not seemed to have had much attention in his life and hadn't learned to expect any; consequently he was all response. She coaxed him out of being intimidated by her; taught him to give his own enthusiasm a chance. Soon he would have abandoned his graduate studies, or anything else, to please her. They never quarreled—had nothing to quarrel about. He kept a certain meekness in regard to her, even after they had been lovers for over a year. It was a measure of his regard, and it made Emma feel her age. Watching Richard, she began to understand the appeal of youth. He had a shy smile, uncynical eyes, long tense legs. He was eager; he brought a freshness to any action. He had never been seriously disappointed, had not grown critical, and had no reason to dislike himself. To Emma he was fresh as dew—he never saw her as the sagging, heavily used woman she felt herself to be.

She had such light, nice times with Richard that she even began to feel sorry for her bedraggled husband, who was looking wearier and seedier every month. He could have had a nice easily impressed girl who might have been able to make him feel he was someone special, and instead he had stuck himself with a woman more neurotic than his wife.

Flap knew vaguely that Emma must have a lover, but he was in no position to inquire. He couldn't manage Janice, and he began to talk to Emma again, and even to take an interest in his children, as an escape. He had even begun to have the vague suspicion that Janice had a lover, and he didn't feel up to confronting even one infidelity, much less two.

Richard was as awed by literature as he was by sex, and discovered a new great writer almost every week. Emma could not resist tutoring him, and with her help his grades improved. As usual, it was her mother who called her attention to the flaw in her arrangements.

"I'm sure he's a fine lad," Aurora said. "My dear, you are so very impractical. This is first love for him, remember? What are you going to do when he wants to carry you off to some very cold town in Wyoming? You're not happy being the wife of a college professor, what chance do you think you'd have with a high sch teacher? These things have to come to some resolution, y

pot's talking to the kettle, on the kettle's money," at have you ever resolved?"

nent, Emma," Aurora said. "Marital arrange- interest me, that's all."

nd less," Emma said.

"The point is that they interest men," Aurora said. "My men are too old to make much of a fuss, no matter what I do. Young men are not so easily put off."

"I don't want to talk about it anymore," Emma said. It was a statement she used more and more often. The illusion that talk was a means to change had left her, and she felt cloudy in her spirit when she found herself talking too much or too hopefully about what was going to happen.

Luckily, though, she made a friend in Kearney. She had felt so isolated from the college community, partly by Flap's affair and partly by her own disinclinations, that she had not supposed she would be making any friends. She had Richard and her kids, and she expected to read a lot. But then one day at a P.T.A. meeting she met a big gawky Nebraska girl named Melba, the wife of the high school basketball coach. Melba was all teeth and elbows, but she was irresistibly friendly; the two of them quickly became fascinated with one another. Melba seemed to have vast unused energies, despite having five boys, all under twelve. She had many nervous habits, one of which was stirring coffee constantly while she sat at Emma's kitchen table. She only stopped stirring long enough to take large gulps. There was something slow and Nordic about her. In her way she was as awed by Emma's ordinary two-story house as Emma had been by Patsy's mansion in Beverly Hills. She thought Emma led a romantic existence because her husband taught college; she was fascinated by the fact that Emma's children read books instead of throwing balls around constantly, as her boys did.

Emma, in turn, was intrigued to discover that there was someone whose domestic situation was on a lower level than her own. Melba's husband Dick had no interest in anything but drinking, hunting, and sports—his general disregard of Melba made Flap seem almost oppressively considerate. Emma often felt like telling Melba that it was all relative, only Melba wouldn't have known what she was talking about. Emma soon found that she couldn't resist titillating her friend, and she confessed her affair—dangerous as that was.

"You mean a young guy?" Melba said, crinkling her large forehead as she tried to imagine it. She tried to put herself in Emma's

389

place, tried to imagine sleeping with someone other than Dick, but it didn't work. She couldn't imagine anybody. All she could imagine was Dick killing her when he found out. In a vague way it worried her that Emma would pick a young guy, but it was so different from anything she might do that her imagination never got a good grip on it. All she knew was that if Emma was doing it it must be very romantic. From then on she referred to Richard as "your Dick."

"Richard," Emma said over and over again. "I call him Richard." But Melba never made the switch. In her world all Richards were Dicks.

It was a minor flaw, though, for no one was better-hearted than Melba. She would offer to keep the boys at the drop of a hat, if Emma even looked like she might be getting sick. The only problem there was getting the boys to go, for her boys regarded Melba's boys as uninteresting louts—a judgment with which Emma agreed. With Melanie, Melba was less sure of herself. She seemed to regard Melanie was an exceedingly delicate creature.

"That kid's about as delicate as a truck," Emma said, but it didn't matter. Melanie found Melba scarcely worth the charming. Melba's whole life, it seemed to Emma, was spent hoping that the prices of things at the supermarket wouldn't go any higher. If they went any higher her husband would gripe at her for buying them, and yet they had to eat something. She was like a big walking ticker tape of commodity prices; when she walked into Emma's kitchen the first thing she said was, "Pork's gone up twelve cents. Twelve cents!" And yet she seemed to be a happy woman—Emma never heard her complain about anything *except* prices—and her energy was extraordinary. Emma watched her shovel snow one day, and she cleared a driveway almost as quick as a snowplow would have. "Emma, you don't exercise," she scolded. "I don't think you could shovel out a driveway if you had to."

"I believe in professionals," Emma said. "Fortunately my boys are professionals."

ON THE morning of Melanie's third birthday Emma baked a cake and got everything ready for a little birthday party they were having. It was Melanie's first party. Unfortunately, Emma had forgotten and scheduled an appointment for both of them to have flu shots and checkups that morning, something that didn't suit Melanie at all. "No shots, it's *my* birthday!" she insisted, but she got a shot anyway.

"I don't want you sick," Emma told her.

Melanie dried her tears and sat on a little stool eating a lollipop and kicking at a filing cabinet, much to Emma's annoyance and the doctor's. Emma was getting her shot.

"She's big, two shots!" Melanie said vengefully, removing her lollipop and pointing it at her mother. Her eyes were still dark from her recent anger.

"She has a keen interest in justice," Emma said.

"What's this?" the doctor said. He was named Budge, a fat sexy-ugly man with enormous patience and a way with women and children. He began to raise one of Emma's arms up and down while probing her armpit.

"What?" Emma asked.

"You have a lump in your armpit," Dr. Budge said. "How long has that been there?"

"I don't know," Emma said. "Stop it, Melanie. Stop kicking that cabinet."

Melanie kicked more lightly, pretending that she was only swinging her legs. When her toes happened to bang into the cabinet again she looked at her mother and tossed her curls innocently. Dr. Budge turned and looked at her sternly.

"I'm three," Melanie said cheerfully.

Dr. Budge sighed. "Well, you have two lumps," he said. "Not very big ones, but lumps. I don't know what to make of that."

"I didn't even know they were there," Emma said.

"They're not very big," he repeated. "They're coming out, though. The question is when. I have to be out of town for a week and I hate to leave them that long."

"Goodness," Emma said, feeling her armpit gingerly. "Do I have to be scared?"

Dr. Budge frowned. "Be scared," he said. "Then you'll be that much happier when they turn out to be nothing."

"What will it turn out to be if it doesn't turn out to be nothing?"

Dr. Budge was probing her other armpit. He shook his head and gave her a thorough examination. Melanie watched with mild interest, sucking greedily and audibly on her lollipop. She had been that way nursing, Emma remembered; she could be heard in the next room.

By the time he was finished Dr. Budge had regained a cheerful demeanor. "Oh, well, you're lucky," he said. "They're just in your armpits. Some people have lumps in their brains."

"I can read," Melanie said, jumping up and grabbing Dr. Budge by the pants leg. "You want me to read?"

THE BIRTHDAY party worked fine, where the kids were concerned, but it never quite worked for Emma. She was a veteran of a good score of birthday parties and managed the games and refreshments and even the gaiety with expertise; yet she was partly not there. She kept feeling her armpit. Her mother called, and Melanie had to babble away about her birthday to Aurora, Rosie, and even the General. Vernon was in Scotland, to Melanie's annoyance. "Where's Vernon?" she wanted to know. "What's he doing? Let me speak to him please." By the time Emma got the phone she had begun to feel very tired.

"I'm in postparty collapse," she said. "Have you ever had lumps in your armpit?"

"No, why should I?"

"I don't know," Emma said. "I do."

"Well, I believe there are a lot of glands in that area, if I'm not mistaken. Probably your glands are just stopped up. It's no wonder, the way you eat."

"I eat fine," Emma said.

"I know, dear," Aurora said, "but you're always so prone to malfunctions."

"Mother, don't generalize about me like that," Emma said. "I just have my ups and downs."

"Emma, what do you think our lifelong argument has been about?" Aurora said.

"I don't know!" Emma said, furious at being picked on when she had just given a birthday party.

"About keeping yourself up, of course," Aurora said. "Now you've let your glands stop up. Are you still seeing that young man?"

"I'd rather you didn't mention that quite so casually," Emma said.

"Well, I forgot," Aurora said. in fact, Emma's news had upset her, and she was casting about for a normal explanation.

"What kind of hospitals do they have in Nebraska?" she asked.

"Perfectly good ones," Emma said. She had grown patriotic and had begun to defend Nebraska against her mother's constant attacks.

When Flap was told about the lumps, he winced. "I'm glad we're insured," he said. "Remember that tonsillectomy?" Emma remembered. Teddy's tonsils had kept them poor all one winter in Des Moines.

It was a very minor operation, taking out the lumps. Dr. Budge seemed embarrassed that he had made her stay in the hospital overnight. "I could have practically done this in my office," he said when she had been stitched.

"What were they?" Emma asked.

"Little tumors. Marble-sized. We'll do a biopsy and you'll know soon."

Flap had a committee meeting and was late getting to the hospital. He had had a fight with Janice, who thought Emma was only trying to get sympathy. Janice made whatever emotional capital she could out of whatever marital conventions Flap still chose to honor. The fight and the meeting together had left Flap looking more in need of a hospital than Emma.

"They're doing a biopsy," Emma told him. "That's the modern way of casting bones."

Flap had bought her roses, and she was rather touched; she sent him home to make the kids hamburgers, and settled in with the two Graham Greenes she had brought to read. Then her armpit began to ache and she took the pills that had been given her and drowsed off. It was her own remark about casting bones that was in her mind when she awoke. It was four in the morning; there was no wind. She lay awake imagining her little lumps in a test tube and wishing she had someone to talk to.

The minute she saw Dr. Budge, late that morning, she knew how the bones had fallen. Until then she had somehow pushed away the concept of cancer. "You could have cancer, you mean?" Flap said at one point, and she had nodded, but they took it no further.

"Old girl, you have a malignancy," Dr. Budge said very kindly. He had never called her old girl before. Emma felt herself dropping, as if a bad dream had ended, or was starting.

FROM THAT day, that moment almost, she felt her life pass from her own hands and the erring but personal hands of those who loved her into the hands of strangers—and not even doctors, really, but technicians: nurses, attendants, laboratories, chemicals, machines.

Her escapes were brief: a week at home before she went to Omaha for serious tests. It was not lost on her, in the six days she spent in Omaha, that her doom was being sealed in the city where poor Sam Burns had hoped to take her in marriage. Dr. Budge had been frank; he feared she was melanomic and she was, but his fears had been understated.

"I'm riddled," she told her husband, for that was more or less the case. For a few days she was haunted by the fear of endless operations, but the bones had fallen too definitely even for that. "It must be like measles, only they're inside," she told Patsy, trying to put it comically, for the doctors had given her almost that feeling.

"Don't say things like that," Patsy said, appalled. She went to her own doctor the next day.

Aurora Greenway had listened gravely to the first news. The lumps had not been quite out of her mind since Emma first mentioned them. "Our girl is in trouble," she said to Rosie when she hung up the phone.

"You're not leaving me here," Rosie said. "Somebody's got to take care of them kids."

That was exactly what Emma wanted of her Houston forces. She had never liked visiting hospitals; the awkwardness of visits had often seemed worse than the disease—any disease. Her mother and Rosie were to stay in Kearney and keep the household functioning. Everyone agreed that Flap would stay at the faculty club for a while—a pure convention, since there was none. He stayed with Janice, who managed to be jealous of Emma's illness despite its seriousness.

In the few days that she was home after her first operation, Emma hid her own bewilderment in order better to cope with the bewilderment of her children, her lover, and her husband. Flap at once chose to pretend that she was really not very sick—doctors were often wrong. He was one himself, he knew, he often said. Emma let that ride, because it was what the boys needed to believe. To Melanie it was just a party. Grandma and Rosie were coming. "An' Vernon," she insisted. "Vernon's coming, sometime."

Richard was the hardest to deal with—much the hardest. Emma didn't know then whether she was really dying or not, but some cold instinct told her that Richard must not be allowed to attach himself any tighter. She didn't want Richard's life to be haunted by her, whether he lost her to death or life. She didn't, and yet she had not the strength to coldly banish him. Richard was desperate; he wanted to cure her with love, he made it a test of himself. Emma was touched; she made a show, but she was glad they only had a few chances to meet. She had too much to do and think about. Only, at moments, Richard's fervor did make it all seem silly, really silly, an illusion of the medical profession. As yet she had felt no serious pain.

That arrived in Omaha, where it turned out she was going to be hospitalized. Dr. Budge didn't have sufficient machines; he couldn't administer radium, which she was told was necessary.

"All right, but is it going to stop anything?" she asked.

"Oh, sure, it will arrest it," her new young doctor said. "Otherwise we wouldn't do it."

Her mother had come with her to Omaha. Flap had his duties and Rosie was quite adequate to the children. Vernon was going to come when he could. Neither Emma nor Aurora liked the new young doctor, whose name was Fleming. He was small, neat, and very articulate. He told them both a great deal about the behavior of various cancers; his method was to give his patients more information than they could assimilate. Much of the information was, of course, totally irrelevant to their own illnesses.

"That little person is too self-satisfied," Aurora said. "Must we stay here and deal with him, dear? Why won't you come to Houston?"

"I don't know," Emma said. At night she often wondered herself, for it might be nice to go back to the softness and sogginess of Houston. Yet she didn't want to. What was happening might take months; to go to Houston would mean relocating her life, and she didn't want to. Even though she was riddled, nothing was certain. New chemicals were being tried, and even Dr. Fleming wouldn't predict the outcome. It was all confusing, but she did understand that the new chemicals were her ultimate hope. On certain metabolisms they had been known to cure rather than merely arrest.

If they didn't work, she had it in mind to go home. Even one day in the hospital was enough to make her dream of home, and she wanted to be in her home, not her mother's. She wanted her own bedroom and the smells of her kitchen.

That was her dream, though, before she had had any serious pain. After the radium, and the failure of the magic chemicals, her will to go home weakened. She had never been in pain before and hadn't realized how completely it would come to dominate her. One night not long after she started radium she lost her pills, knocked them off her bed table in the darkness, and found that her bell was out of order. She couldn't get a nurse—all she could do was lie still. Combined with the terrible ache inside her was a sudden deep conviction of helplessness; no one was going to come and help her. For the first time in her life she felt beyond the efficacy of love; all the loved ones she had couldn't help her as much as the little pills lying somewhere in the darkness under her bed.

Flat on her back, Emma began to cry. When the night nurse looked in on her an hour later there were puddles on the pillow, on both sides of her head.

The next morning, the memory of it still in her eyes, she asked Dr. Fleming to allow her extra pills in case she spilled some again.

"I can't cope with that much pain," she said honestly.

Dr. Fleming was studying her chart. He looked up and took her wrist efficiently. "Mrs. Horton, pain is nothing," he said. "It's just an indicator."

Emma could not believe she had heard him right. "What did you say?" she asked.

Dr. Fleming repeated it. Emma turned away. She told her mother, who made life harder for Dr. Fleming whenever she could; but Emma knew that even her mother didn't really know what she was talking about. She had never been painfully ill in her life.

By the time she had dealt with pain for a month she had already lost what everyone healthy would have called life—i.e., health. The night of helplessness had turned her away from more than Dr. Fleming. From then on her energies went into an effort to balance herself somehow between drugs, pain, and weakness. The thought of going home no longer appealed to her at all. She would have been terrified at home, and she knew it was foolish to pretend that she could function there. She couldn't deal with children, husband, or lover; an hour's conversation a day with her mother and weekend visits from the kids soon became her limit. One day her hair began to fall out—an aftereffect of the radium —and as she was holding a mirror and weakly brushing it she began to laugh.

"I've finally found the answer to this hair nobody ever liked," she said. "Radium is the answer."

Aurora was stricken speechless.

"I was joking," Emma said hastily.

"Oh, Emma," Aurora said.

THERE WAS another problem; sometimes when she was alone the thought of all the things in life that were not like one imagined they would be amused her. In her case, the old childish fantasy of dying and having everyone suddenly sorry for their mistreatment began to come true. For a time Melanie was the only one who wasn't awed by her decline. Suddenly everyone was sorry for her except Melanie. Tommy wouldn't allow himself to show that he was sorry, but he still was. Melanie chose to treat her mother's move to the hospital as a kind of caprice, and Emma was glad. She was weary of being offered pity and would have preferred it if everyone had criticized her as they always had.

But she rapidly became very weak, and being weak made it easier to attend to her turning away. Aurora, after her first horror, began to try to fight her daughter's increasing passivity. For a few days she tried to goad Emma into living, but it didn't work.

"This room is too bleak," Aurora said bitterly. Indeed, it was quite bleak. That night she called the General, who was ailing himself.

"Hector, I want you to bring the Renoir," she said. "Don't argue, and don't let anything happen to it. Vernon's going to send a plane."

Vernon came occasionally to the hospital, though usually he stayed in Kearney and helped Rosie with the children. His sandy hair was sprinkled more with gray, but he was as scrubbed and as energetic as ever and, as ever, totally deferential to Aurora.

Emma was more comfortable with him than she was with her mother, for Vernon seemed to accept her weariness and weakness. He didn't demand that she live. Then one day all three came: Aurora, Vernon, and the General—who seemed older but no less straight. When he talked it was like someone was cracking walnuts. Vernon carried the Renoir, wrapped in many papers. At Aurora's instructions he unwrapped it and hung it on the white wall, right in front of Emma. Seeing it again, particularly in Nebraska, caused Aurora to weep. The two brilliant young women smiled into the sad room.

"I'm giving it to you," Aurora said, deeply upset. "It's your Renoir."

She felt it was the last and best thing she had to offer.

Too many people came, it seemed to Emma. Melba came one day, driving all the way from Kearney in a snowstorm. It took her two days. She had bought Emma a paperback copy of the *Iliad*. It was said to be important, and she knew Emma read such books. Also, it was poetry. She crinkled her brow at the sight of her wasted friend, left the *Iliad*, and drove back to Kearney.

Also, Richard came. Emma had so hoped he woudn't. They had not been great talkers anyway, and she didn't know what to say to him. Fortunately, all he wanted to do was hold her hand for a while. He held her hand and pretended she was going to get well. Emma rubbed his neck and asked him about his grades. When he was gone she had troubled dreams about him; it had been bad of her to let him get so in love, but it was one among a great many mistakes.

Then one day she awoke and Patsy was there, fighting with her mother. They were fighting about Melanie. Patsy had offered to take her, to raise her with her two girls, but Aurora bitterly opposed it. Flap was there too. Emma heard him say, "But they're my kids." Patsy and Aurora completely ignored him. He was not relevant.

Watching them, Emma's head really cleared, for a while. "Stop it!" she said. They stopped with difficulty, two extremely angry women. To her puzzlement, she smiled; they didn't realize she was smiling at them.

"They're my blood," Aurora said. "They're certainly not going to be raised in California."

"That's very biased," Patsy said. "I'm the right age, and I like raising children."

"They're *our* children," Flap said, and was again ignored.

Emma realized that that was what she had been forgetting in her grogginess: the children. "I want to talk to Flap," she said. "You two take a walk."

When they were gone she looked at her husband. Since her

illness he had almost become her friend again, but there was still an essential silence between them.

"Listen," Emma said. "I tire easily. Just tell me this: Do you really want to raise them?"

Flap sighed. "I've never thought I was the sort of man who'd give up his kids," he said.

"We're thinking of them," she said. "We're not thinking of how we'd like to think of ourselves. Don't be romantic. I don't think you want that much work. Patsy and Momma can afford help, and you can't. It makes a difference."

"I'm not romantic," Flap said.

"Well, I don't want them living with Janice," Emma said.

"She's not so bad, Emma," Flap said.

"I know that," Emma said. "I still don't want her exercising her neurosis on our children."

"I don't think she'd marry me anyway," Flap said.

They looked at one another, trying to know what to do. Flap's cheeks had thinned, but he still had something of his old look, part arrogant, part self-deprecating—though the arrogance had worn thin after sixteen years. Somehow that look had won her, though she couldn't remember, looking at him, what the terms of endearment had been, or how they had been lost for so long. He was a thoughtful but no longer an energetic man, and he had never been really hopeful.

"I think they better not stay with you," Emma said, watching him, willing to be dissuaded. "I just don't think you have the energy, honey."

"I'll really miss Melanie," he said.

"Yes, you will,"' Emma said.

She reached out and picked at a spot on his coat. "I'd like her better if she kept your clothes clean," she said. "I'm just that bourgeois. At least I kept your goddamn clothes clean."

Flap didn't counter. He was thinking about his children—about the life he would have without them.

"Maybe we should let Patsy take them," he said. "I could spend my summers at the Huntington."

Emma gave him a long look. It was the last time Flap really looked her in the eye. Ten years later, rising from the bed of a dull woman in Pasadena, he remembered his wife's green eyes, and he felt all afternoon as he worked at the Huntington that he had done something wrong, wrong, wrong, long ago.

"No," Emma said. "I want them with Mother. She has enough gentlemen around to control them, and anyway Patsy's just being loyal. She might want Melanie, but she doesn't really want two boys."

The next day, alone with Emma, Patsy sighed and agreed. "I just hate to see your mother get her hands on that little girl," she said. "I'd love to raise your little girl."

"I'd let you, but Teddy can't spare her," Emma said.

That was the big ache, the only emotional pain that compared with the pain in her vitals: the thought of Teddy. Tommy was fighting; he had already girded himself into a tense, half-desperate self-sufficiency; but that was all right. He was half convinced that he hated his mother anyway, and maybe that was all right too, although it was painful. They had not given in to one another in a long time, she and Tommy, and maybe the fact that he kept himself braced against her was good; maybe it was even some kind of anticipation.

As for Melanie, her golden-haired daughter, Emma scarcely worried at all. Melanie was a little winner; she would make her way anywhere, with or without a mother.

But what would ever, ever become of Teddy? Who could he find to love him as much as she did? His eyes were the only eyes that haunted her. If she could have lived for anyone it would have been for Teddy; the thought of how he could take her death filled her with fear. He was always prone to assume all blame; probably he would feel that if only he had been a better boy his mother would have lived. She spoke of it to Patsy, who didn't disagree.

"Yes, he's like you," she said. "Innocent and guilt-ridden."

"I wasn't so innocent."

"I wish you wouldn't use the past tense," Patsy said. "Anyway, I'm having those kids out to visit a lot. She can't object to that."

"I'll make her agree," Emma said. She was thinking that her friend looked wonderful; only she seemed sad. It was hard to believe it, but Patsy too was thirty-seven.

"What's wrong?" Emma asked.

Patsy shook the question off. Emma persisted.

"I don't think you realize how I've depended on you," Patsy said finally. "You and Joe. Sometimes I think I'm in love with Joe instead of with Tony. He's drinking himself to death, despite me, and now you've got cancer, despite me. I don't know what good I am."

There was no answer to such a remark, and the two of them sat silently, as they had often sat when they were younger.

Then Patsy went off to Kearney to bring Rosie and the kids for a visit. "Bring my *Wuthering Heights*," Emma said. "I always ask for it and they always forget it. And bring me Danny's book if you can find it."

"YOU'RE TO let her have those children now and then," Emma said. "She's my closest friend and she can take them to Disneyland and show them a great time."

"I was thinking of taking them to Europe this summer," Aurora said.

"Take your boy friends to Europe," Emma said. "The kids will have more fun in California. Send them to Europe when they're in college."

It was inconsiderate, she thought, how blandly people mentioned the future in sick rooms. Phrases like next summer were always popping out; people made such assumptions about their own continuity. She pointed that out to her mother.

"Yes, I'm sorry," Aurora said. "I'm sure I'm the worst offender."

ALONE, EMMA didn't think about much. She didn't like pain and asked for drugs, and they were given her. Most of the time she floated; the effort of allowing tests, complying with shots was all she could manage usually. She sometimes watched scenes occurring around her, almost without emotion. Once her mother drove out an old religious fanatic who had tried to come in and leave a Bible. Emma watched, detached. Even when her head was clear she didn't really think. In two months she found that she had almost forgotten ordinary non-hospital life; perhaps the drugs had affected her memory, because she couldn't remember it clearly enough to yearn for it. Sometimes it occurred to her that she was through with most things—sex, for instance—yet the thought didn't hurt much. It bothered her worse that she couldn't go Christmas shopping, for she was a person who loved Christmas, and she sometimes dreamed of department stores and Santa Clauses on street corners.

Once, picking up the copy of the *Iliad* that Melba had given her, she chanced upon the phrase "among the dead," and found it comforting. Even counting people she knew, there were a lot of dead to be among: her father, for one, and a school chum who had been killed in a car wreck, and Sam Burns, and, she guessed, Danny Deck, the friend of her youth. She supposed him dead, though no one really knew.

Mostly, though, she didn't think. She floated; and when she roused herself at all it was to cope with doctors or visitors. She noticed that everyone in the hospital assumed that she was finished. They were polite; they were not really perfunctory, but essentially they let her be. It was her own people, not the doctors, who kept pressuring her to get well enough to go home for a while. They all seemed to think it must be what she wanted, but Emma resisted. If she had had a chance she might have gone home and dug in, but she knew she had no chance—knew it from what she felt, not from what she had been told. Once she accepted that, then she accepted the hospital. For those who could be cured, it was a hospital, but for her it was a depot, a kind of bus station; she was there to be transported out of life, and because it was ugly and bare and smelled bad and was run impersonally by hired functionaries, that which was never easy—a departure—could at least be handled efficiently. She didn't want to go home, because at home the warmth and good smells of her life would be overpowering. Her children would drag at her, with their love, their brilliance, and their need. She would become vulnerable to her little joys: her soap operas, washing Melanie's fantastic hair, Tommy's newest book and Teddy's hug, a nice dawdle with Richard, some Hollywood gossip from Patsy. If she went home it would hurt too much to die; also it would hurt those who were losing her. She wanted to slip away from her children as she had when they were tots, while they were somewhere else in the house happily playing with their baby-sitters. Then perhaps, before they really missed her, they would already have partly learned to do without her.

Still, as had been true so many times in her life, she was not as strong as her principles, nor up to executing any of her best theories. When faced after a few weeks with what she knew would be last visits, she could only get through them by pretending they weren't last visits.

Most heart-rending of all, more terrible even than her youngest son, was Rosie. She had not come to the hospital much; she hated them. "They spook me," she said nervously when she did come. "I was never in one myself in my life, except to have babies."

"Momma should have left you in Houston," Emma said. Rosie had brought her a box of chocolate-covered cherries. The sight of Emma, the real darling of her life, shook her so badly that she couldn't speak. She had accepted stoically the eventual death of Royce—from pneumonia—and of her oldest girl's baby, but the sight of Emma's bloodless face was too much. She couldn't talk and was too strung out to cry. The best she could manage was a few observations about the children, and a hug. For the rest of her life she was to regret, often to Aurora, that she had not managed to put her feelings into words that day.

The boys Emma saw together, after Rosie left. Melanie was in the hall playing with Vernon. The General had caught a cold, and Aurora was seeing that he got a proper shot.

Teddy had meant to be reserved, but he couldn't manage. His feelings rushed up, became words. "Oh, I really don't want you to die," he said. He had a husky little voice. "I want you to come home."

Tommy said nothing.

"First of all, troops, you both need a haircut," Emma said. "Don't let your bangs get so long. You have beautiful eyes and very nice faces and I want people to see them. I don't care how long it gets in back, just keep it out of your eyes, please."

"That's not important, that's just a matter of opinion," Tommy said. "Are you getting well?"

"No," Emma said. "I have a million cancers. I can't get well."

"Oh, I don't know what to do," Teddy said.

"Well, both of you better make some friends," Emma said. "I'm sorry about this, but I can't help it. I can't talk to you too much longer either, or I'll get too upset. Fortunately we had ten or twelve years and we did a lot of talking, and that's more than a lot of people get. Make some friends and be good to them. Don't be afraid of girls, either."

"We're not afraid of girls," Tommy said. "What makes you think that?"

"You might get to be later," Emma said.

"I doubt it," Tommy said, very tense.

When they came to hug her Teddy fell apart and Tommy remained stiff.

"Tommy, be sweet," Emma said. "Be sweet, please. Don't keep pretending you dislike me. That's silly."

"I *like* you," Tommy said, shrugging tightly.

"I know that, but for the last year or two you've been pretending you hate me," Emma said. "I know I love you more than anybody in the world except your brother and sister, and I'm not going to be around long enough to change my mind about you. But you're going to live a long time, and in a year or two when I'm not around to irritate you you're going to change your mind and remember that I read you a lot of stories and made you a lot of milkshakes and allowed you to goof off a lot when I could have been forcing you to mow the lawn."

Both boys looked away, shocked that their mother's voice was so weak.

"In other words, you're going to remember that you love me," Emma said. "I imagine you'll wish you could tell me that you've changed your mind, but you won't be able to, so I'm telling you now I already know you love me, just so you won't be in doubt about that later. Okay?"

"Okay," Tommy said quickly, a little gratefully.

Teddy cried a lot, but Tommy didn't—he couldn't. Later as they were all walking down the hospital sidewalk—all except the General, who had gone to the motel in a cab to nurse his cold—Tommy felt like he wanted to run back upstairs to his mother, but instead Teddy was babbling something about cub scouts and he suddenly said bitterly that he had never been a scout because his mother had been too lazy to be a den mother. He didn't mean to say lazy, or to say anything bad, or even to speak. It just slipped out, and to everybody's horror his grandmother turned and slapped him so hard that he fell down. It astonished everyone—Melanie, Teddy, Rosie, Vernon—and before Tommy could help himself he burst into tears. Watching his face finally open was a great relief to Aurora, and before he could run away she grabbed him and hugged him as he went on crying helplessly.

"That's a boy," she said. "That's a boy. It just won't do to criticize your mother around me."

Then her own heart left her for a moment and she glanced around at the ugly brick hospital.

"She was always a proper daughter," she said, looking up helplessly at Rosie and Vernon.

Melanie was the first to recover herself. She saw Vernon and Rosie smiling and decided it was some kind of joke. She ran to Teddy and slugged him with all her tiny might.

"Ha, Grandma hit Tommy!" she said. "I hit you, Teddy." She hit him again and he wrestled her down on the cold grass and held her down while she giggled.

With her mother a few minutes earlier she had been equally gay. The hospital interested her. She had toddled off down several halls, and a nurse had let her try out some scales. A doctor had even lent her a stethoscope, and she sat on her mother's bed, occasionally listening to her own heart. Emma watched her contentedly; even her little white teeth were adorable.

"How's your dolls?" she asked.

"Very bad dolls, I spank them a lot," Melanie said. She had always been a stern disciplinarian where dolls were concerned.

"I was in you," she said suddenly, poking at her mother's stomach.

"Who told you that?" Emma asked.

"Teddy," Malanie said.

"I could have guessed. Teddy's a blabbermouth."

"Un-uh, you're a blabbermouth," Melanie said. "Tell me the truth."

Emma laughed. "What truth?"

"I was in you," Melanie said, nodding her head affirmatively. She was very curious.

"Yes, you were, now that you bring it up," Emma said. "So what?"

Melanie felt triumphant. She had confirmed a secret.

"So what, so what, so what," she said, and fell on her mother. "Let's sing some songs."

They sang some songs, and Rosie, walking in the corridor, heard them and began to weep.

EMMA WAS glad when the visits ended. The healthy didn't seem to know what claims they made. They didn't know how weak she was, what an effort it was to give them her attention. Dying took all her attention. The boys went off with Patsy on a ski trip; the General's cold got worse and he had to retreat to Houston; Rosie settled down in Kearney to take care of Flap and Melanie; only her mother and Vernon stayed in Omaha.

"I wish you'd go home," Emma said. "You're losing weight."

"It's the one advantage to Nebraska," Aurora said. "I can't find anything to eat. At long last I'm becoming slim."

"You weren't meant to be slim," Emma said. "I feel guilty thinking of you and Vernon sitting in some dinky motel playing cards every night."

"Oh, no, often we go to films," Aurora said. "Once we even went to the symphony. It was something of a first for Vernon."

Her mother continued to come every day. Emma entreated her to go home, but in her weakness she was no match for Aurora. She always dressed in gay colors. In time, as Emma faded, her mother became lost in the Renoir. Often Emma couldn't tell whether there were two shimmering women in the room or three. Sometimes she felt her mother hold her hand; other times she found herself talking and when her vision cleared found that her mother had gone and only the picture remained. On weekends she sometimes roused herself to Flap, but only briefly. She had stopped wanting to read, but she sometimes clutched *Wuthering Heights*. Sometimes she dreamed she was living in the picture, walking in Paris in a pretty hat. At times she felt herself awaking in it instead of in a bed covered with hair that had fallen out during the night. Her flesh was departing in advance of her spirit; her weight had dropped to ninety pounds. Aurora, for the only time in her life, ceased talking of food.

For a time Emma was ready but the cancer wasn't. She had cut her ties, she was poised to leave, but the cancer retreated a step, became quiescent for a week or two. When she was rested and confused, it came back. Then she began to hate it, hate the hospital, hate the doctors, hate most of all the slavery of living when she had stopped wanting to. Her heart and her breath wouldn't accept her weariness. They wouldn't stop. She began to dream of Danny Deck. Sometimes she opened his book, not to read it, just to look at the pages or his signature on the flyleaf, to try and have him vivid again. Her mother noticed.

"I thought the boy was going to be your great romance," she said. "He didn't have much staying power."

Emma declined to argue. Danny was hers, like Teddy; only those two had liked her entirely. As she slowly began to forget her life, his memory returned. In her dreams they began to have conversations, though she could never remember where they had talked or what they said.

The cancer went too slow, much too slow. When the drugs wore off she felt like she had inside her a diseased and aching tooth, only a tooth the size of a fist. In February she grew impatient with it. She began to nurse a vision. Outside the wind blew steadily from the north. Often there was snow but always there was wind. To Emma it became like a siren song. She could hardly tell her mother from the Renoir; she felt the wind had come for her, off the ice, over the barren lands, across the Dakotas, straight to her. She had thought perhaps to save enough pills to kill herself, but that was hard. Saving pills meant being in pain, and besides the nurses were too shrewd. They watched for such tricks. Anyway, the wind was more appealing. In pain, she told her mother of her dream. Some night she would get up, rip out all the needles and tubes, throw a chair through the window, and let herself fall. She was sure that was best.

"I'm not a person, I'm just an expense now, Momma," she said.

Aurora didn't argue. She was ready to see her daughter at rest. "My dear, you couldn't lift a chair," she said. "There is that practical aspect to it."

"I could if it was the last thing I had to do," Emma said.

She thought about it. She convinced herself she could do it. It seemed like something good, something with a little style. The part of the vision she liked best was ripping out all the needles and tubes. She hated them worst of all—they brought everything into her body except life. She was only a candle, a weak flame. If she could only break the window the wind might come in and blow her out. She could die like a winter traveler, blown over with snow.

She thought about it. She looked at the chairs a lot, looked at the window.

The thought of Teddy stopped her. It was a question of who determined, who had final claim: her children or the cancer. Teddy might go out a window himself someday if she gave him an excuse. He was so loyal he might even do it as a way of following her—or out of guilt.

Emma gave it up. She took her pills. Pain was easier to escape than parenthood. Even though their lives were lost to her, they were still her children. They got to have final claim. In clear moments she scribbled a few more notes to the boys, drew Melanie some funny pictures. Several weeks later she died in bed.

EMMA WAS buried in Houston on a warm, rainy March day. Mrs. Greenway and Patsy, smartly and almost identically dressed, stood together at the grave. Melba had come. In a desperate act of loyalty she had taken money out of her family's savings and risked both divorce and her life—by flying in an airplane for the first time—to pay her respects. Joe Percy had escorted Patsy. He was standing with Vernon, the General, Alberto, and the boys, telling the boys how movies were made. In that regard he had been very helpful. Flap sat in a limousine wiping his eyes. With her death he had recovered all his first feeling for his wife; he seemed a broken man. Melanie was chattering at a heartbroken Rosie, trying to get her in the mood to play. Patsy and Aurora both cast watchful looks in her direction, for Melanie was apt to dart off without a moment's notice, and Rosie was too bereft to pay attention. Melba stood apart, almost as tall as a tree.

"I don't know what we're to do with that poor woman," Aurora said.

"I'll make Joe talk to her," Patsy said. "Joe can talk to any woman."

"I don't know what you're doing going around with him," Aurora said. "He's old enough to be one of mine."

"Well, he takes care of me," Patsy said.

Neither of them particularly wanted to move—to get on with it.

"She often made me feel I was faintly ridiculous," Aurora said. "Somehow she just had that effect. Perhaps that was why I remained so unremittingly critical of her. Actually, I suppose I am."

"Am what?"

"Am faintly ridiculous," Aurora said, remembering her daughter. "Perhaps I felt she would have been a little happier if she had been . . . faintly ridiculous . . . too."

"It's hard to imagine," Patsy said, thinking of her friend.

It had stopped raining, but all around them the great trees were dripping.

"There's no point in us standing here like bookends, my dear," Aurora said, and they turned and went to attend to the children and the men.